Ere àwòrán

Ere àwòrán

Ere àwòrán (pronounced: EH-reh ah-WOR-AN) = Little Statue

To ▬▬▬▬

I heard that you love to read

Enjoy!

Michael Jay Nusbaum

Cover Illustrated By: Gil Balbuena Jr.

Library of Congress Control Number:		2015902321
ISBN:	Hardcover	978-1-5035-4263-1
	Softcover	978-1-5035-4264-8
	eBook	978-1-5035-4265-5

Print information available on the last page

Rev. date: 02/13/2015

To order additional copies of this book, contact:
Xlibris
1-888-795-4274
www.Xlibris.com
Orders@Xlibris.com
704579

CONTENTS

I dedicate this book to the millions of innocent Africans who died and were enslaved in the four hundred years of brutal mistreatment of the African people and to all human beings who continue to be enslaved today.

To Rabbi Joachim Prinz (May 10, 1902–September 30, 1988). As a young rabbi in Berlin, Rabbi Prinz was forced to confront the rise of Nazism and eventually immigrated to the United States in 1937. He became vice chairman of the World Jewish Congress and was a significant participant in the 1963 Civil Rights March on Washington, where he marched hand in hand with the great civil rights leader Rev. Dr. Martin Luther King, Jr. Growing up, I was blessed to have him, as my rabbi, friend, and teacher. As his last professional act before retirement, he, along with Rabbi Barry Friedman, officiated at my bar mitzvah and ushered me into manhood on December 9, 1978. It was through his guidance that I developed my strong conviction that all men and women are created equal in the eyes of God and that no human being should ever be subjected to enslavement by another. He told me the stories of slavery in the South. He told me of Harriet Tubman and Box Brown. He was the one who told me the truth that I would not learn in school.

PROLOGUE

IN ORDER TO understand the story of slavery in America, one must look at the history of slavery in general. As I began to delve deeper into my research, I was stunned to find out facts of which I had been previously unaware. Many of us were taught the horrors and atrocities that took place during the years of slavery here in the United States. What we were not taught in America were the staggering numbers and the horrendous dehumanization of those enslaved and those who died as a direct consequence of the slave trade itself.

Beginning in the ninth century and continuing into the nineteenth century, the continent of Africa hemorrhaged its human occupants from every available route. It began with at least ten centuries of slave exports to Muslim countries with some four million enslaved Africans being exported via the Red Sea, an additional four million taken from the Swahili ports of the Indian Ocean, and as many as nine million ferried out along the trans-Sahara caravan route to all manner of destinations. From the fifteenth to the nineteenth centuries, an additional fifteen million Africans were enslaved and forced to endure the Middle Passage in which they were transported across the Atlantic Ocean to a life of bondage in North America, South America, and the Caribbean islands.

The slave trade was mostly the result of endemic warfare, which existed between the African states and, on occasion, their neighbors. Some Africans made a business of capturing other Africans from neighboring ethnic or tribal groups and selling them into slavery in return for manufactured goods from Europe. Others simply took their captives of war and sold them into slavery directly. Many others were obtained through raids or kidnappings, most of which occurred at the points of European guns held by African warriors. Selling slaves to Europeans ensured that the flow of weapons and manufactured goods would continue to go to certain African leaders.

In 1494, the Portuguese king had entered into agreements with rulers of several West African states to allow trade between their respective peoples. This deal enabled the Portuguese to gain peaceful access to the African economy. By the mid-1500s, the Portuguese began to colonize numerous islands, beginning with the Canary Islands located just off the western coast of Africa. Initially enslaving Canary Islanders, the Portuguese found slave labor to be very effective in maximizing their profits from the land they had converted to the production of wine and sugar. As they continued their territorial expansion, the Portuguese acquired many more islands throughout the Atlantic. Their plan was to use slave labor to maximize production from these new fertile island acquisitions.

Thus, the transatlantic slave trade began in about 1502 with the Portuguese acquiring slaves themselves directly from Africa. This was soon followed by the second Atlantic slave trade system, which consisted of Africans enslaved by mostly British, Portuguese, French, and Dutch traders. The main destinations for these slaves were the Caribbean colonies and Brazil. By the eighteenth century, the British, Portuguese, and French were responsible for nine out of ten slaves abducted from their homes in Africa and transported across the Atlantic.

The peak of the Atlantic slave trade occurred during the last two decades of the eighteenth century both during and after the Congo civil war. States along the Niger River declared war on one another, leading to a series of bloody campaigns, providing fresh new slaves to export and to help continue the financing of the bloodshed. As the kingdom of Dahomey and the Oyo and Asante Empires set out to expand their holdings on the African continent, the supply of enslaved peoples rapidly expanded to surplus levels.

Many of the slaves transported across the Atlantic were first sent to seasoning camps for their first year. These camps were found throughout the Caribbean, but Jamaica was home to one of the most notorious of these camps. Here, the enslaved people were tortured for the sole purpose of breaking their spirits and conditioning them to their new reality of lives as slaves. Their brutal captors set out to break them through a process they felt similar to that of breaking the spirit of a wild horse. As the 1860s approached, the slave trade to the Americas and Caribbean had been substantially curtailed.

In the years from when the Portuguese first began to bring captured Africans over to the Americas until the time the last known slave ship set sail, some fifteen million human beings were forcibly taken from their homes in Africa and forced into a life of bondage. Only around 6 percent of those slaves transported across the Atlantic were destined for the shores of the United States, while the other 94 percent went to the Caribbean islands and South American destinations. Approximately 10 percent of those transported did not survive the Middle Passage. This mortality rate combined with the five million who died upon arrival or in the seasoning camps led to a total of some six and a half million dead of the original fifteen million abducted. Still, many more Africans died as a result of the slave raids themselves at the hands of their African abductors. In total, the death toll from four centuries of the Atlantic slave trade is estimated at nearly ten million.

This story is told through the eyes of both fictional and non-fictional characters, but the names, dates, and events in history are all real.

FOREWORD

THIS STORY IS told from the perspective of Michael Joshua Smith, a young New York City native who joins the United States Navy in hopes of broadening his horizons. Instead, he is thrust into the battle over slavery in the United States. Brought up in a liberal Northern family, he is both morally and ethically opposed to the institution of slavery. The journey he embarks on not only places him in the midst of the Civil War but also introduces him to a remarkable man named Osumaka. This man who was abducted from Africa, enslaved in the South, and escaped to freedom teaches him about honor and perseverance. Ultimately, this story is based on the recounting of Osumaka's tale told to Michael on his journey to Liberia to be reunited with what is left of his family.

Michael Joshua Smith:

"As I gaze upon the delicate diminutive ivory statuette sitting on my writing table, I realize that I have told the story of my role in the Africa Squadron and my encounters with a heroic man named Osumaka many times before, but in doing so, I now feel the events of those days have become increasingly vivid. I frequently find that my thoughts revert to a time gone by, and I find myself wandering back to those days, those events, and those places. The smells and sights push forth from the recesses of my memory as if I were experiencing them now. I can feel the pain, the anguish, the loss, and the love of those I have encountered in my journey through life. Now, in the latter prologue of my life, I put pen to paper in an attempt to record the events which shaped my life and the lives of many more. This also is a most humble effort to ensure that the record is set straight and that no generation ever forget the injustice done to the brave and honorable people of Africa. In the Passover Seder,

Jews recount their exodus from the bonds of slavery in Egypt under the guidance of Moses, so too do I hope that the Africans develop such a tradition so that they never forget. The reason for retelling the story of the Jews' exodus from Egypt is so that we never forget the bitterness of slavery and to ensure that it never happens again to any human being. History tells us, however, that men easily forget the evil done to other men. Our memory as a species rivals that of the ant when it comes to human atrocities, and yet with the individual capacity of memory of the bold giant elephants who roam the continent of Africa, we fall short of that capacity."

CHAPTER 1

Personal Log

Capt. Michael Joshua Smith, July 1, 1868

"POTENTIAL MEANS NOTHING without the realization of one's own abilities. But remember, son, a man is judged by his deeds and actions. Make certain that the good far outweighs the bad before your time on this earth is over." This was the last piece of advice given to me by my mother before I left home. How many people have been thought to have great potential but never lived up to that measure? I have pondered this ever since she uttered those words. It has come to me now, after seeing so much good and bad in this world that the advice was meant to have me look at myself with a critical eye. It was intended to force me to recognize my abilities and to harness them to do good in order to realize my full potential in life. I can only hope that I have done so. The journey, which I now embark upon, will, I hope, mark the pinnacle of that potential.

The night is crisp and the ocean air fresh with a light breeze coming off the ocean waves; only the whirring of the machinery and the paddle wheels of our steamship attempt to disrupt the calm of this beautiful evening. Their mechanical rapidity seems to fade into the background as the moonlight plays off the waves and a myriad of stars illuminate the night sky. The temperature is refreshing and a light coat is barely needed. We are on an important journey, one that I consider the culmination of my life. The civil war in the United States has ended and as her coastline fades past the horizon, I know in my heart that the forces of good have prevailed but at a great cost. Some say that our nation will never heal and others say that it never could have healed without this war. Either way, it has taken its toll on both sides.

As our ship steadily pushes through the waters and the occasional cloud passes by, I can hear the songs of our passengers who have settled in for the long journey below. They are songs of freedom and songs of longing, which rise up to the night sky and envelop our vessel. What incredible people they are to have lost so much for having been set into the bonds of slavery and yet remain dignified and hopeful for the future.

Our journey to the African continent should take half the five weeks that it took me upon my first visit there eight years ago. We are lucky to have secured a steam-powered vessel. The days of being reliant on the winds have now passed into the history books. What a marvel of technology! What a shame that this ship, along with so many others, was built for war; a war between brothers in what was nearly the end of our great nation. We have prevailed not only for the North but also for the South. Now with the war ended, it is my sincere hope that we can reunite this once great country and perhaps repair the damage left by the horrific institution of slavery.

"Captain," a voice calls out from behind me as I peer back at the horizon, hoping to get one last glimpse of home. It is Osumaka standing behind me. "Why do you do this?"

Osumaka is an African with a strong and muscular frame with an even six feet in height. His dark-skinned body is mostly devoid of hair save for patch on his chest and a mat of short curls of dark black hair upon his head. His body wears numerous scars, the origins of some of them are not entirely clear. At least two of the scars appear to be deliberately placed across his chest. I say this due to the symmetric nature of the scars and the high improbability that neither an animal nor an assaulting warrior could create such a symmetry. He also bears the marks of his captivity as a slave. His back is riddled with lash marks from his former master's whip. The scars are heaped one upon the other, coursing in every way. His ears are slightly larger than most, but his nose was neither as wide nor the openings nearly as prominent as that which I have observed of his countrymen. He has high cheekbones and a firm, angled chin. His voice is deep and calm, no doubt reflective of his strong constitution.

"Do what?" I asked.

"Why do you help us return?" Osumaka asked.

"It is the least I can do to help you," I replied.

"But why would you or any other white man help me return home?" Osumaka asked.

"I do it . . ." I said, but I paused.

"Out of guilt?" he asked.

"Because it is the right thing to do," I replied.

"That has not been my experience," he said as he took a deep breath. "Some white men are good, but most are not. Some wear their hatred for us openly, while most others just look the other way as if we are not there. How many times have whites seen me, yet they did not really see me? They look at me, but they do not notice me. They know I am there, but they ignore my existence. They knew I was a slave, but they thought if they did not see me, then no wrong was being committed. Just because they did not participate in my enslavement didn't make them less guilty of my enslavement."

"I understand," I replied. "Inaction can make one as guilty as the one committing the crime."

"Yes, this is so," Osumaka said.

"That is why this country was nearly destroyed."

"Because of slavery?" he asked.

"Because many of us looked away for too long, we let it go too far. We did not stop slavery when we could have—when we should have."

"Yes, for too long," he replied solemnly.

"For too long," I responded as I glanced back.

"I met a man once. A very important man," Osumaka said. "He told me, 'If there is no struggle, there is no progress. Those who profess to favor freedom, and yet depreciate agitation, are men who want crops without plowing up the ground. They want rain without thunder and lightning. They want the ocean without the awful roar of its many waters. This struggle may be a moral one or it may be a physical one or it may be both moral and physical, but it must be a struggle. Power concedes nothing without a demand. It never did, and it never will.'"

"That is clearly a very wise man," I replied. "Who was he?"

"His name is Fredrick Douglass. Have you heard of him?" he asked.

"I have. Many have. He is truly a very wise man," I said.

"He said one other thing that has stayed with me, 'The white man's happiness cannot be purchased with the black man's misery.' Do you understand this?" Osumaka asked.

"I do, and I agree with him and with you," I said solemnly.

"You look back from where we came. Why?" he asked.

I smiled and responded, "Yes, it is hard every time I must leave."

"Ah," he said, "but it is not hard for me to leave." He paused. "It was much harder for me to arrive."

"I have meant to ask you," I stated. "I hoped to learn more about you. About your life and your journeys . . . to put in my memoirs. Hopefully to retell your story someday."

"There is not much to know about me," he replied. "I am but a slave; one of many . . . who do not look upon your country favorably."

"You speak eloquently for a former slave," I stated.

"I learned English from a slave who used to be a freewoman and school teacher. She was taken by bounty hunters from her home in the North and forced into a life of slavery in the South. She risked her life to educate me and several other slaves on the plantation. In the end, it was her way of defying her masters," he replied with a large grin.

"Well, I am favorably impressed!" I replied as I motioned to the deck seat, which was within steps of us. We sat down. "Can you tell me about your home?"

He paused and then began. "The memories of home are as clear as those of today. Every night since I arrived, some eight years ago, I have dreamed of my family, my wife, my children, and my home. I know that they are with me every time I close my eyes . . .

These are the memories and words from Osumaka himself, set to pen and paper by me after his retelling of his journey:

His story took me back to April of 1861, some eight years ago and five months after I had set sail on the USS *Saratoga* for Africa.

On the continent of Africa, Lower Guinea, in an area known as the Congo lived the Matamba. A tribe of the BaKongo, I was told, lived in peace and that their unique geographic location placed them away from the wars, which had torn the continent apart. They had heard of the wars from stories related to them by travelers who occasionally passed through their village peacefully. There existed a village, which had been present in this particular location for untold generations. It was situated on an elevated plateau and surrounded by palm groves and fertile fields, which expanded out to the horizon and in which the village grew their food. The village itself, consisting of some fifty thatched huts, were situated in two long rows on either side of a central open space. Within the center of the open space was a communal meeting area, where a fire was maintained by the tribe and never permitted to die out. The smell of heavy smoke was forever present and made its presence known as if it managed to meander through the village on its own accord. The sparks from this terrestrial eternal flame rose far into the sky as ash fell gently to the ground and covered the pounded dirt of the village square like a gentle flurry of snow.

In this village of peace and harmony there was a man named Osumaka whom I encountered through my life's journey and from whom my knowledge of such things exist. He lived there with his wife, Likana. She was of statuesque form. Her body was much leaner than most with, as Osumaka put it, mounds upon her chest, reminiscent of gentle rolling hills. Her skin was of similar hue to Osumaka's. Her hair was short and curly and kept very neat. She wore a beaded band across her forehead, and her smile could make others smile by its mere presence. They had two children: the elder a boy of six years of age named Bwana and a four-year-old daughter named Nzinga. Bwana was a most affable child with a friendly demeanor and an inquisitive mind. His face wore the distinct mix of features from both parents. He too was lean but was tall for his age. Their daughter Nzinga, whom I can only relate from description alone since I never had the fortune to meet her in person, was equally affable in nature and loving of animals of any kind.

Every time the sun arose, the village slowly came to life each morning. An average day consisted of a separation of tasks not much different from that of the naval service in a vessel upon which I would spend a good portion of my life. Village women primarily engaged in the processes of preparing food. This included harvesting of the rice and cassava with the children's help. This is followed by the separating of the rice grain from its husk by mixing up quantities of it with coarse gravel followed by a rudimentary mortar made of wood. The women would then use the mortar to punch and grind the harvest. Then the children separated the grain and sand by tossing the mixture by hand into the air. They seemed to make a game of it, singing and laughing while performing such an arduous task that many of my childhood friends back in New York City would find akin to the hard labor of a prisoner, yet these children enjoyed the task at hand and made game of it with competition to see who was the best at creating separate piles from the components. All the while, the women in the village sang songs of hope and prayers to their deity, Fa.

The men of the tribe congregated separately. When they were not hunting, they would sit upon their heels, talking and telling tales of their exploits. Most spent the time honing their blades with stones as they spun their tales. The sounds of metal upon stone, buoyant voices, and the rhythmic beating of the work of the women filled the village. Upon occasion, a child or wife would head over to the men to give their head of family a bite to eat or a gentle touch of affection.

Osumaka was the most successful hunters of the tribe, and he would often lead the village men out to stalk game from which they would feast. On the morning of one such excursion, Bwana approached his father.

"Why must you leave us again?" young Bwana asked his father.

"I must hunt for food so that you and your mother and your sister have something to eat," he replied.

"Can't we just eat the foods from the plants that mother collects?" he asked.

"Of course, but we need meat too, and we need the other parts of the animals for other things," Osumaka responded as he lifted his son onto his lap.

"I'm afraid that you may get hurt or you may not return to us."

Osumaka took out a small item from the pouch on his hip. It was a small carved figurine of a warrior made out of ivory. Osumaka had been working on it for weeks and took pride in the craftsmanship of the figure, which stood no more than three inches high. Despite its diminutive appearance, it was rich in detail with a spear and a hip pouch similar to his own. Osumaka handed it to his son. "I made this ere àwòrán ("little statue") for you. It is a piece of my spirit, which I will entrust to you. Keep it close to you, and I will always be right here with you."

Bwana took the figure and examined it closely. "It doesn't look exactly like you," he replied. "I like the spear."

Osumaka responded, "It is me, and it is for you. I will always be with you, and I will always love you. No matter what, I will always find you as long as you have this."

"I will, Father. I will keep it safe, and I will never let it go," Bwana replied as he held it tight.

"What did you give him?" asked Likana.

The young boy held out the figure to show his mother.

"So beautiful," she responded. "Let's attach a piece to make it a necklace. That way you will always wear your father close to your heart." Likana approached her husband. "This is a good thing you have done, my husband. He is so afraid to lose you."

With that, mother and son went into the hut as the father finished sharpening the tip of his spear.

Suddenly, from the hut, Nzinga ran out. "What about me? I want one too."

"I don't have another, my dear," her father replied, "but I will make you one too if it will make you happy."

"It will. It will," she gleefully responded, "but I don't want a spear on mine and can mine have long braids?"

"Certainly, my dear," he said as he dropped his spear and picked up the young girl. "Anything for my little princess," he added as he held her tight and gave her little kisses all over her face. She giggled in delight.

"I love you too, my brave father," she said as she kissed him back.

Osumaka placed the little girl back on the ground, and she ran into the hut. He followed close behind.

"I must go now, my love. We will return before the sun sets."

"Be safe, my husband," replied his wife.

Osumaka picked up his spear and headed back out.

A group of men had gathered once again in the center of the village around the area of the fire pit. Osumaka joined them. They each recited a prayer to Fa for a good hunt and a safe return and then headed out. They filtered into a single column and headed down a path through the palm groves and out into the distance. As they headed away from the village, the children followed, but only to the edge of the palm grove since they knew not to stray too far from the village. They called out to their fathers and then sang a song of luck, calling upon Fa to protect and watch over them.

Not more than an hour after they left, the sky began to darken. The sounds of thunder in the distance approached the small village rapidly. Soon, the sky seemed to open as a torrent of water poured down upon them. The rain came down with such intensity that it almost appeared as one solid sheet of water. The fire at the center of the village sizzled as the water hit its hot embers, and it struggled to burn. Soon, water mist pervaded their little huts. It was unclear if the mist was coming from the roof, the reed walls, or from the entryway. Osumaka's two children huddled next to their mother as Bwana grasped her with one hand and the little statue in his other. She began to sing a song to them. This was a song with which they had become very familiar, which Osumaka had made up when Bwana was born. The song, which contained Bwana's name and later lengthened to include Nzinga's name, was created just for them by their father. It used a popular African melody of the time, the simplicity of which might be closest to the American children's tune "Mary Had a Little Lamb," although with a slightly different cadence. Likana sang the tune to them over and over as the storm approached. When the thunder and lightning increased as they passed over them, she sang the song to them even louder as if to drown out the noises with the sounds of her soothing voice.

"I'm scared," Nzinga cried out to her mother.

"I know, my little one," Likana replied as she pulled them closer. "I know."

"Why must it be so loud?" Bwana asked as he put his hand out of the hut to feel the strength of the stream of water.

"It is Fa nurturing the land and helping the ground give us what we need. Without it, nothing would grow, and we would not survive," she explained. "It is Fa's way of taking care of us."

"But why must it be so loud?" Bwana cried out as another loud crack of thunder emanated from the palm groves not too far away.

"My son, it is not for us to ask. It is the way that Fa makes the water we need to live. We must not ask the ways of Fa for fear of offending him. We must just be thankful for that which he gives us to sustain us."

"But, Mother, the water which comes down is so heavy, and there is so much of it. How could it stay up in the sky without falling?"

Likana did not know what else to say to her young son. It was as much a mystery to her as it was to him. "I do not know, my son. It is Fa who provides all for us."

"I hope that our animals are all right," young Nzinga said to her mother.

"I'm sure they are, my dear. Fa will protect them as he does us."

MICHAEL JAY NUSBAUM

Just as suddenly as the rain had started, it was over. Steam rose from the ground, which had been baked by the sun relentlessly for the past several days. Puddles strewn through the village were ever present since the ground was unable to absorb the deluge. Out from the huts came the mothers first, as they looked around to ensure that the area was safe. Not soon after came the children who ran out into the puddles and began to splash in them as if they had never seen such a sight before. Several of the women ran to the fire, which had nearly been doused by the flood. They stoked it back to life and fed it until it roared back stronger than ever.

Several hours later, Osumaka and the men return. He and two other men were each carrying small- to medium-size gazelles. This was clearly a successful hunting trip. The men headed to the center of the village to give them to the women to prepare the carcasses. No sooner did they place the animals on the ground did they hear a volley of loud thunderous noises coming from all around the village. They initially looked at the sky, assuming that the noises were thunder once again approaching.

One and then two and then three of the men fell to the ground for no apparent reason. Osumaka turned to see other African warriors approaching at full speed with long sticks spewing fire and lances coming from the direction of the palm groves. He grabbed for his spear only to realize that they had surrounded the village and that he was greatly outnumbered. Prepared not to go down without a fight, he pulled back his spear. Just then, he heard the screams of Bwana. He hesitated as he looked toward his home. Three warriors had grabbed his wife and children.

The men rounded up the villagers and forced them to the center of the area. Osumaka maintained his spear level and was ready to kill. The men who initially fired had now reloaded and had closed in the circle upon them. They trained their weapons on Osumaka and the surviving members, now huddled together like sheep.

"Put it down, you snake," one of the men called out to Osumaka as he readied to fire. "Move and I will end you in a cloud of smoke."

Likana, who had been thrown into the group with her children and the rest of the villagers, placed her hand on his shoulder. "Not now, my love. There are too many of them."

Osumaka lowered his spear as the warriors grabbed the men first and began to bind them. They were followed soon after by the women and the children. Infants were heard screaming in the huts, which the marauders soon set ablaze. The infants' screams then turned to more violent cries as the mothers and fathers fell to their knees in tears. Unable to help their babies, they wept.

The men of the village were then bound to wooden yoke collars, which were secured around their necks, and then bound with iron pins. Each one bound to another and then chained between them to form a train of enslaved humanity. Long thin sticks were used to beat both man and child into compliance. Once fully formed, with the men at the lead, the women in the middle, and the children at the very end, the string of captives was forced to march forward. All in tears, many still struggling to free their limbs from bondage and the women and children crying, they were marched away.

Osumaka strained to look back to see his wife and children but was unable to turn his head to do so. All he could see was the home, which he had known for his entire life, burning. He cried out, "Likana! Likana! Likana!"

"I am here, my love. I am here." Likana struggled to get a word out through her tears and emotions.

"The children. The children," Osumaka called out.

"They are here too, my love."

"Mother! Mother! Father!" the two children called out, along with all the other children.

It was too hard for either Osumaka or Bwana to distinguish the sounds of their children from the constant cries of the others.

"Quiet! Quiet!" one of the men shouted out as he whipped the children with his cane until they became silent.

The villagers, now captives, were marched away to an unknown fate.

The slavers used the same collars on the men as they did on the children. Many of them cried out as the loosely fitting yokes carved at the skin on their shoulders. The children cried out from the pain of iron cutting into their flesh but mostly from fear and loss. As they continued to march, the blood began to flow from their open wounds.

CHAPTER 2

The March

THE NEW CAPTIVES marched for two days through all manner of bush and vegetation. There was no chance to rest, no food, only an occasional stop by a stream for water, and unremitting pain and anguish. To them, the sky may as well have been continuously black as night.

"Likana?" Osumaka called out.

One of the guards ran up to him and beat him with a stick. "Quiet!" he shouted.

Many others tried to call out for their loved ones but were beaten repeatedly as well.

Osumaka strained to look back. He could see that one of his friends was behind him.

"Is that you, Adofo?" Osumaka said in a low voice. "My brave friend."

"Yes, it is Osumaka."

"Please ask whoever is behind you to pass word down to Likana."

"Yes, Osumaka. What is it?" Adofo asked.

"Ask her if she and the children are all right."

"Yes, Osumaka," he replied and then he whispered to the man behind him.

Soon, messages to be passed along came to Osumaka, all asking similar questions, but none yet from Likana.

Finally, a word came back from Likana.

"Likana says the children are with the women behind us, tired and hungry but fine," Adofo reports.

"And what of you, Adofo? Would you like me to send a message along?" Osumaka asked.

"No, my friend. My family is no more. They are all with Fa. I am all that remains."

"I am sorry, my brave friend," Osumaka replied. "You are strong, my friend. Find out who is behind you. I will find out if any of our hunters are in front of me. Get word to them that we will fight back at the right moment. Have them await my signal. Tell them, 'Osumaka is prepared to fight with anyone who will follow him.'"

"I will, my friend. I will," Adofo responded.

Word was spread up and down the line. Soon, Osumaka had his response. Many of the hunters were prepared to fight. They awaited Osumaka's word. They knew not how or when, but they were prepared. Once hunters, now they were warriors ready to fight for their family and friends.

Along the way, one of the children was no longer able to keep up.

"Unleash him!" shouted one of the guards to another. "Cast him off and leave him as feed for the beasts."

The other guard removed the child, no more than six years of age, from the human chain; his ankles bloodied and raw from being dragged along with the mass of humanity. His listless body was thrown to the side of the trail.

"I will carry him!" one man shouted from his bound position. "He is my nephew. Please . . . please allow me to carry him."

The guard closest to him took out his stick and whipped him in the face. "Quiet, slave!" he shouted at him as he laughed and nodded to the other guard.

The man began to weep. Not for himself but for his now orphaned nephew left to die at the side of the trail. "I will kill you!" he shouted at the guard. "With my last breath, I will see you draw your last."

Osumaka closed his eyes in the hope that the horror would fade away. With his mind filled with anger and his veins with the fury of revenge, he felt invigorated by the very thought of fighting back. He plotted his attack over and over in his head. Would they release his neck first? Or his hands? If he could just get his hands free. His heart pumped, and his blood boiled with purpose.

Their feet continued to pound the uneven surface of the well-worn path. Osumaka heard the sounds of whimpering from the women and children. The journey seemed unending and with no idea of where they were or where they were going, Osumaka began to pray to his god. *Fa, give us the strength to get through this. May I be given the chance to avenge my village? May my wife and children get through this ordeal*, he asked.

As they reached a downhill slope, Osumaka could see many losing their footing, relying upon the attachment to their fellow villagers to keep them upright. He strained to look back to see how his children were doing. He knew that his daughter, Nzinga, was neither sure of foot nor strong of stamina. No sooner than he tried to turn back did he hear a familiar voice.

"Father! Father, help me!" the young girl cried out.

Osumaka knew the sound of his daughter's voice well even though it was from far away. "My child!" he cried out.

"Father! Father help me!" she repeated.

"What is it, my daughter?" Likana cried back through her tears.

"My ankle. It is my ankle. I have done something terrible to it. It does not work," Nzinga cried back to her mother.

"Please, child, try to use it," Osumaka cried back.

The guard lunged forward and whipped him on his neck with his stick, "Quiet!"

"I can't. I can't," Nzinga cried out as she repeatedly fell, only to be dragged along by her chains. "Help me, Mother. Help me, Father. Help me. Help me," she continued to cry out.

One of the guards approached her. "This one is done. She will not make it," he said to another.

"Cut her loose and tie her to that tree," another instructed him.

The guard separated her from the chain of her fellow villagers. He tugged at her as she fell to the ground. The human chain kept on going.

"Father, Father, help me!" she repeatedly called out.

The guard dragged her across the ground, her legs too weak for her to stand. He pulled her into the edge of the trail and then tied her to a tree along the side of the path.

Soon, there was a rustling in the woods. The guard looked up to see a branch move but was unable to see the creature that had done it. He too became afraid and rapidly finished his task. He walked backward away from Nzinga and the creature that had been stalking them.

"No, please!" she shouted. "Father, Mother, help me!" she repeatedly cried out.

Her arms were wrapped around the tree. Unable to move, she kept calling out, "Father, Mother, help me."

Likana wept as she strained to look back at Nzinga. She was unable to create a single intelligible sound.

Osumaka called out to her as he struggled to break free of his bonds.

The guard who bound her to the tree shouted to the others, "The beasts will enjoy that treat very soon!"

Osumaka's body shook with overwhelming emotion. He turned his head to look back and tried to slow his movement and that of the men attached to him. The yoke cut into the skin of his neck as he strained to see his daughter. He could feel his chest tighten and couldn't breathe or make a sound. Tears began to flow from both eyes, not for the pain he was feeling, but for his daughter. Amid the tears, he managed to shout out, "NO! NO! My daughter . . . I LOVE YOU, my little one!" He struggled even harder to break free as the strength in his body seemed to fail him against the iron restraints. He would rather be dead than let his little girl die. She was his princess, his little Nzinga, his life. Yet he felt helpless to do anything for her.

The human train continued to march on. As they left, they could hear Nzinga screaming for help. Osumaka knew what fate awaited his little girl as he heard her blood-curdling screams, "Father! Mother! Help me!"

Osumaka's blood boiled even more, and he found a resurgence of strength. He pulled at the chains around his wrists. The metal cut into his skin, but he kept trying. The blood, as it flowed, seemed to lubricate his wrists, and it seemed as if he might break free, but with each try, the pain just became worse. He could not free himself, and he could not help his little girl. He broke down and, for the first time in his life, cried uncontrollably.

Likana was equally devastated. She marched in a daze, neither unaware nor unaffected. The loss of her daughter had made her numb. She could hear the sobs of her husband and this too cut into her very soul. Tears ran down her face, but she showed no emotion. Only the thought of her son Bwana kept her going. She had to continue on for him.

Along the path, they passed a female slave who had been stabbed in the chest and was lying on the path. Not soon after, they passed another woman who had been tied by the neck to a tree, and her lifeless body remained anchored in place. Still further down the road, the body of a man lay on the side of the path. His frame was emaciated, and he had clearly succumbed to the effects of starvation or disease.

They stopped only occasionally when they came upon a small stream for water. There was no food for them. It would be water or nothing at all.

Finally, they reached the edge of a wide river. Men in long dugout canoes awaited them. The men were all eerily similar to each other. They were all dark-skinned men in their twenties with muscular bodies, short curls of hair on their heads, and a very distinctive blue-striped tattoo going from their hairlines to the tips of their noses. The men spoke a very strange language. Even though they appeared as if they could be from the next village over, they were so different.

The villagers were separated into groups of six, still bound to one another. The groups were then loaded into the canoes and sent down river. Along the way, the strangely tattooed men called out to one another.

Osumaka tried to reason with them, "We are peaceful, and we are as you are. You must help us and set us free. Why would you do this? We have done nothing to you."

The men kept paddling and spoke to one another in a rhythmic tone that matched their strokes.

Several others tried to reason with the strange men as well but also without luck.

Osumaka repeated his pleas. Finally, one responded to him in his own language. "We are not Ango. We are not Mahi. We are not Sobo. We are not Fon. We are not you. We are Kroo. You are slaves. You are to do as you are told. You are not to speak. If you do, you will be beaten. If you do not take heed of your beatings, then you will be put to death."

CHAPTER 3

The Beach

THE CANOES PULLED up to a beaching area of smooth tapering sand as the mouth of the river widened rapidly and joined the sea. Many of the captives had never seen the ocean before. The sound of the waves fascinated many, while it terrified others. The sounds of screaming and metal banging on metal echoed through the seaside outpost. The beach was wide as the tide was and exposed a large swath of beach. It was growing. The day grew late in the day, and the sun was beginning to make its journey past the horizon. The smell of the ocean was thick in the air. The shoreline was so flat that Osumaka could see for miles in either direction from the mouth of the river. In addition, the captives could see a slave camp. They could see that there was some kind of structure set up at the edge of the jungle as it reached the beach. It protruded out from the vegetation that marked the beginnings of the inland forest. It was surrounded by sharpened spear-tipped trunks from hundreds of trees.

The captives were taken out of the canoes and led to an area where a blacksmith stood. As Osumaka's fellow villagers approached still bound together, the blacksmith took a branding iron out of the hot fire. He seared it into the flesh of each person who was marched in front of him in chains. The sound of the iron sizzling as it burnt into the skin could be heard all the way back to the landing area as others arrived. The men were brought to him first. Some of the men cried out, while others held their tongues to show their strength. Osumaka could see that the blue-striped men were unhooking the yokes from their necks after they were branded. He watched intently to see how they were handling his friends and neighbors as they shoved them into the holding pens. He noted that there was a gap in time from the point at which they unhooked the yokes from the two attached men to the point when they grabbed the men separately and threw them into their confinement. Osumaka believed that he and Adofo would be freed simultaneously. If there were enough warriors who were freed but not yet crammed into the pens, then Osumaka and Adofo may have the ability to attack the blue-striped men and free enough of the others to overwhelm them.

Osumaka whispered to Adofo, "Do you see what I am seeing?"

"No, my friend, all I see is that they intend to burn our arms. What do you see?" he replied.

"I see them freeing two men at a time with only two blue-striped ones guarding them," Osumaka retorted.

Adofo looked again, "I see, my friend."

"Can you take the one who will be unlocking you?" Osumaka asked.

"Yes, I see he has a knife in a pouch hanging from his waist. I will seize him by the neck and use his knife against him," Adofo said quietly.

"Yes, I too see that now. They both have knives. I will do the same. I can see at least six of our fellow warriors in the cage to the left. If we can hold them off long enough, I can try to free them."

Osumaka and Adofo were led up to the area where the blacksmith and two Kroo men were. The blacksmith took out his iron from the coals and pushed it on the flesh of Osumaka's upper arm. The intense pain traveled from his arm to his spine. It felt as though his entire body had been burned, but Osumaka did not make a sound. Adofo was next. He let out a muzzled growl. Both men seethed—their hearts pounded, their muscles flexed and readied, and their senses heightened as they had been when they hunted a thousand times before. Now, again, they would turn into the hunters. Their reflexes would be swift. Their actions decisive. They waited for their moment.

The Kroo men began unlatching the yokes. Osumaka caught the eye of one of his friends who had just been released. Osumaka nodded as he was released. His friend kept a close eye on him. The blacksmith turned to place his iron back in the fire. His Kroo man looked down for a second. He turned to see Adofo released too.

"NOW!" Osumaka yelled.

With that, Osumaka and Adofo grabbed the Kroo men closest to them. They held their left arms tightly around the necks of the blue-striped men and grabbed their knives and drove them deep into the men's chests. They fell to the ground as the others, about to be locked into their cages, pushed their way back out and overpowered the Kroo men guarding them as well.

Suddenly, the blacksmith turned to strike Adofo.

"Look out!" Osumaka called as he threw his new weapon. It flew through the air and into the chest of the blacksmith before he could strike Adofo.

Adofo flinched as the knife flew past him and into the blacksmith. Stunned, he responded, "Thank you, my warrior friend."

The sound of a trumpet from the Portuguese-run station blared out the alarm. Soldiers with muskets poured from the gate of the fortified center and streamed toward the melee.

Osumaka retrieved his knife and ran toward the other Kroo men leading the next set of captives up the beach. They abandoned their human cargo and ran toward Osumaka, Adofo, and their six warrior friends.

Likana's canoe was just pulling in. She could see the fighting and could see her proud husband Osumaka leading the charge. Her heart soared with excitement and pride.

Osumaka's knife struck the knife of a Kroo man as they raced toward each other. Osumaka placed a leg behind the Kroo and threw him over it and on to the ground. He drove his knife deep into the man's abdomen and cried out, "My friends, we fight! We fight for our families! We fight for our village! We fight for our *freedom*!"

The other villagers soon overwhelmed and killed enough Kroo to arm themselves. They headed toward the canoes to free the women and children. They jumped into the water and easily dispatched the Kroo still trapped in their canoes. The Kroo who had jumped out of the canoes swam underwater toward Osumaka and his warriors.

Adofo cried out. A Kroo man had stabbed him through his thigh from underwater. Adofo drove his knife into the water, striking his target.

They helped their loved ones from the canoes and on to the beach; however, lacking both the skill and the proper tools, they were unable to unchain them.

MICHAEL JAY NUSBAUM

Osumaka got Bwana and Likana out of their canoes, now floating away without a Kroo man to direct them, and brought them onto the beach.

"I'm frightened, Father," Bwana cried out as he threw his arms around Osumaka.

"I am proud of you, my warrior," Likana said as she, also still in chains, embraced Osumaka.

The men caught their breaths as they watched the Portuguese soldiers running over and lining up into a formation to the left with the ocean behind them.

"Do you have the ere àwòrán?" Osumaka asked Bwana.

"I do, Father. It is right here," he replied as he pulled out the necklace with the statue on it.

"Keep it close to you, my son. As long as you do, I will be there with you," Osumaka said as he kissed Bwana on the forehead.

He sang the song that he had composed for his children to Bwana to calm him. Bwana, terribly afraid, reluctantly joined in.

The soldiers were now in full formation and were marching toward the canoe landing area. They advanced in two rows with twenty men armed with long guns in each row.

"I must go, my wife," Osumaka told Likana. "Our job is not yet done."

"I know, my love," she replied as she kissed him and placed her forehead against his. "I will always love you."

"I will always love you, and I will never stop . . . till we are together again," he answered.

Osumaka stood and motioned to the others. They formed next to him as they walked further up the beach and away from the women and children. The formation of soldiers adjusted their line to form two parallel lines facing the band of lightly armed warriors.

"What are we to do?" asked Adofo.

"We are now warriors!" Osumaka called out. "We fight for our families! We fight for our village! We fight for our *freedom*!"

The men responded, "We fight for our families! We fight for our village. We fight for our *freedom*!"

With that, they charged the formation of Portuguese soldiers. The first row of soldiers knelt and took aim. The second row then lowered their rifles and took aim.

The men called in unison as they charged the line, "We fight for our families! We fight for our village! We fight for our *freedom*!"

As they drew closer, the first line of soldiers fired. Adofo and three others instantly fell to the ground. Then the second row fired. Osumaka was hit in the arm but continued to charge. He and the others who had survived both volleys lunged toward the soldiers who struggled to get their bayonets directed to their attackers. Osumaka slashed one and then two. Then the butt of one rifle was thrust into the back of Osumaka's head. He fell to the ground unconscious.

Likana cried out, "OSUMAKA! MY WARRIOR, MY HUSBAND!"

The men were cut down until none was left standing. The soldiers dragged the bodies to a pile on the center of the beach. Realizing Osumaka wasn't yet dead, one raised his bayonet to finish the job.

"Hold!" The Portuguese officer stopped the soldier.

The soldier protested, "But, sir—"

"He is worth more alive than dead, is he not?" the officer asked.

"But, sir, he killed two of our men and . . ." he replied, holding the bayonet over Osumaka still ready to strike.

"He is worth more alive than dead," the officer repeated as he motioned for the soldier to lower his weapon. He then pointed, "You two, take him there," directing two of the surviving Kroo to drag Osumaka's limp body into the holding pen.

"This warrior has more heart and more courage than all of you put together," the officer said as he pointed at the soldiers. "Had I a hundred men of his character and strength, who knows what I could do."

"Sir," the soldiers replied.

"Now, clean this up," the officer ordered. "Get those women and children up here as well before they kill you too."

The villagers were unchained and locked into separate holding pens. Iron bars held them in. Many of the captive men lay dead in a pile on the beach. After a few hours and after the sun had already set, Osumaka came to inside of the cell.

"Are you all right, Osumaka?" one man asked.

"Yes, I am," he replied as he looked around. He could see the pile of bodies on the beach only feet from their cell. "Where is Adofo?"

"He is there. Dead with the others." The man gestured.

Osumaka looked around further. He could see the others behind iron bars in separate pens.

"Likana," he called.

"I am here, my love," she replied.

"And Bwana?" he asked.

"He is with me," she assured him. "I love you, my husband," she added.

"And I love you, my wife," he replied.

"What are we to do now, Osumaka?" the man asked.

"I do not know," he replied.

"What is next for us?" the man asked.

Osumaka did not respond. What was next for them? How could they ever escape these pens? Who were these men with pale skin?

"For now, we rest," Osumaka decided as he sat back down at the edge of the cell. "For now, we rest and gain our strength for the next opportunity."

"Father," Bwana called out.

"Yes, my son?" Osumaka called into the darkness. He could hear his son's voice coming from one of the other cells but could not see him.

"I'm frightened," Bwana wept.

"Be strong, my son. Now is the time for you to rest and gain your strength."

Still scared, Bwana nonetheless replied, "Yes, Father."

With the sunrise, the men arose to the sight of a ship off shore. None of them had ever seen anything more than a canoe. The sight of the immense ship unsettled them.

"Osumaka," one man nudged Osumaka to wake up.

Osumaka opened his eyes.

Most of the men were at the bars, peering out at the sight of this huge craft sitting upon the water.

"What is it?" the man asked.

"Some kind of sea creature?" another asked.

"It is so large and does not seem to move much," yet another observed.

Osumaka did not answer. He peered out at the ship, which was now fully illuminated by the sun rising over the land behind them.

"I see things moving on it," one called out.

"I think those are men," another replied.

"That is not possible. They are far too small to be humans," the first responded.

"No, I think he is correct," Osumaka stated. "I see them too."

They were all weak by now. None of them had had food or water for almost two days. The young were lethargic, and the weak became ill.

The seaside slave station seemed to come alive with the arrival of four canoes of Kroo men who came from the ocean. They beached their craft, walked up to the cages, and peered in at the captives. Soon, the gates to the fort opened and soldiers came out led by the Portuguese officer.

He walked over to one of the Kroo men who seemed to be the leader.

"How many?" the Portuguese officer asked the Kroo.

The Kroo indicated with his hands thirty and then only men.

"Thirty," the officer replied. "Tell your captain $100 per man."

The Kroo man bowed and took his men back to the ship. This time, they came back with not only their canoes but also with one of the slave ship's launches and the first officer. The boat and canoes landed on the shore, and the first officer approached the Portuguese officer.

"I hear you have thirty men for us," he said as he approached the Portuguese officer.

"I have thirty men for you, but we have many women and children as well."

"We are only taking men on this trip. The plantations require only men as laborers. We need no women or children," the American slaver explained.

"I have some young boys who are sure to grow into strong young men for the fields," said the Portuguese officer, attempting to bargain.

"We already took a few youths at the last slave post," said the American slaver. "Our holds are only half empty. We need many more men to have a full cargo."

"This is all we have for now." The Portuguese officer shrugged.

"Well, we will take all you have for now and continue up the coast until our quota is met." The American motioned for another sailor to bring the chest. "It's $100 per head I'm told."

"Yes, they are all strong and without disease," the Portuguese officer affirmed.

The American slaver instructed his subordinate to hand over the chest. "Here is your payment. We need to load them as quickly as

MICHAEL JAY NUSBAUM

possible. We have been filling up for the past four days, and my captain grows weary of this poor harvest."

The Portuguese officer opened the chest. "It is all here," he replied. "Thirty males," he called out to his Kroo men.

Three at a time, the villagers were removed from the pen. Osumaka stood at the back. Likana and the others began to weep and cry out.

"My husband," Likana cried out as she watched the pen empty. The Kroo entered the pen and dragged Osumaka out.

"No!" Likana cried.

Bwana screamed, "Father!"

"My husband, NO!" she sobbed again.

Osumaka was chained to the other two and dragged to a canoe that had been pulled up onto the beach.

"My wife, I love you!" Osumaka shouted to them, hoping that his voice would carry over the sounds of the waves. "My son, be brave and strong. I will find you both. I will never stop looking until I find you!" They removed the men, chained them together in groups of three, and loaded them onto the canoes. The Kroo from the slave ship then paddled the canoes out to the ship they were working for and started loading them.

"I don't trust these Kroo," the sailor said to the first officer from the slave ship.

"Neither do I. They sell their countrymen into slavery and think nothing of it. They come to our ships and pretend to help us, but I have no trust for these soulless heathens," the first officer responded.

"They seem to enjoy taking the other Negroes into slavery," the sailor noted.

"Too eagerly, I would say," the first officer agreed. "Keep a close eye on them both here and on back on the ship. I will be happy to be rid of them and head home with our holds filled with cargo."

The sound of the waves soon drowned out the cries of the women and children. Osumaka tried to look back to catch one last glimpse of his family. He could not raise his hands, for they were chained to the back of the man in front of him. He could barely turn his head to see as the Kroo paddled out to the ship. The surf tossed the men in the canoes from side to side. Suddenly, one large wave hit one of the other canoes. Osumaka could see the front of the canoe rise up straight into the air. The men, chained and unable to hang on, fell out of the canoe and into the sea. The canoe crashed back down upon the water with only two stunned Kroo at either end but without paddles and without their cargo. The slaves struggled to keep their heads above water, but their chains prevented them from using their arms to stay afloat. The Kroo men panicked as they looked for their paddles to get to the men in the water. Unable to swim and without the use of his hands, the first man slipped below the waves. Soon, the second and then the third man were pulled below as well. The Kroo jumped into the water to get their paddles, completely ignoring the drowning men. They turned their canoe back around and headed back to the beach.

As Osumaka's canoe approached the ship, the sailors were already loading up the men from the canoe in front of them. The chain in front would be handed up, and the men were lifted and then dragged onto the deck. The first canoe pulled away, and now, it was time for Osumaka's canoe to unload. The ship was huge. He had never seen anything so large before in his life. It groaned and made sounds he had never heard before. The two men in front of him were pulled onto the deck, dragging him hands first upward. He struggled to stop from being dragged over the edge, but he had no sure footing. His arms came over the top first as his shoulder and right side were scraped along the wooden hull. His skin was ripped from the fresh wound on his side as he was pulled onto the deck. Three large gashes were clearly evident and now oozing blood.

Osumaka looked around. The masts of the ship seemed to soar up to the sky higher than any tree he had ever seen on land. The white-skinned sailors all spoke a strange language that he could not understand. He saw ropes everywhere and more white-faced men with swords. They led the captives/villagers through an opening in the deck and down the stairs.

"Up onto this platform!" one of the sailors shouted to the first man in their trio.

"I need one over here," a sailor called out from the other side of the hold.

"I have three," the sailor loading them responded. "You can have the last one here."

The first sailor unchained Osumaka from the other two captives and pushed him over to another sailor. The sailor pointed to the space on the rack, which was empty.

"Here, fill this space," the sailor said to Osumaka even though he knew that Osumaka had no idea what he was saying. "This one died last night. We need to fill all the gaps."

Osumaka was laid down next to the feet of two men. He was then chained to them.

"That's all from this post," one of the sailors called out.

"Good. Let's get away from this horrid stench," the other replied.

The white-faced men headed back up the steps. Osumaka strained to see where they were going and what was happening. The ship was rocking slightly from side to side, and Osumaka felt dizzy. Suddenly, the hatch closed and the hold became pitch-black with only a few beams of sunlight penetrating small gaps in the deck. Osumaka and the new captives found breathing difficult as the stagnant air filled the place with the odor of feces, urine, and fear.

Back on shore, the American slaver confronted the Portuguese officer.

"Three of those men just drowned," he argued.

"That is not my problem," the Portuguese officer replied in English and again in Spanish.

"How is that not your problem?" the American slaver responded. "You owe me $300."

"No, I owe you nothing," the Portuguese officer replied. "The Kroo men who took those slaves were yours, not mine. They allowed the slaves to fall over and drown. Therefore, they owe you the money and not I."

The four soldiers with the Portuguese officer lined up behind him. The American slaver looked at the Portuguese soldiers with rifles in hand. He looked back at his two sailors armed with only knives.

"I suppose that you are correct," he replied with bad temper. "We will have to fill that loss at the next outpost."

With that, the sailors and Kroo returned to the boat. Two Kroo pushed the American's boat off and out past the break and then got into their canoes and paddled back to the ship as well. When the sailors reached the ship, two lines were cast down. The small boat was hoisted up as the sailors and Kroo climbed onto the deck.

"What happened?" asked the captain.

"We only loaded twenty-seven," the first officer responded.

"What happened? We paid for thirty!" the captain shouted.

"Yes, sir." The first officer was still angry with the Portuguese.

"You demanded reparation?" the captain asked.

"I did, sir, but they refused to pay, stating that the Kroo had allowed the cargo to fall overboard. Therefore the Kroo were responsible for the loss and not them."

"Damn swine Portuguese!" the captain of the slave ship swore. "Had this been another time, another ship, and other circumstances, I would open fire upon that post and level it with my cannon. But I have not the firepower to take them on this godforsaken ship!"

With that, the captain stormed away into his quarters, and the ship set sail for the next slave post.

CHAPTER 4

Separation

B ACK ON SHORE, the women and children were weeping at the loss of their husbands, sons, and brothers. Some women dropped to the ground and began feeding sand into their mouths.

"Mother, why do they do that?" Bwana asked.

"I am not certain, my son," she replied.

"Won't they get sick?" Bwana was persistent. "This dirt is strange. It is white and scratchy."

"Yes, my son, it is. I know not why they do that."

"It makes no sense, Mother," he replied.

"Perhaps they are trying to take some of our homeland with them by eating it," she replied.

"Mother, I think that they are trying to kill themselves with it," he replied.

"I do not think that they believe that they will die if they eat this strange dirt," she responded.

"Where do you think they are taking Father?" Bwana changed his focus to a new subject.

Likana was irritated by his questions and unsure about what would happen to them, so she thought carefully about how to answer the question. She knew that Osumaka was not going to a good place, but she did not want her son to worry.

"They are taking him to a place to train as a soldier," she lied.

"So father will become a soldier like those we saw with the fancy outfits and the sticks of fire?" he asked.

"Yes," she replied, "they need to teach him how to use the sticks of fire."

"I bet he'll be the best soldier they ever had!" Bwana decided cheerfully. His mother's untruth had worked to relieve his worry.

"I am certain of that, my son," she replied. Likana pretended an optimism she could not feel. Where was her husband going? Would she ever see him again? What might her future bring?

They watched as the ship holding Osumaka sailed off. First slowly and then rapidly, it seemed to diminish in size as it headed north up the coast in search of more slaves to fill its holds.

Four Kroo came by the pens with water and pieces of fish for the slaves. They poured the water into the outstretched hands of the women and children as they lined up at the bars.

"Mother, Mother!" Bwana called out, "I can't get any water!"

His mother had some in her hands. "Here, you drink this, my son. You need this more than I do," she said as she gave him all the water that she had received.

Soon, the Kroo were tossing pieces of fish into the pens.

"What is this?" Bwana asked as he picked up the sand-covered piece of fish.

"Eat it, my son. This may be all we get for a while," she replied as she bit into a piece herself.

"Oh, this is terrible!" Bwana complained. Used to eating land animals, the child was repelled by the new flavor. "I can't eat it. It smells bad; like it's rotten."

Likana also did not care for the fish but knew they had to keep up their strength. Her greatest fear was that if Bwana became weak, she would lose him as she had Nzinga. She began to cajole him, trying to mask her terror. "Please, Bwana, you must eat. You can have mine. There is no white dirt on mine," she said as she exchanged their pieces of fish.

"Must I?" He pouted. Likana's dissembling was working. Her son was being a normal picky eater with no sense that refusing the smelly food might doom him.

"You must, my son," she replied. "You must so that you may live." Bwana was taken aback and stopped whining.

They both ate the pieces of fish. Many of the villagers could not stand neither the smell nor the taste, but they were so hungry that they would eat almost anything.

MICHAEL JAY NUSBAUM

Within hours, another ship approached from the south. This ship was even larger than the last. It had three large masts and sleek lines.

"Oh, Mother, look at that one!" Bwana alerted his mother.

The ship was the *Nightingale*. She had been sailing up and down the coast as the others did, loading her cargo. The boat drew closer and then seemed to remain fixed in position. Just as before, the blue-striped Kroo approached the shore in canoes, but this time, two white boats joined them from the ship.

"Look, Mother. Look!" Bwana shouted.

"I see, Bwana," she replied.

"I wonder what they want?" he asked out loud.

"I do not know, little one," she replied. Likana tried desperately to remain composed for her son, but she knew they would be taken aboard this new ship as her husband had been taken earlier.

Just as before, the Portuguese officer met the men from the ship. Again, they exchanged money and greetings. This time, the Kroo headed over to the pens where Likana and Bwana were held.

"I think that they are coming for us," one woman stated.

"If I cannot be with my husband and son, I do not wish to live!" another shouted.

The Kroo began binding up the women and children. Likana was grabbed first.

"Bwana!" Likana cried out, terrified. "Come here!" Her son was the only family she had left—she could not lose him.

"I can't, Mother! I can't get to you!" Bwana began to panic.

He struggled to get to her, but other children blocked his way. The Kroo had chained at least a dozen women and children before they got to Bwana.

"Mother!" he began sobbing. "Mother! Don't leave me!" Bwana began to understand the gravity of the situation, and he grew increasingly frantic.

"I'm here, my son. I'm here," she called back into the crowd but could not see him. "It will be all right!" Likana knew that the Kroo might kill Bwana as they had Nzinga if he did not calm down.

"Mother, I'm scared!" Bwana screamed.

"We will be together!" Again, she tried to reassure him while fearing a dreadful fate. "We will be together on the island which floats out upon the water."

"All right, Mother," Bwana cried, still terrified. He was slightly soothed by his mother's confident voice. "I will be there too. Wait for me."

"I will, my sweet son. I will wait there for you," she responded as tears poured down her face. She tried to sound brave for her son, but her knees were weak, and she feared the worst. She hoped Bwana couldn't hear the tears in her voice.

The Kroo loaded the first groups of villagers onto the canoes and rowed out to the ship. Everyone was crying. Mothers had been separated from their own children but tried to comfort other women's children as best as they could, knowing that their neighbors would be doing the same. One ten-year-old child next to Likana was crying, "Mother, Mother. I want my mother."

"I know, child. Your mother will be with you soon," Likana assured the young girl.

"Why? Where did she go?" the girl asked.

"She is right behind us," Likana replied. Likana regretted the small lies she was telling but knew that the children's spirits had to stay up. "She asked me to take care of you until she could get to you. Is that all right?"

"Did she really?" the child asked as she gasped for breath in between sobs.

"Yes," Likana nodded comfortingly. "I will take care of you till she can get you."

"Oh, thank you," the girl said as she tried to stem her tears.

The canoes approached the boat. Although the villagers could not read the name on the side of the boat, it read Nightingale. Bound together in pairs, they were taken out of the canoes and led onto the deck where men with pale white faces and odd clothes waited for them. The villagers looked up at the tall masts and at the strange men who had no color to their skin. They had never seen anything so tall before or anyone so pale before. Trees don't grow that large in Africa, and the people with the white skin were so odd looking. It all seemed overwhelmingly strange. They were brought to an open hatch, which appeared to be a dark hole leading down into the ship. Here, the white-faced men unshackled them from the person behind them. Each woman turned and looked back at those behind them as they slowly descended the steps leading to the dark and foul-smelling place. They took each step in fear, not knowing whether or not they were being led to their deaths. Some, uncertain of where they were or where they were headed, hesitated before entering the opening. Those who lingered too long at the entrance were pushed down into the hold. The space was dark and the air stagnant and stale. The villagers were quickly stunned into silence by both the stench and the darkness. Their captors gave no instructions that the women could understand. They just pantomimed, "Get in there!" Finally, mothers were able to reunite with their children, and despite the dankness, there was brief joy in the hold. They sought out others whom they knew and formed little groups inside the dark and cramped space. The height of the ship's hold was at most five feet. Only the small children could walk upright, while everyone else had to duck and crouch in order to move at all. Only the light coming from between the wooden planks above and from the open hatch illuminated the cramped space.

"Mother!" Bwana shouted as he ran to Likana.

"Bwana, MY SON!" Likana yelled back. The little boy ran into her with a force that nearly knocked her over. She knelt down on both knees and held him tightly against her. Whatever happened next, they would be together.

"I feared I would never see you again!" he said to her as he held on just as tightly.

"I will never let you go again," she said to him. "From now on, we stay together."

Likana wasn't sure whether she meant only until the journey was over or not. "Yes, Mother. Yes, I like that idea," he replied.

They headed to a corner where several other members of their tribe—three other women and two children—were gathered, having found a space against the side of the ship between two of the ship's ribs.

"Likana," one called out.

Likana clutched Bwana's hand and made her way over to the gathering.

"Hello, my friends," she responded as she sat down next to them.

"What is this place?" one asked the group.

"I do not know," another responded.

"It is a floating island," Likana replied.

"Where do you think they are taking us?" a third asked.

Soon, more and more captives were ushered into the hold. Space soon became very cramped and there was no longer room to move about. Likana suddenly missed her son who had slipped his hand from her grasp.

"Bwana, come here!" Likana screamed.

"Yes, Mother," he replied.

"You must stay with me, remember?" she asked.

"Yes, but we were going to play over there on those things," he replied. After their reunion, Bwana had lost much of his fear and began to behave again like a normal six-year-old with his friends.

"No, you must stay with me. Soon, there will be no room to move about, and we might get separated again." Likana and the other mothers tried to contain their panic while ensuring that the children understood their situation. Every woman feared being separated from what was left of her family.

"Yes, Mother," he replied. Although Bwana wanted to play with his friends, the thought of being separated from his mother again subdued him.

More people continued to climb down the steps, filling the hold. Soon, there was no more room. They all struggled to find a place to sit. Mothers tried to protect space for their children, but the crowd soon pushed the gaps closed, and the children were forced into their mothers' laps.

"How can they put more down here?" one woman asked.

"There's no more room," another called out.

"Perhaps they don't know that there is not room left for any more?" another woman across the hold wondered.

Soon, the hatches closed, and even the brief flashes of light ended. Children started to cry as the dark enveloped them. The mothers found it difficult to soothe their children, not knowing what was in store for any of them.

CHAPTER 5

Michael Smith

New York City, Michael Smith, November, 1860
(*Five Months before Osumaka's Capture*)

DRESSED IN A United States Navy uniform, I walked briskly
along the busy New York City street, staring intently at a
book in my left hand. My fingers followed the handwritten words,
which I had scribbled in my notebook titled The Story of My Life.

From it, I reread the words in my journal entries:

"I have, unfortunately, not held a plethora of robust convictions in
my life. Like other men, I feel that I share a checkered history of both
good and bad. It is ultimately, I believe, the deeds and actions in life
that define us. Only through those who do not tolerate injustice and
who stand up on the side of freedom is true good is done on earth. I
must also endeavor to clarify that I am not, nor have I ever been, a very
religious man, to the great disdain of my parents.

While I do believe in the idea of God and a creator, I personally
feel that religion has divided us, and that it tends to bring out the worst
in mankind rather than the best. That one man could enslave another
is just such an example. It bewilders me that human beings have yet
to learn the lesson taught so many years ago. God directed Moses to
lead his people out of bondage, and the descendants of those people,
Christian, Jew, and Mohammedan alike, should know better than
anyone else that slavery is unjust and should never be tolerated. Yet we,
as a small nation, accepted that evil, partook of its vile bouquet, and
wallowed in its rancor.

I was born Michael Joshua Smith in New York City on May the ninth the year of our lord 1835. Our family had little in the way of means. My parents had come over from Romania, looking for a better life. My father is Romanian Catholic, and my mother of German Jewish descent. This did not go over very well with either family. The backdrop of their marriage was the hatred of Jews that was reaching a fever pitch in Europe. Many were being beaten, killed, and raped. The anger seemed to be without reason other than the alleged cultural differences between Jews of Europe and the rest of their neighbors. This difference seemed to be enough to allow those who incited violence to rise up and blame the Jews for all the problems that existed. My father recognized this even though my mother and her family refused to admit that the home they had loved for generations no longer welcomed them. He did not wish to leave, but his love for his wife prevailed, and he chose to leave for freedom in the United States. My father's last name was actually Fieraru which means "one who works with iron." Being new to this country and wanting to assimilate more easily, my father decided to change their surname to Smith, the English meaning of Fieraru. They had very little in the way of possessions when they arrived. Most of what they did own, they wore on their backs. The one prized item which they brought over was a box with all sorts of needles and threads. My father was a tailor, and my mother a seamstress. Together, they took in clothing from their neighbors and repaired or tailored them. When they saved up enough money, they would buy more thread and pieces of scrap fabric with which they make garments. They specialized in women's dresses.

As for me, as a child, I became no stranger to trouble. The city was a bustle with activity and offered many ways for a young man to stray from the path of righteousness. Since we did not have much, I found it incumbent upon myself to seek additional forms of income. My inner moral compass, however, refused to permit me to engage in the acquisition of wealth by outright theft. Instead, I found myself to be quite adept at the art of gambling. The thing of it was that my skills in the art of risk were admirable over a wide range of games of chance. It is quite possible that my young age and seemingly innocent appearance led many of my opponents to be lulled into a state of overconfidence. Despite my age, I acquired a rapid and comprehensive knowledge of the art of cardsharping. One important event in my life occurred in an establishment that was better known as a house of ill repute than for its reputation as a gambling institution. It was there that I fell in love for the first time. While I never acted upon my feelings of love, they were nonetheless strong. One evening, I entered with a friend of mine with the intention of separating some drunken fools from their hard earned pay. As I entered the establishment for the first time, I laid eyes upon Emily. She was hardly much older than I yet had an air about her of worldliness and sophistication. Her hair consisted of corkscrews of blond curls on either side of her face. Her delicate face was similar to a small child's baby doll that I had seen in a shop window. She wore a dress with both shoulders exposed to all. The curve of her neck gently tapered to her chest, where she accentuated her womanly breasts with a tight corset and deep cleavage. My eyes were naturally drawn there. Emily was the first woman whom I had ever truly looked forward to seeing on a regular basis, although I did not learn her name until I had seen her several times. I noted every change in her coiffure and the shade of her dresses—oh, how they emphasized her eyes! I noted every subtle tone in her voice. Day after day, I observed her from afar. Each time I saw her, a smile grew upon my face and warmth in my heart. I became so attuned to her laugh that I hardly had to turn to find her in the crowded room to see her. After several weeks, I had the opportunity to finally speak to her.

Her first words to me were rather prosaic. "Hello, young man. What brings you here tonight?"

I didn't know how to respond or what to say. I found my eyes once again drawn to the valley of her bosom, which I had only viewed from the other side of the room. I wanted to speak, yet nothing seemed to come out and then I managed to utter just a few words in response, "Ma'am, I'm not as young as you might believe."

"Not so young as you might believe," that was the best that I could come up with. Me, a sharp-witted master of the game of chance and an experienced man about town. She let out a little laugh and placed her hand on my shoulder. The energy from my body seemed to drain, my head spun in a mass of confusion, and I was unable to speak once again. No sooner did I finish chastising myself for the inept response than did a gentleman of much advanced age and in much finer garb came over to court Emily.

"It was nice talking to you," she said as she turned and blew me a kiss. She then sauntered off with the old roué and headed up the set of stairs. I hoped, meanly, that their congress upstairs failed because he was unable to perform up to Emily's undoubtedly high standards. I fantasized that she laughed at his efforts. I not-so-secretly wished that I had gone up those steps with her. But as Emily was not my goal for the evening, I let go of my prurient fantasies and focused back on the task at hand.

The next evening, I returned in hopes of redeeming myself to Emily and to myself. I entered at the same time that I had done many times before and listened for that distinctive sound, but it never came. I searched the room, but she was nowhere to be found. My friend chided me to join him at the table and to make our wages for the evening, but I couldn't focus. Perhaps she was upstairs with that old man again. I waited and watched while couples came and went from the rooms upon the landing but no Emily. Finally, I gathered up the courage to ask one of the bar maids.

"Pardon me, but is Emily here tonight?" I asked.

"Emily? No, I have not seen a hair of her since the other night. Quite odd for her since she is never one to stray far." The overly padded and scantily dressed woman stated as she looked around the room as well. "Perhaps she wasn't feeling well," she surmised as she walked away.

Despite her disappearance, I couldn't get my mind off Emily. In just a few short encounters, she had become my muse and my reason for being. She featured in many dreams and became the obsession of my ascension into manhood. I returned every day for the next three days, hoping to see her. I couldn't gamble. I couldn't do anything but think of her, but she never showed. I eventually asked the barkeep to tell me where she lived. It cost me two nights' earnings, but he eventually gave me her address.

That evening, I headed over to her flat, which was in a part of town I can only describe as derelict even for someone with my limited resources. Not knowing which window was hers, I peered at the four-story building, hoping to get a glimpse of her. I spent quite a few hours across the street until my eyes could stay open no longer. I headed home, intent upon returning the next day. With my decision, I stumbled, half asleep back to my parents' home. I may have fallen asleep before my head and pillow met. I was still fully dressed.

MICHAEL JAY NUSBAUM

Late the next morning, I arose to find the place quiet. My parents had left and gone about their daily business without arousing me from my slumber. This was not a small feat since our home consisted of three rooms with one being a washroom, the other half bedroom and half kitchen, and the other half congregating space and half tailor's workroom. My mother was unable to have more children after my birth. Her infertility weighed heavily upon her, but I did not regret the fact that I was an only child. I occasionally considered the joys a sibling would have brought to my life, but then I would see how my friends and neighbors fought with their siblings. The parties used such vigor and venom that I would be certain that one of the two would not survive the engagement. Then I would see them shortly thereafter no longer malicious or vicious. Sibling relationships were quite strange relationships, and clearly, I lacked insight into their dynamics.

Once I found the strength to accommodate the growls of my innards, I put myself together and headed out in search of Emily. The neighborhood in which she resided was even worse than I had thought upon my initial visit. My previous perch was now occupied by a vagrant whose rank odor seemed to permeate several hundred feet in all directions even without a breeze. I could not distinguish his smell from that of the horse dung in the middle of the road. I suspect that the heaviest of rains would be unable to wash this poor wretch clean even if it continued upon him for forty days and forty nights. As a result, I found compelled to enter the building and search for her apartment, which was on the third floor.

The stoop consisted of four steps with at least as many rodents. Two termite-infested doors of questionable craftsmanship that hung askew from broken hinges were the immediate obstacle and passing the threshold of the building placed me in no better circumstance. What appeared to be either a very sleep-deprived or dead cat lay in the corner of the hallway just beneath the landing to the stairway. Paint and paper peeling from the walls cast shadows and ripples no different from what I have witnessed in the harbor. The only light to guide my way came from a broken window at the midway landing heading up the stairs. I turned to look at the first doorway number three. I looked up the stairwell to see how high my climb would take me. As I came upon the next landing, I heard a door open. No sooner did I hear the siren's voice I sought than I heard the burblings of a young boy. I froze in place, unable to move. She was leaving her home with her son. I rapidly turned and ran back down the stairwell. They came down the stairs after me, but luckily, they were too far away for her to identify me. I headed out the door and across the street, past the malodorous vagrant and into the entry of an alley. I turned and noticed her exiting the building. She was dressed modestly in a long dress with a high bodice. Even her blouse covered her neck all the way up to her chin. I watched as they headed down the street and then followed. No one spoke to her, and she only spoke to the young boy in her tow. I marveled at the contrast between the vivacious Emily of the saloon, a person who lit up the room with her mere presence, and this Emily, a woman who blended into the background of the downtrodden so well. I watched as she stopped at a fruit cart and selected one apple, a tomato, and two potatoes. She continued on as she headed out of her neighborhood. I hoped that no one would witness my surveillance of this woman, lest they think I had malicious intent toward her. I struggled to stay far enough behind not to be noticed but not too far away to lose sight of her and the young boy.

I was happy to have seen her in this way, but I soon found myself embarrassed by what I was doing. So I decided to leave satisfied with having seen this side of my Emily. As I rounded the corner, I noticed a group of boys, around the same age as me, directly across the street. They were huddled around a young black boy and were clearly harassing him. I slowed my pace as I watched what was going on. I counted six of them picking on the one black boy and shouting out racial epithets against him as they shoved and pushed him. This scene was a familiar one for me, as I had been in that boy's position way too many times. If you're a Jew in New York City that dares to go outside of your neighborhood, you learn to defend yourself as a matter of survival. The result is that I had become quite adept at fighting and equally intolerant of such a situation. Before I knew what I was doing, I had crossed the street and inserted myself between the young black boy and the crowd of angry youth.

"Who the hell are you?" the most aggressive of the boys asked with a thick Irish accent.

"What's your name?" I asked the boy being picked on while ignoring the others.

He looked at me unsure why I was asking him his name but kept his eyes on the others very carefully.

MICHAEL JAY NUSBAUM

"Nathanial," he responded with a quavering voice.

"I'm talking to you!" shouted the lead bully.

"This may not end well," I said to Nathanial, "but two against six are better odds!"

While Nathanial was digesting what I had just said to him, I turned and landed a punch square on the jaw of the lead bully. He immediately dropped to the ground, and his cohorts didn't hesitate to insert themselves right into the fight. I took on three of them, landing punch after punch while taking a few hits myself. Nathanial was holding his own until one of the two boys on him pulled out a club. I quickly jumped to his aid and grabbed the boy with the bat from behind, placing him in a chokehold. Two others began to punch me in the back and head as I held tight to the neck of the boy with the bat.

"Nathanial," I shouted, "grab the club!"

The boy soon dropped the club, and Nathanial picked it up. Now, three of them were on me while I felt blow after blow hitting my head. I wasn't sure how many more of those hits I could take before I might black out. I could hear Nathanial screaming at them and saw him swinging the bat like one of those baseball players. *Crack!* was followed by another *crack* as his bat found its targets. Before I knew it, Nathanial had managed to drive all of them off.

"Are you all right?" Nathanial asked me as he leaned over me.

I was on all fours on the sidewalk and was struggling to stay awake. "Not sure."

"Come with me," Nathanial said as he reached under my arms and helped me up. "You are one crazy son of a bitch."

"Yes, well, I couldn't just walk by. I've been in your spot way too many times."

"Wow, you're really bleeding," Nathanial said as the blood from my scalp now ran down my face. "Here," Nathanial said as he took off his white shirt and used it as a bandage. "My parents' apartment isn't far from here."

I held the shirt to my head as Nathanial kept me steady. We rounded the corner and headed down the block.

Even though it was only a few hundred yards, it felt as if we'd journeyed miles. "We live here," Nathanial said. "My parents' apartment is on the fourth floor. Do you think you can walk up?"

"Sure, I'm fine," I replied as I walked through the opened door. I looked up the stairwell and started walking. I don't know how far I walked up since the next thing I knew, I was waking up in Nathanial's parents' apartment.

"He's waking up now!" a woman's voice called. "Nathanial!"

My vision was still blurred, and only the sounds were clear. I could feel someone's hands on my head and someone wiping the blood off my face.

"Hey there," the woman's voice said softly. "How are you feeling?"

"Where am I?" I asked.

"You're in my parents' apartment," Nathanial told me. "You passed out in the stairs on our way up. My father had to help me carry you up here."

"I have to sit up," I said as I was feeling pressure in my head.

"I think it's best that you continue to lay down," the female voice said.

"I really need to sit up," I repeated as I started to sit up.

"My mom is a midwife. She knows quite a bit. I think you'd best listen to her," Nathanial replied.

"What's your name?" asked Nathanial's mother. She was an attractive slender woman with long black hair, caring eyes, and a soft motherly touch.

"Michael," I replied. "Michael Smith."

"Well, Michael Smith, you've lost quite a bit of blood, and it's best that you stay lying down for a while," she said.

"You are one crazy son of a bitch!" shouted Nathanial. I seemed to remember he'd told me that before. Or did I?

"Nathanial!" His mother reprimanded him. "We'll have none of that talk in this house."

"Yes, ma'am," he replied sheepishly.

"What's goin' on with the white boy?" asked an older man from the room's doorway. I guessed he was Nathanial's father. He was a large man with a bit of a belly and a deep husky voice.

"He's awake," replied Nathanial.

"Thank Jesus!" he shouted. "We can't have no white boy dying in our apartment. Jesus only knows what would happen."

"I'm fine, sir," I said.

He leaned over me and lifted the towel off my head to look at my wounds. "You are one crazy son of a bitch!" he told me gleefully.

Nathanial's mom took a swing at him and hit him in the back, "Carl! I'll have no cussing in my home!"

"I know. I know. But he is one crazy son of a bitch!" the father said, laughing as Nathanial let out a chuckle as well.

Nathanial came over and pulled up a small chair. I was on the couch in what appeared to be a single-room apartment.

"I just wanted to thank you for helping me out back there," Nathanial said.

"My pleasure," I replied. "I've been there myself, and I've had the crap beaten out of me too many times for me to recall."

Nathaniel's father laughed and said, "I told you. He's one crazy son of a bitch!"

"Carl!" the mom shouted out. "Now I know where Nathan gets it from."

"I was just curious. Why were those kids attacking you?" I asked Nathanial.

"All I did is ask a white girl where she got the candy she was eating. The next thing I knew, they surrounded me and wouldn't let me leave. I tried to get away, but they kept shoving me back, calling me names and telling me they were going to kill me," he replied.

"Where do you live, Michael?" Nathan's mother asked.

"Quite way from here, ma'am," I replied.

"I could've told you that!" shouted the father from the other side of the room. I suspected that his booming voice would be comforting in normal times, but not when my head felt as if it might split open.

"Your mom must be worried sick that you're not home," she said.

"No, she's used to me staying out late," I assured her. "Besides, I don't want her to see me like this."

"Well, you can stay here until you're feeling better," she said.

"I'm not sure," Carl argued from the kitchen area.

"But, Dad, he needs our help," Nathanial replied.

"Carl!" The mom scolded him. "He's going to stay here, and we are going to take care of him until he feels better."

"I'm not sure. I just don't want anyone . . . thinking the worst and accusing us of kidnapping him or something."

"Dad, he's like this because he helped me," Nathanial said. "Besides, he can sleep in my bed."

Nathanial pointed to a pile of old blankets in the corner of the room. There weren't any beds in the room. I wondered if I had missed something or if there were doors to other rooms that I couldn't see.

"I don't want to put any of you out," I said as I sat up slowly. "I'm feeling better already."

"Here, have some soup," the mom said to me as she spoon-fed me the soup.

"Um . . . It's very good," I replied sincerely.

"My dad gets like this sometimes," Nathanial said quietly to me as he put his hand on my shoulder. "I thank you."

The father walked over to me. "Look, Michael, it's nothing personal. I'm thankful to you that you helped Nate out. It's just that the police are just lookin' for any reason to arrest black folk like us, and havin' a beat-up white boy in our apartment is just enough reason for them."

"I understand, sir," I replied.

"You don't know what it's like for us," Nathaniel said.

"No, you're right. I don't, but I think I have an idea," I replied.

"These kinds of things happen to us all the time. If they aren't spitting at us, then they're beating us up, and the police certainly aren't here to protect us. I thought things would be better for us here in the city. Most of the time it's fine, but you never know. I mean for us, not you," he said solemnly. "I was born a slave and know how the world really is. My wife and son were born free here in the North and don't feel the same as I do. They haven't seen the things that I have seen. Our skin color makes us too easy to be seen and too easy to be nasty to."

I looked at Nathanial and then back at his dad. "I don't know what to say."

"There ain't nothing for you to say. It's just the way of the world. What chances do you think Nathan has? Oh sure, he could find work as a butler if he's lucky. More likely, he'll be sweeping the streets like his dad, washing dishes in restaurants we're not even allowed in."

I didn't know how to respond. He was right. I knew that he was right, and I had felt quite a bit of discrimination myself just for being half-Jewish.

"I've felt some of that. Clearly not at the same level as you," I replied.

"And how would that be?" he asked.

MICHAEL JAY NUSBAUM

"Well, I'm half-Jewish on my mom's side. I'm not allowed in certain places. I'm not allowed to go to many schools, restaurants, or even hotels. I'm not even allowed to go to many hospitals. I've had people beat me up simply because 'I'm a Jew.' I do get it."

"I had no idea," the dad replied as he looked at me more closely. "You don't look like a Jew."

I really wasn't sure what he meant by that.

"That's fine," the mom told us. "Our Lord Jesus was a Jew too. You're welcome in this home anytime."

"Thank you, ma'am. I appreciate it. By the way, I'm sorry. I didn't get your last name," I said looking at Nathanial.

"Smith," he replied with a smile.

"Really," I asked.

"Yup," Nathanial said.

"Isn't that somethin'," His father seemed amused.

"Well, thank you, Mr. Smith, Mrs. Smith," I said.

"You're welcome, Michael, and you're welcome back here anytime," said Mrs. Smith.

"It's not you, son," the father said to me. "In a world where you can't even make eye contact with a white person without being accused of being uppity or dangerous, where you are suspect simply because of the color of your skin and where you are judged based on your appearance and their prejudice rather than your character—there is little hope for us here."

I stayed with them for a few more hours. We had dinner, and we talked. We talked about racism and slavery and how discrimination isn't always in the open here in the North, but that it is hidden in the shadows. We talked about friends of theirs who were abducted and never heard from again. We talked about their ancestors and the history of this country when it comes to slavery. They woke me up to what was really going on. I had always thought that only the South was the problem. That slavery and racism were relegated to the southern half of this country. That evening, I came to realize that racism in the United States had no boundaries. I never did see Nathanial again after that, but my day with him changed me profoundly.

I came to realize by my sixteenth birthday that my options in life were quite limited. Given the fact that I was quite tall and muscular for my age, it was very easy for me to pass myself off as being eighteen. I would frequently visit the ports in New York City, where various ships moored and where their more naïve crew members were an easy target for my gambling skills. One day, a few months into my sixteenth year, I found myself being pursued by a number of unsavory characters to whom I think that I may have been in debt to about $80. The storefront in which I sought refuge from my pursuers just happened to be a United States naval office. Given my belief that everything happens for a reason, I threw caution to the winds and decided to sign up. I added two years to my age to meet the recruiting requirements. Thus at age sixteen and just a few weeks after my encounter with Nathaniel, I entered the United States Navy completely unaware of what that entailed. Over the next seven years, I traveled extensively with the navy. My deployments took me from the Caribbean to South America and to numerous ports within the United States. I paid close attention to detail, learned all that I could, and impressed my superiors. Over this period of time, I worked my way up the ranks and served on several ships. On November 5, 1860, I was assigned as second lieutenant to the USS *Saratoga*, which was recently recommissioned.

We departed the port of Philadelphia on November 15, 1860, and set sail for the west coast of Africa. During this journey, I endeavored to keep a log in my book—a log separate from the ship's log, not quite a diary, but more of a log of events, emotions, and feelings. I felt as though I was about to embark upon an epic journey; an epic equivalent to Homer's *The Odyssey*. I understood that the endeavor set before me is one in which uncounted lives could be positively affected.

My world is a turbulent one, and our country is on the cusp of a new age. The British have already abolished slavery, thus our northern neighbor Canada and British colonies in the Caribbean are free of the scourge of slavery as well. The political tide turns, I hope, toward emancipation of slaves here in the United States.

We are frequently reminded by those who favor slavery that only 6 percent of all those taken from the shores of Africa ended up in these United States and that the vast majority of those enslaved were taken to the islands of the Caribbean and to South America, not to our United States. This fact should not diminish the severity of the offense. The children born of these slaves were also forced into slavery, thus the ranks of the slaves within our borders have swelled.

Until next March, our president is James Buchanan. Since I have come to follow politics closely, I have made an effort to read as much as I could about our president. He is an odd man to say the least and one whom many referred to as a "Ms. Nancy." He was unmarried and lived with his best friend William Rufus King, a man of questionable masculinity, for over a decade. It was not uncommon for some to refer to the two of them when they were in public together as "Ms. Nancy" and "Aunt Fancy." His unmarried status caused quite a stir in Washington and quite a problem for the White House staff. Because of his lack of a wife, President Buchanan imported his niece into the White House. Her charm and well-bred social graces served her well in this role as surrogate for a president's wife. It is well known that the White House staff, uneasy as to the unusual situation, approached President Buchanan and asked him how they should address his niece. He simply stated, "Refer to her as my first lady."

Buchanan's intolerance and personal distaste for the institution of slavery is, alas, matched by his strict adherence to the Constitution. He is fond of saying, "I acknowledge *no master but the law*," and refuses even to consider that the institution of slavery can be ended by people outside the South . . . Buchanan seemed to be tolerant of slavery. Thus, in his 1860 State of the Union Address, he said, "The incessant and violent agitation of the slavery question throughout the North for the last quarter of a century has at length produced its malign influence on the slaves and inspired them with vague notions of freedom. Hence, a sense of security no longer exists around the family altar. This feeling of peace at home has given place to apprehensions of servile insurrections. Many a matron throughout the South retires at night in dread of what may befall herself and children before the morning." His inaction certainly leads many to believe that if the Southern states do secede and civil war results, it should really be known as Buchanan's War.

My love for politics, by this point, had become a bit of an obsession for me. I found myself fascinated by the debates between politicians over the issue of slavery. Beginning with a series of very public and highly publicized political debates back in 1858, the then-former Rep. Abraham Lincoln, in his campaign for a U.S. Senate seat, openly opposed slavery. I soon found myself admiring this man Lincoln. Unfortunately, Mr. Lincoln lost that election to Stephen A. Douglas for the Illinois senate seat, but he continued the debate opposing slavery. It was during the presidential race of 1860 when Lincoln came from political obscurity to secure the newly formed Republican Party presidential nomination. The Southern states were now in turmoil. Were this man to win the presidency, they felt, he would tear the country in two, and without any significant support from the South, Lincoln took the election by sweeping the North. The proslavery Democratic Party was outraged, but it made no difference. I look forward to Lincoln's presidency to right some of the deepest wrongs of our country. It was widely reported that Buchanan said to Lincoln upon his departure, "If you are as happy to obtain the office as I am to leave it, then you are a very happy man indeed!"

Fearing that Lincoln would end slavery, seven Southern states who were totally reliant upon slave labor announced their secession from the Union by February 1861. This defection had significant political implications as the secession from the Union led to the departure of the proslavery democratic congressmen and senators from the South to take up their new positions in the Confederate States of America. Thus the antislavery Republican Party took firm control of Congress, and its more radical leaders refused to yield on their stance. The result was that no compromises could be achieved and no reconciliation was possible on the question of slavery.

In his second inaugural address, President Lincoln stated, "Both parties deprecated war, but one of them would make war rather than let the nation survive, and the other would accept war rather than let it perish, and the war came."

We set sail for the west coast of Africa before President Lincoln was to be sworn into office on March 4, 1861. Everyone on board the *Saratoga* knew that tensions were increasing at home, but none of us knew how bad it was actually getting. We were trained as sailors of the proud United States Navy. We were brothers in arms, and we came from all across this great land. The question of abolishing slavery was now all that anyone spoke of at home. I know that this single issue will set our nation and our friendships on a course that could not be plotted. I have no idea what lay before us, but I knew the cost of freedom will be high.

CHAPTER 6

USS *Saratoga* Sets Sail for Madeira

Log of Michael Joshua Smith:

Port of Philadelphia, November 15, 1860

W E SPENT THE last week provisioning the *Saratoga*. We took on supplies necessary to keep our crew for the next month, including soap, cordage, cloth, water, rum, charcoal, salted beef, butter, salted pork, sugar, molasses, raisins, cheese, pickles, flannel, pine planking, white jackets for the sailors, and pantaloons for the marines. Guthrie and I made certain that the stores were full for our voyage. We even loaded a few items to add to the comfort of our journey. Once everything was stowed and secured, we prepared the ship for the open seas.

The weather leaving the northeastern coast of our homeland was cold and dreary. We left to overcast skies with temperatures in the upper thirties and easterly winds gusting to thirty knots. This is the kind of weather which tests a man's constitution. Were one of a frail nature, this is certainly not the land in which to reside. The gusting winds make the temperature feel much below freezing, resulting in the ocean mist freezing to the most inopportune mechanics upon which we rely. Sailors are charged with the duty of picking off the buildup before the ice infringed upon our ability to respond to commands from the helm.

The easterly gusts also hamper our departure. We are a crew, who unfamiliar with each other has set before us two tasks— one to man this ship and the other to establish a rhythm by which we can work together—each task does not appear to be going smoothly from our outset. First Lieutenant Guthrie seems set upon whipping the men into shape in rapid order. My leadership approach is far different. I prefer to begin more mildly followed by escalating levels of sternness based upon the cooperation received by the crew member. It will be interesting to see, in the end, whose approach is most effective.

November 16, 1860

Refreshed after a night's slumber, I arose to the sounds of song atop deck. I rapidly dressed and headed on deck. I encountered a delightful breeze and pleasant weather, which pushed the previous day's dreary disposition into the recesses of my memory. Today, my goal is to make acquaintance of as many of the crew as possible.

My first encounter was with Master's Mate, Madison, a portly fellow in his late thirties, I would suspect. His limbs were of normal caliber, but his abdomen was so protuberant as to lead me to suspect him pregnant of a litter of puppies. His voice was deep and had an air of knowledge and experience about it. His hair was dark and curly yet remarkably well kept for a man of his stature. His neck was as wide as his head and one might argue where one stopped and the other started as the blubber of far too much drink swallowed his chin.

"Master's Mate." I began as I approached.

"Yes, Leftenant," he replied.

"Fine weather we have today."

"Aye, sir. Much improvement over yesterday, I must say."

"Aye, true enough words were never spoken," I replied as I leaned upon the rail.

"How many days do you guess to reach the coast of Africa?" he inquired.

"Less than thirty," I replied. "Many have made the crossing in just over twenty."

"Aye, but they must have had the favor of the winds all the way," he responded.

"True," I replied. "Our lot will improve as we pick up some favorable winds."

"Aye, sir," he responded as he motioned for a crew member to come over, "time to take a reading."

The crew member responded, "Aye, sir." He threw over the bucket attached to a rope and called out, "ten knots!" Followed soon by, "Sixty fathom!"

The master's mate called out, "All sail set from topgallant studding sails to courses!"

"The weather will significantly improve as we approach the lower latitudes," I said.

"Aye, sir, were it only to happen sooner."

"Aye, from whence do you hail?" I asked.

"Maryland, sir," he replied. "From a sea-faring family."

"Ah, and how long in the navy?"

"Two hitches. I left for happier seas and joined the merchant marine after four years in the navy only to return."

"Not what you expected?" I asked.

"Not hardly," he replied. "The opportunities were limited, and the excitement was nonexistent."

"I could see that," I replied.

"I returned to the navy two years later, wiser to the world than when I left."

"A certainty for sure." I nodded. "Family?"

"Never married, lest I came close one time. She wasn't fond of seamen and would have had me work at a position of her choosing."

"And in a position of her choosing it sounds."

"Aye." He chuckled. "Ain't that be the truth, sir."

Several of the crew members slushed the masts, greasing them so the yards would slide smoothly up and down. Some worked on the rigging while others scrubbed the decks.

One of my many jobs was to furnish and maintain the wardroom prior to our departure. I had asked the other officers what types of chairs they preferred. Based upon my previous experience, many officers were beset with chronic aches and pains for which a comfortable chair would become a respect. I had found a merchant who would supply the most comfortable of armchairs for the mere addition of a dollar per chair. No officer took advantage of the offer, but I made certain to place an order for myself. The wardroom of the *Saratoga* was the location where a dozen commissioned and noncommissioned officers dined with the captain. The room was richly appointed with two tables with six chairs each. The captain's table, however, was adorned with additional carvings and was slightly longer in length to accommodate the captain's chair at the end. The most senior location was at the starboard end of the after table. This was reserved for Lieutenant Guthrie, the captain's second in command; a man of whom I was still uncertain yet determined to figure out. The junior "steerage" table was left for those with lower rank or experience and for the master's mate.

Our officers' staterooms were adjacent to the wardroom. They were of significantly less grandeur, but they had far more space than the quarters of the crew. Mine was on the starboard side next to Guthrie's. I shared it with Lt. Curtis Stanton of whom I know little other than he comes from a prominent family in the South. He is about the same height as I, five feet ten, but with a slightly heavier build and with a weight that I would estimate to be a hair under two hundred pounds. Unlike my dark hair and green eyes, his hair is blond and his eyes as blue as the sky. Just forward of the wardroom was where the enlisted crew slept, and they ate in the grand open space of the berth deck. The enlisted crew did not enjoy the furniture of the officers. They would eat on crates, barrels, or any other elevated platform that appeared suitable for a temporary dining table. Still, others not bound to the convention of eating off the floor were content with a piece of canvas laid on the deck itself. In fair or moderate weather, the crew slept in canvas hammocks slung between two hooks lest they do the same below deck if weather does not permit the former. The remainder of the officers consisted of the midshipmen, the surgeon, the purser, the gunner, the boatswain, and the carpenter.

Upon entering the wardroom, I found Lieutenant Stanton engrossed in the pages of Prescott's *History of the Conquest of Mexico*.

"Stanton," I announced as I entered, "What have you there?"

Initially unresponsive to my question, he slowly lowered the book from his face, just enough for his eyes to peer over. "It's Prescott."

"Planning your next conquest?" I joked.

"You might say that. I certainly wouldn't expect a Yankee to understand." He then pulled the book back up to shield his eyes from me.

Stanton's cold reception led me to believe that this would be a long voyage.

MICHAEL JAY NUSBAUM

November 17, 1860

Favorable winds carried us along at ten knots. Later in the day, the wind carried us right into a heavy squall. The darkened sky revealed no way to avoid her. We reduced sail to double reefed fore and main topsail, furled mizzen topsail, and hauled down the jib with hoisted fore topmast staysail and hoisted fore topsail but no main.

The squall lasted several hours to spit us out on its backside with not a breeze to fill a single sheet. We lay lull in irons. The calm wind and sea was a dramatic contrast to the tumult from which we had just exited. The temperature, which had been a delightful seventy degrees before the storm, now became stifling with the lack of wind or wave and the overabundance of sun.

Lieutenant Stanton and I have exchanged few words since our brief conversation over Prescott. We remained cordial and professional in our interactions, but I am perplexed as to why an aristocrat from the South would be in the navy, let alone on a mission to interdict ships carrying the very slaves that have made him so wealthy. My opposition to slavery is so strong that I fear it may blind my ability to reason with him. I will strive to control myself when around him. He is fond of making derogatory references to the African people. His every outburst makes me eager to lash out in response, but I endeavor to take the higher road and curb my emotions. Despite my best efforts to avoid conflict, I feel that I must grow to understand the rationale that drives him. It is but a matter of time before we engage in heated debate over the evils of slavery and his warped view of these human beings.

Heading to the deck, I noticed Stanton on duty. He seemed preoccupied by the lack of activity upon the waters but his demeanor was that of a misbehaving child dreading the return of his father and the reckoning for his misdeed.

"Stanton, how goes the watch?" I asked as I walked over to join him.

"Without the benefit of a breath from the Lord, we might just rot here till the end of days," he answered my query in the most serious of voices.

"Oh, it's not all that bad. I'd rather this than the squall we just visited." I returned. "Perhaps we should give the men leave to take a swim or do some fishing. Clearly we are going nowhere at quite a rapid pace."

"Perhaps. The sun is beginning to weigh on everyone. The temperature has risen fifteen degrees in the past two hours."

He was correct. The temperature had risen quite rapidly. It seemed all the more correct to permit the crew an hour or two of downtime until we could get back underway.

"I am in agreement," Stanton stated. "Give the word," he said to the master's mate who stood close by, eavesdropping on our conversation, eager to hear an affirmative answer to my suggestion. With orders in hand, the master's mate relayed the command.

Stanton turned back from monitoring the waters to address me. "So what's your story?"

Astonished, I hesitated. "Where to start?"

"Clearly we're not going anywhere, so we have time. You can start at the beginning." Still serious, he let a small teasing note enter his voice. Perhaps this conversation wouldn't be as bad as I feared.

I told him of my upbringing in New York City, my encounter with a woman by the name of Emily, who I thought to be the love of my life, and my lifelong/long-held desire to go to sea.

"And what of your stance on slavery?" he asked me, and for the first time, he looked me square in the eyes.

"I'm opposed both morally and ethically to the practice of slavery."

"I see," he responded calmly. "So you believe that this country could have and would continue to grow without the use of slave labor?"

"Well," I responded as I formulated my answer, "I would agree that the human beings who have been wrongly enslaved have contributed to the wealth of our growing nation, but only to the effect that they themselves did not prosper from the fruits of their own forced labor."

"I see," he said condemningly. "You're an idealist but not a realist."

"And you on the subject? You come from a family of means and clearly benefited from the fruits of slave labor. Why would you agree to embark on such a venture?"

"Interdicting slave ships and halting the import of slaves?" he asked arrogantly. "That's a simple answer. We have too many slaves already. They breed faster than we do, and their children fill the slave houses. Soon, they will outnumber us and will descend upon our fields like locusts, consuming all that is in their path."

"I see. So you loathe them," I replied. His position was becoming clearer. Not only did he think that slavery was a just system, but he

MICHAEL JAY NUSBAUM

could not be swayed from his belief in the supremacy of the white race as well. We seemed not to have any common ground.

"I do not. I have had many a slave whom I felt quite impressed with in both character and ethic. I cannot say that of most, yet the need to halt the flow of slaves to our shores is an imperative, and I wholeheartedly support the effort."

"Although with warped motives I see." I tested.

"I hardly see that," he retorted.

I decided to call him out. I was heartened that he felt our mission was legitimate, but his dismissal of blacks' humanity baffled me. "You benefited from and took advantage of the slave labor. Yet you now agree to halt the import because you feel that too many have been imported already and that their numbers grow because you enslave all future generations of those born to them in captivity."

"And your point is?"

"I find your rationale to be hypocritical at best, while your motives are clearly questionable," I responded.

"Do you know the history of our country?" Stanton's ire was beginning to rise.

"I most certainly do," I responded.

"The U.S. Constitution limited the practice of slavery by calling for its abolition within twenty years of the date of its signing. So as a compromise of its time, the Constitution limited the importation to a two decade window after 1787." He held onto his calm. "Did you know that?"

"I did," I replied.

"Well, there were two schools of thought regarding the abolition of the slave trade at the time. One in whom the idea of slavery was contrary to the entire basis of freedom set forth as the cornerstone of our great nation—people like you." He could not hold back a small sneer with that description. "The other side adhered to a belief that the slave trade had gone unencumbered for thousands of years and was deemed a necessity to ensure the financial success of our fledgling nation. It was the Portuguese who really began the slave trade to the Americas in the fifteenth century, and this group of proslavery, mostly Southern and learned gentlemen, believed that their participation in the practice should not be condemned by countrymen who benefited from the financial fruits of their labor. The condition in the Constitution was, ultimately, a grand compromise born from these two schools of thought," he said.

"I would agree with that assessment." Although I could not agree with the idea that slavery was ever necessary. His interpretation of the constitutional compromises seemed apt.

"Then you can see that both sides were hypocritical, we in the South for using the slaves to do the work and you in the North for allowing the practice to continue to build our nation," he taunted me with a grin.

"I hadn't looked at it that way," I responded. The truth was that I hadn't. I had always been morally opposed to slavery. I just had not seen the lack of action as a moral failing until he presented the idea to me.

"Have you studied the subject of slavery in the Americas? I have. What do you really know about the subject?" he then asked me. At this I felt on much firmer ground.

"Here," I said as I opened up a paperback I kept in my back pocket. "March 22, 1794: Congress passes the Slave Trade Act of 1794. This act of Congress, passed with the fervent support of our founding fathers and backed by George Washington himself at the twilight of his career, endeavored to right this act of wrong to the people of color. The act 'prohibited any ship to be used in the act of the slave trade.' In doing so, the act launched the fervor of antislavery speakers. John Brown, a citizen of these United States, was found to be engaged in the slave trade and was promptly detained. He was tried and convicted of slave trading on August 5, 1797. He was forced to forfeit his ship the *Hope* but was never sentenced to prison."

"Let me see that!" Curtis growled as he grabbed the booklet from me.

"What are you doing?" I asked, surprised at his outburst.

"Typical damned Yankee abolitionist propaganda," Curtis swore as he threw it to the deck.

"It isn't. These are the facts. You just don't want to admit to them," I said as I retrieved the booklet. The truth was that it was handed to me by an abolitionist back in New York, and I had attended quite a few abolitionist rallies, but the antislavery bias didn't change that the facts were still facts.

"Your example only serves to illustrate my point precisely," Stanton responded. "They acted, but they didn't act. In the end, all they did was take away his ship. Complicit."

"All right," I responded as I opened the book to a section where I had dog-eared the page. "Then look here. April 7, 1798: Congress passed an act to impose a $300 fine per slave on any person convicted of the now illegal importation of slaves. Pres. John Adams promptly accepted and signed the act into law."

Stanton laughed. "Do you really think that a $300 fine, which wouldn't have even been imposed on a regular basis, would stop them?"

"It was an effort." I tried.

"And how many $300 fines were issued?" Stanton's confidence was growing again.

"I do not know," I admitted.

"Don't you get it yet? These were all half measures." Curtis was nearly triumphant at his imminent victory.

I had, in fact, gone to quite a few abolitionist events and I struggled to recall the salient points of those meetings. Then the perfect riposte came to me, and I flipped through the booklet until I came upon the evidence I was looking for.

"Give it up, Smith. Your little book won't help you win this argument," Stanton said smugly.

"All right," I replied. "December 12, 1805: Sen. Stephen Rowe Bradley of Vermont puts forth a bill to 'prohibit the importation of certain persons there in described into any port or place within the jurisdiction of the United States of America from and after the first day of January 1808.' This bill, designed to enforce the provision in the Constitution that had been specifically written to protect the slave trade for a maximum of twenty years, was set before Congress. It was later elucidated 'certain persons' were indeed 'slaves.'"

Stanton listened but did not respond, so I continued reading aloud.

"March 2, 1807: The House passes a bill, explaining the Senate Act HR77. The two measures are then bonded together and approved by Congress. The bill is called 'an act to prohibit the importation of slaves into any port or place within the jurisdiction of the United States: HR77.' It failed to abolish the act of slavery, but it was a first step in ending the practice. Later on that very day, Pres. Thomas Jefferson signed the bill into law."

"But it failed to abolish slavery. Does that not speak volumes to you?" Stanton's confidence had not wavered in the face of my arguments, but I would not let him win this debate!

It all started coming back to me. I remembered the emotions that poured through me when I heard a Quaker speaker describe the first steps in the attempt to stop the importation of slaves to the United States. These were the facts that had motivated me to join the navy in the first place. Now they were ammunition that I could use to repel a fervent slave owner's attacks, so I fired them off at him one after another.

"In 1807, the blockade of the African slave trade begins. Britain outlaws the act of slave trading and the Royal Navy established a presence off the coast of Africa. Soon after, the West Africa Squadron is formed initially with two ships from Portsmouth, England.

"In 1813, the USS *Chesapeake* sets sail for the west coast of Africa to interdict American vessels engaged in the act of slave trading. This was the beginning of the Africa Squadron, to which we are now assigned.

"In 1818, six British warships entered into the service to interdict and prevent the exportation of slaves from the west coast of Africa. They established a naval station at Freetown in British West Africa, then created supply bases first on Ascension Island, then in Cape Town."

"You can quote me from your little book all day. There were no teeth to any of these acts. Yes, the British opposed slavery, but they already had their slaves as well as the empire they helped build. British abolition in 1837 means nothing to the United States."

My mind opened as if inspired by a higher power. All the facts seemed to be at my fingertips. My argument was undeniable. My facts were accurate. I needed to ensure that Curtis was not able to hide from the truth. He obviously didn't know everything. Perhaps if I educated him he would see the light.

"Right," I responded, "but in 1819, Congress established that the 'importation of slaves into the United States is to be deemed an act of piracy. Furthermore that any citizen of the United States found guilty of such "piracy" might be given the death penalty.

"Later that year, the role of the navy was expanded to include patrols off the costs of Cuba and South America in an attempt to interdict such activity, clearly showing that a resolve was building," I added.

"Irrelevant," Curtis stated as he looked away as if he was losing interest in the discussion.

I was determined to educate this man. Surely, if presented with enough facts, he must understand. I was not going to give up! I flipped to a section of the booklet that had the origins of our mission as well as the origins of the Africa Squadron itself.

"In 1842, the Webster-Ashburton Treaty established an agreement that the United States and Britain would work together on the abolition of the slave trade, which was now deemed piracy by both nations. They agreed to commit at least eighty guns apiece to the endeavor.

"In 1843, Cdre. Matthew Perry is placed in command of the Africa Squadron. Richard Stockton became the commander of the first U.S. steamer *Princeton*. Perry's Africa Squadron now consists of the USS *Yorktown*, USS *Constellation*, and the USS *San Jacinto*." I closed the book. Curtis was just staring at me with his forehead furrowed, and his eyes were mere squinting slits.

"I know the history of our mission," he growled at me, "but it wasn't until 1850, some seven years later, that a total of twenty-five ships with only two thousand personnel and only one thousand sailors were engaged in the effort to stop the slave trade." He concluded as if that were enough to the argument.

"I will not deny you the fact that our government was slow to act and acted with weak half steps, but President Lincoln is going to be much better than either Buchanan or Tyler!"

"Ah, your President Lincoln," he replied.

"He's our president," I responded.

"No, he most certainly is not. He is *your* president. He means to tear this country apart."

"He does not," I retorted. "He means to right a moral wrong—slavery in America."

"He means to destroy the economy of the South! He means to tear apart that which built this country. He means to destroy the very fabric of our nation and set friend upon friend. This country has never been so divided." Stanton was becoming quite heated now. From his apparent disinterest, he'd renewed his argument with vigor. He was no longer defending hypothetical ethics but arguing for his personal future.

"I would say that we have been divided for quite some time. President-elect Lincoln is merely the first to step up and do what is morally right." I replied. "Besides, less than 2 percent of our nation's citizens own slaves. Why should we let an elite few destroy our nation?"

"He will be the one remembered as the destroyer of our nation," Stanton replied as he walked away. "Mark my words."

I wondered whether we would be able to maintain amity for the rest of our mission. I saw Stanton as willfully backward and maybe even evil while he was sure I was trying to end his way of life. What would it take to make him see?

December 14, 1860

"Land ho," one called out. The crew headed to port side for the first sight of Africa.

"Not too bad," Captain Taylor said. "Just under thirty days, given the poor conditions and lack of favorable winds."

"Aye, Captain," responded Stanton.

We dropped anchor off the coast of Funchal on the island of Madeira just before sunset.

The next morning, boats from a Portuguese frigate came out to assist us entering the harbor and achieving a better anchorage. As we approached, we exchanged gun salutes with the Portuguese garrison on Madeira. The sounds of the cannon echoed as thunder. We slowly reached our ideal spot within the harbor and set anchor. No sooner the anchor was down than we were inundated by bumboats filled with fresh vegetables, meats, and wine for the crew. The African men who manned these boats were all young and possessed a very distinctive blue-striped tattoo going from their hairlines to the tips of their noses. The captain made certain that we provisioned the vessel before he granted the first rotation of shore leave. We took on barrels of bread, fruits, salt pork, and salt beef. We took on thousands of gallons of fresh water to refill the metal tanks on the lowest deck. Having listened to some of the traders, the captain soon expressed his concern and called a meeting of the officers.

"There have been numerous reports of disease outbreaks coming from the coast. I personally have two theories for the outbreaks, but I have ordered that the crew not eat the local fruit and that they wear their flannels at night."

"But, sir, the temperature. Won't the flannels be too warm for these tropical climates?" asked Guthrie.

"They are, but the evenings result in a drop in temperature, and I fear that after sundown, the men many succumb to the ravages of the ethers in the evening air." Captain Taylor was unyielding. The crew would spend some uncomfortable nights.

"Aye, Captain, winter flannels after sundown," Lieutenant Guthrie replied.

"Set teams to paint the hull and black the rigging," the captain ordered as he took out a map of the African coast and opened it up. "This is our patrol area."

"My God," I marveled. "That's thousands of square miles. It will be like finding a needle in a haystack."

"Precisely," the captain replied. "That's why we need to be wise about how we enforce our orders."

"How so, sir?" Stanton asked.

"Yes, how so, sir?" Guthrie added.

The captain pointed at the map about ten miles from our current location. "We will begin here and sail, following the coastline. Our patrol will end here and then we will reverse course and head back toward Madeira. We will pause at the mouths of these rivers. Reports are that slave ships load up as many slaves as they can and then move onto the next slave post in order to fill up the remainder of their holds. We will catch them as they go from station to station to load their human cargo. One more thing," Captain Taylor added glumly, "under the treaty with the British, we cannot stop any ships flying their flag."

The men looked shocked, but none dared speak.

"I know," he replied to the concerned looks. "It gets worse. We must take care not to fire upon any ship which does not fly our flag."

"How could that be?" Stanton was incredulous.

"I don't question our orders. Neither should you. The politicians deal with that. Thank the Lord we don't have to deal with those burdens. We are here to follow orders and that is what we will do. We may board ships flying flags other than ours, but we may not fire upon them. The British have the same problem. They may not fire upon a ship flying our stars and stripes. Think about how they must feel. The real trouble is that the vast majority of the slave ships are Portuguese."

All responded in unison, "Aye, sir."

"That is all. Dismissed." The captain turned away.

As the others filed out of the wardroom, I stayed behind to study the map.

"You have concerns, Lieutenant?" he asked.

"I do, sir." I started.

"Feel free to express them." He allowed.

"Sir, we have so few ships and so much territory to cover. Our orders are only to interdict ships flying our flag?"

"Correct," he replied.

"Then the odds are stacked against us," I stated. My visions of a noble and successful mission were fading quickly.

"This is true. There is a bounty to be paid to the crew for each slave we can free. This should also act as incentive." The captain was offering boons, but they did not interest me.

"For some that will be true," I commented.

"But not you?" he asked. The captain did not seem surprised at my declaration.

"No, sir. I do not seek to free them for any prize."

"No? Then what for? Duty?" He seemed amused at my fervor.

"Yes, duty and . . ."

"And?"

"And moral obligation, sir." I finished.

"I see," he responded as he looked up at me. He shook his head. "Oh, to be young and full of ideals."

"Ideals and moral obligation," I repeated.

"Yes, yes. Moral obligation," he agreed. "I do not have the luxury of considerations of morality and obligation, but I know my duty is to carry out orders as instructed. They are not open to interpretation by me and neither should they be to you as an officer in this fleet. Understood?"

"Aye, aye, sir," I replied.

"If that is all, you may leave," he told me. "We set sail in four days."

"Aye, aye, sir." I saluted and then left his quarters and closed the door behind me.

December 18, 1860

Having left the safety of the port of Madeira, we came upon the famous Peak of Tenerife, which is clearly visible as a perfect cone from a distance of no less than twenty miles. The view disappointed no one on board, and it continued to reveal its full grandeur as we drew closer. At

MICHAEL JAY NUSBAUM

a speed of seven knots, the rapidly approaching shore gave way to this monumentous geographic formation of the volcanically formed island. The island of Tenerife is known for women who wear white mantillas, its well-laid out town, and is often the first place American sailors can see camels in use.

Day after day, we patrolled the waters of the west coast of Africa. Days turned into weeks, and weeks into months. Apart from boarding the occasional fishing vessel, we have not seen a single slave ship.

There is one undeniable fact that this mission is becoming more and more tedious and tiresome with each passing day. It is quite evident that the novelty with which we were all first engaged has rapidly worn off as a result of the continuous repetition of task and the character of the individuals with whom we are forced to encounter while in this land.

CHAPTER 7

Africa

March 14, 1861

T HE DAY OPENS with fine weather.
The coast of Africa can now be seen again.
Back home it has been ten days since Lincoln was sworn in. I wonder how grand the ceremony was. Someday, I wish to see that in person. Oh, to be in the nation's capital and witness such an event.

Mail is most unlikely to reach us out here. I've been told by the more seasoned sailors that ships leaving from home are given sacks of mail to pass off to other ships if they were to cross paths. It seems random, but I'm told that it will happen eventually, and we will get word back from home. Even the thought of news makes me long for my carefree days in the city. Best I focus on my duties lest I wander off into dreams of those days gone by.

March 15, 1861

Light winds and calm seas—nothing special to report here or in the official log.

In an effort, no doubt, to reduce the tedium of the evening, the drum and fife were laid out and operated upon. Most men laid about while a handful arose to partake in the revelry. Performing what was half jig and half spastic movements, they attempted to keep to the time of the music. Half-amused, the Kroo men, who have stayed aboard to assist us, have joined in. They gave representation of what we believed to be their type of dance. What best could be described as a war dance not dissimilar to those of American Indians. Their movements consisted of representations of killing wild animals, ambushes, and enemy attacks, all of which are extremely fascinating to me.

Upon returning to our quarters, I noticed Curtis unsheathing his dagger.

"What are you doing?" I asked of him.

"I slumber with one eye open on the Kroo men. Too many stories of natives turning on sailing crews exist for us not to take notice. I lay with my dagger at hand in case of a surprise attack by those we sought to help us," he said as he settled in.

I looked at my dagger sheathed and hung with my uniform. My logical side told me to leave it as is and that Curtis's behavior was simply prejudice. Ultimately, my fear overcame my logic. I slid out of my bunk, unsheathed my dagger, and slid back into bed.

"Wise decision," Curtis said from his bunk. "Best you keep one eye open as well."

"Do you really think that they would attack us?" I asked.

"They play both sides. They help us now, but they are known to be slave traders. They abduct their own people and then sell them off like cattle. I would not trust them at all. I do not trust them at all. Were I captain of this vessel, they would not be allowed on board," Curtis replied.

March 16, 1861

Arose earlier than usual and earlier than most. Still alive and no insurrection to note. Kroo men wide awake well before most of the crew not on station.

I can't help but think about what Curtis said last night. Why would they enslave their own people for money? I must learn more about these Africans.

Air calm and light, scattered cloud—remainder of the day a complete blank as to incidents.

March 17, 1861

Weather remained calm. This midday, we let our anchor off Dixcove in twenty and a half fathoms veered to a forty-fathom chain.

Dixcove is a British station on the Gold Coast with a formidable fort erected upon the most desirable eminence and commands the cove in its entirety as well as a distance of at least two miles beyond to open waters.

As a matter of course, we exchange a salute of seven guns.

As second lieutenant, it is incumbent upon me to set the cadence for leave. Lest I forget to ensure that Curtis accompany me on our reconnaissance.

March 18, 1861

Since we were in the second order, Curtis and I were to make shore this morning. He seems keen to inspect Dixcove Fort, which is clearly the first prominence to attract anyone's attention here given that it is at least sixty feet above sea level. Its walls are not as thick and reinforced as I would have suspected from the cove. It boasts at least a dozen twelve-pound long guns with several smaller calibers in reserve.

March 19, 1861

I awoke early to take the first watch of the day. Several men decided to go fishing off the port bow. Their efforts were not in vain. They pulled out what appeared to be a fifty-pound grouper, and to my astonishment, the line did not break. The commotion, however, woke up the remainder of the crew. I had not heard such jubilant noise from these men in quite some time. It wasn't soon before Lieutenant Stanton came out to hear what the commotion was about.

"What's going on, Smith?" Stanton questioned with a large grin on his face.

"The men seem to have been very successful at their fishing endeavors."

"What did they catch?" Stanton asked.

"Well, from what I can tell, it appears to be a good-sized grouper. You should've seen them trying to pull their catch onto the deck. It was quite a sight." I grinned with him.

Curtis sauntered over to where I was standing. He looked up at the sky and stretched his arms out wide in a full-body yawn. "It is a beautiful day, I must admit."

"Aye, it is at that," I replied.

"Do you think we'll see any action anytime soon?" Curtis asked as he peered over the horizon.

"I certainly hope so. Captain Taylor seems to know what he's doing. Our plan is to head to the capes of Gabon in three days. According to all reports, our best hunting will be done in those waters. You never know, however. We might get lucky before then," I replied.

"You know I don't hate the Negroes," Curtis began. "I have known several with very admirable qualities. On the other hand, I have also seen many who have had the demeanor not unlike wild animals."

I wasn't really sure how to respond to that statement, and Curtis didn't say anymore after that, but I did begin to wonder about what he really thought. Did he really think of his slaves as subhuman beings?

"You didn't know that they can be civilized?" I asked Curtis.

"I do know some Negroes more than others. The plantation where I grew up had hundreds of slaves. I only got to know a few of them while I was growing up. They were house servants in particular, some of whom I remember fondly. One in particular, called Esther, was my wet nurse and caretaker throughout my childhood. She was actually very intelligent and very compassionate. I would actually say that she was there for me more than my parents were." Curtis remembered.

"And what became of her?" I asked.

Curtis answered slowly, "I'm not entirely certain. Soon after my eleventh birthday, she was taken away abruptly, and I never saw her again. I remembered feeling a great sense of loss at her absence. It was actually many years before I would fully recover."

"Well, what do you think happened to her?"

"Years after the fact, I had heard some rumors that my uncle may have forced himself upon her during one of his many visits to our plantation. According to the stories, my father had little tolerance for such behavior and sold her off."

"Your father punished Esther for his brother's sin. I say again, I don't really understand how you can be proslavery." Nearly everything Curtis said could come from the mouth of an abolitionist like Mrs. Stowe, yet he accepted the most heinous conditions because he was used to them.

"It's what I grew up with. It was the way things were and the way things are. I do know that without the slaves, the plantation would never be able to function. The entire economy in the South is dependent upon slave labor. I wouldn't expect someone from the North to understand that. Indirectly, everyone in the country—including you—benefits from the very slaves that we have and that you so conveniently condemn us for having."

"But I'm trying to understand your perspective. I think I understand that over here is more of an economic reality for you and your family. I just have a really hard time accepting the fact that anyone could put another human being into bondage." I countered.

"Have you ever seen the way they live? I mean, how they live over here," Curtis asked as he put his hand on my shoulder.

"No more than what the Kroo have shown us on this voyage. I'm only beginning to learn how they live over here," I responded. I wondered whether Curtis really knew how Africans lived or whether he had been fed stories by self-serving advocates of slavery.

"They live a much better life back home with us than they ever would over here."

"You don't truly believe that, do you?" I asked.

"Absolutely, I do! Back home, we take care of them. We feed them, provide them with shelter, care for them, and even make some of them part of our families. In return, all we ask is that they do the work that we ask of them," he replied. I decided that he had accepted the standard proslavery rationale preached by Southerners. Even so, I was flabbergasted at his naiveté and protested, "Curtis, they are slaves. They must do as they are told, live where we put them, and can be sold away from their families because of someone else's lust. That is not freedom!" I pointed to the coast in front of us. "Here, they are free to do as they wish. They are not forced to labor in the fields for others and not see the profit of their labor. Can you truly not see the difference?"

Curtis remained unmoved, however. "Michael, they are much better off with us than they are over here. Someday, you will learn that. Perhaps when we get home, you can come visit our plantation and see how well they live. See how well they're being taking care of. I think then you will realize that we are doing them a favor," Curtis said as he patted me on the back and walked away. Apparently, Curtis was amused rather than offended by my naiveté.

That conversation bothered me for the rest of the day. I wanted to understand where he was coming from, and I truly wanted to understand his perspective. I believe that deep down, Curtis is a good man, but he seemed utterly blind to the inhumane realities of slavery. I am just wondering how it is possible to change the minds of people who grew up accepting slavery. Is there any way to make them think otherwise?

Later that day, I heard Curtis speaking with one of the crew about Lincoln.

"What was that about the president?" I asked.

"Oh, sir, nothing, sir. We were just sayin' . . ." the sailor stopped and decided. "I should get back to my post."

"Carry on," I said as the sailor hurried off, leaving Curtis leaning on the starboard rail. "So what was all that about?"

"Nothing," he replied.

"Really?" I asked calmly. "I know that you don't like our president."

"It's not that I don't like him." He corrected me as he stood upright and addressed me. "But he's bad for our country. He's tearing us apart with all this talk of freeing the slaves and equality. He means to destroy the South."

"I see." I looked him square in the eyes. "What you don't understand—what you fail to understand is that there is a fundamental difference that exists here. You see, my parents, and your grandparents too for that matter, came to this country for a better life voluntarily. Mine came to escape religious persecution, and I'm sure your family came for a better life and more opportunity. The problem is that slaves did not come here by their own free will. Even if Lincoln were to free them all, and I hope that he does, the legacy of slavery will impact their children and their children's children for generations to come. It will remain a stain upon this great nation and a void in the hearts of those whose ancestors were forced to come here. When they hear stories of the founding fathers and of generations of immigrants who voluntarily came over here to live, they will know. They will know in their hearts that this was not true for them. It was not true for their ancestors who were forcibly taken from their homes, from their families, and from their loved ones and brought over to work in a foreign land in bondage. They will know. Generations of their descendants will know and feel the pain of what their ancestors went through. They will never be able to relate to stories of parents like mine. How could they? How could we ever expect them to? They were brought here against their will as slaves. Generations that follow them, free or not, will feel the same, knowing that it could have been different. Even our country's founding fathers are not their fathers. They were just a bunch of old white men, some slave owners, in a room that had an idea that could not have included them. They did not have representation at the signing of the Constitution. The difference is, and this is what we need to recognize, is that the Constitution was made for everyone. Everyone was and is to be considered equal under the eyes of the Constitution of the United States. There was no mention of skin color, race, or religion from which anyone was to be treated differently. You must see that. That is the ideal to which Lincoln is trying to aspire." I had grown more passionate with each sentence and, despite my best intentions, was nearly shouting at Curtis now.

"I really don't want to debate you when you clearly do not understand the subject Michael." Curtis remained unruffled and unmoved by my exhortation. He turned to walk away.

Realizing that yelling at him was not going to change his mind, I tried to regain my composure. As he turned away, I held my hand out as a gesture of openness. "I don't mean for it to be a confrontation but more of a discussion. I apologize for losing my temper. I am honestly curious to hear your opinions on these matters. We come from such different backgrounds."

"What you probably don't understand is that I don't see you and your kind as American either. To have you, a half Jew, preach to me about how we wronged the Negroes is insulting. I'd just as soon have you and your kind go back to where you came from," he responded coldly and started to walk away.

My first reaction to Curtis's anti-Jewish remark was to feel flush with anger, and I felt my fist clench as a matter of reflex. I was startled by his prejudice but not surprised. Nevertheless, I reached out to him again. "Ah, but that's where you are wrong. I can preach to you about the wrongs being committed upon these people. My people, the Jews you refer to with such disdain, were also wrongly enslaved. Enslaved by the Egyptians long ago. We are raised never to forget the bitterness of bondage and to make sure that it never happens to us or anyone else ever again. The Jewish part of me that you seem to hate so much is exactly that part of me that is against slavery in any form and to anyone. It is in my blood. The sad thing is that I have no doubt that, despite us being taught never to forget, it probably will happen again someday. Someday, Jews will be forced into bondage and killed as they were in the days of pharaoh. We are taught to remember lest we forget and then history will repeat itself. I pray that the descendants of these slaves will never forget either. I pray that they create their own exodus story and that they pass it down from generation to generation as my ancestors did. It is that important that they do not forget and that they celebrate and revere the day they are set free. If it is not to be by this president or if it is not to be in my lifetime, when it happens it should be exalted to the same levels of the story of the exodus from Egypt. The question is not if it will happen, but rather when it will happen and to whom they credit for their release from bondage. They will have their Moses. If not Lincoln, then someone else will come along one day and free them. This I am certain of." Once again my temper had flared and passionate but intemperate words spilled out of me in a rush. Surprisingly, Curtis was still listening, but his temper then began to rise.

"And it will mark the end of this nation. If Lincoln does what he says he will do, this country will be permanently divided. Heck, most of the South announced their plans to secede from the Union before we left. By now, who knows, I may not even live in the same country as you do."

"You may not be. Certainly our opinions on slavery are a world apart."

Curtis began to walk away but turned back for one last volley, "The South will never give up its rights to have slaves. And without the South, the North will collapse. These are truths that you won't understand. We drive the nation with what we produce. Mark my words."

March 20, 1861

Not much to report today. I think that if something doesn't happen soon, the crew might go mad.

Suddenly, the alert to general stations is sounded. I reentered the helm to see what was happening. The officer of the watch had his scope out.

"Over there! Off the port bow!" he shouted.

"What is it?" I asked.

"I'm not sure. Never seen anything like it," he handed me the scope.

I put the scope to my right eye and peered out to see the cloud on and above the water, rapidly approaching our vessel.

"What in God's name is that?" I asked. "Could it be a flock of birds upon the water?" As I spoke, I realized that birds could not be moving so quickly, but I really had no idea of what it could be.

Curtis came to my side and motioned for the scope. "Sorry about what I said before," he stated as he placed it upon his right eye and examined the dark cloud as it began to obscure the view of land. "I have no idea what that is." Curtis shook his head, as puzzled as I was.

Within a matter of seconds, the cloud was upon us. It was locusts. Millions of them swarming in a vast cloud that spread out over the ocean. They quickly engulfed the entire ship. The men batted them away from their faces. You would need nearly choose to put your hand up and swipe it to get a handful of these persistent creatures. The noise that came with it was deafening. I could hear them bouncing off the hull of the ship. Many more were hitting our sails and falling to the deck below. Soon, the deck was covered with them. The entire attack lasted but a few minutes. When it was over, every square inch of the vessel was covered in locusts. Following closely behind the cloud was a flock of seagulls making easy prey of the clumsy insects. The birds let out shrills of delight. We welcomed the sound after the ominous buzz of the insects.

Some of the birds stayed behind with our vessel and helped clear the insects off the decks.

"Stand down from general quarters!" the officer of the watch announced.

I turned to Curtis and said, "I was just thinking that if something exciting hadn't happened, these men would all go mad."

Curtis looked at me and laughed. "Oh, so it is your fault. I had best remind you next time to conjure up something a little less biblical in nature." It was strange how we could remain civil to one another despite his dangerously backward opinions.

MICHAEL JAY NUSBAUM

The men spent the rest of the day cleaning the boat of the carcasses left behind from the swarm that had engulfed us.

March 21, 1861

Today we set sail for the Cape of Gabon at first light. The men are anxious for some action that doesn't include insects, but we haven't seen a single ship in days. Captain Taylor has plotted a course, which should take us to the cape by first light tomorrow.

Feeling encouraged by our brief conversation about the locusts, I endeavored to engage Curtis in another debate over slavery.

March 22, 1861

Early morning, the Cape of Gabon was clearly visible. Stories tell of many ships laden with slaves coming out of the mouth of the Gabon River. Our hope is that we may catch such a prize.

"Bring us in to a distance of five miles," called out Captain Taylor.

"Aye, sir," came from the helm.

Standing orders from Commodore Perry were that ships of the Africa Squadron were to anchor several miles from the shore and to never permit any crew member to spend a night ashore. We were also not permitted to sleep on an open deck when in eyeshot of shore. We were also forced to use charcoal drying ovens to reduce the oppressive humidity. This turned below decks into a dry oven, and most of us hated the infernal device. The oddest of Perry's orders were for all to wear a flannel undershirt night and day. This, according to Perry, was an effort to minimize exposure to the "bad air" of West Africa. The officers obliged to comply with the strange orders and followed the instructions albeit grudgingly. The remainder of the crew were mixed. Our ship's surgeon thought it wise to wear the flannel simply because it was too thick for insects to get to our skin. Most of us secretly felt that Perry must have suffered permanent delirium as a result of his bouts of fever during his previous African expeditions.

"Guthrie," Captain Taylor called, "when the ship is put away and the weather braces checked, we will hove anchor and lay just outside the mouth of the Gabon River. Make certain that you check your fathoms repeatedly as we approach. I do not want to hear the hull scraping anything. The bottom is very rocky and uneven as you get closer."

"Aye, Captain," Guthrie replied.

"Let go larboard anchor in no less than five fathoms," the captain ordered.

"Aye, Captain," Guthrie replied. "Did you hear that?" Guthrie asked me.

"I did. All of it," I replied.

"Very good. Let's make it so and not let him down."

"Do you think it wise to venture inland?" I asked.

"Wise?" Guthrie looked at me. "I'm not certain. Why do you ask?"

"Well, Perry gave the entire fleet these orders not to venture too close to shore with the ship"—I paused as a crewman walked by—"and not to spend any time overnight on land."

"Right, and your point is?" Guthrie was still taken aback at my questioning the captain's orders.

"Well, we will have to sleep at some point, and if the vapors will make us ill when we sleep on land, why would they be any different when we're inland on the river?" I asked.

"Perhaps you should hold your breath upon our voyage upriver." He snapped.

"I'm just saying," I replied, "it makes little sense and seems a contradiction in orders."

"The captain has his reasons," he replied. "I would guess he knows something that we do not, or he would not order us to directly disobey Perry's orders for the squadron."

The next day, we took on board a local pilot to help us proceed up the Gabon River. There is a long history of missionaries traveling up this river, and they have significant experience in navigating these waters. The entire crew was eager to capture a prize, and the commander was even more eager than we were. I had thought it unusual when the commander ordered us upriver. This area was heavily incurred upon by the French. Because the French had so many conflicts with the natives, many of us fear that the Africans in this area will have formed a negative impression of white men—that they will not welcome us despite our mission to help keep their people out of slavery.

Guthrie and I then heard the order, "All officers in the commander's ready room!"

We assembled at the captain's table.

"We are going to venture up the Gabon. François here will assist us in navigating the river. The French established Fort d'Aumale in 1843 not far up this river. They obtained a questionable-at-best treaty with King Glass some twenty years ago, establishing French sovereignty over the area. We've heard reports that a ship flying a U.S. flag headed up these waters three days ago and has not been seen coming out."

All at the table stirred with excitement.

"I can take you as far as the French station," François stated. "Beyond that, I am not an expert. The river is navigable for ships of up to fifteen feet draught to the distance of sixty miles. Above that for boats of five feet draught to the distances of over a hundred miles!"

"So that's it. We will proceed upriver to the French station some ten miles."

"Aye, Commander!" we all replied.

We left with excitement. This was our first great lead, and the crew is eager to make this journey worth their while. We weighed anchor and proceeded up the river. Along the way, we saw small native villages.

"Do you see that?" asked Curtis with excitement. "I had no idea."

"I do," I replied as I gazed out at the thatched huts, and the natives running toward the shore of the river to observe us. There were many canoes beached along the edge of the river. They had brightly colored clothing, and the women were topless but wore extravagantly beaded necklaces, which clearly demonstrated their skill as artisans. Children ran up to the water's edge in excitement at the sight of the large ship. A woman, dressed in a white-feathered skirt, followed the children up to the water and scolded them, I presume, telling the children to keep their distance. Mothers' scolding is universal. Given the history of the slave trade and recent abductions, I was not surprised at her response. In fact, given the same circumstances, I would have done just as she did. It was strangely conspicuous that I did not see any men in the village. I wondered the possibilities.

The men manning the boats towing us upriver strained at the oars. They swatted away all sorts of insects while they battled the current. We saw forested areas and lowlands inhabited by elephants and hippos.

Soon, we came upon a village by the name of Quindah. It seemed to be a much larger village than what I had assumed to be the standard size African village. Not comparable to the American cities I was used to but with just as many huts as our large cities had houses. Here there were small ports, way too small for our vessel, but enough to do commerce. Crates of European manufactured goods lay empty upon the dock. Perhaps the crates would later be filled with items for trade; however, my distinct impression is that trade between Europe and Africa is far out of balance. They seemed keen to trade their most valuable natural African resource—human beings—in return for manufactured goods. An asymmetric trade arrangement if there ever was one. Here, too many of the natives either observed us from places of protection or they simply didn't care about our presence.

Next, we came upon the town of Glasstown. The human presence on either bank of the river was the greatest we have seen to date. François, our navigator, informed us that the French garrison lay a mile or two further up river and that it is maintained by fewer than a dozen officers. As we turned the bend in the river, we observed a three-masted schooner at dock. Excitement reached a fever pitch on board the *Saratoga*.

"Hold!" Guthrie ordered. "Alert the captain."

"Aye, sir," Willis responded as he ran to get the captain.

"What have we here?" asked the captain.

"A three-masted schooner off the starboard bow. She is actively loading slaves," Guthrie reported as he handed the spyglass over to the captain. Guthrie's voice betrayed his excitement.

The captain peered at the schooner. "We can do nothing," he replied as he lowered the scope.

"But, sir," I protested, "she is actively loading slaves. We must act."

"We can't, Smith. We are under strict orders. She flies a foreign flag," he replied, shaking his head. I remembered our previous conversation about rules of engagement and grew frustrated all over again.

"What shall we do?" asked Guthrie.

"We can do nothing, and she knows it," Taylor replied as he walked resolutely back to his cabin.

"What is going on?" asked Willis. His excitement had not ebbed.

"We do nothing," Guthrie replied, shaking his head.

"What?" Willis argued. "We could lay waste to her with our twenty pounders, and she knows it!"

"She does," Guthrie replied. "She also knows that we can't touch her so long as she flies a foreign flag."

"I do not understand that line of thinking at all!" replied Willis as he marched away in disgust.

"Odd rules of engagement," I said to Guthrie.

"Odd indeed," he replied.

Stanton approached. "Word is we can't touch her."

"Very true," I replied.

Curtis wore a smug look. "How will we ever be effective if our hands are tied?" he asked.

"Orders are orders," Guthrie replied as the three of us stared at the prize we were denied.

"Look," Curtis said as he pointed to the ship, "they're acting as if we aren't here. They haven't even paused their loading of the slaves. Unbelievable!"

"There's nothing we can do, Lieutenant," Guthrie stated.

"Too bad we can't give her a salute with our cannon. Just to wake her crew up to the fact that we're here," I suggested.

"Wouldn't do any good," Curtis replied.

"Unless of course the salute was with fully loaded eighteen pounders," I replied.

Curtis chuckled in agreement. "Wouldn't that be a sight?"

"Well," I said to Guthrie, "if we can't take her, and we can't scare the pants off her, then what are we to do here?"

"Point well taken, Lieutenant," he replied. "Should I ask the captain if we should head back downriver and out to open water where our luck might improve?"

"Especially since we are so limited as to the rules of engagement," I stated, still frustrated at having been denied our prize.

Guthrie headed to the captain's quarters, relaying the captain's orders on his return: Head back to open waters and resume our patrol.

I decided that I wanted to learn more about these seemingly contradictory orders. I headed over to the captain's quarters and knocked.

"Enter," Captain Taylor said. As I stood at attention, he asked me, "Lieutenant, what can I do for you?"

"Sir, I am confused over our orders."

"I see. Have a seat." He sighed out of frustration with me. "What is your confusion?"

"Well, sir, we are out here to stop the slavers, but we can't stop most of them, so . . ."

"So you were wondering?" He prompted.

"Sir, I was wondering who we were really out here to stop, and why we can't go after that ship," I blurted this out in a rush.

"Lieutenant, are you familiar with the Webster-Ashburton Treaty?" he asked.

"Of course. It settled the border dispute between the United States and the British over the Canadian borders."

"That was certainly part of it. Under the treaty, the British and the Americans were each obligated to maintain a naval force of eighty guns off the western coast of Africa. Given our limited resources, this ship and the few others in this Africa Squadron are the best we can do. We are limited to the maritime rules of engagement set before us. We are permitted to interdict any ships who fly our flag, that is all. It is not my duty to question our orders, and neither is it yours to question me. We do our duty with honor, and we do the best we can do in the name of our great country." The captain's tone left no doubt that he would not greet more questions with the indulgence he had shown me thus far. I could sense his annoyance, not with me, but with the limited rules of engagement that so restricted his command. I took my leave.

CHAPTER 8

Patrol

April 18, 1861

WIND SSW IN light breezes. Our heading SSE on patrol. At one fifteen, lookout reports sail ho. Sail identified to the westward. Unfurled all sail from topsail. Sail ahead steering a perpendicular course. The chase is on.

While in pursuit of this vessel, I can't help but recall the sorties of ships in the first incarnation of the African Squadron. In 1821, some forty years earlier, the *Alligator* encountered a similar situation. An unidentified vessel, upon sighting the *Alligator*, lay to instead of continuing on her way as she awaited *Alligator*'s approach. Lookouts on the *Alligator* soon reported that the mysterious vessel was wearing a distress flag instead of her colors. As her duty calls, the *Alligator* approached the distressed ship in an attempt to assist her. Once the *Alligator* entered into her gun range, the purported distressed vessel opened fire upon the warship. Lt. Robert Stockton loaded his guns, let off one volley and then began chase. Heavily outranged by the mysterious ship, the *Alligator*'s crew was forced to lie flat on the deck while Stockton steered his ship into her. Despite the hail of cannon fire and with the suffering of several casualties, the *Alligator* finally had the rogue ship in range of her own guns. Her next volley sent the rogue ship's entire crew below deck for cover. The *Alligator* valiantly poured broadside after broadside into her enemy, which was responded with equally furious volleys. This exchange continued for twenty minutes until the adversary struck her colors of surrender.

Oh, to be involved in such a glorious battle! No doubt such a battle would be the highlight of my naval career.

At two fifteen, our prey eludes us. Despite our endeavor to pursue, she appears to be pulling away. All sheet available to us, yet alas, she is faster than we are.

At four o'clock, our prey disappears over the horizon, and the captain calls off the pursuit.

April 19, 1861

The day opened clear and pleasant. We got under way at an early hour and made for the coast as far as the wind would allow of it. We plan to anchor near the mouth of the Congo River at Cabinda, Angola. God willing, we will make it there before nightfall tomorrow.

My thoughts wander again to the tale of the American merchant schooner Mary Carver. In these very same waters in 1844, the locals murdered the crew and then plundered the trading schooner. It was Commodore Perry who then took strong action against the locals responsible for the heinous crime. Perry had gone ashore with Joseph Jenkins Roberts, the governor of Liberia. They attempted a palaver with King Ben Cracow. Unfortunately, the meeting went awry and erupted into a melee in which the commodore was stabbed. The Americans grabbed King Cracow and scurried back to their launches. Meanwhile, their landing party fought off the two hundred or more natives and then burned the village in retreat. Upon returning to the ship, the commodore, his uniform soaked in his own blood, gave orders to level the village. A fierce bombardment of the village and surrounding woods ensued. Aboard the Macedonian, the king died of his wounds. Perry, in his rage, landed his party a good twelve miles down the coastline. He then marched his marines the entire length back along the shore, setting houses and villages ablaze along the way. When he made it back to where he had begun, he was met with white flags of capitulation and expressions of amity. Many of us know the story, and we remain vigilant in our stead.

April 20, 1861

Wind from northward and westward, fresh too. It does, however, render the weather particularly unpleasant with the frequency and heaviness of the rains here.

At three thirty, now staggering under studding sails at the rate of 9.4 knots per hour. All on board hope that land comes into sight soon.

At 7:00 p.m., fine breezes abound, and that's about all that could be boasted for now.

At 7:15 p.m., alas, land ho proclaimed to all. Land on the horizon and a heaviness lifted off us all.

At 7:30 p.m., Finally! A vessel flying our stars and stripes is observed loading slaves near the mouth of the river. It appears that they have been loading for a while. The captain has ordered us to sail away from the vessel with plans to reverse course after sunset and sneak up upon her.

At 9:00 p.m., we arrive near the mouth of the Congo River at Cabinda. It being moonlit, we stood on until it was considered prudent to come out and ventured as close as we dared to the other ship. This was done in thirteen fathoms of water with two and a half knots current.

April 21, 1861

We began our raid just after midnight the next day. The location of the darkened ship, which the captain had previously observed, was noted. Captain Taylor instructed two boats be launched silently into the water. I took the command of the first. Lt. James J. Guthrie took command of the other. Curtis came on board with me in the former.

We approached the vessel silently. Guthrie motioned that I take port while he maneuvered around and broach from starboard. Captain Taylor had loaded all port guns of the *Saratoga* for broadside in the event we were repelled. I hoped that the captain saw fit to let us clear before he opened up.

Grappling hooks tossed topside, we clambered aboard. The clipper was the *Nightingale*—we could see her name marked clearly on her hull and her American flag hanging off of her stern. I reached the deck starboard side as I saw Guthrie's stern brow rise from the port side.

Cold steel and muskets drawn, we faced the crew of the *Nightingale*, aroused unexpectedly from their slumber stagger to their feet in a half-wakened daze. Several, unable to stand still, stagger slightly like sailors after a night of drunken revelry. Curtis and I headed for the captain's quarters. Curtis breached the entryway with his boot as the doors swung violently inward. Curtis and I heard the crash of glass and witnessed the captain of the *Nightingale* throwing something overboard from his cabin portal. Suddenly, a crew member armed with a hatchet lunged at Curtis from the corner. Being two steps behind Curtis, I raised my pistol and let a shot fly. My shot struck the man just behind his left eye but above his left ear. The man was blown back toward the corner and away from Curtis. We ventured forward toward the captain's table and the light within. The captain of the *Nightingale* stood frozen in position. Despite his precarious position, he stood firm and defiant. I could then see Curtis's face, powder-burned from my shot.

Deafened by the shot, which had ignited mere inches from his right ear, Curtis turned to thank me. "I'm indebted to you, my friend."

What we had seen the captain throwing overboard was a handkerchief tied up with the ship's papers and other incriminating documents. This, weighed down with a handful of musket balls, sunk to the depths taking with it much of the evidence we needed for a successful prosecution of the captain and crew. No matter—we would be able to free the poor souls below.

Guthrie called out to me as Curtis lunged forward and wrestled the captain out of his quarters and onto the open deck. Hardly noticed at first, but clearly apparent now, the stench of God knows what permeated the thick air. Curtis shoved the captain in with his crew as our marines trained loaded muskets upon them.

No sooner had Curtis called out to me than he opened the hatch. Sensing possible rescue, the slaves bound up within the bowels of the ship let loose a jubilation of shouts and voices beneath our feet. The sound could be heard not only on the *Saratoga* but also no doubt for miles in all directions.

Guthrie pulled steel upon the ship's captain and laid it upon his nape. "I demand your papers, sir," Guthrie growled. "I have none to give, and you will never get them," the captain sneered, still defiant.

"The swine threw them overboard before we could detain him," Curtis explained as he turned back to peer into the darkened hold of

MICHAEL JAY NUSBAUM

the ship. "Light. Light," he called as the moonlight was insufficient to penetrate the darkened passage.

The stench from below was so great that it was impossible to stand for more than a few moments near the open hatch. Several of our crew began to open the rest of the hatches in curiosity.

Curtis stood fixated at the opening unable to move. I could hardly stand the smell coming from the hold, and I was yet several feet from him. No sooner did I pull out a cloth with which to cover my nose and mouth from the smell than Curtis descended into the abyss. With all hatches open, several other men ventured down below but were forced up sick and retching within moments of their journey's beginning. Curtis, however, remained below and attempted to render assistance.

"Call for the blacksmith!" Curtis shouted from below. Being at the entrance myself, I could not only hear him but also see the horror for myself. Some eight hundred—nay, nine hundred—or more human beings with the darkest of skin lay chained to racks or packed into corners with barely enough room to breathe and hardly any to move.

Curtis cried out again, "For God's sake, get the blacksmith over here!"

I had never seen Curtis cry. For all the time I have known him, he has been a rock of a sailor devoid of emotion even while arguing slavery with me. Now, I witnessed tears streaming down his face as he tried to undo the iron chains with his bare hands. Pulling with all his might, he was unable to break the chains of these imprisoned souls. One marine provided a hatchet liberated from a member of the *Nightingale*'s crew. Curtis hacked furiously at the chains and the posts holding the captives. His body writhing in a rhythmic full force effort to break the bonds. Near exhaustion, he finally achieved success. The first anchor of the chain for some fifty men was released through the sheer brute force of Curtis's fury. Now, with the personnel of several more launches and the *Saratoga*, which had pulled alongside, the full complement of marines boarded the *Nightingale*.

The ship, having only racks for bunks, which were hastily made for a slave deck, had a total of 961 Negroes chained between her decks. The Africans were men, women, and children. The women and children were packed into separate holds from the men. The sight of the children shocked the most steadfast worthy man on deck.

Soon after, we learned from one of her officers that the *Nightingale* was a clipper ship designed and built at Portsmouth, New Hampshire, in 1851, almost ten years after our ship, the *Saratoga*, had been launched. She had been preparing to load even more slaves before getting underway for the Americas when we boarded her.

We were told by her crew that the male slaves were chained in a confined space to prevent the stronger from strangling the weaker. Having heard abolitionists speak of the Middle Passage, I thought I was prepared for the reality of the slaver's hold. The horror endured by these human beings, who were placed in conditions not suitable for animals, made us question the humanity of their captors. The thought that they would have faced these conditions for an entire journey across the ocean in their noisome hole was something that not one of us could ever have fathomed.

We struggled to get the Africans topside for fresh air and medical care. I witnessed Curtis carrying young children one by one to the deck. Where he got the strength, I will never know. He made over fifty trips below to bring up the imprisoned from their hellish entrapment. Several were already in a weakened state, and our ship's surgeon separated out the most severe so that they may receive the most attention.

Curtis seemed to latch onto one young boy. I'm not quite sure why, but he held the child close as if he'd appointed himself the boy's protector. I was astonished to watch as Curtis wept. Casks of fresh water were brought on board from the *Saratoga* and fed to the recently freed.

Soon, a woman timidly approached Curtis. She motioned that the boy he held so closely was her son. Curtis helped her down as he handed the boy into her lap. Unaware that I had observed the entire exchange, he rose from the spot, turned away from the woman and boy, and wiped off his tears with his sleeve. He then headed over to me.

"I have never seen such vile treatment before," Curtis said in a low and angered voice.

The inhumanity of the slavers had stunned me, but I hadn't expected Curtis, who was such a defender of slavery, to have reacted so viscerally. Deep down, I hoped that seeing this might be enough for him to change his views.

Once all the captives were brought topside and care was rendered, we focused on imprisoning the *Nightingale*'s crew in our brig. Although there were too many to hold there, we bound them with the very same chains that they had used to bind their prey.

The captain soon came on board to witness the horror himself. Captain Taylor then called a meeting of the officers back on the *Saratoga*.

CHAPTER 9

Journey to Monrovia

The officers meet in Captain Taylor's quarters:

"GENTLEMEN," HE ANNOUNCED, "have a seat." We sat down ready to hear our instructions for moving forward.

"Lieutenant Guthrie, you and Lieutenant Smith will take the *Nightingale* to Liberia. Unload the passengers in Monrovia. You will then await there for further orders."

"Aye, Captain," we responded. We all rose from our seats to leave and follow the captain's orders.

"Smith," Taylor called.

I waited as the rest of the officers left, "Aye, Captain."

"Smith, I want you to pick the crew. Guthrie outranks you, but I have confidence in you. I have given him orders to command the ship on your voyage to Monrovia, and you are to be his first officer and second in command."

"Thank you, Captain," I replied. "I'm honored by your trust in me." And I was. Despite my twice questioning orders, the captain thought I was enough of a strong leader to pick a crew and assist Guthrie.

"Once in Monrovia, I need you to unload your passengers and then sanitize, decontaminate, clean the living quarters. Give Guthrie all the assistance you can."

"Aye, Captain," I replied.

"Most likely, we will rendezvous with you in Monrovia. I will send word back to command of our capture of the *Nightingale*. She is a worthy ship and will make a nice prize," Taylor said as he lit his prepared pipe. "Dismissed."

I could not help but think to myself about the captain's use of the word "prize." This was not about the prize for me, but rather what I was meant to do in this life. For me, it was for morality; for Curtis, it was for duty; and for others, it was simply about the money.

April 22, 1861

With Lieutenant Guthrie in command, and I as second, we prepared the ship to set cloth for Monrovia. The passengers are weak from their captivity aboard the *Nightingale*. Some reports from the imprisoned crew of the *Nightingale* indicate that many of the Africans have been on board for five days and many with minimal food and water. Others were brought on board as recently as the day before her capture. Their fragile state concerned me. Many of the men on board the *Saratoga* have chipped in parts of their pay to acquire additional provisions for our freed passengers. I pray that we make it to Monrovia with our full complement.

The commander asked me to handpick our crew, so the natural choice for second lieutenant was Curtis. We had grown to rely upon each other, and the thought of him not joining me on this journey was unfathomable. I also needed the skill of the doctor's assistant, Willis, so I saw him as an integral part of our new crew.

April 23, 1861

During the latter part of the day, we weighed anchor and made sail for Monrovia. Our stores are sufficient for the journey and the handpicked crew is up to the challenge.

A strong breeze had us at a speed of ten knots. Very rapidly, Kabenda faded into the distance.

The water is an emerald green between the latitudes of 20' odd N to 17' long and 15' and 17' westerly.

That evening, we saw a lunar rainbow. Not a very common evening spectacle. If I were superstitious, I would wonder if it were a portent.

The next morning, the water's color changed to a turbid blue.

Curtis seems to be particularly concerned with the well-being of one of our young freed captives. The boy to whom he grew attached in the initial rescue now appears particularly ill.

I walked over to Curtis who was caring for the boy. "What's this?"

"Michael, he's very ill," Curtis said with genuine concern. "He's burning up with fever."

"Many of them are ill," I responded. "We will do everything we can for them."

"I know, but I'm not sure if this young boy will make it," Curtis said.

"What's his name?" I asked.

"His name is Bwana. His mother's name is Likana. She went to get him some fresh water and food."

"We will do everything we can to help them," I repeated.

"Well, I'm going to give him my rations," Curtis stated as the boy's mother returned.

"That's very admirable," I replied, "but there are many who are ill on this ship right now. Two of the crew have succumbed, and I am concerned that more will fall under the ethers of this plague before we reach Monrovia."

The boy's mother Likana sat down next to him and tried to feed him some fresh water. The water poured from either side of his mouth, and he appeared to swallow very little. Curtis took the cup from the boy's mother and attempted to get some fluids into him.

"Please, Bwana, you need this water or you will die," Curtis pleaded with the boy. "You are burning up with fever and the fresh water will help you." Of course, neither Bwana nor Likana could understand Curtis, but Likana nodded in approval at his tone.

Likana began to rock back and forth with her hands on her head. Then she started to sing a song to Bwana. The melody has many words to it, but I could only make out two names, Bwana and Likana, and two other words, Nzinga and Osumaka. Beyond that, I had little idea of what she was saying to the boy, but it seemed to soothe both of them.

Curtis remained with the mother and child throughout the day and night. He fed and washed him and was rarely seen elsewhere. I hadn't the heart to force him back to his duties just yet. Were I to do so, I would certainly be the focus of his anger should the boy succumb to his illness.

April 24, 1861

Day 2 of our voyage to Monrovia

Any of the crew has already become sickened. I did not have to tell Curtis of the change in his duties. He was to assist Willis now in caring for the sick. It wasn't long before he and Willis had a small ward of ill passengers and crew under his care.

"Curtis, how goes the hospital you and Willis are running?" I asked.

"Well, I think," he responded, "the little boy Bwana is now taking water and keeping it down. His eyes are less sunken, and he seems to be responding to his mother. I think that he has formed an attachment to me. Whenever I leave him, he calls my name to come back."

"He does?" I asked.

"Well, the best Stanton he can get out. Sounds more like 'Stadon,' but the message is there," he replied with a grin.

"And how are your others?" I asked Curtis.

"There are many in different stages of the disease. Based on Bwana's progress, I feel that the best course of action is fresh air on the deck whenever possible combined with as much fresh water by mouth as possible. I've taken to boiling the water and adding a bit of citrus from the stocks of lemons," he explained. "I hope that you don't mind. I assume we can replenish the stock when we reach port."

"No, I don't mind. Sounds like an interesting potion you have come up with," I stated as I looked at what now appeared to be nearly half of my crew laid up with this pestilence.

"Doc Willis has been showing me what to do," Curtis mentioned as he tended to two of the crew.

"Where is he?" I asked.

"In the wardroom. He's been tending to some of the most severely ill. There are several who are burning up with fever, and he's been letting their blood."

"I'll see if there is anything I can do to help him. Keep up the good work," I replied as I headed over to the wardroom. I could hear the moaning of many of the crew. I paused at the door to listen.

"Had I only had the proper setting and a staff to assist, this would be a great deal easier," I could hear Willis telling the two crew members who were helping him.

I opened the door. The smell was overpowering, and I asked tightly, "Doctor, don't you think it best to get these men out into the fresh air?"

"I wouldn't quite call me doctor," Willis replied.

"Well, for now you are the doctor on board this ship," I replied sternly.

I could see Guthrie laid out on the mess table motionless. Other crew members were lying on other tables and on the floor.

"Aye, aye, Captain," Willis replied.

"What of Guthrie, Doctor?" I asked.

"I fear that he will not make it. He was hallucinating for the last twelve hours and has now become quite lethargic. He no longer responds to my questions and refuses all food or drink."

I grabbed one of the midshipmen who had been helping the doctor tend to the ill. "You, Gabre, tend to Guthrie," I ordered. "He is to be your number one priority. Help the doctor with the others when you can, but make certain that Guthrie survives."

"Aye, sir," Gabre responded and headed directly to Guthrie's side.

The new doctor himself appeared to be slightly ill with sweat beads pouring down his forehead and a look of malaise upon his face.

"It looks like you're in command now," stated the doctor.

"It looks that way. I wish someone had informed me that the lieutenant—I mean, that the captain—had taken ill." I reproved the doctor. "You must make certain that he survives."

"I'm doing the best I can, Lieutenant. The fever comes up very quickly, and I haven't had time to make regular reports," he grunted. "These men here are the most sick, and I felt it best to keep them from the rest."

"You don't look well yourself, Doctor," I stated.

"I'm not, Lieutenant. I believe that I've succumbed to the ethers of this plague as well."

"Well, Doctor, do the best you can and try to at least keep the hatches and these pocket doors open to let in some fresh air," I said. "I am going to set up canopies out on the deck for all who need refuge from the stale air."

I left and headed back to the main deck. Most of the crew were now unavailable for duty, leaving just a handful to man the ship. I had the purser Vanderbeek and the boatswain Druskin fashion canopies from all the available cloth. This created enough of a shaded area to cover most of the crew who by now were becoming delirious.

"Boatswain!" I called.

"Aye, sir," he responded.

"Take account of all the sick and dead. I need to know where things stand."

"Aye, sir. I will get right on that," he replied as he scurried off.

I returned to Stanton's side. Curtis was doing the best he could to take care of the sick passengers and crew members who were now outside under the canopies. I noticed that Bwana was awake and talking. He appeared to have taken a turn for the better within the last hour.

"I see that your young patient is looking quite well." I congratulated Curtis.

"He is. He is," Curtis replied, smiling a little. "He's actually been helping me. He's quite a remarkable young boy."

The boatswain Druskin returned. "Sir, I have your report."

"Yes?" I asked.

"It's not very good, Lieutenant." He began.

"What is your report?" I repeated, dreading the news.

"I'm sorry to say that sixty of the Negro passengers and one crew member are dead, sir," he told me.

"And of the sick crew?" I asked.

"That's the problem, sir. More than half of the crew is now fevered or so weak that they can barely take care of themselves."

I shook my head, dismayed at the boatswain's news. This was not how I saw my first command beginning. "We are still more than two days away from Monrovia at this speed. Unless the winds become more favorable, then I fear we may take too long to get sufficient help." I worried.

"Aye, sir. The midshipmen have been taking turns at the helm. I'm sorry to say that two of them are down with the fever, and the third was at the helm when he became delirious"—the boatswain took a deep breath—"it is not clear how far he may have set us off course."

This news distressed me greatly, and I wondered why this was the first I'd heard it. "Then who is plotting our course?" I demanded.

"Lieutenant Guthrie was, but the purser Vanderbeek took over as there was no one left to do it." Reacting to my anger, the boatswain's voice grew softer.

"What happened?" I asked, trying to modulate my tone.

"We have been tacking into the wind, and it appears that we were set off course," he answered.

"Are we back on course now?" I asked.

"Aye, aye, sir. We are most definitely." Druskin was happy to give me this news.

"Right. Meeting of all the well-abled officers in the captain's quarters in fifteen minutes," I ordered. "Spread the word."

I headed to the captain's quarters and opened the log. I had to record the events for today as well as my plans for the rest of the journey. The situation is this: I am unaware of our current position, our normal complement of crew is unfit for duty, and the mission's commander, Guthrie, is amongst the very ill. I, therefore, must take command of this ship and get us safely to port. I wondered idly whether Captain Taylor could have foreseen these circumstances when he made me second in command. I determined our current position after taking several readings with my sextant and chronometer. I repeated the measurements several times for accuracy's sake.

There was a knock at the door.

"Enter," I said as I sat in the captain's chair and considered my plans.

The remaining officers entered.

"Gentlemen, here is our current situation. Our captain, Guthrie, is taken with fever and has been incapacitated. As a result, I have taken command of this ship," I stated. "Wait"—I looked around the room.—"Where is Lieutenant Stanton?" I asked.

"Not certain, sir," the purser replied.

"Well, bring him here right now," I ordered.

"Aye, aye, sir," he replied as he darted out to the deck.

"We are now a half day off-course thanks to one of our midshipmen who failed at his duty. I am happy to say—"

Just then the door opened and Stanton entered.

"Glad you could join us, Lieutenant. Is everything all right?" I asked.

"Yes, sorry. I had a quite a few patients to attend to." He apologized.

"Understood. As I was saying, we are now off course by at least a half a day's journey given our current speed. I am happy to say, however, that we are now back on course, but Monrovia is at least two days' journey from our current location. Given that half our crew is unfit, we need to be clear on what needs to be done."

The officers paid close attention.

"How many deceased?" I asked.

The purser replied, "Sir, all of the sixty deceased passengers have been released to the depths. Our deceased crewmate has been wrapped, awaiting a formal burial at sea, sir."

"Right, so we will attend to that immediately. Stanton will continue to assist the doctor in caring for the ill. Vanderbeek will help me with controlling sanitation as well as careful distribution of the remaining food stores. The two remaining midshipmen fit for duty Rieber and Carter will take shifts at the helm. I will take every third shift. The doctor, Willis, wants all those who are not responding or too ill to be taken to him and kept away from the passengers or remaining healthy crew. With the Lord's help, we will make it to Monrovia. Dismissed."

The American Colonization Society (ACS) was founded in 1816 as a way to support the "return" of free African Americans to what was believed to be greater freedom "back home" in Africa. It counted among its founders: Henry Clay, Charles Fenton Mercer, John Randolph, and Richard Bland Lee. The society was made up of mostly evangelicals, Methodists, and Quakers who supported abolition but did not wish to socialize or in any way interact with free blacks. Many of their supporters had good intentions. They hoped to give freed blacks a better chance for full and rewarding lives in Africa, while others feared the growing numbers of slaves in the United States and wished to limit their numbers for fear of a possible uprising.

In 1822, the ACS, with the help of the U.S. government, established Liberia with its capital Monrovia after a failed attempt to start a colony for freed slaves further north along the coast. They purchased several hundred square miles of territory around Cape Mesurado.

(By 1864, the ACS had assisted in the repatriation of nearly fourteen thousand free slaves to Liberia. No longer seeing a need for its existence, the ACS formally dissolved later that year and then transferred all of its documents to the Library of Congress.)

The U.S. government had its own reasons for supporting the establishment of Liberia. They were following the model set previously by Great Britain in Sierra Leone.

CHAPTER 10

Osumaka's Middle Passage

O SUMAKA HAD BEEN placed inside a ship with almost six hundred other African men all bound for a notorious seasoning camp in Jamaica. The conditions were far worse than what Likana and Bwana would have experienced had they not been liberated by the USS *Saratoga*. On this ship, human cargo was treated as livestock. The racks below deck were hastily made and were no more than large shelves stacked upon each. Each man was forced to lay naked next to two others, but with their bodies alternating head to toe. The racks were three shelves high with barely three feet between each shelf. The shelves were six-feet deep, which meant that those who were taller than six feet were forced to either dangle their feet over the edge or bend their knees to avoid having their heads dangle.

Beyond being cramped and unable to sit upright or partake of any significant movement, the men were forced to endure horrid living conditions in the dark bowels of the ship. The smell of feces and urine was ever present. Many of the men, unaccustomed to ocean travel, vomited what little they had in their stomachs. This regurgitation would either end up on them or on the feet of their neighbors. Conversations were difficult in the cramped quarters, and most of them could not understand each other's language, but Osumaka tried desperately to find out their fate.

"Friend," Osumaka called to the man on his left beyond the feet of the man between them. "Friend, I am Osumaka. What is your name?"

"Olaudah," the man replied. "You sound like you are BaKongo. My grandfather dealt with the BaKongo and taught me your language. I am Olaudah."

"I am called Osumaka," he replied. "Where are you from and how old are you?

Olaudah responded, "I am Mande and am twenty-five years of age, and you?"

"I am twenty-eight years old and am BaKongo," Osumaka replied. "I have a wife and two children." He began and then sadness welled up inside of him. "I had two children, but the raiders left my daughter for dead in the wood on our journey to the sea. I know not if she is still alive, but I heard the sounds of her screams as they forced us to march away. I still hear her voice screaming for me to help her, to save her, every time I try to sleep. She is always calling to me, and I am never able to help her."

"I am sorry, my friend," Olaudah replied sympathetically. "I too was about to have a family. They killed my wife when they raided our village. Then they placed a spear through her belly where my baby slept. I will never know that child nor see my dear wife ever again."

"I too am sorry, my friend."

"What of your wife and other child?" Olaudah asked.

"I pray to Fa that they might be alive," Osumaka responded as he tried to get enough slack on his chain to wipe his eyes. "My wife Likana is twenty-five as well, and my son Bwana is six. My daughter Nzinga was four. We were separated at the fort by the sea."

"I don't know Fa, but I too was separated from my family. My sister and her husband were taken at the same time that I was. We made it to the fort by the sea, but then they pulled me away from them."

"Where are we going?" Osumaka asked. "Have you any idea?"

"I have none my friend. I suspect we are to die," Olaudah responded.

The old man between them grumbled in a low shallow straining voice, "We are going to the place of evil where we will be fed to wild beasts."

Osumaka looked at the man's feet and his legs. He could see that the man was much older than they were, and he sounded ill.

"What is your name?" Osumaka asked the old man.

"Katana," he responded in a low voice followed by a bout of coughing. "Katana, and I am old enough to be the father of both of you. I know both the Manda and the BaKongo and have had honorable dealings with both."

"Sir, do you know where we are headed? Has someone told you?" Olaudah asked.

"The white men are taking us away, but no one has ever returned. So I know not what awaits us or where we are going," he replied and then broke into a long bout of raspy coughing.

Olaudah turned to the man whose head was on his other side. "Friend, I am Olaudah, who are you?"

"I heard that you are Olaudah and the other is Osumaka. I also heard that you are Mande, and we do not speak to the Mande."

"But we are here, prisoners together. I have no quarrel with you. Should we not try to befriend all who we can?"

"No," the stranger replied sharply, "we do not. When we get to where the white devils are taking us, I will kill as many of them as I can or I will die trying."

"I feel the same," Osumaka replied. "I am BaKongo. I do not believe that you have any quarrels with BaKongo."

"That is true," the man replied. "I am Bakude, and I am a warrior."

"I can see that," Osumaka replied. "Your spirit is strong."

"It is!" Bakude shouted back. "I have killed many, and I will fight again."

"You will, my friend, but we are not your enemy," Osumaka stated. "We must all work together to get through this."

"Neither you nor anyone else on this thing will give me orders. I am Bakude. I am a warrior." With that declaration, Bakude turned his head away.

"A foolish young man, that Bakude." Katana breathed. "He will not survive this journey with that belief."

"You do not sound well, sir," Osumaka replied.

"I am not, my son. I became ill in the fort by the sea and feel weaker with each painful breath."

"When will they feed us?" Olaudah asked. "We have not eaten since they bound us here in this space. The sun has set and risen since we saw our last meal and our last chance to drink."

"I too am hungry and thirsty," Osumaka responded. "I know not when they will feed us, but I fear that we will all pass to Fa if they do not feed us soon."

"Fa, Fa, Fa!" Bakude shouted out. "Neither your Fa nor his Allah nor anyone else can do anything for you now. Only you can do for yourself. You look after yourself, and you may just survive this. If not, you will certainly perish like the others who are as weak as you."

"That may be true, Bakude," Osumaka replied.

Suddenly, the prisoners heard a sound coming from the deck above. Since they were in the middle bunk, they were unable to see through the planks in the decking. Nevertheless, Osumaka and Bakude strained to look toward the source of the sounds. Just then, the hatch to the hold was opened and light poured into the cramped space. Fresh cool air rushed in, and the prisoners gulped the clean air with gratitude. The bunks on which they lay were constructed along the hull of the ship. The men, stacked three high, lined the outer perimeter of the hold. The space within the center, between them and the men on the other side of the ship, seemed to be filled with cargo. Boxes and canvas sacks were stacked high and served as a wall, separating the two sides of the ship.

Three white men descended the stairs from the deck and into the dank, stale, and putrid air of the bowels of the ship. The air down here was heavy with the smells of human waste, festering open wounds, and decaying bodies. The sailors shouted at their prisoners through the cloths covering their noses and mouths against the stench. Osumaka and his friends were unable to tell what they were saying, but it was clear from their actions that the smell was bothering the white men as much as it did them. One man held a large ladle, and the other two held a large pot each—one filled with rice and the other with water. They slapped the scoops of rice into the hands of the men. As each prisoner struggled to get the rice to his mouth, he pulled the chains of the men next to them and prevented them from reaching their own. Many spilled the rice before they could get it to their mouths. Only the strongest were able to get the most of their sparse meal. Many tried to pick up the food that had fallen on their bodies and bring it to their mouths. Others tried to steal their neighbors' food. The man with the water followed behind with another ladle. He poured the water onto the faces of the men whose heads were closest to him, but those who had their heads to the hull of the ship strained to reach the short instrument delivering the water they desperately needed to survive. Most received barely a mouthful, while others got none at all. Osumaka and his friends could hear the men on the other side of the ship in a frenzy trying to get their food. He could only hope that they would come to his side of the ship as well. As he continued to strain to look out of the open hatch,

MICHAEL JAY NUSBAUM

he saw three more white men coming down the stairs. They too were carrying large pots and ladles. They began at the back of the ship and worked their way forward. Osumaka and his friends lay midship within the hold. Bakude was first to get his.

"How is it?" Osumaka asked.

Chewing, Bakude did not respond at first.

Osumaka repeated, "How is it?"

"It tastes like animal feed!" Bakude responded with disgust. He then received his scoop of water. "But I am so hungry. I would eat anything right now."

Soon, Olaudah received his food. "It does taste like animal food." Then he received his scoop of water as well. He joked. "I would never marry a woman who would cook this badly." His friends laughed.

Katana received his meal and then Osumaka received his.

"No wonder they are so white," Bakude shouted. "If I prepared food this poorly, I too would turn white and look as ghostly as they do!"

With that, the men began to laugh out loud.

Suddenly a banging noise—metal striking metal—was heard on the other side of the ship. The men strained to see what was going on.

"What are they doing?" Olaudah asked. "Can anyone see?"

"They are breaking the chain of the men on the other side," Bakude replied.

"For what purpose?" Osumaka asked.

"I have no idea, but when they break mine, I will use the chain to break their necks." Bakude decided.

Olaudah could see the men on the other side leading the captives, still chained to each other up to the deck above. "They are setting them free?" He sounded doubtful.

"I don't think so," Osumaka replied. "I think we are still upon the water."

Once all the men were above deck, the sound of splashing water was heard, followed by water pouring through the planks from the deck above and through the open hatch.

"They are drowning them!" Olaudah shouted in fear.

"I don't think so," Osumaka replied.

After several minutes passed, the men were led back to their racks at the bottom. Then the sailors released the chain on its end with the pounding of the hammer against the metal. Soon, the next group was led to the deck and the prisoners heard the splashing again. This process repeated until the middle rack on their side was freed as well. The men were pulled out of their rack. Katana was too weak to move on his own, so Osumaka and Olaudah helped him out to his feet.

"My legs no longer work. Leave me," Katana argued

"We will help you," Osumaka responded.

"Leave me to die. I have not the strength to continue."

"Olaudah, you hold his right arm up, and I will hold the other," Osumaka instructed.

"Leave you to die, old man?" Bakude shouted. "I would be happy to were we not all chained together. You are lucky that I am not chained to one of your arms. I would as soon tear it off to be free than to help you."

The men helped Katana to his feet and up the stairs onto the deck of the ship. The light was too bright for their eyes, and they strained to keep them closed or covered with their chained hands. The men were lined up along the railing of the ship as a row of sailors stood ready in front of them like a firing squad.

"Buckets up!" shouted one and then, "Heave to the wretches!"

As the buckets of sea water were splashed upon the captives, the salty water burned their eyes. Osumaka could feel the salt water seeping into the fresh burn wound on his arm from the recent branding. As the salt water burned others' wounds, many men screamed in pain.

The sailors began to laugh as the men cried out.

"I guess that it hurts them to be clean!" one sailor shouted out as the rest reveled in his insults.

None of the captives had anything covering them. They were completely exposed and humiliated by the experience.

Once again, the prisoners heard the shouts, "Buckets up!" and then, "Heave to the wretches!"

By the second dousing, many of the men were prepared and had their eyes already closed. "The burning from the wounds could be no worse this second time around," Osumaka thought out loud.

In a few minutes, they were led back down the hatch and into the hold. They were instructed to get back into their racks.

When it came time for Bakude to climb back in, he refused.

"Up to your space," the sailor demanded.

Bakude stared at him defiantly, all his muscles flexed and ready to pounce like a fierce lion upon its prey.

"I said, up to your space!" the sailor repeated and then he reached for a leather strap. "One last time, you dog. Up to your space!"

Bakude held his ground. The look in his eyes was that of pure rage. Had his hands and feet not been bound, the sailor would not have survived beyond the next few moments.

"I said up!" And with that, the sailor whipped the strap across Bakude's bare back. Bakude did not flinch. "I said up!" said the sailor as he whipped him over and over.

Soon, blood was pouring from the cuts on Bakude's back, yet he did not budge.

Suddenly, Katana spoke, "Now is not the time, young warrior. You will have your time, but this is not it. Return to your place, and I assure you that you will eventually have victory over these devils."

At that, Bakude reluctantly returned to his place, the blood still pouring from the three deep gashes in the skin of his back. Then each man returned to his own place.

"Why did he do that?" Olaudah asked Osumaka. "It served no purpose."

"But it did," Osumaka replied. "It did for Bakude. He showed the white man that he would not be broken. That he would do what he wanted when he wanted."

"But he wanted him to get back to his prison. Bakude did what the devil wanted. He had no choice. I still say that it served no purpose."

Katana chimed in, "It served no purpose to you or me, but Bakude needed to do that for himself. The pride of such a strong warrior can never be broken. Never by captivity and never by a white man with a whip.

The routine of feeding, cleaning, and the dousing on deck repeated itself each day for nine days. On the morning of the ninth day, Osumaka arose first.

Soon Olaudah woke up.

"How are you this morning, my friend Osumaka?"

Osumaka's voice was thick with unshed tears. "I dreamed of my daughter calling out for me again. I have heard her screams for me every night. Each time, I am unable to reach her."

"I am sorry, my friend," Olaudah replied. "I too am haunted in my dreams."

"Katana, are you awake?" Olaudah asked.

The old man made no response. Olaudah and Osumaka have helped him out of his rack and onto the deck every day since their journey started.

"He was very weak yesterday," Osumaka reminded his friend. "I had to hold up more of his weight yesterday than I had ever had to before."

"I thought he was just getting lighter from his lack of eating. He hasn't had much of an appetite." Olaudah reasoned.

Olaudah reached out to feel Katana's leg.

"He feels very cold to me," Olaudah said. "Osumaka, feel his legs."

Osumaka reached out to feel Katana's ice-cold leg. He squeezed hard. Katana made no response, and Osumaka could feel no life in his friend's leg.

"I believe that he has passed to Fa," Osumaka stated sadly. "His journey has ended."

"The old man is better off," Bakude commented. "He was never strong and would have died anyway."

"Perhaps so," Osumaka said to him. "He is free now."

"What will they do with him now?" Olaudah asked. "We need to tell them."

"They will not care," Bakude said. "Our people line the walls of this boat. We are stacked like timber."

"He's right," Osumaka said. "We can try, but they do not understand us, and we do not understand them. Even if we could speak their tongue, their ears would ignore our pleas."

When it came time for them to go topside to get washed off, Osumaka and Olaudah carried Katana as they had before. They released him just before the water hit them. Katana's body was lowered to the deck, pulling their arms down with him.

"Get up, old man!" one sailor shouted. "UP, UP, UP, UP, UP!"

"I think he's dead," another sailor said in response.

"He's not dead. He's just as lazy as the rest of them."

"No, I think he's really dead."

"Great. This will be the tenth one in only nine days at sea. The captain will be furious at the loss of our cargo," the first sailor said to the other. "Let's free him and toss him over before the captain knows."

"That's crazy. What about the count?" the other asked. "The inventory will be short. We must tell him."

MICHAEL JAY NUSBAUM

The other sailor then took out a large machete and raised it high. "At least we should make as little work of disposal as possible."

He brought the machete down upon Katana's arm, severing it at midforearm. Then he raised it again and repeated the blow on the other side. Katana's arms fell while his hands and wrists remained in the chains.

"Oh, that was not necessary," replied the other sailor. "Now you take his hands out of those shackles."

"That's fine. I will," said the other, raising the hatchet again. "Just as soon as I free his feet from his body as well."

Soon, all four limbs were severed from the chains. Two other sailors removed a section of the side rail so that the opening was flush with the deck. Then one of them grabbed Katana's head and slid him over the side into the open sea. He replaced the railing.

"See. That was easy," the sailor with the machete chuckled.

"You forgot the rest of him. Finish cleaning up," the other replied.

"Oh, right," the machete responded as he took the severed body parts and threw them over the side of the ship.

Horrified, Osumaka and Olaudah can only look at each other. "These men are monsters," Olaudah said to his friend.

"These men have just marked their own fates," Bakude growled. "Someday I will avenge what they have done. But when I do, the white devils will still be alive to see me doing it to them!"

They headed back down below deck and back to their spaces. Katana's space stayed empty, reminding them all how fragile their new lives were.

Day after day the process repeated itself. One day led into the other, and soon, they lost count of the days. Was it twenty days? Or twenty-one days? Or twenty-two? No one was sure at this point.

One day, Osumaka and the other captives heard a commotion on the deck.

"LAND HO!" one sailor shouted.

The rest of the crew cheered in excitement.

"What are they celebrating?" Olaudah asked.

Osumaka lifted his head up and turned to see. "I am not certain. It sounds as if they celebrate, but I cannot be sure. They are a strange tribe, these white men. It does sound like celebration though."

ERE ÀWÒRÁN

"Could it be that we have come to the end of our journey?" Olaudah asked.

"It could, but why would they celebrate that? We are the ones who are suffering."

Several hours later, there were strange sounds coming from outside the ship, which was by then barely moving. All noticed the new sounds and wondered what was happening. Soon, the hatch opened again. As had happened every day for the saltwater dousing, some sailors came down to bring the captives to the deck. As always, the light blinded them. When their sight returned, they could see that they had reached a new land. The new land had many white men, all engaged in some important activity.

"What is this place?" Olaudah asked Osumaka.

"I am not sure, but it looks very much like that which we left on beyond the waters."

They could hear screams coming from the walls of a structure to their right.

"What is that?" Olaudah asked.

"I am not certain, my friend, but I fear that we will soon find out," Osumaka replied.

"I hope it is the shouts of the white men as one of our countrymen is exacting his revenge upon him," Bakude replied.

The other men did not share Bakude's optimism. "I have a strange feeling about this place," Olaudah stated timidly.

"I do as well, my friend," Osumaka replied.

The men were led in their groups off the ship and onto the dock. Each looked in a different direction, trying to figure out where they were and what was in store for them. There were other ships docked and unloading. Most of the Africans being taken off the ships appeared to be men.

"Where are our women and children?" Olaudah asked.

"I do not know," Osumaka responded as he too was perplexed by the scene. He had almost hoped to reunite with Likana and Bwana at the end of the journey. He wasn't sure whether to wish they were all together or be thankful his wife and son were not observing and experiencing this horror.

The men were then marched single file into the fort and taken to the center of the structure. They looked around at the high walls and saw other chained captives. There were captives chained to posts with white men whipping them. Others were kept in cages no bigger than themselves. The air stunk of a sweet putrid smell mixed with feces.

Soon, they saw Africans who were not chained and who were wearing the white men's tattered clothing. That group of Africans approached Osumaka's line. Rapidly, they began to scrub the naked men down with soap and water using large sponges.

"Where are we and what is this place?" Osumaka asked the African who was washing him. He received no reply.

"Where are we and what is this place?" Osumaka asked the man again.

"Do not speak," the man said to Osumaka. "They will beat you if you do."

"Please, friend, you must tell us where we are and what happens to us next," Osumaka pleaded.

The man looked around and then started to scrub Osumaka's neck and face. Quietly he said, "You are in Jamaica, in a slave preparation port. You will be cleaned, shaven, oiled, then placed in a seasoning camp. When they find you ready, you will be taken to the slave market and sold at auction. That is all I can tell you."

"But what is Jamaica and where are we? What is a seasoning camp?"

The man ignored Osumaka and kept scrubbing him. Next, another man came up to him with a knife. Osumaka stepped back, wary of what the African could do with the sharp blade.

"I am just here to shave you," the man reassured Osumaka.

"But where are we? And what is going to happen to us?" Osumaka repeated. He heard "Jamaica" and "seasoning camp" but could make no sense of the terms. He needed fuller explanations.

"You are here to be prepared for the slave markets where you will be sold," the man with the razor replied.

"Sold to whom and for what purpose?" Osumaka asked.

"That depends. I hear that most go to the islands to harvest sugar cane. Some others work in the fields of America and harvest cotton, rice, or tobacco, of course," he responded.

"That is a woman's work," Bakude replied as he pushed the man away from him and refused to be cleaned or shaven.

"But you must, or they will torture you," the man pleaded with Bakude.

"Then they must torture me," he responded.

The overseer heard the commotion. "What is going on here?"

"This one is refusing," the other stated.

"Oh he is, is he? Do as we tell you, or we will beat you till you do."

Bakude refused to move.

"Whip him to his knees!" the overseer shouted. "You are not the first to come through here who refused to obey, and you will not be the last. We have created ways to break stubborn ones like you."

Another white man approached with a long whip that soon began cracking across Bakude's back. Within a few cracks, the old scars reopened and blood again began to flow from his back. The whip struck him over and over.

"Again!" the overseer called out. "Again, again, again!" Then he said, "Give it to me."

Bakude stood firm as the overseer took the whip. Bukade's face showed nothing but pure anger. Soon, his muscles began to twitch with each lash, but still, he stood firm. Pieces of flesh began heaping up on his back. Then pieces of skin began flying off as the whip cracked across Bakude's back. Blood began to splatter onto the white man's skin. Then a piece of Bakude's flesh flew and landed on the overseer's cheek. The overseer temporarily stopped the whipping to wipe the blood and the piece of Bakude from his face.

"Had enough?" the overseer asked as he wiped his face with the bottom of his shirt. "No?" he asked when he received no reply from Bakude. "We have other treats in store for you then. His voice was menacing. Although Osumaka and Olaudah could not understand the words, the overseer's threat was clear."

"Please, Bakude, just let them do it," Olaudah pleaded.

"He's right, Bakude," Osumaka agreed. "Now is not the time."

"If now is not the time, then when is the time?" Bakude responded. "Katana died and that wasn't the time. We're here in this horrid land of evil white people, but now is not the time? I will not wait for them to chop off my hands and feet. Now is the time. I will not yield!"

After Bakude's impassioned proclamation, the overseer instructed the African helpers to bind him separately and remove him from the chain of men.

"You will love what I have in store for defiant ones like you," the overseer gleefully stated.

MICHAEL JAY NUSBAUM

"What will they do to him?" asked Olaudah of Osumaka.

"I do not know, but I wish that Bakude would just wait for the right time." Osumaka could not have known that Bakude was essentially correct—there was no "right" time for rebellion. But unlike Bakude, Osumaka still cherished a small hope that he would see his family again.

"Quiet you two!" The overseer barked out at them, not understanding a word that they were saying to each other, but ready to stifle any more defiance.

Osumaka and Olaudah watched as the men took Bakude to the other side of the fort. There stood a large wooden frame as if for a house, but it had no sides and no roof. They attached his leg irons to yet another chain. Then they pulled on a wheel with spokes coming out of it until Bakude was left hanging upside down from the structure and swinging suspended under it. The leg irons cut into the skin of his ankles. Blood began to flow down his legs, yet Bakude remained silent. The blood from his back flowed past clumps of ripped tissue.

Osumaka looked around. All he could see was evil and death. Then he noticed two men pushing a cart past the newly arrived group of captives. The cart was filled with bodies of dead Africans. Their bodies were emaciated and their limbs tangled together.

"We have arrived in hell." Olaudah decided.

"This is not hell," Osumaka disagreed. "This is a place of the evil of the white devils, but this is not hell."

They watched as the bodies were dumped off the cart and into a smoldering pit. Smoke billowed out of the pit. It was then that they realized that the putrid sweet smoke they had smelled when they landed was that of burning bodies in the pit.

"What have we done to deserve this?" Olaudah cried.

"I do not know, my friend. I do not know," Osumaka replied.

Once cleaned, they were taken to the next station. Here they were rubbed down with oil. A claylike substance was spread over their open wounds so as to hide them. The clay stung as it filled the gaps in the men's flesh.

Osumaka looked down at his own legs as the irons were removed from his ankles. As the leggings were taken off, he could see maggots moving over his wounds and the irons themselves. He looked at Olaudah's legs to see the same horrific sight.

"It is not a bad thing," the slave in white man's clothing stated. "They keep the wounds clean. See, look, very clean."

Another came over to wipe down their legs, brush off the maggots, and cover their wounds with the thick clay. All the while, their arms remained bound behind them.

Suddenly, the crack of a whip could be heard again. The men turned their heads to see not one but two men whipping Bakude as he hung upside down.

The sounds of Bakude being tortured could still be heard, yet he didn't make a sound. The men were then led through a gate in the wall and into another courtyard of the fort. There, a white man sat in a chair on a platform. The slaves were marched in front of him.

"A," he called for the first one as a white powder mark was placed on his chest.

"C," he said for the next.

The next man in line spat upon the African in white man's clothing.

"F," the white man said.

Two men came over and unchained the spitter from the rest. They dragged him by his feet with his back scraping against the pounded dirt ground of the fort, through the gate from which they had just come.

"A," the white man pointed to Osumaka.

"B," he called for Olaudah.

On he went down the line as the men wrote letters onto the slaves' chests.

"What does this mean?" asked Olaudah.

"I do not know," replied Osumaka, "but I suspect that we will be separated since your mark does not match my own." Osumaka knew that he was about to lose the only friend that he had left in the world.

They were then marched through another wall and another gate. This time, the courtyard was filled with holding areas bound with walls of iron bars. Each man was released and placed into a cell as they passed.

First, Osumaka was released from the chain and thrown into a cell with at least twenty other men. Then Olaudah was unhooked and thrown into the neighboring cell. The cells had a common wall of bars, so Osumaka and Olaudah met at the wall between them.

"I'm scared," said Olaudah.

"I know, my friend," Osumaka replied. "I am frightened too." What could happen next?

Just then the other men in the cells jumped up and ran to the front of the holding pens, stretching out their hands as two men came by and ladled food into their cupped hands.

"Get up!" Osumaka called to Olaudah. "We haven't eaten and need to keep our strength up."

Then men pushed through to get their hands out as well.

Olaudah received his scoop only to realize that a bar remained between his two hands so that he was unable to get the food through. He separated his hands trying to keep as much in each hand as possible, only to see most of his only meal fall to the ground. No sooner did it hit the dirt than another man scooped it up, dirt and all, and ate it. Seeing Olaudah's struggles, Osumaka made sure to put both hands through one slot to capture the full meal. He ate most of it and headed back to the common wall.

"Here," he said to Olaudah, "have some of mine."

He handed over the remainder of his meal to his friend. Olaudah gladly took the food and placed it in his mouth.

Night fell as they lay in the holding cells. No one spoke to each other with the exception of Olaudah and Osumaka. The flies were now joined by swarms of mosquitos that landed on every part of their naked bodies. The men started slapping their skin to kill the vile insects.

Osumaka asked another man in his cell, "Where are you from?"

The man looked at him and responded in a strange language.

"These men are speaking a language I don't understand," he said to Olaudah. "I wonder where they're from."

"We had best get some rest, Osumaka." Olaudah yawned.

"Let's keep our backs to each other. If something happens, then wake me," Osumaka replied.

The men tried to sleep but could not. The noises and the smells kept them awake for hours. Eventually, Osumaka found himself drifting in and out of sleep. Soon, he could not tell the difference between the two worlds.

"noooooooo!" Osumaka shouted.

A hand reached through the bars and touched his shoulder. "Wake up, my friend," said Olaudah. "You are having a bad dream."

"Yes, I was." Osumaka tried to regain his composure.

"Was it of your daughter again?" Olaudah asked.

"Yes, the dream is always the same," Osumaka replied, still shaken. "I no longer wish to sleep. There is nothing good that waits for me there. You sleep, my friend. I will keep watch."

Olaudah slept as Osumaka refused to close his eyes.

Morning came too quickly. The camp was awakened to the sounds of screaming once again, but this time, the screams came from men who had been tied to posts in front of the cages.

"What is happening?" Olaudah asked. "Is it Bakude?"

"No, it is two other men. I have never seen them before."

The guards whipped the two men as they remained tied to posts anchored firmly in the ground. Then the white-faced guards came over to Osumaka's cell and pulled out one man. They handed him a whip and instructed him to whip one of the men tied to the post. The prisoner looked back at the men in the cells and then at the bloody man tied by his wrists, his legs without strength. The guards, both African and white, shouted at him to use the whip. He hesitated. One African guard took out a stick and hit the man in the head and demanded he use the whip. Another guard, this time a white man, came up to the man holding the whip. He placed a gun to the prisoner's head and instructed the African guards to tell him to whip the man or be shot. The man lifted his hand and feigned an attempt to whip, but the leather never left the ground. The white guard repeated his demand and the African guards repeated their shouts. The white man shouted again and then fired a shot into the prisoner's head. The man was blown several feet away and his blood splattered over the white man that he appeared red-skinned, his clothes saturated in bright blood. Everyone in the cells fell silent as the sound of the gunshot continued to echo.

"You see!" the white guard shouted, but no one understood his words. "You see what you get when you do not obey!"

The African guards translated his shouts.

"What kind of people are these?" asked Olaudah.

"I do not know," Osumaka replied. "Have they no soul?"

The guards came to the cell door and motioned for Osumaka to come out.

"Do as they say," pleaded Olaudah. "Please do as they say."

The guards instructed him to place the body in the cart and wheel it to the pit.

Osumaka picked up the body and carried it to the cart nearby. He looked at what was left of the man. Half of his head and face were gone. Were it not for the arms and legs, one might mistake the lump of flesh for a half-eaten meal of a lion.

"And the pieces!" a guard shouted. "Don't forget the rest!"

Osumaka went back and picked up the bloody pieces of bone and flesh and then carefully placed them on the cart as well.

Olaudah watched intently as his friend was instructed in the gruesome task. He nodded his head in approval when Osumaka caught his eye. Then the guards led Osumaka through the gate and into the other area. Osumaka saw a new group of slaves being marched in and inspected. He passed them, heading into the first courtyard where he saw another group of fresh slaves being washed down. Then he caught a glimpse of Bakude. He was still hanging upside down, bloodied, and his body looked limp. His eyes were closed and there was no sign of life from him. Osumaka lost his last piece of hope. They had broken Bakude, and he knew he was doomed. He wheeled his cart to the pit and dumped the body in without finesse. The smoke was thick and bellowed out when the body hit the hot coals at the bottom. The guards motioned for him to return the cart to the cells where they had started. Osumaka turned and began wheeling the cart back. He turned his head to look over at his friend one last time. Bakude's eyes were now open, and their eyes connected. Bakude smiled and blinked both eyes. Osumaka was pleased. A large grin formed on his face. His back straightened, and he walked tall and proud, knowing that his friend had not been broken. Osumaka swore at that moment that they would not break him either. Osumaka pushed the cart past the new arrivals who looked around them in astonishment. He marched past the white man assigning letters for the slaves as he separated them. Then he entered back into the compound where his friend was, but he was gone. The entire cell had been emptied. The men from his cell were being led out. Osumaka looked around, but he could not see Olaudah anywhere. He and the other men were gone. The guard motioned for him to leave the cart and join his group. Osumaka was chained to the last man as they were marched out of the fort.

They were brought to a port by the sea. Once again, tall ships stood in the harbor. Flashbacks of his journey across the great ocean flooded his mind. Before he knew it, he was back inside the bowels of another ship. Osumaka found himself very much alone once again. Bukade had been taken away from him, but they could not break him. Olaudah had been taken away from him, and he feared for him as he knew that Olaudah was not as mentally strong as he was. He had no one to talk to, so he closed his eyes and dreamed of his family.

Eventually, the new ship arrived in port. Osumaka had lost track of time. He was unsure of how many days had passed, and at this point, he could not care. As they were led off the ship, he followed in the footsteps of the person in front of him. In this new land, there were many Africans walking around in white men's clothing, all bustling about. The line of men was stopped at the end of the road before a large gate. Two African women, the first he had seen since he had left Africa, came up to the men with large mops and pails. The first woman dipped the mop into the pail and drew it out filled with oil. She then painted each naked man with the mop. Finally, she got to Osumaka. He stood straight and proud, reminding himself of his vow. The woman looked at him and smiled. Her skin was as dark as his, and she appeared healthy and well cared for.

The line was then marched down the road and into the town. There were many buildings, and now, they could see many white people. They saw horses and carriages, shops, children, and dogs. It was a village Osumaka decided. A white man's village. The white men brought the slaves to a platform, where one by one, the Africans were forced to stand and turn around as white men yelled things at them.

"What an odd thing," Osumaka said out loud.

Each of the slaves was taken away when the white men were done shouting at him. Soon, it was Osumaka's turn. The men seemed to shout even louder at him and at the white man up on the platform with him. They waved their hands at each other with such fury.

"How odd they are," Osumaka said to himself as he stood, proud and unbroken.

Then he too was ushered away and loaded into a wagon with five other slaves. A white man walked around the wagon, speaking to two Africans dressed in white man's clothing. The white man's speech confused Osumaka. He wondered if it was the same language the white devils had spoken in Jamaica.

MICHAEL JAY NUSBAUM

One of the Africans dressed in European clothing spoke to them in Osumaka's own language. "Your name will be Peter," he said to the slave in front of Osumaka.

"Brother, you speak our language!" Osumaka exclaimed. A glimmer of hope returned.

"I am not your brother," he replied.

"But you are one of us!" Osumaka protested as he motioned to the others in the wagon.

"Your name will be Paul," the African said sternly, "and I am not one of you."

"My name is Osumaka," Osumaka replied.

"Your name is now Paul."

"My name is Osumaka," Osumaka stated defiantly.

"Your name is now Paul," the African repeated and moved to the next man.

CHAPTER 11

Arrival in Liberia

WE SET SAIL for Liberia on April 22. It is now the seventh day of our journey, and I fear that we may lose more of our freed passengers before we arrive. Several days ago, I made an entry into the logbook that I had taken command of the *Nightingale* as its captain. This I did with great hesitation. It was only when Captain Guthrie was struck down with fever and delirium that I stepped in to assume command. Lieutenant Stanton has performed admirably through this most difficult of times. Without his concerted efforts, in fact, we might have lost many more of the crew and our passengers. I have noticed that he has become rather attached to the young boy Bwana, whom he met in the first frantic minutes of the rescue. I am glad to see that through Curtis's nurturing, Bwana appears to be recovering well. So well in fact, that the young boy has been assisting Curtis with his endeavors to care for both passengers and crew.

"I see you have quite the eager helper there," I said to Curtis.

"Indeed, and he has recovered quite well I think," Curtis replied.

"He has, indeed, as a result of your efforts," I added. Despite our differences of opinion, I valued Curtis's contributions to the order of the ship.

"How far away are we?" Curtis asked.

"Not far, I suspect. Based on our latest positioning, we should arrive sometime later today."

"None too soon," Curtis replied. "We are running low on provisions, and the passengers and crew need to be taken off this ship."

"I know," I replied. "Were it not for your care and keeping all above deck, I am certain that we would have lost more."

"I will stay with the boy. He can have my rations until we arrive," Curtis said as he went back to the mother and son.

Curtis took Bwana in his arms and held him. His mother, Likana, did not object, recognizing the growing bond between Curtis and her son. She herself was feeling weak and welcomed Curtis's help.

April 29, 1861

We arrive in Liberia!

As Curtis most eloquently stated, "Not a moment too soon."

The port was alive and bustling with activity. I was shocked to see such a port here in Africa. There were admirably built docks with warehouses and shops. There were churches and homes resembling those I had seen in the Southern United States. There was quite a bustle of activity with carriages and wagons. Many ships were anchored within her harbor. Upon sight of the port, both passengers and crew arose to behold the sight. The few crew who had remained strong enough to work dropped sheet as we settle into position to dock.

We were greeted by nearly a dozen African men. They wore clean white shirts and were apparently eager to help us. Lines were thrown across to them, and they helped pull our ship into position. Many on board were too ill to move.

"We have many ill passengers," I shouted out to them. "We will need your doctor if you have one."

"Aye, Captain," one man responded. "I will fetch him."

I turned back to the *Nightingale*. "Set the ship for dock," I ordered the crew. "I will go ashore and find provisions for us. The purser will come with me."

"Aye, aye!" replied the boatswain.

I called down to the dock crew, "Can we get some fresh water and some provisions?"

"Right away, Captain," the lead dockhand replied.

"There must be a governor of the city with whom I can negotiate some provisions on behalf of the U.S. Navy," I said to Curtis.

"I'm certain that there is," he agreed.

"Keep an eye on things, won't you?" I asked of him. "The passengers as well as our crew. We need all to disembark so that we can clean the ship."

We disembarked as the dock crew handed up casks of fresh water and rum to the crew members. Liberia was quite a strange place. I was surprised to be greeted by so many Africans who spoke English, and some quite well. We headed out of the port and into the city proper. I counted three Protestant churches within the immediate downtown area and all within sight of each other. I asked myself, "Could there be so many here?" The air was thick with the smell of spices and all manner of food, familiar and strange, in front of the many shops.

"Excuse me?" I asked one very distinguished-looking African gentleman who approached us with a confident and steady gait. He was dressed impeccably in a three-piece suit, top hat, and walking cane and wore a pocket watch at the ready. His appearance was almost European in nature with strong features and was incredibly well groomed. He was quite light-skinned for an African over here, and I suspected that he was a mix of races. "Could you direct me to a representative of the United States?"

"We have no formal embassy here," he replied as he pointed to a large domed building. "There is the building that seats the government and our president."

"President?" I asked.

"Of course, what would you expect?" he replied. "We are a civilized country with a government not dissimilar to your own."

"What do you know of him?" I inquired.

"Of our president?" he asked.

"Yes," I replied.

"I know much," he responded. "Stephen Allen Benson is our president. He was elected to office in 1856 as our second president of Liberia. Prior to that, he served as our third vice president from 1854 to 1856 under then president Joseph Jenkins Roberts. President Benson was born in Cambridge, Maryland, to free Negro parents. His family left the United States in 1822 to seek a new life of equality for all in the newly created country of Liberia. Through the efforts of the American Colonization Society (ACS), they left the United States on the ACS brig Strong.

The tone of his voice changed, "Unfortunately, he and his relatives definitely picked the wrong time to come over here. It truly wasn't very long after their arrival in August 1822 that the colony was overrun and totally under the control of some very aggressive African natives. He and his family, along with many other African colonists, were taken hostage by these African warriors and held captive for more than four arduous months. Once they were freed, he worked his way up from a lowly shopkeeper all the way to the private secretary of Thomas Buchanan, the last of Liberia's white governors. Stephen Allen Benson wasn't an idle man. He was extremely dedicated to Liberia, so in 1835, he joined the militia to help regain control of Liberia from its invaders. He became an incredibly prominent figure in the newly founded Liberia and was even a delegate to the colonial council for Liberia's independence in 1847."

"How do you know so much about the president of Liberia?" I asked. I certainly did not have the same fluency with facts about the life of Abraham Lincoln.

"Because I am Stephen Allen Benson," he replied with a grin.

Astonished, I knew not what to do other than salute him. "It is an honor, Mr. President."

"And you are?" he asked.

"Acting Captain Smith, sir," I replied.

"Acting captain?" he asked.

"Yes, sir. Our captain, Guthrie, took ill along with more than half our crew and the many natives whom we rescued," I replied.

"I see. Then you are with Commodore Perry's Africa Squadron, are you not?"

"Yes, sir. Off the USS *Saratoga*, sir," I responded. "We were patrolling off the coast when we came across the *Nightingale*. She was anchored off a known slave trading post. We boarded her at night and took her. While liberating the ship, we found her holds filled to the deck with captive Africans. The conditions were abhorrent. Many were ill. Soon, the illness spread and nearly half of my crew were struck with fever."

"Well, Captain, I will make sure that you get the help that you need as well as the provisions required," he replied.

The president motioned for two African soldiers standing nearby to come over. "Have the garrison assist the American sailors with the freed captives on the ship *Nightingale*. Have the infirmary send over nurses and the garrison's surgeon to care for the ill on board. Also, make sure that they have provisions so that they may return home soon."

"That is much appreciated, Mr. President," I replied.

"In the meantime, I would like to invite you and your officers to the capital for a welcome dinner," he requested. "Of course, those officers who are not ill and are up to attending."

"That would be very much appreciated," I replied. "We had best return to our ship now that we have secured your most gracious assistance."

"That is understandable. I will have my assistant relay communications between your ship and my office. You are welcome to stay here as long as you need to, Captain. Rest and recover your crew." He smiled again as he tipped his hat and walked away.

We headed back the way we came, through the center of town, past the bustling warehouses and then back into the port. We could see that many of the freed slaves were gathered on the dock while others passed us as we approached. Some bowed before us, in thanks, as we walked to the *Nightingale*. I could not understand what they were saying, but the meaning was still very clear. They were eternally grateful to us for rescuing them. It was gratifying to know that we could help so many with just a single act.

When we arrived at the edge of the *Nightingale*, there were crew members laid out all over the dock. Curtis was directing the still sickened crew off the ship and onto the dock. His eager junior assistant remained at his side.

"What goes on?" I asked Curtis.

"We are trying to get everyone off the ship. She must be cleaned, and the holds reek from human waste," Curtis called from the railing.

"How goes it?"

"We have all the freed slaves off and are working on getting the sickest of our crewmates off as well."

"And Guthrie?" I asked.

"Not good, Captain. I fear that he may not survive," Curtis replied solemnly.

I told the purser to stay on the dock and assist with the off-loading of the ship while I board and see the status of the remaining ill crew members as well as Guthrie.

I climbed on board with the aid of Curtis's outstretched arm.

"He's not well, Michael," he whispered to me.

MICHAEL JAY NUSBAUM

"How many of the crew are fit for duty?" I asked.

"Not enough, I'm afraid," he replied. "We might be here for quite some time until enough of them recover to have a full active crew."

"Take me to Guthrie," I said.

We headed through the maze of crew members who were moaning in agony and shaking with fever. They were all laid out under canopies of cloth, which luffed in the light breeze of the port. We entered the makeshift hospital of the officers' mess. Tables had been pushed to the sides and two and three men lay on each. Guthrie was straight ahead being attended to by the doctor. A moist white cloth lay across his forehead, and his body shook from the fever.

"Guthrie?" I whispered into his ear. "Guthrie? Can you hear me?"

There was no reply. "We've made it!" I exclaimed. "We are in Liberia. They are eager to help us. We will soon get supplies from the local infirmary. We'll get you well and head home soon."

Guthrie made no indication that he had heard or understood me. I assumed he was too weak to respond, but I hoped he was alert enough to hear what I had said to him.

"Doctor, how is he doing?" I asked.

"Not well, Captain," he replied. "If he makes it, and I'm not saying that he will, it could be weeks or even months before he is fit for duty again."

"But we have help coming," I explained. "The president of Liberia has personally granted us all the assistance we need."

"Well, that's a bit of good news," the doctor replied.

"As ship's surgeon, what is your estimate of our readiness to return home?" I asked of him.

He looked up at me from beneath his spectacles. With a raised eyebrow, he responded, "Estimate? Estimate? We have more than half our crew laid out all over the dock and deck with half of those so dehydrated that I am doubtful of their very survival."

"I understand," I replied. I'd known our situation was bad, but the doctor's assessment was far worse than I had thought.

"Assuming we can nurse the majority of them back to health"—he paused—"I would say three to four weeks at the earliest."

"Three to four weeks," I repeated.

"At the earliest," he emphasized. "And that's assuming we get some help as I am outnumbered and understaffed."

"Understood, understood. Help is coming. They should arrive soon. We will nurse the crew back to health and ensure that the freed slaves get to where they need to go. We will make the best of this," I declared as I looked around the room.

There was a knock at the open door.

"Help has arrived, Captain," the purser announced from the open doorway.

"What manner of help?" I asked.

"All kinds, Captain. You name it, and it's here," he replied gleefully.

I turned and walked out of the stifling air of the ward and onto the open deck. It was filled with African women all in white garb, tending to the crew. Young African men, also in all white, scurried about, assisting the women as they went about their nursing duties. More men with buckets and mops headed down into the holds of the ship to clean the fetid quarters below. Out on the dock, a line of men handed off cases of goods one to the next until the cases were stacked neatly alongside the *Nightingale*. Stamped on their sides were the listings of their contents.

"This is excellent!" I exclaimed.

I could see Curtis on the dock with the little boy and his mother, so I walked over to him. Curtis was on his knee, hugging Bwana as the mother placed her hand on Curtis's shoulder and nodded her head in thanks.

"I will miss you, Bwana!" Curtis said as he placed his hands on either side of the little boy's face.

The boy reached out again and hugged Curtis tightly. Curtis let out a grunt and a sigh.

"I will truly miss you, my little helper," he said.

The boy released Curtis and began to say something to him with great enthusiasm.

"I don't understand what you are saying," Curtis said to him, but he continued to ramble on enthusiastically.

Curtis turned to me, "I don't have a clue of what he's trying to say to me."

"I have no idea either. I think that Gabre knows some African dialects. Perhaps he can help," I replied as I called Gabre over to us. "Gabre, come over here!"

"Yes, Captain," Gabre replied.

"We need you to interpret what this boy is saying to Stanton," I said.

"Yes, Captain," Gabre said as he crouched down closer to the little boy.

"Well?" asked Curtis.

"It's not that easy, sir. There are hundreds of different dialects in Africa, perhaps more. There are some words I can make out."

"Yes, yes," Curtis said.

"He's saying something about a fever dream or a . . ." Gabre paused.

"Well, what is it?" Curtis barked out.

"He's saying that he saw his father in a fever dream, and he told him to give something to a pale-faced man with gold hair and eyes like the sky. He believes that the person his father told him about is you."

"Give me what?" asked Curtis.

The boy then embraced Curtis again and looked at his mother. He said something to her, and she nodded back her approval. He then reached for something around his neck and pulled a rope, with a white object attached to it, off from around his head. It was a little ivory carving of a soldier of some kind with a leather strap so that it would hang off one's neck. The boy looked at his mother one more time and then placed it around Curtis's neck. Curtis looked down at it as he held it in his hand.

"What is it?" he asked as he pointed to the figure.

Gabre translated for him.

The mother responded, "Ere àwòrán."

The little boy spoke too, but I had no idea what he was saying, and it all came out so fast. He grabbed Curtis again and held him tightly. Then he kissed the statue and stepped away.

"What is he saying?" Curtis asked Gabre.

"I have no idea. He's speaking too fast for me to understand a word," Gabre replied.

"I guess it is something important to him," Curtis said to me.

"I guess it is," I replied.

"Thank you, Bwana. Thank you, Likana." Curtis bowed to the family, touched by the gift.

With that, Bwana and his mother walked away. As they did, the little boy kept looking back at Curtis. Curtis waved to him, and the boy waved back very enthusiastically. They headed off the dock and out of sight. Curtis didn't leave that spot for several minutes. I'm not quite sure, but I think that I saw him shed a tear as little Bwana walked away.

ERE ÀWÒRÁN

As they walked away, Bwana's natural exuberance returned, and he peppered Likana with questions.

Bwana asked his mother, "What do you think Father is doing right now?"

Likana tried to keep her son's hope alive. "I know that your father is a great warrior, and he is probably organizing the men who are with him to revolt, escape, or kill the evil men who have taken him. I know your father will meet up with us again." Secretly she wondered whether she would ever see her husband again in this world.

On their journey with the other freed slaves, Bwana and his mother talked of the old days back in their village. They talked of times with the other villagers, women gathering and sitting around, telling stories and cooking vegetables, and the men going out to hunt. They wished they could go back to the tribal festival, chanting songs around the fire. Bwana was supposed to be initiated into a manhood ceremony a long time from now, but she didn't see how it would be possible without her husband and the other men from the village.

Bwana's questions came quickly now that he felt safe, "Mommy, remember when we used to climb the trees? Remember when you used to cook my favorite meal? I wish we were back in our village with the whole family."

Likana answered absently, "Yes, my son. I wish that too."

Bwana kept talking, "Do you remember when me and my sister, Nzinga, used to play hide and seek? I miss Nzinga. When I go to sleep, I dream that she is still with us and that we are going to the other village to meet our friends . . ." The excitement in Bwana's voice began to fade.

Likana tried to reassure him, "I know, my son. I dream the same dreams."

Bwana was quiet for a moment then asked, "Why do the white people hate us mommy?"

Likana answered slowly, "The bad men were afraid of us because we are different from them. We look different, we speak different, and we act different. They hate everyone who is different. It is not just us, my love."

Bwana thought about that then said, "But some must be good. Like the white-haired white man."

Likana agreed, "Yes, my son. Some are good like your friend Curtis, but I do not trust anyone anymore."

MICHAEL JAY NUSBAUM

CHAPTER 12

Monrovia

W E ENTERED THE president's residence that evening in our dress uniforms. We were greeted at the door. The small welcome dinner I had expected turned out to be quite a social gathering with a who's who of Monrovian society in attendance. My officers and I struck up conversations with as many of the attendees as possible. I was curious to find out more about this city and country.

One of the women, wearing a beautiful dress, told us of her experience as a slave in Atlanta. She explained that many times, the fashionably rich would actually borrow slaves to serve at parties because they had beaten their own slaves so badly that their flesh putrefied and their bodies were so broken that their presence would be inappropriate for a formal party.

We heard story after story of the beatings, whippings, rapes, and torture experienced by those who had fled the states for a better life back in Africa. I could see that Curtis was clearly moved by the stories. The entire time we were there, he never once announced to anyone at the party that he had grown up with slaves nor did he admit to the fact that he had only recently changed his mind regarding slavery.

"Captain!" a voice called.

"Mr. President," I replied as he approached.

"How do you two like our reception for you?" he asked, smiling.

"This is for us?" Curtis replied. I had not told him all about my dockside encounter with the president, only that he would be helping us arrange medical aid and provisions.

"Why yes," the president responded. "And you are?"

"I am sorry, sir. I have forgotten my manners," I replied. "This is Lt. Curtis Stanton, my second in command."

"Lieutenant," the president said.

"Sir, it is an honor," Curtis replied, bowing his head.

"I must thank you again, Mr. President, for all of your help," I said.

"It is my pleasure," he replied.

"It is remarkable that you are able to help the people we free from bondage," I stated.

"They return all of the freed slaves here, but this is not their home," he told me with a hint of reproach. "They know that they are not really from here. They are from all over Africa. You dump them all here, but they speak different languages— they come from different tribes. You think that they are black and that they are African, so just bringing them back to Africa and dumping them here in Liberia is good enough. It is not. They do not get along with each other. They fight here as they do across all of Africa, only here they are on top of each other."

"I had no idea. I mean that our orders—" I started.

"Yes, I know. Your orders are to capture the slave ships and release their human cargo here in Liberia," he replied.

"Yes." I nodded.

"I understand that you are just following orders, but what your commanders do not understand is that all Africans are different. Just as a white man from Boston is different from the white man from Atlanta," President Benson explained.

"Well, we are not all that different. We just have different ideas about things," Curtis argued.

"Yes, you do, and the same is true for the people you bring here. They have different ideas, customs, and even languages from each other. Yet you deposit them on our shores, and we are forced to deal with those differences. Many of them come from warring tribes. Others come from areas with deep-seated hatred for their neighbors. Yet we must accommodate them all in this very small land." President Benson was shedding a different light on the colonization movement. I was taken aback at his arguments and realized that my simplistic view of Africans as a group was nearly as bad as Curtis's previous dislike for their race.

"But I thought that the whole idea of Liberia was to have a safe haven for slaves who had been freed so that they did not end up right back on those very same ships," I said.

MICHAEL JAY NUSBAUM

"Yes, indeed, that was the intention. A good one at heart but not very practical, I'm afraid," he replied solemnly.

"What else would you have us do with them?" I asked.

"First and foremost, stop the slave trade altogether. That would stop the problem," he replied.

"That is easier said than done," I said ruefully.

"Why would you say that, Captain?" he asked.

"Well, first of all, the area we patrol is too large. You could have a thousand ships, and I doubt that you could stop every slave ship from getting through." I began.

"And . . ." He prompted.

"And our rules of engagement hamper us greatly. They limit our powers," I continued.

"How so?" he asked.

"Well, we are only permitted to interdict ships flying American flags. So even if we find an American vessel, they can simply change their flag to say Spain and then we have no jurisdiction over them," I replied.

"That does sound very frustrating, indeed," President Benson commented. "What you've described is certainly part of our problem. If the United States Government only employs half measures such as the ones you just described, then I fear the slave trade may never end."

"Yes, I believe that you are correct, Mr. President," I agreed sadly.

"It's not an easy solution." Curtis put in.

"How is that so, Lieutenant?" he asked.

"Sir, this is an international problem. The United States cannot be expected to solve all the problems of Africa nor can we be expected to end what amounts to thousands of years of a slave trade coming out of Africa," Curtis replied. Capturing the *Nightingale* might have changed Curtis's views on slavery, but he still refused to see that the South bore a major responsibility for the very existence of the slave trade.

"I see. So you believe it to be more of an internal African problem than an American problem?" the president asked.

"Sir, I would say that it is a problem for many nations, but our country is a small fraction of the problem, and we lack the resources to solve it by ourselves." Curtis said confidently. I listened to their conversation with interest. How might President Benson address

Curtis's confidence? I had been unable to shake Curtis for nearly six months now. Perhaps the president could do better.

"I see," the president repeated. "There is no question that many of our people sell those from rival tribes or regions into slavery. This has, indeed, been going on for many, many years. We are not a united people here in Africa, as I explained to your friend, Captain Smith. There are many regions within this very large continent. There are many languages, many customs, many kings, and many beliefs. What I am saying is that if the demand was gone, if slaves were no longer needed or wanted, if no one was willing to trade goods for people, then the slave trade would surely end."

Curtis looked like he was going to say something but stopped himself. "I understand, and I can see your point." I jumped in. I worried what Curtis might say next.

"You have an opinion on this?" the president asked Curtis.

"No, sir, your points are well taken," Curtis replied.

"I hear a Southern accent in your voice," the president commented.

"Yes, sir," Curtis answered.

"Surely you must have an opinion," he asked again of Curtis.

"Sir, I do, but I fear that you may not take kindly to my answer," he replied.

I sensed Curtis becoming extremely uncomfortable, so I stepped in. "Perhaps these issues should be left to the politicians."

"True, but I am curious to hear the lieutenant's opinion on this. It isn't often that I get a chance to meet a Southern gentlemen. Not many seem to find their way over here." the president tried a little joke. "Please, Lieutenant."

"Well, sir, I fear that the South will not give up their labor force without a very vigorous fight," Curtis stated.

"Why would you say that, Lieutenant?" the president asked.

"Sir, the economy of the South, and thus a significant part of the economy of the United States, is based on agricultural goods, which rely upon the work of slave labor to produce. If you were to eliminate that labor force, then the economy would collapse," Curtis explained.

"And what if the enslaved laborers were not eliminated but rather set free and paid a fair wage for their work?" the president asked.

"Sir, have you ever been in a cotton field?" Curtis asked.

"No. No, I have not," he replied.

MICHAEL JAY NUSBAUM

"Well, sir, it is very harsh work. The profits that come from cash crops like cotton only exist because of the slave labor force. In fact, if a slave picks less than 250 bushels a day, the plantation starts to lose money. There is a cost to maintaining a slave labor force," Curtis replied.

"I am certain that there is a cost to that," the president agreed. "The only question is how high of a cost."

"Sir, I am not trying to insult you in any way," Curtis pleaded.

"No insult taken," said the president easily.

"I am just saying that if the slave labor force were set free, there would be no incentive to do the work. Even if a plantation owner could pay them for their day's work in the field, I highly doubt any of them would work voluntarily," Curtis said confidently.

"So you grew up on a plantation? You know these things to be true?" he asked.

"I did, sir. I did grow up with slaves, but I have recently changed my position on the subject," Curtis replied.

"Well, Lieutenant, I am very glad to hear that you have changed your position on the subject of slavery, but I must say that the freedom of the slaves in America is not a possibility, but rather an eventuality." The president had lost his jocular tone and was speaking almost sternly.

Just then, a finely dressed African man approached the president and tapped him on the shoulder. He whispered into his ear and the president nodded yes.

"Well, gentlemen, duty calls, and I must be going. I would very much like to continue this conversation another time."

"Yes, we would as well," I replied.

"Very good. Perhaps the two of you could join me at my home for a dinner so that we may discuss these issues in a more private setting," the president stated.

"It would be an honor," I replied.

"Yes, an honor, Mr. President," Curtis stated.

The president was escorted away by several men, but no one else in the room seemed to pay his departure any attention.

"What was that?" I asked.

"What?" Curtis asked.

"That whole Southern economy thing," I replied.

"Why, he asked," Curtis replied.

"Look, this is not home. While we are invited guests, you have to remember that we're officers in the United States Navy, and neither your opinion nor mine matters. We can have these discussions between ourselves, but we're ambassadors now." I scolded him. In truth, I had lost sight of our diplomatic status because of my interest in the discussion between Curtis and the president.

"I'm sorry, Michael. I didn't think," Curtis sheepishly replied.

"Let's just be more careful and present more of a united front the next time we speak with him." I concluded.

"Right. Will do," Curtis replied.

The rest of the evening passed without incident. President Benson did not return to the soirée.

May 12, 1861

We arrived at the president's home for the promised dinner and a chance to meet more of our gracious Liberian hosts. Tonight, we expect to meet some local members of the American Colonization Society. The president's assistant informed us that their ship had arrived this afternoon and that their representatives would be attending tonight's dinner.

The night was crisp and clear. Even though the sun had gone down, it remained in the low eighties with a slight breeze. We headed from our ship to the president's home as instructed. Again, we were greeted at the door as honored guests.

"Captain Smith and Lieutenant Stanton," the man at the door announced as we entered.

Everyone seemed to pause their conversations as they turned to look at us as we walked into the ballroom. Several of the Americans approached us.

"Captain, Lieutenant," one finely dressed white man said in a strong Boston accent while another man accompanied him to greet us.

"Sir," I replied as I reached out to shake his hand.

"Bartholomew Baldrich," he said, "and this is Richard Below, a fellow abolitionist."

"Sir, sir," Curtis said as he shook the hands of both men.

"Sir," I said as I shook Mr. Below's hand.

"No doubt you will be returning home posthaste," Mr. Below said as he paused to look at a passing woman. "Given the conditions back home I mean."

"What conditions would those be?" I asked.

"Are you not aware?" he asked, surprised.

"No, sir, what has happened?" I asked.

"We just received word from a newly arrived ship. She left Maryland on April thirteenth. It's war!" Below exclaimed. "Civil War."

"War?" I asked as I looked at the purser.

"Yes! Soon after Mr. Lincoln took office in March, the Confederates attacked Fort Sumter on April 12. The attack seemed to have rallied the North against the South and inflamed the already high tempers of the fire-breathing secessionists."

"My God," I was astonished by the news. "I had no idea. We have received no news from home since we left last November, just after the election."

"I'm sorry, son. The war has been underway for at least a month now. News is slow to come here. Word from the States is easily four to six weeks old by the time it gets over here," Mr. Baldrich said.

"I see," I said. Despite knowing that war was inevitable, I was still shaken to consider that I might soon be fighting against my Southern friends on the *Saratoga*.

"It's really no surprise." Mr. Below reproved me. "Before you left for Africa, the air was thick with talk of civil war."

"You will probably be ordered to return to New York immediately," Mr. Baldrich told us.

"I would think so, if it were really true," I stated in disbelief.

"Oh, it is true," Mr. Below stated with a smile, "and long overdue, if I do say so myself."

"Now, now, Richard. There'll be none of that tonight," Mr. Baldrich said as he scolded his friend.

Curtis didn't say a word. He looked more stunned by the news than I felt. I had no idea what was going through his head, but I suspected that he feared that the Southern way of life was in jeopardy even if he no longer agreed with any of it.

"And you, Lieutenant, you have not uttered a word," Mr. Below said.

"I'm as stunned by the news as my captain," Curtis managed.

"Have you no opinion on the matter?" asked Baldrich.

"No, sir, I'm a sailor. I simply follow my orders," Curtis replied.

"That must be nice," said Mr. Below. "To be able to stay out of all the ugly politics of slavery, I mean. Given that you're a Southern gentleman and all."

"That's a luxury that neither the lieutenant nor I have," I interjected. "Our opinions are solely with regard to our orders and protecting our country." I was beginning to wonder if Mr. Below was trying to start a fight.

We noticed the president walking in our direction.

"I see that you have met my Colonization Society friends," the president stated as he patted them both on the back. "Have you heard the news?"

"Yes," I replied. "They just informed us."

"War. Civil war. In the United States. Unbelievable," the president stated.

"Unavoidable." Mr. Below countered.

"Inevitable." Mr. Baldrich concluded.

"Have you been ordered to return yet?" asked the president.

"We have not yet received any such orders. However, given the news, I would say that we will be leaving first thing in the morning," I replied.

"I will have our people help you with the provisioning of your vessel," the president said.

"That would be very kind indeed," I replied.

I looked at Curtis, and he back at me.

"I only hope that my crew is well enough to make the journey," I said.

We set sail for New York late the next day. It had taken far longer to get our ship provisioned than I had thought. Many of the men sailing were still sick, and we had to leave others, who were far too ill to travel, behind in Liberia.

June 15, 1861

Our ship arrived in New York Harbor some three weeks later. During our journey, fever broke out again on the ship, and nine crew

MICHAEL JAY NUSBAUM

members succumbed to their illnesses. Our mood somber, the voyage home was difficult for us all. My crew did their jobs and did them well—that was all I could ask of them. After we docked, my crew packed up their belongings. It was not long before reality set in for all of us.

"This may be the last time we see each other," I said to Curtis.

"I know, my friend," he replied.

"What will you do?" I asked.

"If they let me, I will head back home," he replied.

"You will fight?" I asked.

"I will defend my land and my family." He corrected.

"But this war is over slavery," I argued. Surely, after his experiences on the *Nightingale* and his friendship with Bwana, he would have changed his mind about this evil institution.

"Yes, and you know how I feel about it now. But I must defend my home and my family," Curtis said as he packed the last of his personal items.

"Stay with me. You can stay with my family. There is no loss of honor by staying here and not going back South to fight for something you don't believe in."

"You'll never understand the South, Michael. There is honor and tradition. I have family and generations of relatives. There is a culture—our culture, my culture—that Northerners will never comprehend. I must go. I must fight. I am sorry. We have been through so much together."

"We have," I agreed.

Curtis put his sack on the deck and reached his hand onto my shoulder. "You are my friend. You always will be. You were right about slavery, and I was wrong. I am not returning to my home to defend slavery. I return to defend my family and my land."

"I guess I understand," I replied, although truly, his attitude still puzzled me.

Curtis stood at attention and saluted, saying, "I hope that we never have to meet in battle, my friend." He then picked up his sack, threw it over his shoulder, and headed out.

CHAPTER 13

Union Blockade

MORE THAN A year has gone by since I last sailed in the Africa Squadron. The war has dragged on longer than most had hoped. The Union Navy is now actively engaged in a blockade of the Southern coastline. This blockade was designed to cut off any aid to the South, but also to prevent raw goods from being exported to Europe from the Confederacy. If we could stop these goods from being exported, then we could cut off the lifeblood of the South. I now find myself captaining one of these blockading ships. We are stationed outside of Savannah's harbor.

"Keep a sharp eye out," I told my crew. "The moon has retreated behind the clouds and this would be the perfect time to try and run our blockade."

"Aye, aye," responded several of the crew.

It was indeed dark out. Not a star in the sky could be seen. The moon was completely blocked by cloud cover, and only the reflection of a few lights from the shore could be seen reflected in the waters. I speculated that if there were ever a time to try and sneak by us, this would be it.

"Do you think that they would really try to get past us?" asked the first lieutenant.

"The South is desperate and getting more so with each passing month. Scott's plan seems to be working. If we can cut off the South's supply lines, then they will lose the resources to fight," I replied.

"I agree, Captain. General Scott's plan is a good one. I just can't believe that anyone would be foolish enough to try to get past us, especially when there are three other Union ships within sight of each other."

"Perhaps not foolish enough but certainly desperate enough. Given the order to break the blockade at all cost, I would give it a shot. Tonight seems like the perfect time to do it given the cover of darkness."

"But, Captain, we have been on station here for four days and have yet to see a ship try to break our blockade."

I gazed out over the waters, "True, but this is the first night where the weather is on the Confederates' side."

"I hope that they do try," responded the first lieutenant. "I have yet to see elephant in this war, and I'm ready for a fight."

"That's because you are young, Lieutenant. When you get older—and certainly wiser—you'll realize that fighting is ugly and distasteful and results in the senseless death of too many young men such as yourself," I replied. "I hope that I am wrong, but I sense that you will see the action you so much desire very soon."

"I hope so," the eager young lieutenant replied. "We are ready. The crew is ready. I have drilled them daily for the last month. We will fight as one when the time comes."

My warnings had not dampened his enthusiasm for the glories of battle. I wondered if anything could. "Battle does strange things to men. I hope that you are right, but I also hope that no Confederate captain is willing to take the risk of sneaking past us this evening."

"Captain!" shouted the crew member in the crow's nest, "I think I see something—over there off the starboard bow!"

I ran over to the starboard railing. "I see it!" I shouted, "ALL HANDS PREPARE STARBOARD GUNS TO FIRE!"

No sooner did I shout out the command than the darkened vessel opened fire upon our warship. We could hear the whirring of machinery coming to life and then we could see a paddle wheel churning the water to white.

"She's a steamer!" the master's mate shouted.

Cannon fire rained over our heads. The darkened ship lit with bursts of orange and white. Ball and chain flew over our heads.

"They are shooting for our rigging," I called out.

One crew member to my left hadn't the time to move when a direct shot from the Confederate ship ripped his body into two. His blood covered the first lieutenant and me. Pieces of the sailor's flesh were blown into the lieutenant's face as he dived to the deck.

"Take cover," I shouted as my crew was forced to lie flat on the deck while we steered the ship to broadside the blockade runner. With the hail of cannon fire from the first volley of the Confederate ship, we had suffered several casualties.

"Cannons at the ready," came from below.

"FIRE AT WILL!" I ordered.

Our first volley ripped into the Confederate ship. Bodies were sent flying, and pieces of the ship were thrown into the air. This sent the blockade runner's entire crew belowdecks for cover. We valiantly poured broadside after broadside into her but received an equally furious return of fire from the steamer. This furious exchange of volleys continued for some ten minutes, yet it seemed to take an eternity. Then one shot hit the axle of her starboard paddle, and we could hear the sound of metal upon metal. I worked my way to the helm and ensured that we maintained our position for optimal broadside. As our cannon fire ripped into her hull, I noticed that fewer and fewer guns were returning fire.

"Concentrate your fire on the remaining cannons!" I ordered.

"Aye, aye, Captain."

"Lieutenant," I shouted, "instruct the lower deck of guns to fire upon her waterline!"

"Aye, Captain," he responded as he dashed away below deck. Shortly thereafter, I saw that our fire was concentrated at the steamer's waterline. Neither the first lieutenant nor his men had lost their heads in the chaos of battle. I was impressed by their composure and proud of their effort.

Shouts of "FIRE!" could be heard from both ships.

Soon, the Confederate ship began to take on water. She listed heavily to starboard where our cannon had blown numerous holes under her waterline. Taking on water, she broke deep. With a final shudder, her bow began to drive into the water as her still functioning port paddle wheel seemed to drive her deeper. A searing sound was followed by a massive explosion that lit up the night sky. The blast pushed me backward while it knocked others on my crew to the deck. I could feel the heat of the explosion upon my face as if it were the midday sun. I shielded my face with my right arm and then felt the burning of hot knives as several pieces of shrapnel plunged into the meat of my arm.

"Hold your fire!" I shouted, but my crew let off a few more shots before the word to cease fire could reach them. I could see the ship's crew jumping off her decks and into the water. The last few shots from our cannons ripped into many of the men who were merely trying to survive.

"Cease fire!" My order was finally heard by my entire crew.

Suddenly, only the sounds of men screaming for help, both from the water and from our decks, could be heard.

"Tend to the injured!" I shouted. "And prepare to take on prisoners!"

"Sir, your arm," the boatswain said, "you've been injured."

"It seems I have," I replied as I looked more closely at my right arm.

"Here, let me help you," he said as he took out his knife and cut off my torn and bloodied sleeve. "Surgeon!" he shouted. "The captain has been hit!"

"I'm fine. I assure you. It looks much worse than it is," I said to him.

"Captain, it is best that we get you to your quarters. We can handle the rest from here," the first mate said to me as the boatswain agreed and began to lead me to my quarters.

"All right, the first lieutenant is in charge," I called. "Tend to our wounded and bring the prisoners on board one at a time. Be sure to disarm them and chain them before permitting the next one on deck. Have the marines stand guard with loaded musket shot at the ready."

"Aye, Captain, we can handle this," the first lieutenant replied.

"Let me take a look at that," the surgeon demanded.

"Doctor, I need you to tend to the crew who have been more gravely injured than myself. This is merely a flesh wound."

"I'll be the judge of that. Last I checked I was the surgeon on board, and you were the captain, and unless I miss my guess, your knowledge of medicine is comparable to my knowledge of captaining this vessel." The doctor scolded me gently. He then pulled out pieces of my jacket and shirt from the wounds. "You are very lucky indeed, Captain. The major blood vessels have not been hit and the metal which pierced the skin was so hot that it cauterized as it entered. I will have the boatswain bandage you up as I tend to the rest of the crew."

"Very good. Thank you, Doctor, and please get reports back to me regarding the status of the injured."

"Aye, aye, Captain," he replied as he hurried out to the deck.

The boatswain began wrapping my arm while exulting. "It was a glorious battle. I've never seen such fury concentrated into such a small period of time. My heart is still racing a mile a minute!"

"Yes, a glorious battle," I said dryly. "When I was your age, I too looked forward to such things. Now, I only see death and destruction. Brother killing brother."

The boatswain finished wrapping my arm.

"All done, Captain," he told me.

"Very good. Let's get out there and help."

"Aye, aye, Captain."

We headed out to the deck to see seven men having succumbed to their injuries laid out neatly on the deck. Four others shouted in pain. Each was being attended to by other crew members. Meanwhile, we took on survivors of the Confederate ship. As instructed, the marines stood guard over them as they came aboard and were shackled and set into a tight grouping. One by one, the sailors came up, bloodied and weary. They looked like my men. No different in appearance or age other than the color of their uniforms.

Suddenly, I saw a familiar face. I could hardly believe my eyes—it was my good friend Curtis. Despite many new wrinkles and gray hair, which had not existed the last time we were together, I still recognized that face.

I wanted to run over to Curtis and embrace him as a long-lost friend, but I restrained myself. *What message would that send to my crew?* I thought. I could see he had achieved the rank of captain as well, but he had aged so much. I headed over.

"No need to shackle him," I said to the marine.

"Aye, aye, Captain!" the marine barked.

I saluted him, "Captain Stanton, I presume."

Curtis straightened his back, stood upright, and returned the salute. "Captain—no—Commodore Smith!" he exclaimed. "Damn, happy it was you who blew my beautiful ship out from under me and not some other salty Yankee." His crew members chuckled at his proclamation.

"And I'm damn happy that I blew her out from under you and not you with her," I replied and extended my left arm.

"Sorry about that," he replied as he realized that my injured right arm was no longer fit for shaking.

"Previous injury?" he quipped.

"Sorry to say, no, this is the result of our latest debate," I replied.

"My ship, your arm. I guess we can call it even then," Curtis said with a smile.

"Are there any more survivors?" I asked him.

"I made certain that all my surviving crew got on aboard before I came aboard," Curtis replied.

"Very good," I stated. "Marines, secure these men in the brig. I will escort the captain to my quarters."

"Aye, aye, Captain," they replied in unison.

We headed away, and I noticed one of the marines and the boatswain following us.

"May I help you gentlemen?"

"Sir, shouldn't we come with you? I mean, the captain is a prisoner and . . ." the boatswain's voice trailed off.

"And what? He might kill me?" I asked, one eyebrow raised.

"Sir, Captain, you are injured . . . he is not . . . and he is our prisoner." The boatswain's confusion rendered him incapable of speaking in complete sentences.

"True enough, but Captain Stanton and I go way back. I think that I am safe in his hands, and he in mine."

"Aye, Captain." They conceded as they stopped their pursuit of us.

As Curtis and I continued down the passageway, I asked my old friend, "So how are things?"

"They were great up until an hour ago." He chuckled.

We entered my cabin. I gestured toward a chair. "Have a seat, Captain."

"How's your arm?" Curtis asked.

"Burns like hell."

"No doubt."

"Drink?" I asked.

"Definitely," he replied.

"Rum is all I have to offer."

"Rum will do just fine," Curtis agreed.

I took the decanter out from the cupboard with my left hand but struggled to turn and place it on the table.

"Here, let me help," Curtis said as he jumped to his feet, grabbed the decanter, and reached for two glasses.

"Thanks. Keep forgetting that this wing isn't working right now."

"No problem," Curtis replied as he poured the rum, and I took my seat again.

He held up his glass and said, "A toast."

"Yes," I replied.

"To good friends on different sides of the wrong battle. I am truly happy it was you over anyone else!"

"To good friends." I echoed as we clinked glasses.

We both took a deep and long savory sip of the rum and let out simultaneous sighs of contentment.

"Seriously, you blew the heck out of my ship." Curtis chuckled.

"Well, you did open fire upon us first." I reasoned.

"True, true." He allowed. "I actually didn't think that we would drift so close to you though. We were under sail to sneak by you, but when I read the Made in Boston, legend on your cannons I realized that we would have to shoot our way through."

"I see," I replied as I took another sip of rum. "I would much rather you had said 'Oh, shoot, it's Smith. Let's just surrender.'"

"Um . . ." He pretended to consider my suggestion. "I'm not sure how well that would have gone over with my crew or back at headquarters."

"True. But my arm would have appreciated a more civilized form of surrender."

"And my ego as well." He chuckled.

I lost my joking demeanor. "Seriously, how are things with you?"

"I'm sure that you know"—he paused—"things are not going well. Scott's blockade was a joke for the first few years, but now, we are struggling to get supplies in and goods out."

"I think that was the idea," I replied.

"Right. I know it's working. Now give me some more rum." Curtis tried to revive the light atmosphere, but I needed to tell him some things.

"It was hard for me to see you walk away when we hit the port in New York."

"I know. I didn't want to make a scene and get emotional with all you guys," he said as he took another long, slow sip. "You and the rest of the crew basically stayed as you were, and of course, you clearly received a well-deserved promotion."

"You as well."

"Right, but when I made it back, I found that there wasn't much of a navy, and they were hard up for officers, let alone anyone with enough experience to captain a ship. Damn, we have fishermen without a lick of command training captaining some of our ships," he complained.

"And your family?" I asked.

"No word for a while," he replied. "It's been over a month now. Last I heard was that Sherman's army was headed to Savannah."

"I hadn't heard that."

"I'm not sure what is going on other than Sherman marching not far from here, but I do hope that this war comes to an end soon. I'm not sure I even care who's victorious." Curtis had lost all forced jocularity.

"I'll drink to that," I said as I clinked his glass yet again.

"Do you remember the *Nightingale*?" he asked.

"As if it were yesterday."

"I know. Hard to believe that years have passed."

"True."

"And our debates about slavery?" he continued.

"I do," I replied. "I remember how you took care of that little boy from the *Nightingale* too."

"Bwana."

"I hadn't remembered his name."

"Bwana. I haven't forgotten his name nor his face," he mused. "I think of him often and wonder how he is doing—what has become of him."

I noticed the wedding band on his left hand. "I see you got married."

"Yes," he said sadly as he spun the ring upon his finger. "She was killed not too long ago. We were not blessed with children."

"Was this someone you had known long?" I asked.

"Yes," he replied. "We had grown up together. We were well-matched, I suppose. And you?"

"I have not yet had the time to settle down and find a bride. I suspect that after this war is over, I will return to civilian life and find a wife. Settle down and have children."

"I see," he replied.

"So where were you headed out of the harbor?" I asked. "Officially, I mean."

"Ah, we were loaded with cotton bound for Cuba to trade for supplies from the British."

"Interesting," I responded. "They trade with us as easily as they do with you. I suspect that they quite enjoy seeing us at each other's throats."

"No doubt," he responded. "Their disdain for us is only surpassed by their need for cotton and tobacco."

"She was a nice ship," I noted.

"She was at that. Twice as fast as this cloth hanger I would say."

"Truly?" I exclaimed.

"Oh yes. She is—was—a fast little girl." He corrected himself regretfully.

The conversation turned stale. I sought a new topic of conversation, but the pain in my arm and the rum I had drunk hampered my ability to think clearly. Moments passed. "And what of Guthrie?" Curtis finally asked.

"Guthrie," I nodded. "Guthrie succumbed to his illness in Monrovia."

"Poor Guthrie." He lifted his glass in memory.

The conversation grew stale once again. Only the sounds of the crew moving about on deck and the creaking of the timbers of the vessel as she rocked from side to side broke the uneasy silence between us.

"What next?" Curtis asked. "What do you plan to do with me and my crew?"

I took another sip of rum. "Well, in the morning, we will hand you and your crew off to another ship. We'll remain on station to enforce the blockade."

"I'm done, Michael," Curtis stated sincerely. "Really, I'm done. I fought to defend my homeland, to defend the South, but I don't defend the reasons for this war. No matter what the politicians are saying now, the South is fighting for slavery. It's always been about slavery, not states' rights, not tariffs, but the right to own other human beings."

"I know," I replied. "I know. The recent developments in Confederate strategies prove that while there may have been other reasons stated, none was as important as maintaining your utterly amoral slave system."

"True," he replied softly.

"Had we not picked you up, had you been able to swim to shore, what would you have done?"

"I would have gone home. Home for a while. Home just for a break from all this."

"If I were to let you go tonight, and I'm not saying that I will, but if I were to let you go, you would head home?"

"I would," he replied.

"I see. Well then, we will need to figure out a way for you to escape that doesn't implicate me." Had he announced his intention to rejoin the fruitless battle, I would have turned him in to prison authorities in the morning. But I trusted the sincerity of my old friend, and I knew he would stick to his plan.

"Um," he replied as he emptied the rum decanter into our glasses. "I guess this is the last of the rum."

"Well, we need to come up with a plan before we finish it all!" I joked.

We mulled various options. Curtis suggested, "What if I were to hit you over the head with this decanter and knock you unconscious, then slip into the night?"

I didn't like that plan for a few reasons. "Right, well that would not bode well for me as I turned down the offer to have a marine with us and keep an eye on you. Also, I had them leave you unshackled—also a problem for me if you were to escape."

"I see." He thought some more. "What if you were to ask for shackles for me and place them upon my wrists but not completely lock them? Then have me stay, presumably shackled, in an officer's quarters, once again showing me the respect due another ship's captain. Then, in the middle of the night, I somehow manage to escape from my bindings, slip out a porthole, and swim to shore undetected."

"That might work," I replied. "Not bad. I had better slip a key into your pocket as well just in case the shackles do lock or something else were to go wrong."

"Agreed." He smiled. "Why are you doing this for me?"

"Wouldn't you do the same for me if the roles were reversed?" I asked.

"I would." He realized. "I would."

"Good then. It is all set." We made one last toast and downed the last of the rum.

I called the marine into my quarters. The boatswain came as well.

"Shackles for the captain?" I asked.

The marine walked over to Curtis to attach them.

"I'll do it," I told him as I reached out for the bindings.

"Aye, Captain," the marine said as he handed them to me.

"Turn around please, Captain," I ordered Curtis as I stepped behind him and placed the shackles loosely upon his wrists.

"Shall I take him below?" the boatswain asked.

"No, he will be staying in the first lieutenant's quarters. His cabinmates will be on watch tonight, so the room will be empty. One marine will guard the door until we can transfer him and his crew to another ship in the morning."

"Very well, Captain," the boatswain replied.

I led Curtis to the first lieutenant's quarters and slipped a key into his pocket. "We will see you in the morning."

"I thank you for your hospitality and your kind treatment of my crew," Curtis replied.

"Not at all. After all, we are all Americans," I said as I closed the door.

"Marine, you will stand guard at this door. No one is to enter and no one is to leave. Is that understood?"

"Aye, Captain," he responded.

"Good. Now, I suggest the remainder of us take a rest as our prisoners are safely tucked away. Ensure that the watches are set and that our cannons are loaded and ready just in case another ship tries to sneak by us tonight."

"Aye, aye, Captain." The boatswain saluted crisply.

CHAPTER 14

Curtis's Escape

A FEW HOURS passed before Curtis decided it was time to affect his escape. He could see through the keyhole that the marine remained stationed at the door. The gentle rocking of the ship on the waves was in stark contrast to the turmoil that had existed on the water just a few hours before.

"I must make my move soon before the sun rises, or I will never have the opportunity to escape," he said to himself.

Curtis unlocked his shackles and slipped slowly out of the porthole. He made sure to enter the water equally slowly so as to not make a sound. The water was cool but not cold, and the surface was relatively calm. Debris from his ship still lay in the water about him. He found a hatch that had broken free from his vessel and was floating unattached. He used the hatch as a raft and slowly swam toward shore.

When he neared the beach, he remained in the water for a few minutes, making sure that no one was there to see him. He wasn't sure exactly where he had landed, but he knew that he was somewhere north of the harbor. He stood up in the gently breaking surf and walked onto the beach. When he looked back, he could see the silhouette of Michael's ship along with three others, barricading the harbor entrance. There were few lights on shore, and the area in which he landed was unpopulated. He shook some water off his clothing and headed inland.

The brush was heavy as he headed up the sand dune. To his left, he could now see the lights of Savannah. His goal now was to simply head home.

When he and his crew had set out to sneak past the blockade, it was well after nine at night. He thought he's met Michael around 1:00

a.m. Now, based upon the position of the moon, Curtis estimated that it was several hours past midnight. The sky was barely broken clouds, but when the nearly full moon broke through, it lit up everything. He continued through a marshy area until he reached a road. Once on the path, he headed back South.

No sooner than he had begun his journey down this road than he heard the beating of hooves and the noise of a carriage. Curtis darted off the road and into some brush. A procession of six horses all ridden by Confederate soldiers escorted a carriage. The group quickly moved past his hiding place. He waited awhile, making sure that there were no riders behind them. Except for the chirps of cicadas and frogs, the night was again silent. He set back out onto the road.

His thoughts wandered. He considered his friend Michael, who had risked everything to set him free, and the adventures and horrors of his time aboard the *Nightingale*. He recalled his harshly worded debates with Michael over the subject of slaves and slavery. He remembered Likana and more importantly, her son, Bwana. Thinking of the little boy, he reached into his pocket and pulled out Bwana's ere awòrán. He held it in his right hand, looking at it as he continued to walk down the road.

As he held up the statue, he noticed a fork in the road ahead. The sign indicated that Savannah was to the left, but he could not read where the right path led. Just as he pondered his decision, the light of the moon caught the ivory statuette. The right side of the carving gleamed in the moonlight. Curtis took this as a sign not to head toward Savannah but to take the other unknown road.

"Bwana," he whispered, "I hope that you are correct. I hope that this thing is truly showing me the way to go." With that, he placed the statuette around his neck, tucked it under his shirt and walked briskly down the road.

The road was lined with farmland on either side. There was no man-made light that Curtis could see, but the moon continued to provide him with just enough light to see his way. He had walked many roads like this before. He was close enough to home that the topography was familiar, but he was alone, unarmed, uncertain of his exact location, and he ran the risk of running into a Yankee column at any time.

Now, the moon reappeared further to the west, showing him that he had been walking several hours. It was nearly four in the morning.

Curtis's muscles ached, and he was losing his strength. As he walked along the road, he noticed a cart filled with hay in one of the fields. As he could see no structures and was feeling tired and chilled in his still-damp clothing, Curtis decided that the cart would be the best place to rest. He climbed into the cart and arranged the hay to make some bedding for himself.

"I've slept in worse," he said to himself.

When he awakened, the sun had already risen. The dew, which had covered him during the night, was now beginning to burn off. The air smelled so familiar. He could not be very far from his plantation at all.

CHAPTER 15

Escape from Slavery

1864

O SUMAKA WAS SENT directly to a plantation in South Carolina after his experience in the Jamaican seasoning camp. It has now been three years since he arrived on the plantation. He has witnessed the horrors of the slave masters and overseers—their torture of slaves—and seen the tragic ends of many of his fellow slaves. He worked hard, tried to stay out of trouble, and kept his eyes and ears open. Thus, when a slave named Peter came to him with a plan to run off with several others, Osumaka was skeptical. He had been trained by his slave masters to never trust another slave. The conditions in which he was living combined with his overwhelming desire to be united with his family someday led him to agree despite his apprehensions.

"So will you go with us?" Peter asked.

"I will," Osumaka responded. "I would rather die than remain apart from my wife and my child."

"Good," Peter said. "Several of us will leave tonight. I was speaking with one of the house servants, and she told me of a place where there are people who will help us escape. We leave near midnight."

"I am with you, my brother," Osumaka replied as he resumed his labor in the fields.

The sun beat down upon them. Their muscles ached, their backs were sore from bending, and their hands blistered from the harvest of the crops. Despite all this, Osumaka remained steadfast in his belief that someday he would be reunited with his family.

Later that evening, after all had gone to sleep, Osumaka lay awake, waiting for word from Peter. Then he heard a sound to his left.

"Os," the voice said. "Os." Osumaka loathed this shortening of his name, but it was the least of the indignities he'd suffered since being kidnapped nearly four years before.

Osumaka sat up to see Peter at the doorway. He motioned for Osumaka to come with him. Osumaka got up and headed for the door, still wary that this could be a trap of some kind. He stuck his head out the door to see Peter standing there and then looked around.

"Is it just us?" Osumaka asked.

"No, there are more. We must hurry. We will meet them at the edge of the west fields," Peter said quietly as he crouched down along the wall.

Peter slowly made his way to the road, leading to the west fields. All was quiet, and the sky was filled with an almost full moon. Shadows danced along the ground in front of Peter and Osumaka as they walked to the rendezvous point. Sure enough, there were several slaves waiting for Osumaka and Peter when they arrived. There were two other men, one child, and a house slave woman whom Osumaka recognized as Harriet, someone whom he had met when he first arrived at the plantation.

"You are Paul, no?" Harriet asked Osumaka.

"No," he replied. "I am Osumaka."

"Yes, but the master calls you Paul?" she asked again.

"They may call me what they wish. I am Osumaka, a warrior with a warrior's name." Harriet, a slave born on the plantation, looked confused at this, but any further comment was forestalled by Paul's urgency.

"Come all, we must go," Peter announced to the group.

The little girl was as old as his daughter Nzinga would have been had she still been alive. Her skin was lighter than the others, and this was clearly evident even though the only light by which to see was the moon itself.

"What is your name?" Osumaka asked the little girl, but she shook her head and did not respond.

"She doesn't speak," explained Harriet.

"What do you mean she doesn't speak? She has what, seven years? And she cannot talk?" Osumaka was dumbfounded.

"We don't know. She just doesn't. She did. Then about a year ago, she just stopped speaking and hasn't uttered a sound since," Harriet said. "Her name is Pepper. She is the daughter of a house slave who worked with me and had the affection of the master himself. Soon, after she had this child, the master's wife noticed the color of Pepper's skin and forced the master to sell her momma off."

"You're too pretty not to speak," Osumaka said as he rubbed Pepper's head in the affectionate way he used to rub Nzinga's head.

"Where are we headed?" one of the men asked Peter.

"We are headed to the old bridge that crosses the brook. We are to meet a man named Isaac who is to be our conductor."

"Our conductor?" Osumaka asked.

"Yes, our conductor," Harriet responded. "I met him two weeks ago when the missus and I went into town. He helps direct slaves to freedom."

Osumaka knew not what to say, but he still followed and remained cautious over the entire prospect of escape. Finally, they reached the bridge, but no one seemed to be there. Peter motioned to them.

"Get off the road," he said. "We must hide here until he arrives."

The group followed Peter into the woods along the side of the bridge. The little girl, who had stayed close to Harriet the entire way, now clung to Osumaka. He reached over her and held her close as he used his skills as a hunter to listen for movement.

"I hear something," Osumaka whispered. "Over there . . . someone is over there." He pointed out to everyone.

Peter stood up slowly to look. Osumaka was correct. A man stood silently next to a willow tree along the bank of the brook.

"I will see if it is him," Peter announced as he made his way back onto the road and over to the other side of the brook where the man stood silently.

The little girl clung more tightly to Osumaka, and her hands grasped his left arm firmly.

Then Peter motioned for them to come over. Osumaka stood as the others began to walk over to Peter and the mysterious figure. Pepper refused to move.

"What's wrong?" Osumaka asked the little girl.

She shook her head no.

"We must go," he told her, but she shook her head no again.

Growing worried about the success of their plan with such a stubborn child, Osumaka asked Pepper, "Will you come with us if I carry you?"

The little girl looked at Harriet who had now stopped and turned to see why they had fallen behind.

"Come." Harriet motioned sternly to little Pepper.

Pepper held her hands up in the air and Osumaka lifted her onto his chest. She wrapped her legs around him, clenched her hands together around his neck, and laid her head on his left shoulder.

Osumaka stood with the little girl wrapped around him.

"I guess she likes you," Harriet said to Osumaka as she put her hand on Pepper and patted her back. "Will you be all right holding her?"

"I am," Osumaka replied. "She reminds me of my little girl," he explained as they walked over to the rest of the group.

"Is this all of you?" the man asked.

"Yes, this is it," Peter answered.

"All right then. My name is Isaac. I will be your conductor. I will take you to the next stop and hand you off to the station master there."

"Station master?" Harriet asked, confused. "I thought you were going to help us to escape."

"The station master is a white man sympathetic to our plight. He helps many who run off make it to the promised land."

"Why don't you run off?" queried Osumaka.

"I am a free man and live under the protection of this station master as a free man."

"But if you must live under the protection of this master, then you are not free." Peter seemed unimpressed.

"But I am free. I can come and go as I please. I could run off with you to the North, or as I prefer, stay here and help as many of you as I can." Isaac reminded them all. He motioned for the group to follow. "Come, follow me."

The group followed Isaac through a path in the woods. "What is this path?" asked Peter.

"It is an old Indian path, and it leads to the station master's property. We should be able to make it there before sunrise, but we must all keep walking. Please do not stop," he urged.

The ground was rocky, and parts were highly uneven. Harriet lost her footing more than one time. Pepper remained plastered to

Osumaka's chest. She kept her eyes screwed closed, not wanting to see anything.

The journey was long, but they finally made it to the edge of a clearing where they could see a home in the distance. It wasn't nearly as large or grand as that of the plantation house they had left, just a small farmhouse in the middle of several fields.

"Come. It is just up here. We are almost there," Isaac announced.

As they approached the small house, a white woman came out with a small lantern. She motioned for them to follow her as she opened a door, which was leaning onto the side of the house. Isaac was the first to reach her.

"We made it," he said to her.

"Wonderful," she replied. "Isaac, take them down below. I'm certain that they must be hungry. Feed them, let them wash up, and I will be down shortly."

"Yes, Miss Shelly," Isaac replied.

They walked down the stairs and into the cellar, and Ms. Shelly closed the door behind them. Then she walked up to the front porch and looked around. She looked down the road, past their barn, and out to the main road. All remained quiet, so she climbed the steps onto the porch and entered through the front door.

The group walked into the house's cellar. The area was nicely appointed for a cellar. It had a large table with six chairs, an area with a dozen beds made up with fresh linens, and some cold food ready on the table.

The two men Joe and Jim headed straight for the food. As was their habit on the plantation, they grabbed as much as they could before they even sat down.

"Behave yourselves!" Peter shouted in a scolding tone.

Harriet motioned for Osumaka to hand Pepper over to her. He walked over to her and tried to loosen the little girl's tight hold on him.

"Oh my, she has a strong grip." Osumaka chuckled as he tried to give the child to her mother.

She shook her head NO and held on to Osumaka even more tightly.

"Fine," Harriet sighed. "Have it your way, Pepper. You always do." She shook her head and threw up her hands in mock despair.

Harriet looked at Osumaka. "Are you all right with that?"

"I am fine," Osumaka replied sincerely. "I miss this feeling."

MICHAEL JAY NUSBAUM

They all sat down at the table and began to eat. Suddenly, the door at the top of a stairwell leading to the inside of the house opened. They all froze for a moment as they turned to face the intruder. Ms. Shelly had opened the door and was headed down with a tray and a pitcher.

"Here, I have brought you some more food and some more fresh water to drink," she said as she placed the rest of the food onto the table. "Isaac, you will help them."

"Yes, Miss Shelly. I will stay with them," he responded.

"Good," she replied. "I will get some milk for the child."

"I can do it," Isaac responded.

"All right then," she replied. "You will all be safe here. Please eat and rest. We will take you to the next station tonight after sundown."

Isaac repeated reassuringly, "Yes, you will all be safe here."

"Isaac, if they need anything then, just let me know."

"I will, ma'am," Isaac responded.

With that, she headed back up the stairs and into the house. They all sat back in their chairs and breathed a sigh of relief. Tensions were too high for the group to view anything unusual with equanimity.

"Joe and Jim, you boys have eaten way too much. Leave some for everyone else!" Harriet slapped big Jim's hand as he reached for some more corn bread.

Osumaka sat down as well and pulled Pepper into his lap. He took a piece of corn bread and held it in front of her. She looked at him and then ate the bread with him still holding it, unwilling to unleash her hands from around his neck.

"Now isn't that a sight?" Harriet exclaimed. "I don't think I've ever seen her do that! She's the most finicky child when it comes to food and who feeds her."

Their bellies full, they washed up and walked to the beds. Osumaka stood there, looking at a bed not knowing what to do. He had never seen a feather bed before. So he pulled a blanket off the bed, laid it on the floor, and stretched out on it. All the while, Pepper remained clinging to him. Harriet watched and shook her head in happy disbelief. Big Jim's feet hung off the edge of the bed as he was clearly too tall. Isaac made sure that they were all comfortable.

"I will leave this lantern on low over here," he stated. "I will be back before sundown. We will eat once again and then head out once it is dark enough."

With that, he headed up the stairs into the house. Exhausted from the journey, they slept.

The sound of the door opening at the top of the step roused them from their rest. All but big Jim were awakened by the sound. Isaac came down followed closely by Ms. Shelly.

"I hope that you all slept well," she said.

"We did," Peter responded.

"Yes, thank you," Harriet answered.

"You are welcome," Ms. Shelly replied with a smile. "We have brought you more food. It is almost time for the sun to set and then you all need to move on."

Ms. Shelly and Isaac walked over to the table and set down the food.

"Eat, my friends," Isaac announced. "I will be taking you to the next station and then we will say our farewells."

"You're not coming with us?" Harriet asked.

"No, he cannot," Shelly replied. "We need him here, as there is another group of passengers that he must guide tomorrow night."

"Who will take us from there?" Peter asked, suspicious.

Osumaka sat up on the floor. Pepper had slept on his chest all night and the sweat from her head had caused his chest to become damp. She lay asleep in his lap.

"I am not certain. We try not to know too much of the railroad so that if we are ever caught, we could never reveal too much," Isaac responded.

Harriet noticed that Osumaka was trapped by the sleeping girl.

"Here, let me take her from you," she said to Osumaka. "Go wash up and get yourself something to eat."

Osumaka took a washcloth from the counter and poured water onto it from the basin. He rubbed it all over his face and then wiped his sweaty chest. He looked over at the table where they all sat down to eat. Big Jim had just woken up and made several loud groaning noises as he yawned and stretched his body. Osumaka then took a seat at the table across from Peter and Isaac.

"So how about you?" Isaac asked of Osumaka.

"What about me?" said Osumaka.

"You don't say much," Isaac replied.

"I have little to say and less to say in English," Osumaka replied.

MICHAEL JAY NUSBAUM

"You are African? You speak well," Peter commented. "How long have you been here?"

"I was taken from my home almost four years ago. Separated from my wife and my children, taken from all I have ever known and loved."

"I am sorry, my brother," Isaac replied.

"Since I was taken, I have seen many horrors," Osumaka went on. "Most white people hate us. Why does this one help us?"

"Who? Miss Shelly?" Isaac asked.

"Yes, why should we trust her or any white person?" Osumaka asked.

"There are many whites who wish to help us and who believe that what was done to you and to all of us was wrong," Isaac replied. "There are even more like her up North. There are few as brave as her down here in the South."

"What is the difference? North or South, they are all white men," Osumaka stated.

"They are not all the same," Isaac explained. "Many are ready to fight for all of our freedom. This country, the white men, the white women—they are all divided. Many speak of this war. Word from other slaves is that the North's General Sherman is marching through Georgia. Many speak of this country separating into two countries, one in the North and the other in the South, simply because of slavery. They struggle."

"They struggle?" Osumaka chuckles without humor. "They struggle. They have kidnapped us. Separated us from our families. Killed our brothers, sisters, wives, children, parents. They force us to work in the fields and beat or whip us when we don't obey. They struggle. How do they struggle? I have seen nothing of good come from a white person until this day. What is a handful to do for us when so many of them despise and imprison us? The whites are no different from our own people. I was sold into slavery by the Kroo who were no different in appearance than you or I. I can't trust those from our home, who look as we do and are from our land. How can we ever trust those who look so different from us and are from another land?"

"Your words are true, Osumaka. I cannot deny what you say. I can only tell you that there are whites who want our freedom and who are willing to fight for us to be free. With that knowledge, I remain hopeful."

"I do not know of these things. All I know is that I must try to find my wife and son and that I would rather die than not try to be with them," Osumaka subsided but still harbored distrust of whites with the possible exception of one or two.

"Someday," Harriet replied, "with God's help, someday you will see them again."

When the sun set, Isaac opened the cellar doors.

"You should all come out and get some fresh air. We are not expecting any visitors," he told them. "Time is short, and we must keep you moving. Your masters will soon be sending out men to look for you and bring you all back."

Once night fell, they headed out once again. Pepper clinging to Osumaka as tightly as ever. They headed through the fields and back onto another old path. That night's journey was just as difficult as the walk the night before. The ground was uneven, and they struggled to keep their footing. About two hours into their journey, they noticed a man up ahead on the trail. Again, the adults froze in fear, but Isaac remained calm and called to the man.

"Who's there?" Isaac asked the shadowy figure.

The man called back, "I am friend of a friend."

"I too am friend of a friend," Isaac returned as he waved to the man ahead.

The two men approached, shook hands, and patted each other on the back.

"It's been too long, my friend." Isaac said.

"Yes, too long, my friend," the man answered. "Who do you have for me? I am told you have five passengers?"

"I do," Isaac replied.

He turned to the group and said, "This man will take you to the next station. Please make sure that you keep up with him. He walks much faster than I do and the moonlight is getting short. You must reach the next station before sunrise."

"Hello," the man called to the group. "I am Ishmael. I will be your conductor to the next station. As Isaac has said, we must hurry. We have a very long way to go still." ·

With that, he turned and began to walk away. Jim and Joe followed close behind followed by Harriet. Osumaka, who still had Pepper wrapped around him, turned to Isaac.

MICHAEL JAY NUSBAUM

"Thank you, my friend," he said.

"You are welcome," Isaac replied. "I hope that you find your wife and child one day. Keep your heart open to those who show you kindness. They do exist, my friend, both dark as me and as white as Miss Shelly. They do exist." Isaac clapped Osumaka on the shoulder in farewell and turned back to the path.

"I will remember," Osumaka said as he too turned and walked rapidly to catch up to the group.

"Good luck, my friends! Good luck!" Isaac called to the group.

They continued down the path, following Ishmael. Pepper slept most of the way but seemed to wake up when the path became more uneven.

"Ah, I see you are awake now," Osumaka said to her. He made a silly face to try to make her smile.

She looked at him and frowned and then placed her finger between his eyes and touched her own forehead.

"Yes, I see you too." Osumaka nodded.

She shook her head no and repeated the motion, but this time, she pulled her forehead up to his and looked into his eyes.

Osumaka smiled, pulled his head away from hers, and kissed her forehead. "You are a silly girl," he said. "Now, be careful or I may fall if I can't see where I'm stepping."

She came back down to his chest and ran her tiny fingers over the scars on his chest. His daughter used to do the same thing, he thought as tears welled up in his eyes. Pepper looked up at him and saw the tears running down his face. She wiped them away with her little hand and then put her head back onto his chest.

They walked for another two hours without a break until they came to another clearing.

"Wait here," Ishmael stated. "I must make sure that the coast is clear."

He headed into the field. Joe and Jim stood guard at the entrance to the woods, careful to look around themselves.

Ishmael came back and motioned for them to come to him. "It is safe. Please hurry! We haven't much time left before sunrise."

They followed him into the field and came upon a road. They walked a few hundred yards down the road and past an old barn. A few hundred feet further down was an abandoned farmhouse with a large wraparound porch. The home was in disrepair: most of the windows were broken, the shutters were hanging in all directions or missing altogether, the roof had a large hole in it, and several sections of the lattice work under the porch were missing.

Ishmael ducked down as he went under the porch via a missing section of the lattice. He motioned for them to follow. They too ducked down and entered the house through a small door under the porch. Once again, they were in a cellar. This cellar was not as well equipped as Ms. Shelly's, but there was food, fresh water, and sleeping pallets already set up for them. An elderly white man stood there with a lantern in each hand.

"Hello, Ishmael," he said.

"Hello, Abraham," Ishmael replied.

"How may do we have today?" the old man asked.

"We have five, Abraham," Ishmael replied.

"Welcome, my friends," Abraham said. "Welcome. What is mine is yours."

Abraham was an elderly white man. His back was bent so that he was unable to stand up straight. His head was permanently cocked to one side as if he was looking at something to the left. He had to turn in order to see straight ahead, and he used a cane to assist his gait.

"Come. Eat and rest," Ishmael bade the group. "We must move again tonight. It is not safe to travel during the daylight. We are getting too close to Savannah to head out during the day."

"Savannah?" Osumaka asked, alarmed.

"Yes, Savannah," Ishmael replied.

"I remember Savannah," Osumaka said flatly. "That is where they first brought me when the boat came ashore. I do not wish to ever go back there."

"You won't, my friend," Ishmael assured him. "We plan on going around it, but we will not go into the city. I promise."

Harriet looked at her daughter, still attached to Osumaka like a limpet. She said, "You must be getting tired of holding her."

"No, it is fine. I will carry her for as long as she wishes me to." In truth, he missed his family so much that he gloried in the little girl's tactile affection.

"Well, for now, let me take her and wash her up." Harriet decided as she reached and took the child.

MICHAEL JAY NUSBAUM

She went over to the wash area and began to bathe Pepper with a damp cloth. Pepper kept a close eye on Osumaka and would not let him out of her sight. She struggled to look past Harriet whenever her mother blocked her sight of Osumaka.

Osumaka found a place in the corner of the room. He was weary from the journey, and soon, he found his mind wandering. He dreamed of his wife and his children. Although their separation had been more than four years ago, the memories remained fresh. He remembered their life together. He could almost smell the aroma of his wife's cooking. He could feel his children's arms as they embraced him, not unlike Pepper. His eyes closed as he drifted back to the life he longed for.

The others washed up and then they too drifted off to sleep.

A few hours later, they were startled by someone knocking at the front door of the house.

Harriet cried out in a desperate whisper, "Where is Pepper?"

They all jumped up to look for the little girl but could not find her. The door to the cellar was slightly open. Osumaka jumped up, hurried to the door, and peered out.

He saw Pepper outside under the porch. He whispered and motioned for her to come back inside, but she didn't move.

Abraham answered the knock at the door, "Yes, may I help you?"

The stranger introduced himself, "Curtis Stanton the Third, sir. I was hoping to get a bit to eat if you had extra."

"I see that you are a Confederate sailor," Abraham replied, wary of Curtis and his uniform.

"Yes, a captain."

"A long way from the ocean aren't you, Captain?" Abraham asked.

"Indeed, I am. I'm headed home. My ship was sunk in the harbor by the Union," Curtis answered easily. "I hope that you don't mind I spent the night in a hay cart in your field. I did not know if anyone was home nor did I think it proper to knock in the middle of the night."

"Certainly," Abraham replied. "Are those soldiers with you?"

"What soldiers?" Curtis asked as he looked in the direction in which Abraham pointed.

"Those soldiers," he repeated.

"No, they are not with me, but I will see what they want," Curtis replied as he turned and headed down the stairs to greet the men approaching.

Two Confederate soldiers approached with rifles in hand. Curtis waved to them, but they did not respond. As they drew closer, Curtis stood his ground at the foot of the steps to the porch.

"We need water and food, old man," they demanded of Abraham, who stood at the top of the porch in front of the front door.

"Aren't you boys forgetting something?" Curtis asked as they drew closer.

They stopped when they noticed the rank on Curtis's uniform.

"Sorry, sir. Yes, sir," they replied as they saluted. "We are looking for some runaway slaves. Word is that there are three male negroes, one female negro, and a small negro girl. Have either of you seen them?"

"I just arrived myself," Curtis explained, "but I have seen no runaway slaves since I left Savannah.

"And you old man?" one of the soldiers asked Abraham.

"No, no one like that around these parts," he replied.

Little Pepper drew ever closer to the opening at the bottom of the porch. Osumaka crawled out to grab her leg and pull her back in. Suddenly, she dashed out from under the porch as if she were playing hide-and-seek. Osumaka's hand barely missed her leg.

Her movement drew the attention of the two soldiers. The men drew their rifles and took aim at the little girl. One crouched down to see Osumaka on the ground under the porch.

"Come out!" the first soldier shouted.

"Wait a moment," Curtis ordered.

"Wait nothing. Runaways are to be shot on sight," the other soldier sneered.

"You're not shooting any child while I'm here," Curtis told the soldiers.

Osumaka slowly came out from under the porch.

The two soldiers took a step back at the sight of Osumaka's large frame emerging from beneath the porch.

Osumaka glared at them with the anger of a fierce animal ready to pounce on its prey.

Suddenly, one shot rang out and hit Osumaka in the leg. Just then, Curtis turned and stepped in front of Pepper, pulling her to his chest to protect her. A second shot fired meant for the little girl but hit Curtis in the back. The thud of the bullet could be heard by all. Pepper felt the bullet hit Curtis, and she freed herself from his arms as he fell. The little girl let out a loud scream and stood there unharmed but terrified. Osumaka lunged at the first soldier while the second struggled to reload. The first soldier lowered his bayonet and thrust at Osumaka, who blocked the rifle with a swing of his left arm down and up. The blade just missed Osumaka's left shoulder. With his right hand, Osumaka grabbed the soldier's neck. With his left, he pulled the rifle from his grasp. He swung the bayonet toward the other soldier and impaled him on the blade. The second soldier dropped his gun and grabbed at the rifle now protruding from his chest. Osumaka threw the first soldier to the ground, keeping his hands around the soldier's neck. The soldier brought his hands up to try to break Osumaka's grasp and thrashed his legs trying to throw off Osumaka, but his effort was futile. His motions began to slow until he was motionless in Osumaka's hands. Osumaka released the soldier and dropped his limp body to the ground.

Osumaka cried, "Pepper!" Then he saw the white man who had shielded the little black girl lying in a pool of blood.

Gurgling sounds came from the other soldier who had fallen to the ground with the bayonet still sticking from his chest. Osumaka turned to the other soldier, rage in his eyes. He leaned over the soldier and grabbed the bayonet and drove it deeper. The man let out another gasp as blood poured from his mouth and both nostrils onto the dirt below. Now, he too lay motionless.

Osumaka turned to Pepper and grabbed her. He held her tight to his chest as he looked at Curtis, now prone in the dirt with blood coming from his back.

Harriet and Ishmael exited the cellar to see what had happened. Harriet covered her mouth and took Pepper from Osumaka's arms.

The others who had not witnessed the short, brutal fight looked around the yard in horror. "What happened?" asked Ishmael.

"The sailor shielded the child from the soldier's bullet," Abraham explained. "Does he still live?"

Osumaka just stood there frozen, looking at Curtis's body. Ishmael reached over to feel for a pulse.

"He's still alive!" Ishmael exclaimed.

"Well, you'd better get these folks out of here right quick," Abraham urged. "This isn't good. There will be more for sure. Especially if anyone heard the shooting."

Joe and Big Jim had emerged as well.

"What do we do?" asked Harriet, still trying to shield Pepper from the carnage.

"We must take you to the next station right away," said Ishmael

"I thought you said it wasn't safe to travel during the daylight?" queried Harriet.

"Yes, but we have no choice now. Come. Leave them. We must go," Ishmael said firmly.

"No!" Osumaka called as the others began to follow Ishmael.

"What do you mean *no?*" said Ishmael, incredulously. "We must go now!"

"No, this man saved Pepper's life. He is brave and worthy of saving," Osumaka said as he knelt beside Curtis. He finally fully believed that not all whites were devils. He was grateful for the help of Abraham and Ms. Shelly, but they had not shielded any in the group from a bullet as this man had.

He looked up at the others and asked, "How many white men would have done the same? This man is worthy of our help."

Abraham gave in, suggesting to Ishmael, "You could take them to Deborah."

"That isn't our next station, and it's not far enough away from here," Ishmael argued.

"True, but her property is huge, and her wealth is vast. She would be able to avoid consequences better than I. She is a friend to us," Abraham replied.

"Fine." Ishmael now gave in. "I think you are crazy, but if you must, then let's go now."

"Come, Jim. Help me carry him," Osumaka beckoned the big man.

The two of them picked Curtis up and started down the road following Ishmael.

CHAPTER 16

Deborah's Plantation

OSUMAKA AND JIM followed Ishmael as they carried Curtis to the next Underground Railroad station.

"How much further is it?" Osumaka asked.

"It's but a mile down this road, but we must be very careful. If we are seen carrying this wounded sailor, we are certain to be killed ourselves. They will accuse us of doing this to him," Joe replied. "We should really just leave him at the side of the road. Someone is certain to come by and help him."

"No!" Osumaka replied. "He saved the little girl's life. He deserves to be saved himself."

Ishmael grumbled, "All right, but it will be up to the station master if she wants to help him." Jim grunted as he strained to hold Curtis's legs. Ishmael continued, "Deborah's plantation is just down this road."

No one passed as they headed down the road. The solitude was unnerving.

The road that they were on connected most of the local plantations and eventually led directly into Savannah proper. The turn to the plantation was marked by a split rail fence, which lay in a state of neglect. The condition of the fence made it clear to the runaways that it had not been a priority for upkeep for several years at least. It extended for several miles along the road and broke naturally to expose a narrow road to the house. The path was an avenue of tall well-developed cedars that created a tunnel through their embracing branches. The main house was not visible from the entrance; to see it required a journey on to the property of some half a mile. The approach had a cool shadiness as a result of the cedar passage. Intermittent beams of sun would illuminate the roadway so that an ambler, if he wished, could count off the distance in beams of light.

"Oh my," a female voice called from the porch in a voice that carried clearly to Osumaka and the others. "Joshua! Get the carriage and help them!"

"Yes, ma'am," he replied as he ran to the courtyard where a horse and carriage stood ready for use.

He drove down the driveway to where Osumaka and Jim were carrying Curtis.

"Let me help you," Joshua offered as he jumped off the carriage.

The men lifted Curtis onto the carriage. Then Joshua turned the carriage back toward the main house, leaving Jim and Osumaka to finish the journey with the rest of the group.

The woman ran down the front steps and yelled, "Lilly, Mary, come quickly!" Although she was dressed in the latest fashion, she did not resemble the white women of Osumaka's experience who spoke softly and gently to their family and servants. Nor did she move gracefully, taking tiny steps slowly. Osumaka did not know what to make of this Deborah. She ran to the carriage before it stopped. Joshua jumped off and tied the horse to the post. The woman opened the door to the carriage to see Curtis lying in blood-soaked clothing.

Osumaka and the rest of the group followed soon behind. After Joshua put Curtis in the carriage, Osumaka had picked up Pepper again.

"He's been shot?" Deborah asked.

"Yes, ma'am," Osumaka responded. "He was shot saving the life of this little girl."

"Who is the little girl to him?" she asked.

"Just a little girl," Osumaka responded.

"And who are you?" she asked.

"My name is Osumaka, ma'am."

"Joshua, you and this man, Osumaka, carry the sailor to the infirmary. Follow Lilly. She will show you where to put him," she told them.

"Yes, ma'am," Joshua responded.

Osumaka handed little Pepper to Harriet.

"Mary," Deborah ordered, "go find Doc Barker. Tell him this time it isn't an injured runaway but a Confederate sailor who needs his help."

"Yes, ma'am," she responded as she ran away.

"Hurry, hurry," Deborah called out as she ran back up the steps and into the house.

Lilly had led the men to what appeared to be an old dining room. Candles and mirrors surrounded a table located in the center of the room. Osumaka placed Curtis on the table then turned to see his image staring back at him from the mirror.

He was stunned by the reflection. He had never been in a house like this and had never seen a mirror. Since he'd been in the United States, he had spent most of his time in the fields or the bunks where the farmhands lived. He stood still in the face of his reflection.

"What happened?" Deborah asked Ishmael. "You were supposed to be their conductor. You were supposed to keep them out of trouble."

"I know, ma'am, but these soldiers came up upon us while we were at the last station. We tried to hide, then the little girl crawled out from under the porch, and they saw her."

"You let her go out to them on her own?" Deborah was incredulous.

"What was I to do?" Ishmael asked. "Before I could do anything, she was already out, and no sooner did she leave our hiding place than did two other soldiers show up. They aimed their guns at the little girl, and this sailor placed himself in the path of the bullets. She would certainly have died had he not done that."

"He's a sailor," she announced as she opened his shirt and examined the wound.

Curtis remained unconscious throughout. He didn't move or speak; the only signs of life were a weak heartbeat and shallow breaths.

"What happened to the other soldiers? I mean, how did you escape them?" Deborah asked.

"Ma'am, you do not want to know," Ishmael replied.

Deborah briefly looked shocked but recovered her poise quickly. "We will leave it at that then. You are right, Ishmael, I do not want to know. In the meantime, we need to get ready for Doc Barker. Start boiling some water and get the knives out, Lilly. Joshua, you need to get some linens."

"Yes, ma'am," Joshua replied as he left the room and headed up the stairs.

Osumaka just stood there, not sure what to do or how to help.

"Do you know this sailor?" Deborah asked Osumaka.

"No, ma'am. I do not."

"Help me roll him onto his front. Doc Barker will need to retrieve the bullet."

Joshua returned with white linens and some bottles of alcohol. "Here, ma'am, I thought that the Doc would want this too."

"Good thinking, Joshua," she said as she opened one of the bottles and poured it over the wound on Curtis's back.

As she finished pouring, Doc Barker arrived.

"What is it, Deborah?" the doctor asked as he entered the room. "A sailor?" he asked.

"Yes, Doc, you must help him! He saved the life of these passengers!"

"I will. Now you leave Joshua with me. He and I will help this man, you take care of the others."

"Yes," she replied. "You, sir, come with me," she motioned to Osumaka.

He left the room with her, and she closed the door behind them.

"Do you need any help? Are you hurt as well? I see that you have a wound on your neck," she asked Osumaka, her questions coming quickly with no pauses. He could not have answered her if he wanted. "Mary!" she called.

"Yes, ma'am," Mary replied.

"Help this man get cleaned up and take care of his wounds."

"Yes, ma'am." Mary nodded.

She motioned for Osumaka to follow her, and they left the main house to go into a smaller house in the back.

The quarters were very nice, nicer than what Osumaka was used to. He introduced himself to the young woman. "I am Osumaka, Mary. Is this where you stay?"

"Yes. Now sit down."

"These are slaves' quarters?" he persisted.

"No," she told him proudly. "We are not slaves here. Miss Deborah freed us all. We choose to stay. These are the living quarters of free people."

"Who is the woman who cares for us?" Osumaka asked.

"She is Miss Deborah. She runs dist home and dist the station master for the Underground Railroad. Her husband and three sons, they were killed in the war, and it is just her and us who remain." Mary went on, "The colonel was always opposed to slavery. They took most

MICHAEL JAY NUSBAUM

us in and treat us like family. We were never ill-treated here. They even gave us all our papers to prove that we are free. The colonel, he used to give money to many of the committees helping slaves who run off. Ever since the Slave Act of 1850, he swore to help us. It wasn't 'til after he died in the war that Miss Deborah started taking in the runoffs. She said she ain't got nuthin' else to lose. She may as well do as she sees fit."

She began to clean the wounds on Osumaka's face and wipe his neck but kept talking.

"We have many visitors—everyday. We must see ten or more runoffs every other day. Most don't stay but one night. Mostly, everyone just move on as they go from station to station, heading up to Canada and the promised land."

"The promised land?" Osumaka asked.

"Yes, the promised land. Many years ago, they done away with slavery in Canada. Now it is the land of freedom for many," she responded. "Where did you start your journey? Who was your agent? Have you had many conductors?" Mary finally took a breath and slowed her speech a little. "I'm sorry, I know that I can go on and on. They make fun of me around here."

"No, that's all right." Osumaka was amused at her rapid-fire chatter. "I was with the others. I saw this sailor protect the little girl, and I knew I must help him since he did an honorable thing."

"Oh, so you just ran away but didn't have a shepherd or agent?"

"No, I was told by Peter that we could get away," Osumaka replied.

"Did you know Ishmael?" Mary asked.

"No, he helped us get here. What is his story?" Osumaka asked.

"Ishmael was a freeman up North. One day, a group of slave catchers headed to Pennsylvania, looking for runaways, and came upon Ishmael. He was runnin' an errand when they done ambushed him. He showed them his paper that proves that he be free, but they burned it in front of him and locked him up like a criminal. The men brought him to a court where the judge took the case, but they paid the judge $10 and he gave them a decision, saying that Ishmael was a runaway, so they done made him a slave. It was Deborah's husband, the colonel, who found Ishmael at another plantation and bought him. He then brought him here and made him a freeman within our home and on this land."

"I know little about this Underground Railroad. I have only seen a railroad but one time, and it was far too large to ever be underground," Osumaka replied.

Mary laughed out loud. "It's not really a railroad, silly. The railroad is a bunch of meeting points with secret routes and safe houses and stations like this one. There are many white people who sympathize with us and many pastors too who help out. The conductors, like Ishmael, help the runaways go from station to station or from station to safe house. Many of the conductors are freeborn colored folk or white people who are apposed to us bein' slaves, still others be former slaves who help so that our race can be free one day. As the passengers, that's the name we give the runaways who come to us to head up North. There be many Quakers and Methodists who help and hide our people in churches. In the beginning, the colonel was just a stockholder."

"What is that?" Osumaka asked as she continued to clean his wound.

"A stockholder?" she asked. "I'm not really sure, but I know that it meant that he just gave people money or sumthin to help us get free, but he didn't want to really do nuthin' that he could get into trouble for."

Just then, Lilly came into the room. "We just got a message," she called out to Mary, short of breath.

"Well, what does it say?" Mary asked.

"Mary, you know that I can't read," Lilly responded testily. She gave the letter to Mary.

"What does it say?"

"It says, 'I have sent via at two o'clock four large chickens and two small chickens.'"

"What does that mean?" Osumaka asked.

"Lilly, go get Joshua." To Osumaka, she said, "It means that there are three adults and two children comin' through on their way to Charleston and that they be at the other safe house since the one you used can never be used again."

"Mary," Deborah called out from the house.

"Miss Deborah is calling me," Mary told Osumaka as she jumped to her feet and ran out of the building. Osumaka watched her run, bemused at all she had said.

"Yes, ma'am," she replied as she approached the main house.

"Mary, I need you to prepare the passengers so that we can move them on."

"Yes'm."

"So I need you to finish with that passenger's wounds and get him ready to leave. We have more passengers arriving at two o'clock tomorrow."

"Yes, ma'am, but . . ."

"But what?" Deborah asked.

"But this one, the one who calls himself Osumaka, isn't with the others. He isn't moving on," she sheepishly responded.

"He's not? Oh. Well, have him come in and speak with me when you're done tending his wounds," Deborah responded as she turned back into the house.

Mary ran back to collect Osumaka from the bunkhouse.

Mary finished cleaning up Osumaka, and then she led him to the house.

"So Mary tells me they call you Osumaka," Deborah said.

"Yes, they do," Osumaka responded.

"Did they not give you a proper Christian name where you ran from?" Deborah asked.

"They did, ma'am, but it is not my name."

"I understand, but wouldn't you like a Christian name? We can give you one," she offered.

"No, ma'am, I am Osumaka," he responded. "Some call me Os, but my name is who I am. I do not believe in your Christian gods, so I don't need a Christian name."

The door to the dining room opened, and Doc Barker emerged. Light poured from the room where he was working. Osumaka looked in. There must have been a hundred lit candles around the doctor's operating table, and the mirrors made the candles look as many as the stars in the sky.

"The bullet hit the spine," the doctor stated as he wiped his forehead.

Deborah put her hands to her mouth.

"I doubt that he will ever have use of his legs again," the doctor stated matter-of-factly.

"Were you with him?" the doctor asked Osumaka.

"I was not with him, but I was there when he was shot."

"I see, because the others told me that there were two shots fired."

"Yes, there were," Osumaka replied.

"Well, then where did the other shot go, I wonder," the doctor replied, looking at Osumaka.

"Whatever do you mean?" asked Deborah.

The doctor pointed to Osumaka's trouser leg. There was a bloody hole in the right thigh.

Deborah gasped and asked, "Is that your blood or the blood of the sailor?"

Osumaka looked down at his leg and noticed for the first time the hole in his pant leg and the blood.

"I am not sure," he said in response.

The doctor motioned for Osumaka to come into the operating room. Osumaka followed him into the candlelit room and got up on the table.

"Lie down and let me take a look," the doctor told him.

The doctor cut open his pants to reveal a gunshot wound to his right thigh.

"Did you not feel this?" the doctor asked incredulously.

Osumaka looked back at him with a blank stare.

The doctor sighed then said, "No matter, it only hit the meat. I'll clean it, and you should heal just fine."

When he was done, he called to Joshua.

"Joshua, take this man and place him in the room across from the sailor."

"Yes, Doc," Joshua responded as he led Osumaka away.

"He's not with the others," Deborah told the doctor.

"No, I suspected as much," the doctor replied.

"What should we do with him if he's not moving on?" Deborah asked.

"Let's see how he mends. He could help with the care of the sailor. The sailor will need quite a bit of care since I highly doubt he will ever walk again," the doctor stated. "Besides, a man who can take a shot to the leg like that and hardly feel it is someone whom we may want to keep around."

"Should I be worried about him?" Deborah asked.

"I should think not. He has a most affable character with a stable demeanor. But I will instruct Joshua to keep a close eye on him," the doctor responded.

MICHAEL JAY NUSBAUM

Soon after, little Pepper came running down the hallway. She saw Osumaka standing there and ran up to him, throwing her arms around his leg. Osumaka knelt down as best as he could, picked Pepper up, and held her in his arms with her head draped over his left shoulder. She wrapped her arms around his neck and held on tight.

Confused, Deborah asked Osumaka, "Is this your daughter?" She had thought he was alone.

"No," he replied as he put his hand on Pepper's back. "But she reminds me of my daughter."

"Well, I see," said Deborah. "She seems very attached to you."

"Why don't you leave her here with Miss Deborah?" Joshua said to Osumaka.

"She stays with me," Osumaka replied. Pepper also did not seem to like Joshua's plan.

"As you wish, if it's all right with you, Miss Deborah," Joshua said.

"It is fine with me. She clearly prefers to be with him," she replied, smiling.

"Very well." Joshua motioned for Osumaka to follow him, "Just this way."

Joshua led Osumaka and Pepper to a room upstairs. As they walked through the hallway and up the steps, Osumaka looked at everything. He had never been inside a white person's home. All he had known in the United States was the slave quarters. This home was very different from what he expected. They paused at the door to see Curtis unconscious in the bed across the hall with Lilly attending to him.

"You can stay here, in this room across the hall from the captain, until you mend," Joshua told him as he pointed into the room. "Wouldn't you prefer to have one of the women take the little girl?"

Osumaka looked around the finely appointed room. "No, she can stay with me. She will sleep on the bed." He was amused by their efforts to take Pepper from him. *As if she would leave me*, he thought.

"As you wish," Joshua replied.

Osumaka looked at the bed and placed Pepper on it. "I will sleep here," he said and pointed to the rug on the floor in front of the bed.

"Please sleep wherever you feel most comfortable," Joshua told him. "I will check on you two later."

Pepper quickly jumped off the bed and onto the floor as Osumaka tried to lie down.

"No, my little one. You need to sleep up there," Osumaka said to her.

She shook her head no and lay down in Osumaka's lap. Osumaka remained seated on the floor, looking at the little girl and remembering his daughter Nzinga. Pepper reminded him so much of her. Within minutes, Pepper slept. Osumaka lifted her and placed her on the bed.

Osumaka stood there, watching her sleep, for several minutes and then lay down on the rug. His eyes soon closed, and he too fell asleep.

Several hours later, they heard screaming coming from Osumaka's room. Joshua ran to the room to see Osumaka sitting up straight, screaming, "Nzinga! Nzinga! Nzinga!"

Joshua ran to Osumaka and shook him. "What is it? What is Nzinga?"

Osumaka focused his eyes as tears poured from them.

"What is Nzinga?" Joshua asked again.

"Nzinga was my daughter, who was killed by the soldiers who took us from our home," Osumaka replied. "My daughter needed me, but I could not help her, for I was bound by chains."

The commotion woke Pepper, and she started to cry. Osumaka jumped to his feet and went over to her.

"It's all right," he said to her, rocking her as she latched on to him once again.

Joshua stood to hear Lilly called from the other room, "Joshua, come here!"

"He's awake!" she exclaimed.

Curtis's eyes had opened, and he'd raised his head from the pillow. Lilly and Joshua stood over him as Osumaka followed Joshua and stood in the doorway.

"Just don't stand here," Joshua told Lilly. "Go get Miss Deborah."

"Yes, sir," she said and ran from the room.

She returned quickly with Deborah.

"I see that you are awake now," Deborah said to Curtis.

Curtis looked confused and frightened. He complained, "I can't feel or move my legs."

"I know." Deborah gave him the bad news. "Doc Barker says that the bullet struck your spine, and he doesn't know if this is temporary or permanent."

Curtis put his head back down on the pillow and stared at the ceiling.

Deborah reached out to touch his hand and told him gently, "We know nothing of you, not even your name."

He flatly recited, "Curtis Bartholomew Stanton III, born December 1, 1835, in Savannah, Georgia, to Melanie and Curtis Stanton II of the Stanton cotton and tobacco family."

"I know of them. You must know a mutual acquaintance then— Miss Lilly Thompson."

"Of the Charleston Thompsons. Yes, ma'am, I do very well," Curtis said as he rose again to look at her.

"You must tell me your story. Where have you been, and what have you done?" Deborah asked. "This man," she gestured to Osumaka, "says you stood between that little girl and a bullet. You must be very brave indeed!"

Curtis seemed gratified by her interest and softened his face. "Well, I was in the navy, serving as an officer on the *Saratoga* for the Africa Squadron before the war."

"What is that?" she asked, settling into a chair next to the bed.

"Well, our mission was to interdict ships off the west coast of Africa and help to stop the slave trade."

"How fascinating. Please tell me more." Deborah hadn't known about the government's effort to stop the importation of Africans as slaves, but she approved.

"We were near the mouth of the Congo River when we came across a ship called the *Nightingale*. She bore three masts and was docked at the mouth of the river. We observed her when we approached the coast but did not see any activity. After nightfall, we boarded the ship by moonlight and found her hulls filled with slaves fresh from inland. My good friend Lt. Michael Smith and I captured the ship, imprisoned the crew aboard our ship, the *Saratoga*, and then sailed the *Nightingale* to Monrovia where we set the slaves free at the colony there. No sooner had we landed in Monrovia than we received word of the beginning of the war back home. We were ordered to return straight away. Our captain had been struck ill, so Smith was promoted to captain, I to first lieutenant, and we set to return to New York immediately."

Curtis took a sip of water and a deep breath. "Once we arrived back home, we parted ways, and I headed back home to serve with the

Confederate Navy. As an officer, I was given my own ship to captain and have been trying to run the Union blockade some days ago. The ship that sunk us was captained by none other than my old friend Michael Smith. Despite the risk to him, he let me escape to return home in the middle of the night."

"Fascinating!" Deborah replied, her eyes wide.

"I'm sorry, may I have some more water? All this talking is making me very thirsty."

"Lilly, please bring the captain another pitcher of water." To Curtis, she said, "Please go on."

Osumaka stood at the doorway with Pepper wrapped around him, looking at Curtis.

"So trying to work my way back home, I found myself upon a group of slaves, hiding under a building. No sooner did I ask the little girl to come out than two Confederate soldiers came upon us. They shouted that the slaves were fugitives and raised their guns. I tried to shield the little girl." Curtis hesitated, asking, "How is she?"

"She's fine," Deborah told him calmly. "Thanks to you."

Curtis looked relieved then continued. "Then I heard the gunfire and felt it strike my back, but I don't remember what happened between then and now," Curtis explained.

"Well, I believe that you owe this man your life," Deborah said, pointing to Osumaka.

"I do? Well, thank you," Curtis said fervently.

Osumaka bowed his head.

"But I'm not feeling very well," Curtis said as he lay back down.

Deborah got up from her chair and put a hand on his head. "You are burning with fever." To Joshua, she commanded, "Get some towels and cool water!"

"Yes, ma'am, right away."

Curtis soon became unconscious again. Joshua returned with cloths and cool water. He wet the cloth and placed it atop Curtis's head.

"I think it's best that we call Doc Barker back," Deborah said as she left the room.

Osumaka watched and asked Joshua, "Can I help you?"

"Yes, thank you," Joshua replied. "Here, do this. Just make sure you keep the cloth cool and wet."

Osumaka sat by Curtis's side throughout the night and kept the cloth cool and wet. Soon, he found his mind drifting back to his family, to his children, and to his home, to the rains and the feeling of having his children clinging to him when the thunder struck. Pepper stayed close to him and wasn't happy unless she was in contact with Osumaka. It wasn't long before he began to sing the song that he had made up for his own children.

Curtis heard Osumaka singing to Pepper as he slept. As he began to awaken further from the fever, Curtis began to hum the song with him.

"What song is that?" Curtis asked, finally fully awake. "Is it a common song in your land?"

"No," Osumaka said, "it is a song I made up for my children."

"I've heard that song before," Curtis recalled. "I heard it on a ship we interdicted heading to South America."

"That is not possible," Osumaka stated. He looked at the sailor with dismay. What was the man trying to do?

"A woman sang it, a woman whose name I can't recall, but I do remember her son's name. It sounded like Bwana. They were on the ship we stopped—the *Nightingale*."

Osumaka's doubt and suspicion fled, and his face lit up with joy. "Bwana?" he asked. "Are you sure?"

"Yes, I am certain," Curtis replied.

"How can that be?" asked Osumaka. "Someone must have told you his name."

"Where are my clothes?" Curtis asked.

"Over there, I think," Osumaka said as he pointed to the corner.

"Get them for me, please," Curtis requested.

Impatiently, Osumaka put Pepper down and grabbed Curtis's uniform from the chair.

Curtis fumbled through his pants and pulled out the small ivory statue given to him by Bwana. He handed the carving to Osumaka.

Osumaka took the statue into his hands and put it to his forehead. He could hardly believe what he was seeing. Were his eyes deceiving him? Was this possible? The statue was indeed the one he had carved himself for his son. "Could it be?" he whispered. Osumaka's face turned blank, then tears ran down his face, and he fell to his knees. "They are alive?" he wept.

Pepper ran over to him and wrapped her arms around him. She began to weep as well.

"How? Where are they?" he asked as he turned the statue over and over in his hands and then held it close to his heart.

Pepper looked in his eyes and could see his tears. She wiped one away and then held him again. Osumaka held her in his right arm as he held the little statue in his other.

"We brought them to Liberia and freed them. They live there as freed people in the city of Monrovia," Curtis replied.

Lilly came to the door. "Miss Deborah!" she called. "Miss Deborah, he's awake!" She continued to call as she ran through the house.

"What is it?" Deborah asked.

"He be awake, ma'am! He be awake!"

"Who?" Deborah asked. "The captain?"

"Yes'm. He's awake and talking to Os, ma'am."

The two dashed to the room to see Osumaka kneeling and crying at Curtis's bedside while clutching the statue.

"What is it?" Deborah asked. "What's wrong?"

"My son!" Osumaka exclaimed.

She noticed that he held the little girl in one arm and the little statue in the other. Deborah looked at Curtis, puzzled by Osumaka's response.

Curtis grinned at her. "Do you recall the story I told you about that ship we stopped?" Curtis asked Deborah.

"Why yes."

"Well, it seems the young boy and his mother were the family of our friend Os here."

"Remarkable," she replied. "Divine intervention if I have ever seen it."

"Indeed," Curtis replied with a smile upon his face. "I don't think I have ever seen anyone as happy as our friend here."

"And you," Deborah asked Curtis with concern, "you are feeling better?"

"I am. Thanks to my friend . . . and you."

Deborah smiled and blushed.

"How long was I out?" Curtis asked.

"Most of the evening and a good part of today," she replied as she drew closer to his bedside. Osumaka remained on the floor, clutching Pepper and the statue.

MICHAEL JAY NUSBAUM

"What made you think of that boy?" Deborah asked Curtis.

"I'd heard the song he was singing to the little girl. I had memorized it on our journey as his wife sang it to his son while I nursed him. A nice turnaround, eh?"

"Remarkable," she replied.

"Someday, I will be with them again," Osumaka stated as he gazed at the statue.

"You will, my friend. You will," Curtis said as he watched the man who had saved his life.

"Are you well enough to eat?" Deborah asked Curtis.

"I'm afraid that my legs are still of no use," Curtis said.

"The doctor said that the bullet hit your spine. He said that you may never walk again," she reminded him.

"Of course. I had forgotten for a moment," Curtis said. "And the little girl?"

"This one?" asked Deborah as she rubbed Pepper's head. "She's fine."

"I am still hungry though," Curtis reminded Deborah.

"I'm sorry," Deborah said as she caught herself staring into Curtis's eyes. "Where are my manners?" She moved to the door and called, "Lilly! Bring the captain some food, please!"

"Perhaps Os could help me downstairs?"

"NO!" Deborah replied. "Doc Barker said that you can't be moved."

"I see." Curtis pretended to quail at her sternness. She made a face at him.

"Os, why don't you and Pepper join the others downstairs for some supper," she said.

"Yes, ma'am," Os replied. "Thank you, sir. Thank you, thank you. You have given me hope."

"No, thank you, Os! I owe you my life. Someday, I will help you find them," Curtis promised.

"Thank you, sir. Thank you," Osumaka repeated.

Osumaka headed out the room, holding Pepper and the ere àwòrán, walked down the hallway and then down the stairs, still in a state of shock.

"How can you promise him such things?" Deborah asked.

"Someday, I will help him." Curtis was resolute.

"But to give him hope where there is none?" she said.

"Why would you say that?" Curtis asked. "Why is there none? There must be hope."

"But . . ." she began then stopped herself.

"But I'm a cripple and can't even help myself?" Curtis raised an eyebrow at her discomfort.

"I didn't say that," she replied.

"They are alive. Someday, when this damn war is over, I will take him back. Even as a cripple, I can do it."

"You have a good heart, Curtis. I'm certain that you will if you set your mind to it." Deborah was impressed that this man that had survived such a life-threatening injury was able to maintain hope, not just for his future but also for a man he had just met.

Lilly appeared at the doorway. "The captain's food, ma'am. Would you liken me to feed 'em?"

"No, Lilly, my dear. I'll take it. I can feed him."

"With all due respect you two, my arms still work." Curtis sounded mildly exasperated.

Lilly giggled. "I'm sorry, sir. You're right. Here. I'll leave it right here for you."

"Thank you, Lilly. That'll be all." Deborah smiled as she dismissed the girl.

"Yes'm," she replied as she left the room.

"Ma'am, ma'am." They heard a voice from downstairs.

"What is it?" Deborah asked.

There was no reply, but they could hear a furious patter of feet, running up the stairs and to the room. Soon, Mary appeared at the doorway. Out of breath, she panted dramatically.

"Ma'am. It's, it's," she panted out.

"Yes? What is it?" Deborah asked, smiling at the maid's tendency to exaggerate.

"It's Sarah! It's Sarah! Word just came that she's not a half a day away."

"Sarah?" Deborah replied. "Oh my. What a wonderful news. It's been too long!"

"Who is Sarah?" Curtis asked.

"Sarah? You don't know Sarah?" Mary asked. "Oh my."

"Sarah is a kind of a legend around these parts," Deborah explained.

"She's the right hand of Moses, she is. The right hand!" Mary, having caught her breath, was exultant.

"Moses?" Curtis asked with a smile.

"Well, not *the* Moses," Deborah told him. "Mary's referring to a famous conductor named Harriet Tubman. She's known as Moses around these parts."

"Really? Why Moses?"

"Because she has set so many of her people free," Deborah stated. "She is a truly remarkable woman, honorable and strong."

"So who is this 'right hand of Moses' then?"

"Sarah. She is one of Harriet Tubman's most impressive apprentices. She has pretty much taken over for Miss Tubman since the war began."

"Taken over what?"

"Why, the Underground Railroad, of course!" Mary exclaimed. She was astonished at the depth of Curtis's ignorance.

"Mary, where are your manners?" Deborah replied.

"I'm sorry, ma'am. But how the captain has never heard of Moses or Sarah . . . I will never know."

"That's fine, Mary. Go alert the others and make sure that the passengers are ready for her arrival."

"Yes, ma'am," Mary replied as she headed back down to the others.

Deborah turned to Curtis again and told him firmly, "You need to eat, and if you won't do it yourself, then I will be forced to feed you."

"Yes, ma'am. I will abide by your orders . . . ma'am," Curtis replied with a smile as he took the plate and began to eat. "Umm. Ummm. Oh . . ."

"Slow down there!" she said. "You're going to choke on that food if you don't slow down."

"Yes, ma . . . ma'am," he replied with his mouth full.

"And don't speak with your mouth full of food."

Curtis swallowed the food. "Yes, ma'am. But this is mighty good cooking."

"Thank you. Now mind your manners. Don't forget who you are."

"Yes, ma'am," he said. "It's just hard, you know. I haven't been home or had a home-cooked meal for so long. And it seems like forever that I've eaten a meal without my men."

"I understand," she replied with a smile.

Curtis continued to eat, mindful not to speak with a mouth full of food. He swallowed and asked, "Who are the passengers you mentioned?"

"Most of them are the runaway slaves who brought you here. There a few more who came before you arrived. Sarah will be taking them up to Ohio. Then to Detroit."

"Detroit!" Curtis exclaimed. "How's she going to get them there?"

"Sarah has her ways, taught to her by Miss Tubman herself."

"That's a long journey from here!"

"It is. She's made it many times, several times a year now."

"That's remarkable." Curtis was impressed.

"It is. Once she gets them to Detroit, then it's a boat ride across the river to Canada and freedom for them."

"Canada?"

"Yes. Canada."

"Why? Isn't the North good enough? I mean, isn't that what this war is all about?"

"True. Ever since President Lincoln's Emancipation Proclamation last January, many freed slaves and runaways have returned from Canada to the North; some to fight with the Union Army for the emancipation of all slaves. Still, many head up to Canada to be absolutely safe."

Curtis nodded his understanding and commented, "It is a cruel and unusual institution, I must agree."

"Yes, it is," agreed Deborah.

"My eyes have only been opened to the horrors of slavery in the past few years. I grew up accepting slavery as fact. Then I saw the ugly side of it. The part they don't want you to see. The part that any sane human being would be repulsed by. I am ashamed of my past."

"I felt the same," Deborah replied. "I too grew up with slavery only to question it in my later years. My late husband, God rest his soul, also changed his views on slavery. He fought for the South because he thought it honorable, but he abhorred the institution of slavery. He spent a great deal of his fortune trying to correct that error. He died leaving me to keep on the cause, and so we do."

"It is an honorable thing you do indeed," Curtis replied as he placed his hand on hers.

She looked at his hand and then into his eyes. "You are a good man, Captain. I can see that. Now it is time for you to finish your meal and then get some rest. It will be dark soon, and we need to prepare for tomorrow. We have much to do. I will send Os back here to keep an eye on you," she said all this with a smile.

Deborah rose from her chair, pushed it back against the wall, and left the room. Curtis watched her as she moved gracefully from his side. His eyes wandered from her long blond hair to her slender waist.

"Get some sleep now," she called to him from the hallway.

Moments later, Osumaka appeared in the doorway.

"What can I get for you, Captain?" he asked.

"Nothing, my friend. Nothing," Curtis replied.

"Miss Deborah," Osumaka stated.

"Yes. She is a remarkable woman," Curtis responded.

"Yes," Osumaka replied. "We had best do what she says. I will stay with you if you need anything. I will be right here on the floor beside you."

In the morning, they awoke to noises from the front of the house.

"What is it, Os?" Curtis asked.

Osumaka went to the window to look and see what was going on. "I think . . ." He paused. "I think it is this Sarah they spoke of."

"You think?" Curtis asked. "Can you not recognize a woman?" Pain, fever, and forced inactivity had caused Curtis to wake with a short temper.

"If this is Sarah, she is not like any other woman I have seen before," Osumaka replied as he continued to stare out the window.

"What do you mean? I can't see from here. Tell me what you see," Curtis demanded.

"Well, Captain, she's a she I think. I mean, she's dressed like a man. She's tall like a man. She looks like a kind of soldier."

"A soldier? What are you talking about, Os?" Curtis was impatient with Osumaka's vague descriptions and burned to get to the window and see for himself.

"Well, she looks like a warrior to me. She holds a rifle like a warrior. She has two revolvers around her waist like a soldier, and well . . . she looks strong."

"Well, then how do you know it's not a man? How do you know it's this Sarah they keep talking about?"

"Well, Captain, I know when I see a woman even if she is dressed like a man. This one, this one you can kinda see that she still be a woman without all that getup on."

Curtis gave up. He would learn nothing unless Osumaka surveilled the situation from close up. He suggested, "Why don't you go down there and help out? Then come back here and fill me in on everything."

"I think I will just do that, Captain," Osumaka replied. "In the meantime, I also see if I can't rustle up something to get you around so that when Doc Barker gives you the all clear to get up, we can have some way of getting you around."

"Right. All right. Now get yourself down there and make sure you don't leave anything out when you come back to tell me what happened."

"Right you are, Captain. I'll be sure to listen to all that is said."

Osumaka left Curtis's side and headed out to the front of the house, descending the stairs to the front foyer. The front door had been left open, and he could see everyone greeting Sarah. She was almost as tall as he was—at least six feet tall. Her face was chiseled and strong for a woman, yet her eyes were soft and as green as emeralds. Osumaka slowly walked to the open doorway. His large frame moving toward the open door caught Sarah's attention as she caught his movement from the corner of her eye. She immediately turned her gaze upon Osumaka. Their eyes met for a moment.

The sun was strong as it was nearing its peak in the sky. Its rays illuminated Osumaka as he exited the door.

"Who is this?" Sarah asked the group.

"This is Os," Deborah replied.

"Oh, so this is Os. You were just telling me about him," Sarah said.

"Osumaka," he corrected as he stood in front of her. His white shirt clung to his muscular frame in stark contrast to his dark skin.

"I see," Sarah said. "And what were you before you were a slave?"

"I am a warrior!" Osumaka barked. "I am not a slave."

"I see," Sarah repeated. She turned to Deborah and commented, "He could be very valuable in our journey."

Deborah looked at Osumaka and smiled, "Os is a proud and strong-willed man. He is very honorable, and I am certain that he would help you in your journey North."

"Is this true?" Sarah asked Osumaka.

"Yes. I will help you take your freed slaves to the North, but once we are there, I must make plans to leave you so that I can find my family," Osumaka replied.

"That is a fair-enough bargain," Sarah replied. "We leave at sundown."

"I will be ready." Osumaka nodded.

"Now, Miss Deborah, if you can show me the other passengers, we can start to make plans to leave," Sarah said confidently.

"They are over that way," Deborah said as she stretched her arm out in the direction of the quarters around the back of the main house.

Sarah walked in the direction of Deborah's outstretched arm. She glanced to her right at Osumaka and regained eye contact with him. This time, he could see a slight smile on her face when she looked at him. Osumaka smiled back, and Sarah looked back down at her steps as she turned the corner around the main house. Osumaka just stood there as the remainder of the group followed them to the rear of the house. Standing alone, Osumaka looked up at the sky. Now that he had an idea of their whereabouts, he wondered how his family were. He considered the sun and imagined the same warmth that he felt on the faces of his wife and boy. To him, at this moment, they were only a journey away. He felt more optimistic than he had at any time since he came back from the successful hunt that fateful day.

He turned and headed back into the house. He ran up the stairs and back to Curtis's room.

"So tell me," Curtis said enthusiastically. "I could barely hear anything!"

"I am leaving with Miss Sarah this evening. She wants to leave at sunset to take her passengers North. She has asked for my help in her journey."

"Then I wish you well, my friend," Curtis said as he maneuvered himself up in bed.

"Thank you, my friend," Osumaka responded. "Thank you for giving me hope that I will see my wife and boy again someday."

"Someday soon, my friend. You will see them someday soon."

Curtis stretched out his arm toward Osumaka. Osumaka shook his hand and held it.

"Godspeed on your journey, Os," Curtis said.

"Thank you again, my friend," Osumaka replied.

A noise from the hallway caused them both to turn their gaze to the doorway of the room. Harriet stood there.

"Os, they are preparing the passengers. Miss Deborah thought it best that I fetch you and send you to them. I will look after Captain Curtis," she said, slightly winded from racing up to get him.

"Go, my friend," Curtis said as he released Osumaka's hand.

Osumaka smiled at them both and then headed out of the room. His large frame filling the doorway forced Harriet to step out of his way to let him pass. He looked back at Curtis and smiled as he walked away.

"Now you should be lying down!" Harriet barked at Curtis. "Miss Deborah would have my head if she knows that I let you get away with everything you want."

Osumaka arrived at the servants' quarters to see Sarah organizing a whirlwind of activity. She had all the runaways, packing their rations for the trip. The scene reminded Osumaka of his preparations for his hunting trips when he and his fellow hunters would gather their belongings and supplies needed for the hunt.

"Oh good. Os is here," Deborah stated.

Sarah turned and looked over her shoulder at him for a brief moment before she continued with her work.

"What can I do to help?" Osumaka asked.

"Come here," Deborah said as she called him over to the children.

In a few hours, the sun began to set. Sarah had prepared her passengers with military efficiency. They were soon set to go. The cicadas began their evening calls as the bullfrogs announced the setting of the sun. Curtis had been brought to the window to send them off. Harriet was in the window next to him, shouting, "Good luck!" Everyone from the plantation stood outside to send them off. Sarah led the way as her human cargo followed. Osumaka was last to leave.

Little Pepper came running out to Osumaka. "No!" she shouted.

"She spoke!" Harriet gasped.

"No, no, no," Pepper chanted as she grabbed Osumaka.

"I am sorry, little one, but it is best that you stay here with Miss Deborah. You will be safe here," Osumaka said to her.

Harriet had tears in her eyes as she put her hands to her face and then over her mouth as she choked back tears.

"No, no, no," Pepper repeated as she clung tightly to Osumaka.

Osumaka let her hold on to him for a while and then peeled her off, knelt, and looked into her eyes. "You will be safe here. I will come back for you someday. I promise, I will come back for you."

Pepper looked at Deborah, who had come out just in time to hear Pepper speak. Then she looked at Harriet. Both women nodded at the girl. They knew already that Osumaka kept his promises.

"It will be all right," Osumaka said softly to her as he gave her another hug.

Pepper clung to him tightly, and then whispered into his ear.

"I promise," Osumaka told her softly.

Pepper ran over to Deborah and grabbed on to her dress.

"I will look after her for you, Osumaka. Godspeed on your journey," Deborah said.

With a sack slung around his shoulder and one of the rifles of Deborah's husband in his hand, Osumaka walked over to Sarah. He raised the rifle into the air and waved it before he turned and followed the rest down the path.

Deborah and Pepper waved as the group walked away. Pepper raised her hands into the air, and Deborah picked her up so that she could see them walk away. She turned to Deborah and touched her face with her left hand. Then she wrapped her arms around Deborah's neck and held on tightly.

CHAPTER 17

Underground

B Y NOW, THE sun was setting, and the light of the moon began to take over. They journeyed through the woods, between plantations, careful not to make too much noise. The next station was a full night's journey, and they needed to take extra care not to be seen. As they approached each road, Osumaka would go ahead and make sure that the way was safe. They headed along the Indian path through the trees and over small streams. Several hours into their journey, they began to hear voices and smell campfire smoke.

"Do you smell that?" Sarah asked Osumaka.

"I do," he replied.

"We will wait here. Scout ahead and see what it is," she commanded.

"Yes," Osumaka replied as he stealthily approached the edge of the forest to see what was going on in the fields ahead.

What he saw chilled him. There were thousands of Confederate soldiers camped in the open fields ahead. He could see lines of tents and corrals of horses. Guns and cannons with wagons of supplies were lined up along the edges of the tent village. Campfires dotted the landscape.

Osumaka returned to Sarah.

"There are thousands of soldiers there," he reported.

"Yankees?" she asked hopefully.

"No," he replied. "Rebels."

"Damn!" Sarah exclaimed. "We needed to cross that field. We will never make it to our next station before dawn."

"Are there any other stations near?" Osumaka asked.

"Maybe," she replied. "If not, we will have to hide out in the woods all day with all those soldiers nearby. That will never work."

"They don't seem to be going anywhere," Osumaka said. "Should we turn back and return to Miss Deborah?"

"No, no. We need to move. This is even more reason to move on," Sarah told him as she motioned for the others to restart their journey.

The woods became increasingly dense, and the path they were following seemed to lead into a road up ahead. They traveled about a mile around the field, away from their previous location, when the path they were on opened up onto a dirt road.

"Damn," Sarah said again, as she motioned all to stop.

"What is it?" asked Osumaka.

"This path ends onto the road, and I don't see where it restarts on the other side," she replied.

She and Osumaka crouched down and moved closer to the opening of the path.

Osumaka looked again at the path and then back at the road. "Perhaps there is a branch off this path back there somewhere. We may have missed it."

"No. I don't think so. I'm always keeping a close eye out for forks in the path. I haven't seen one for quite a while," Sarah said as she peered across the road ahead.

"What should we do?" asked Osumaka.

"We're going to have to head down this road for a bit until we pick up the path on the other side," she replied.

Osumaka looked around a bit. "I don't like it."

"Why, what's wrong?" Sarah asked.

"The bugs have stopped making noises," he replied.

"Well, that's because we are here," she said.

"Perhaps," he replied.

Sarah looked up and down the road carefully. "I still can't see the other end of the path. We'll have to risk it and use this road until we find it," she said as she stood up and motioned for the rest to follow them.

They walked out on to the road. It was the first time in a while that they had a clear view of the night's sky. The stars were visible, and beams of moonlight broke through the trees and on to the roadway ahead of them.

"How long have you been doing this?" Osumaka asked Sarah.

"What? You mean conducting?" she asked in reply.

"Yes. How long have you been helping slaves escape?" he clarified.

"Quite a few years now. I started with Miss Moses and helped her bring some of her family up North, and then she started getting too old to make the trips," Sarah replied.

"So you took over?" Osumaka asked.

"I guess you could say I took over where Miss Moses left off. I'm not the only one though. She trained quite a few of us," Sarah said.

"How many have you . . ." Osumaka barely got out when two men stepped out of the woods right on to their path.

"Well, well!" one of the men stated. "What in Jesus's name do we have here, Billy?"

Just then, three more figures entered the roadway. There were two more men and a young boy, all of them carrying shotguns.

"Looks like we got ourselves a group of runaways," Billy said as he spat upon the ground and raised his gun toward the group.

Sarah stepped out in front of her passengers and flung open her trench coat. "You boys best be moving on," Sarah said boldly. "We have no quarrel with you. Just let us pass in peace."

"What in God's creation is that?" asked one of the men. "Is that a man or a woman?"

"What's the difference?" another said. "They're all worth the same amount when we turn them in."

The men started to maneuver around Sarah and to either side, each with their guns pointed at the group.

"What a ragtag group of runaways," another said, laughing. "We're gonna make a lot of money off of you."

Suddenly, the man named Billy lunged for a female slave. The group turned to see what he was doing as she cried, "No!" As she did, Sarah drew both pistols, one in each hand. She fired so rapidly and accurately with both hands that she didn't even seem to be aiming. After four shots from each gun, all four men lay dead or injured as she aimed both pistols on the young boy, who, although trembling, still held his shotgun.

"You'd best put that shotgun down, child," Sarah said calmly as she cocked the hammers on both of her pistols.

The boy whimpered in fear and slowly lowered his gun. "Yes, ma'am," he said in a low quivery voice.

Two of the men were clearly dead, while the others moaned in pain on the ground.

MICHAEL JAY NUSBAUM

"Just drop it, boy, and run on home. Don't come back here," Sarah said.

The boy dropped the gun and ran off into the woods. The group of runaway slaves were huddled together in a tight mass.

"You let him go!" Osumaka exclaimed. "Why?"

"He was just a young boy," Sarah replied.

"But he will go back and tell others. Then they will be hunting for us," Osumaka scolded his conductor.

Sarah didn't look up as she reloaded her pistols. "You are correct. That is why we need to be moving on now!" Sarah ordered as she put her guns back into their holsters.

"Where are we going?" Osumaka asked.

"We are going to head west, away from them for the next hour or two, and then restart our journey north. I will need you to scout ahead for us."

"Yes, I will be the forward scout," Osumaka replied.

Sarah took the weapons from the men whom she had just shot. "Those two are dead. These two will soon be," she said as she handed the rifles and shotguns to Osumaka and the other men.

"I have been carrying one of these but don't know how to use it," Osumaka said.

"Neither do we," another man said.

"Just hold them for now, but do not touch this part. This is the trigger and will cause it to fire. I can't show you how to use them now," Sarah said.

"I don't feel that it is a good idea that we hold these," one of the men said.

Sarah looked at Osumaka as he shook his head in agreement.

"Fine, here, give them to me," Sarah said as she collected the guns from the men.

"What will you do with them?" asked Osumaka.

"I am going to throw them into the woods where they can't be found," Sarah replied.

She tossed the guns on to either side of the road as they walked away. Osumaka looked back at the now still bodies of all four men. Surely, they will now come after their group. *Hopefully, the boy did not get a good look at us*, he thought to himself.

"Come on!" Sarah said to the group. "I've found a path that will get us off this road and away from here. We must move quickly now and make as much distance as we can before daybreak."

Once they had detoured sufficiently, they restarted their journey North. They were fortunate that the sky was clear, and the moon was almost full. The light was more than enough to help guide them through the landscape.

After several hours of traveling, Osumaka reported back to Sarah, "There is a farmhouse ahead. It is not very large, but they have large fields and no sign of slave houses unless the slaves stay in the barn."

"Is there a lantern in the window?" Sarah asked.

"Yes. One. In the window to the left of the door on the porch," Osumaka responded. "Why?"

"Because the lantern left burning in the window could be a sign that they are abolitionists and friendly to runaway slaves," she explained. "Show me."

After telling the group to stay, they walked about a quarter mile down the road. "Over there," Osumaka said, as he pointed to the house.

"I think that they may be Quakers," she replied.

"How will we know?" Osumaka asked.

"I will go to the door and find out," she replied.

"I can go," Osumaka told her. "It is too dangerous for you to go alone."

"I do this all the time," Sarah said. "I can do it now. But you're welcome to come with me."

With that, the two of them instructed the rest to lie where they were.

"Stay here. If anything happens to us, just continue north."

Sarah and Osumaka left the cover of the woods and headed carefully to the farmhouse. Sarah could see the porch and the lantern in the window. As they got closer, a dog began to bark loudly at them. They both fell to the ground as the door to the farmhouse opened. A white man came out with a shotgun.

"What is it, boy?" he asked the dog. "Who's out there?"

"What do we do?" Osumaka whispered to Sarah.

"Who's out there?" the man repeated as he raised the shotgun and pointed in their direction.

"A friend of a friend!" Sarah called.

MICHAEL JAY NUSBAUM

"A friend of a friend?" the man repeated.

"Yes! Friend of a friend?" Sarah asked.

"I am a friend of a friend," the man said as he lowered the gun and motioned for them to come closer. "May!" He called into the house, "We have a friend of a friend."

Sarah rose and grabbed Osumaka by the collar to come to his feet as well. They timidly approached the house, looking around in all directions.

Soon, a woman appeared in the doorway with the old man. The dog continued to bark.

"Quiet down, Buster!" she shouted at the dog as she pushed him off the porch with her right foot.

"Friend of a friend?" she asked Sarah.

"Yes, ma'am. Friend of a friend," Sarah replied.

"Oh my, poor dear," the old woman said. "How many are you? Is it just you two?"

"No, ma'am. We are twelve in all," Sarah replied.

"Oh my. Twelve, you say? Oh my," she repeated.

"Twelve, you say?" the old man asked.

"Yes, sir. Twelve, including the two of us standing before you," Sarah replied.

"Well, we haven't the room in the house for twelve of you. But you're welcome to use the barn over yonder. May and I will bring out some food for you. You're welcome to stay until dark. Sun's going to be coming up shortly," the old man said reassuringly.

"That is mighty kind of you, sir. A friend of a friend if ever there was one. Jesus be with you," Sarah said to him.

"And with you, my child. Head your flock over to the barn, and we'll get you settled in there," he replied.

"Thanks you much, sir," she replied. "Osumaka, go get the rest of them. I'm going to look into this barn."

Sarah headed over to the barn as Osumaka ran back to the woods to retrieve their group, bringing them back to the barn. Sarah had already lit a lantern inside as they entered.

"It's not much, but it should do just fine," she said.

It wasn't long before the elderly couple came by with some food and two more lanterns.

"You poor dears must be starving," she said as she handed the iron pot to Sarah. "What is your name, my dear?"

"Sarah, ma'am."

"And your strong friend here?" she asked, pointing to Osumaka.

"That is Osumaka, ma'am."

"Well, you dears eat up and rest. I'll be in later after sunup to check on you."

"Thank you, ma'am," Sarah replied. "May I ask you a question?"

"Certainly, my dear," she replied.

"Ma'am, are you Quakers?" Sarah asked.

"Why yes, dear. Why do you ask?"

"No reason, ma'am. I was just wondering," Sarah said.

"You are welcome, my dear," the woman replied,

She left the barn and headed back to the farmhouse.

Sarah closed the door and told the others, "Eat quickly as we need to put out this light before it gives us away."

Everyone grabbed a share of the food. It wasn't long before they were all ready to pass out from exhaustion. Osumaka had not eaten anything. He remained at the door the entire time, peering out through the crack to the field from which they had just come.

"You must eat too," Sarah told him.

"I'm fine," he answered.

"Yes, but we have many days of journey ahead of us, and food will not always be there to greet us. Eat now, that is an order," she said lightly.

"I will eat," he replied, "not because you order me to but because all the others have filled themselves, and this is what remains. It should not go to waste. I will stay here, guarding the door. You should get some sleep."

"As you wish." Sarah shrugged as she moved to the beds of hay the others had fallen asleep on. Sarah lay down with them and soon slept too.

Sarah was startled by a sound and sat up quickly, pulling both her revolvers from her waist. She saw Osumaka still standing guard at the barn doors. She returned one of her guns to its holster, stood up, and walked over to Osumaka.

"What was that noise?" she asked.

"I'm not sure," he replied. "It came from the roof, but I have seen nothing out there." They stood and listened to the noises of the day.

"Have the others been asleep the whole time?"

"Yes. The sun came up a while ago. I saw a few lights go on in the house, but no one has come out yet," he replied.

"I see," she replied as she peered past him and out through the crack. "So what is your story? How long have you been a slave?"

"I am not a slave!" Osumaka replied angrily. "I am a warrior, and I will return to my family in Africa."

"Fine," Sarah replied. "But how do you know that they are still alive?"

"Captain Stanton gave me this," he pulled out the little statue which hung around his neck. "He was given this by my son after he saved them from slavery and death and brought them to a place called Liberia. I will leave here and find them."

Sarah nodded. "A noble cause for sure. But Liberia is many months away, and you must get there by boat. You will not be able to get there on your own," she reminded him.

"I will find a way to get to them," he declared as he looked back outside. "I will find a way."

"I am sure you will, Osumaka," Sarah replied.

"And what of you?" he asked. "Why do you risk your life to save these people? What are they or I to you?"

Sarah looked around the barn at the ten sleeping runaways—men, women, and children. "They are my people, and we have been held in bondage for too long. Moses taught me how to do this. She trained me to help free our people. If the white men of the South will not let them go, then we will free them . . . by force if necessary, but we will free every last one."

"Who is this Moses who trained you?" he asked as he looked into her eyes.

"She is a remarkable woman. Miss Harriet is revered by all of our people and beloved by those lucky enough to know her. She has made it her life's mission to free our people. I am but one of many disciples of hers who have taken up her cause. She is growing old and is not able to make the journeys as she used to. It is now up to a new generation to help her," Sarah said.

"Were you a slave?" he asked.

"I was. I was born into it. I was born in South Carolina on a plantation and then raised on an island called Hilton Head. Moses made a home for herself there and trained many of us from that place. From time to time, she will journey North, but she always comes home," Sarah said. "But I was freed by Moses, along with my mother. I can't remember when, but it was many years ago."

"I would very much like to meet this Moses," Osumaka told Sarah.

"You will, my friend. You will," she assured him.

Osumaka suddenly said, "Someone is coming. It is the old man."

Sarah edged him out of the way to take a look. The man was nearly at the door when she peered out. The door opened slowly. Sarah kept her pistol drawn.

"My friends, are you all right?" he asked.

"We are," Sarah replied.

"Here. Mother has made some fresh bread, and we cooked some beans and ham for you and the others," he said as he handed over the food that weighed down his arms.

"This is very kind of you," Sarah replied as she took the bread and motioned Osumaka to take the rest. "We will give it to the others."

"There is word that a Confederate battalion is camped not far east of here. I'm not certain where they are headed," the old man said.

"Yes, we saw them on our way here. We had to detour to avoid them," Sarah replied.

"Word is that a Union Army battalion is camped not far north of us. I'm told just a few miles away." The old man looked worried. "We are not in a good place if they decide to fight here."

"We will leave first thing at sunset," Sarah told him. "We appreciate your hospitality and will not overstay our welcome."

"Not at all," he said. "It is the least we can do for you. I am a Methodist, and my wife was born a Quaker. I am well aware of the evils of slavery and our moral obligations to oppose and end it. It's just that . . ."

"Yes?" Sarah asked.

"It's just that other churches use Scripture to justify slavery. It is so deeply woven into all parts of our society that I fear this region will never give it up, even if the Union holds."

"Well, I thank you for your help," Sarah said. "You are taking a great risk to help us, and I . . . we truly appreciate it."

MICHAEL JAY NUSBAUM

"It is the least that we can do," he replied. "If there is anything you need, just place this rake outside the door and lean it up against the barn so that we can see it. We will come out and get you whatever you need."

"Thank you again," Sarah said.

The old man left them and headed back to the house.

"Union soldiers just a few miles north!" Sarah exclaimed happily. "This is great news!"

"That is what he said," Osumaka replied.

"That is where we need to go. At the first signs of sunset, we need to head north and meet up with them," she said emphatically. "Let's get these people fed while we wait."

Hours went by until the telltale signs of dusk were upon them. The cicadas began their evening call, and the bullfrogs began their mating songs.

"Everyone, get ready. We will be leaving soon," Sarah told the others.

It wasn't long before it was time to leave. Quietly, they headed out of the barn, across the field, and back into the woods, with Sarah leading the way. She had been trained by Moses to read and navigate by the stars; unfortunately, this night was cloudy and overcast and she could only catch glimpses of the stars. They could all hear distant rumbling. Sarah stopped the group, and Osumaka walked up to the front of the line to speak with Sarah.

"What is it?" he asked quietly.

"I'm not sure. Those sounds seem to be thunder, but I've been fooled before. Distant cannon fire sounds much the same," she said. "If only Moses were here. God would tell her if it was rain or if battle were to break out nearby."

"How would your God tell her this?" Osumaka asked.

"God speaks to Moses every day," Sarah explained. "He tells her what she needs to know, and she follows His commands."

"How is this possible?" Osumaka was dubious.

"I do not know, but He does not speak to me," she noted regretfully, "and we need to know what to do right now."

They heard a loud crack nearby, and the air became turbulent and thick.

"I would say it is rain," Osumaka decided. "And very soon."

"We had best keep heading north," she replied. "The Union camp can't be much further ahead if the old man was right."

"I will find them," Osumaka told her.

Sarah motioned for him to scout ahead and the others to follow. She helped one of the women whom Osumaka had been helping during the journey.

It wasn't long before the rain began. It was a heavy, soaking rain, and the drops from the trees seemed extra large and painful when they struck. Their feet began to bog down in the mud as the ground soaked up the water. Puddles began to form in their path, and their progress slowed. Soon, Osumaka called to stop and for Sarah to come to the front of the line.

"What is it?" Sarah asked.

"A camp is nearby," Osumaka said.

"How can you tell? I can't see or hear anything," she told him.

"Smell," he said. "Smell." Osumaka was proud he had noticed something she had not.

Sarah took a deep breath. "Smoke."

"Yes. Smoke. A camp is nearby," Osumaka smiled. "I will go forward and scout it. If I do not return, head west before you head north again."

"Yes. Be careful," she warned him.

Osumaka continued stealthily through the woods. The smoke grew thicker, and he began to hear the sounds of many men. He had traveled much further from the group than he thought he would have had to.

"Halt! Who goes there?" a voice shouted.

Osumaka did not know what to do.

"Halt! Who goes there?" the voice repeated. "Announce yourself, or I will shoot!"

"A friend of a friend!" Osumaka shouted out. He had no choice and hoped the phrase he'd heard Sarah use would work with the soldiers as it had worked with the farmers.

"Friend? I have no friend! What is your name?"

"Osumaka! I am a friend of a friend!"

"That cannot be!" the voice replied. "Are you a slave?"

"No, no longer. I am a freeman now. I am a warrior," Osumaka replied.

"The only Osumaka warrior I know is long dead!" the voice replied. "Approach and be seen, or I will shoot."

MICHAEL JAY NUSBAUM

Osumaka stood up and headed slowly over to the voice.

"I am a friend of a friend," Osumaka kept repeating.

"Hands above your head where I can see them," the voice ordered.

The rain poured down upon the two men as the distance between them decreased. Osumaka was only a few feet from the barrel of the Union soldier's gun when he could make out the soldier's face.

"Bakude?" he asked. "Is that truly you?"

"Osumaka?" the soldier asked. "My eyes must be playing tricks on me."

"Bakude, my friend. You are not dead!" Osumaka exclaimed.

"Osumaka, my friend. Neither are you!" Bakude said as he lowered his rifle and embraced his long-lost friend.

"Bakude, it is so good to see you."

"And you, my friend. It has been so many years," Bakude replied.

"How are you a soldier?" Osumaka asked.

"I escaped some years ago. I have killed many white devils. It was not easy to make it to the North. I made it all the way to Canada where I lived for several years. When President Lincoln announced the war, he invited all free Negroes to join him. How could I turn down a chance to kill those men who had tortured and enslaved me?" Bakude said.

"And now you are a soldier for Mr. Lincoln," Osumaka said.

"And now I am a soldier for Mr. Lincoln, and he wants me to kill as many of the rebel slave-owning scum that I can," Bakude stated with a grin. "And I am happy to do so."

"I have eleven runaways with me," Osumaka said as he pointed in their direction. "Just back over there."

Bakude called out into the camp for help. Soon, four other black soldiers appeared.

"This man is a true warrior. He is a very old friend of mine, and he has eleven others with him," Bakude stated. "You stay here, keep watch. You three come with us to get the rest."

"It is good to see you, my old friend," Osumaka said as they headed back to the rest of the group with Sarah. "I thought for sure that they would kill you."

"No one can kill me, Osumaka," Bakude sneered. "I told you that many times before. They can beat me and torture me, but they cannot kill Bakude."

"Sarah!" Osumaka called. "Sarah!"

"Yes," her voice responded.

"It is the Union Army," he replied. "They are here to help us."

"Praise be the Lord," Sarah said fervently.

When they were closer, Bakude bowed. "A pleasure to make your acquaintance," Bakude said.

"Who is this?" she asked Osumaka.

"You would never believe it if I told you," Osumaka joked.

"Try me," she replied.

"Sarah, this is Bakude. He and I made the long and terrible journey across the great ocean together and were sent to the same seasoning camp," Osumaka explained. "We were chained together or close to each other many times."

"Too close, many times," Bakude replied, chuckling.

"You are right. I don't believe it. But I do believe that the Lord works in mysterious ways, so I guess it to be true enough," she told Osumaka.

"Can you take me to your commanding officer?" she asked Bakude.

"I can, but what would you want with him?" Bakude asked.

"I have valuable information on Confederate troop movements and encampments in the area and have a letter of introduction to give to him," she replied.

"Excellent! Let's get all of you out of this rain and into some shelter and warm, dry clothes," Bakude said.

They headed back to the camp. Bakude had another soldier take his watch as he brought them to the infirmary tent, the largest tent in the camp. The soldiers were all black.

"Everyone is Negro here?" Osumaka asked.

"Yes. We are a colored brigade, the First South Carolina Volunteers. The rebs fear us more than they do the Yanks." Bakude laughed out, and the other soldiers chuckled.

"Take me to your commanding officer," Sarah ordered.

"Yes, ma'am." Bakude saluted in jest. "Over this way." He pointed to the large tent to the left. To Osumaka, he whispered, "Where on God's earth did you find this one?"

Osumaka smiled tightly. "She found me."

Sarah, Osumaka, and Bakude approached the commanding officer's tent.

"Permission to enter!" Bakude barked at the two sentries guarding the front of the tent.

"Enter, Sergeant," the commander's voice called.

They all entered the tent behind Bakude.

"What can I do for you, Sergeant? And who are your friends?"

"Sir, these are runaways heading north. This woman has asked to speak with my commanding officer. She says she has a letter of introduction and information on rebel troop movements and encampment."

"Approach," the officer said.

Sarah walked to the desk and handed him the paper.

He read the letter. "Major General Hunter?" the commander said. "Well, young lady. He speaks very highly of you."

The officer stood and stretched out his right arm. "Col. James Montgomery of the Colored Brigade."

"It is a pleasure to meet you, Colonel," she replied. "I have eleven contrabands under my care, and I would appreciate it if you could feed and clothe them until the rain lets up and we can get back under way."

"Certainly," he agreed. "Sergeant, make sure that those under her care are well taken care of."

"Yes, sir!" Bakude replied.

"And you have some information regarding rebel troop movements?" Montgomery asked.

"I do," she replied.

The colonel walked her over to a map table. "Show me."

Sarah began to show the colonel where they had come across the rebel camp.

"You gentlemen are dismissed," he said to Bakude and Osumaka.

"Sir, yes, sir," Bakude replied as he tugged at Osumaka to leave the tent with him.

It was still raining hard, and puddles were everywhere. The soldiers tended to the fires to keep them burning.

"Let's get you into some dry clothing too, my friend," Bakude stated.

They walked down a muddy row of tents when Bakude stopped. "It's not home, but it's dry," Bakude said.

They knelt down into the tent. Bakude handed Osumaka a clean dry shirt.

"It is truly good to see you, my old friend," Bakude said.

"And you, my friend," Osumaka replied. "Tell me, how did you end up here?"

"I was not made for captivity." Bakude smiled grimly. "They had to whip me daily, and even then, I would not give in. I was sold a second time and escaped as soon as I reached my new master."

"After seeing you in Jamaica, strung up and still able to wink at me, I had no doubt that they wouldn't break you," Osumaka told Bakude as he took off his wet shirt and put on the dry one.

Bakude continued, "Then I headed north. Made my way through to Maryland where I met up with some abolitionists who got me into the Underground Railroad. Eventually, they brought me north to Canada."

"Sarah is with the Underground Railroad. She is taking us North," Osumaka replied.

"Yes, I see that. Much prettier than my conductor," he said with a laugh.

"So you were in Canada?" Osumaka prompted.

"Yes. Living there as a freeman. Canada abolished slavery many years ago, and many runaways made their way there," Bakude replied.

"Did you live there long?" Osumaka asked.

"I did. Several years," Bakude said solemnly. "I even took a wife."

"You. A wife." Osumaka chuckled.

"Yes. She was young and very pretty. She was born free and very well educated. I didn't speak but a few words of English when we first met. She taught me everything I know. We had a nice few years together," Bakude recalled.

"What happened?" Osumaka asked.

"She died in childbirth," Bakude said.

"I'm sorry, my friend. And the child?"

"He died as well," Bakude said. "So when word came through that Mr. Lincoln was making up all-colored brigades to fight the slavers, how could I say no?"

"I have no doubt that this is the place for you," Osumaka replied, clapping his friend on the shoulder. "No doubt at all."

"You should join us," Bakude offered. "You would be at home."

"I would, but I must find my family. This is a just fight, but it is not my fight. It is not my land, and this is not my home," Osumaka replied.

"That is true," Bakude said. "But a warrior like you would be very valuable to us."

"This is not my fight to fight," Osumaka repeated. "I do not care if one white man kills another or if the South hates the North. They are all white men to me, and this is not my land."

"Well, I had to ask, my friend," Bakude said.

"There you are!" Sarah exclaimed from the front of the tent. "I've been looking for you everywhere!"

"What is it?" Osumaka asked.

"There is a Union wagon train leaving for Maryland shortly. They are granting us passage in one of the wagons," she said.

"There are too many of us for one wagon," Osumaka noted.

"The other men are staying to fight. They are being sworn in and joining the brigade," she replied.

"See? I told you that you should join us," Bakude said to Osumaka.

"Will you join them too?" Sarah asked with a broken voice.

"No." Osumaka stood up and exited the tent. "No. I am continuing north with you and the rest."

"Well," Sarah said, relieved, "good then. Yes. Good. That is the right decision for you."

"Yes. That is the right decision for me," Osumaka agreed.

"Well, then I will meet you over at the wagons shortly," she replied as she clumsily turned and walked away, looking back several times at Osumaka.

"Is she your woman?" Bakude asked.

"Sarah?" Osumaka replied. "No. She is definitely not my woman. I have a wife and a son, and I will get back to them or die trying." Osumaka could not understand how Bakude could assume he would be unfaithful to Likana, especially moments after he had declared his intention to find her again.

"Well, you may not think that she is your woman, but I think that she may think so," Bakude replied with a loud chuckle. "Good luck with that one, my friend."

"Be safe, my friend," Osumaka said as he placed his arm on Bakude's shoulder.

"Don't worry, my old friend. They can't kill Bakude," he replied.

"Be safe, my friend," Osumaka said again as he turned and headed toward the wagons.

Bakude raised his arms and repeated his mantra. "Don't worry. They will never kill Bakude!"

Osumaka waved back to him as he continued toward the covered wagons. He could see Sarah and some soldiers helping the others into the wagon.

"So are you sure that you do not want to stay and fight?" Sarah asked.

"This is not my fight. My fight is to get home to my family," Osumaka said. "I will continue on with you."

"Good," she replied, smiling. "I need your help with these six."

"Miss Sarah!" A voice called out. It was the colonel. "I have a letter of transit for you. This should help you on your journey North."

Sarah opened the letter and read it aloud, "Brig. Gen. Gilman. General: I wish to commend to your attention Ms. Sarah Freeman, a most remarkable woman who has made herself available to the Union through her scouting of Confederate troop movements. She is a woman of courage and is highly useful. She is returning with seven refugees to the North for whom she remains responsible. I am, General, your most obedient servant. Col. James Montgomery, Cmdr., 1st SC Volunteers."

Sarah stared at the letter for a moment then looked up. "Thank you, Colonel."

"You are very welcome, Ms. Sarah," he replied. "God be with you."

"And with you," she replied as she loaded up the wagon and motioned for Osumaka to take his place beside her.

MICHAEL JAY NUSBAUM

CHAPTER 18

Journey North

THEY JOURNEYED NORTH under the protection of the Union Army. There were many stops, and the journey was arduous. Word came to them that Harriet Tubman was staying in Frederick Douglass's home in Rochester, New York. So they headed up to Rochester. Their arrival would be somewhat unexpected, as they were unable to get word to Harriet that they were on their way to see her.

The day was pleasant, and the weather was ideal for travel. It was now late spring, and cherry trees were blooming. There were beautiful wildflowers on either side of the road, and a light breeze carried the smell of trees and flowers alike. Sarah and Osumaka were now on their own and no longer under the protection of the Union Army. They parted from their escort in Maryland and acquired a horse and buggy from a Quaker family in Maryland who had helped both Sarah and Harriet many times in the past.

"I am once again in your debt, Miss Rachel," Sarah said to the kind woman as she handed over the horse and carriage to them.

"It is through acts of charity that God's work is revealed to us, my dear. Just bring her back when you are done with her," Rachel replied.

"I will, Miss Rachel," Sarah responded.

Osumaka held out his hand to help Sarah up. She looked at him oddly and prepared to climb up completely on her own. She grabbed the door handle with her left hand and placed a foot upon the step board. Before she stepped up, she looked at Osumaka once again. His gaze mesmerized her. The sun caught his hair and made his head seem to glow. Suddenly, she found her right hand moving on its own to meet his. Osumaka smiled as he held her hand and helped her into the carriage.

"Where are you headed, my dear?" Ms. Rachel asked.

"We are headed up to Rochester, New York, to meet with Miss Harriet. She is staying with Mr. Frederick Douglass for a while. We hope to meet her there before she moves on," Sarah said as she grabbed the reins.

Osumaka climbed up next to her and took a seat.

"Oh, the thought of the two of them together warms my heart. Such powerful spirits joining forces. The Lord is certainly a wonderful father to us all," Rachel proclaimed.

"Yes, ma'am," Sarah replied. "Thank you again."

"Godspeed on your journey, my child," Rachel called as Sarah flicked the reins and headed off.

"Have you known her long?" asked Osumaka.

"Miss Rachel?" Sarah asked.

"Yes. Miss Rachel."

"I have," she replied. "Miss Rachel and most of the Quakers are very sympathetic to our plight. They have been most active in the Underground Railroad as well as supporting the antislavery movement in general."

"She seems like a lovely woman," he replied.

Sarah looked at him, smiled, and looked back at the road. "Yes. Yes, she is a lovely woman."

They continued to travel north, through New Jersey, on their way to Rochester.

The roads were windy and beautiful, with thick forests seemingly everywhere. One section of their journey took them through a dense pine forest. As they headed further north, the flatlands that they had enjoyed were now replaced by gently rolling hills.

"I meant to compliment you," Sarah stated.

"On what?" Osumaka replied.

"I have yet to meet a slave . . ." she began then stopped herself. "I mean, I have yet to meet a person who has escaped slavery who speaks English so eloquently."

Osumaka smiled at her self-correction. "It was through the kindness of a woman I met while I was held on the plantation."

"Please tell me of her," Sarah said.

"Well, she was actually born a free woman and was raised to be a teacher. For several years, she taught children in a small schoolhouse, probably not far from here."

"In New Jersey?" Sarah asked, surprised.

"Yes, right here in New Jersey. It was a small schoolhouse for Negro children, and she taught there for five years."

"I don't understand. How did she end up on the plantation?" Sarah asked.

"She was abducted by bounty hunters and brought to the South. She told them that she was a free woman and begged them to ask anyone. They refused to listen to her pleas. They bound her and brought her to a slave trading post where they auctioned her off. She told me that she continued to protest her enslavement and even tried to show her new masters that she could both read and write. This only served to anger them. They repeatedly beat her and told her that if she did not stop with her lies that they would have cut her tongue out."

"My God!" Sarah exclaimed. "That happens way too often, ever since that fugitive slave act was passed. They may as well have just sent all of the free Negroes to the South as slaves."

"She was also told that if she ever tried to read a book or if she were caught writing, that she would be beaten. They beat her so many times that eventually, they decided to sell her. She was then sold to my master as a house servant. Her previous masters never told my master of all the trouble she caused. When he asked about all the whip marks on her back, they told him that she came to them with those. So my master took her in and made her a house slave. He never knew that she could read or write better than he could."

"What did she do?" Sarah asked.

"She decided to teach some of us English. At night, she would sneak into our bunkhouse, and she would hold class. We would pour extra dirt on to the floor and learn by scratching letters into the dirt with sticks. Soon, we were learning words and full sentences."

"Did anyone ever suspect? I mean that you must have been able to speak better than when you first arrived? That must have given you away."

"No. She warned us not to change our ways in front of our masters or the overseers. We were to speak 'ignant' and never show them how smart we really were."

"Did she do the same?" Sarah asked.

"She did. She also taught us what she called slave speak."

"What's that?" she asked.

"That is how the masters expect us to speak," Osumaka replied.

"Yes, I understand. I know what you mean," Sarah said.

"Eventually, she would steal books for us, and we would read them out loud to one another," Osumaka said as the memories were clearly weighing upon him. "I remember the first book she brought to us. It was a copy of a farmer's guide. She said it was the easiest book to get, as the master would throw many of them away at the end of each planting year."

"I've seen many of those. I could see how they would be easy for her to get and easy for the master not to miss," Sarah said. She changed the subject. "We should make it north of Trenton by tonight. We'd best plan on finding a station for the night. There are dozens of routes for the Underground Railroad here in New Jersey. I have taken almost all of them myself at one time or another."

"Where will we stay?" Osumaka asked.

"We should arrive at the Aaron Hudson house just before sundown," she replied.

"Where is that?" he asked.

"It's in a town called Mendham. The house is just down the road from the Black Horse Inn off a road called Hilltop. I've brought quite a few passengers there before. They should be able to help us."

"It would be nice to get some rest," Osumaka replied.

This area was wooded too but with open rolling hills filled with crops. Osumaka marveled over the beauty of the landscape. He was used to seeing open flat fields, but these were different. These fields were undulated.

They arrived at the home just before sundown as Sarah had predicted. As they approached, a woman came to the door with a lantern.

"Who is that?" the woman called.

"It is Sarah, Mrs. Hudson!" Sarah called out.

"Oh, Sarah, my dear. It's been too long," she said as she came out to meet them.

The house was large; it had four large columns, a large triangular pediment above those, and everything was painted white.

"Sarah, how are you?" Mrs. Hudson asked.

"I am well. Thank you, Mrs. Hudson," Sarah replied. "This is my friend Osumaka. He and I are traveling to Rochester to meet Miss Harriet."

"Oh my!" Mrs. Hudson exclaimed. "What a long journey. You must be starving."

"We are, and we were hoping that we could stay the night. We will be continuing on at sunbreak," Sarah said.

"Of course, my dear. Why don't you and your friend come in? You can tie up your horse here, and let him get some fresh water," she said.

Sarah led the horse to the trough and tied him up then worked the pump to fill the trough.

"Come, come. It is so good to have guests," Mrs. Hudson told them warmly.

"Where is Mr. Hudson?" Sarah asked.

"He's at the Black Horse Inn right now," she said. "He's always there. All the men meet there and talk politics and business and all those things that men talk about."

"Follow me," she said as she led them to the kitchen. "Please sit. Sit here."

There was a small table with two chairs in the kitchen. Mrs. Hudson poured some drinks and began to lay food out for them.

"Thank you for your hospitality," Osumaka said.

"It is my pleasure," Mrs. Hudson replied.

When they were done, Sarah helped clean up, while Osumaka finished his tea.

"Well, this is quite different from your normal visits. Normally, you have quite the group with you," Mrs. Hudson said. "I'm not sure where you'd like to stay then."

"We can stay in the usual place," Sarah stated. "Please don't put yourself out on our account."

Mrs. Hudson seemed relieved.

"We do appreciate all that you do for us," Sarah stated.

"Why, thank you, Sarah. Here are some blankets and a lantern. The rest is in there. You know where the secret passage is located."

"Yes. Thank you again, Mrs. Hudson," Sarah said.

"My pleasure. Good night, Sarah, Osumaka."

"Good night, Mrs. Hudson," Sarah responded.

"Where are we staying?" asked Osumaka.

"I think that she thought that we might want one of her rooms. I did not want to impose, so we will stay in their secret room that we use for the underground. It is just over here."

"I see. Where is it?"

Sarah pushed a bookcase to reveal a door. She opened the door and motioned for Osumaka to follow. She then pulled the bookcase back and closed the door behind them.

"This is not a very large room," Osumaka stated.

"No. No, it is not. Sometimes, we have had as many as ten in here," she replied.

"They must have slept on top of one another then," Osumaka guessed.

There was one cot in the room, but there were piles of blankets to lie on. The room also had a small oval mirrored vanity with a bowl and a pitcher of water.

"You should take the bed. I will sleep here on the floor," Osumaka stated.

"Why don't we wash up first? Then we can sleep," Sarah replied. She took off her long coat and pulled out the pins holding her hair up. Her hair unraveled into a long train that hung to the middle of her back. She then took off the two holsters holding the revolvers that she hid under her coat. Osumaka watched her as she relieved herself of the layers she carried.

"Have you ever had to use those other than when you killed those men and let the boy go?" Osumaka asked.

Sarah stopped and looked at him. "Yes. Far too many times."

She unbuttoned her shirt to reveal her undergarments. Osumaka looked away.

"Perhaps I should step out and give you some privacy," he said nervously.

"No, no need. I'm not ashamed," Sarah said.

"All the same, I will just turn and face away until you're done."

She then unbuckled her belt and removed the heavy trousers. Osumaka could not help but glance over. Her arms and legs were long and muscular. Osumaka thought her torso could be that of a man but for her breasts, which were also strong and firm.

She washed herself in the basin with a towel that hung over the rack to the left of the vanity. Osumaka could not help but catch the occasional glance of the water glistening on her skin, the long hair, and the curves of her body. He tried to think of something to say to break the silence of the moment, but his mind was blank.

"It is all yours," she said as she finished up and got into bed.

Osumaka got up and went over to the basin. He could smell her scent in the water. First, he washed his face to remove the dirt, and then he removed his shirt as well. He took the other clean towel and wet it. Then he washed off his neck and chest. Sarah made no pretense of not looking at Osumaka. His body was very muscular and well-defined. The water shone off his chest, and she looked away. Soon, she could hear splashing.

"What are you doing?" she asked.

"I'm cleaning my shirt," he said.

"Oh. Well, don't use up all the water."

"Don't worry, I'm using the dirty water. It's still cleaner than my shirt is," Osumaka assured her.

"Oh. Right. Well, let's get some sleep," she replied.

"I am finished," he said, hanging his shirt to dry.

Osumaka laid out a blanket on the floor and then lay upon it.

"Good night, Osumaka," she said as she turned down the lantern.

"Good night, Sarah," Osumaka replied.

A few hours later, Osumaka felt a hand upon his chest. He was dreaming of his village, and in the dream, he was lying with his wife. He slowly woke, feeling that the dream was real. Sarah had lain next to him and was caressing him.

"Likana?" Osumaka managed before her lips met his.

His eyes remained closed as he responded with a deep passionate kiss and put his left arm on her shoulder. She then moved over on top of him, kissing him even more deeply. She placed his right hand upon her left hip. He could feel that she was naked under the long shirt that she was wearing. He slid his hand up her side, feeling her body until he reached her shoulder. Sarah responded as he took his strong arms and wrapped them around her. Her hips moved rhythmically on top of him. He rolled her off of him and to his left side. Now they lay facing and still kissing each other deeply. Osumaka took his right hand and slid it under her clothing again. This time, he ran it up the left side of her body and moving it forward to her breasts. He ran his hands over them, gently caressing each mound. Then he moved his hand slowly down her body until it reached between her legs. She responded with a deep, happy sigh then put her hand on his right hip and began to move it between his legs. She could feel that he was fully aroused by her. Her passion deepened as she quivered with each movement of Osumaka's hand between her legs. She struggled to get his trousers off but couldn't focus as the motions of his hand between her legs caused her to roll over and arch her back. Osumaka continued to touch her in places and ways that she had not felt in many years. Her mind wandered, and then she just focused on the pleasure that Osumaka was giving her. Her hips moved wildly in sync with his hand. Waves of pleasure ran up her spine as her muscles tightened. She let out a loud moan of pleasure and then felt her abdominal muscles contract, her toes pointed downward, and her legs began to quiver until the pleasure in her body reached a climax. Her body continued to shake, even though his hand was no longer stimulating her. Her muscles felt weak as the waves of stimulation slowly left her body. Now she wanted him even more. She rolled back on top of Osumaka. He was fully aroused, and the only thing separating them was the thin cotton of his trousers. She began to work them off, but she noticed that Osumaka's eyes were closed. Finally, having taken off his clothing, she lifted her leg to straddle him.

He held her face and looked into her eyes. "I can't," he told her. "I'm sorry."

She looked into his eyes and asked, a little hurt, "What's wrong?"

"I'm sorry. I shouldn't have . . . I know that my wife and child are alive now. My sole purpose is to find them and be with them again," he said regretfully.

"But you are with me. Here. Now." Sarah could not believe Osumaka had stopped—she could still feel his arousal. But his face was solemn.

"I know. You are very beautiful, and it has been many years since I have been with a woman. But I cannot. I am so sorry."

Her eyes welled up with tears, her body stiffened over his. "I'm sorry. I was wrong."

"No. No! I feel the same about you. You are strong and beautiful, smart and loving. Once that captain told me that my wife and son were still alive, I have not been able to think of anything but our reunion," he said softly.

"I was wrong. I should never have assumed," she said, ashamed, as she crawled back to her side of the cot.

"I'm sorry, Sarah. So very sorry," Osumaka apologized.

He could hear her sobbing quietly, and it pained him to have hurt her. But all his dreams were of his wife and his son.

When Osumaka awoke, Sarah was gone. He quickly dressed and headed out to find her. Sarah was already hitching the horse to the carriage. Osumaka stumbled out into the morning sun, still tucking in his shirt.

"We have to leave right away," Sarah said as she tossed him a piece of bread. "Eat this, and let's get going."

Osumaka ate the bread and got in the carriage. Sarah hopped up and then snapped the reins. They did not speak again until they reached Rochester two days later.

They arrived at Frederick Douglass's house midday. The town was bustling, and his home was on a well-traveled road. Since Sarah had never been there, they had to stop several times for directions.

Sarah pulled the carriage up to the house, jumped off, and tied up the horse.

"Sarah, we need to talk," Osumaka tried as he climbed down from the carriage.

"There is nothing to talk about," Sarah said stiffly. "We are here."

She went to the door and knocked. A short woman opened the door and greeted her.

"Sarah!" the woman exclaimed.

"Miss Harriet," she replied.

"Miss Harriet?" Osumaka said quietly. "Our Miss Harriet?"

"Who's this?" asked Harriet. "A parrot?"

Sarah laughed. "No, this is Osumaka. We have so much to tell you about."

"What be your story?" asked Harriet.

"I'm sorry. I just imagined you much larger," he replied.

"What? You thinks a small woman's no match fo' sum big runaway likes you?" she replied as she turned her back and shook her fist at him.

Sarah laughed and put her arm around her as they turned and walked into the house. Osumaka didn't know what to do. He had clearly upset both of them and was uncertain if he even dared enter the house.

Soon, a man appeared at the door. He was well-dressed like a barrister. His wild graying mane of hair, mustache, and beard contrasted with his dark skin. "You're not going to just stand out there, are you?" asked the man.

"I'm not sure. I've upset them both," Osumaka replied.

"I'm certain that won't be the last time you upset them," the man replied with an arched eyebrow as he walked over to Osumaka with his right hand extended.

Osumaka stepped over to meet him. "I am Osumaka."

"Osumaka. I am Frederick Douglass," the man introduced himself.

"It is an honor to finally meet you, sir," Osumaka said with a smile.

"Why do you smile?" Frederick asked.

"Well, you are more like what I expected, and Miss Harriet, well . . ."

"She is not what you expected?" he asked.

"No. Not at all. I mean, if you look at Sarah, and then you look at her."

"She is small and fragile-looking?" Frederick asked.

"Well, yes. I expected her to be much larger," Osumaka explained.

"Well, her personality is much larger than life, but don't let her small frame ever fool you. And though she be but little, she is fierce!" Frederick replied. "Come on in. I'll help you patch things up with them. After all, that's what I do best."

Osumaka and Frederick walked into the house then over to the parlor. Harriet and Sarah were already seated and talking up a storm. Sarah was telling Harriet of their encounter with the rebels and then with the Union Army.

"You should have seen it, Miss Harriet. We gave them the camp location, positions for their cannons, where their supply tents were, where their scouts were heading. It was glorious!" Sarah exclaimed.

"That sounds just wonderful," Harriet replied.

"I was thinking, you need to come back South with us. With all the people you know, we can get information to the Union Army from so many," Sarah said.

"You means for me to be a spy?" Harriet asked.

"Why yes!" Frederick exclaimed. "That's an incredible idea. You could organize free blacks and slaves to report on the movements of the rebels, and then you can get that information back to the Union

MICHAEL JAY NUSBAUM

generals. It would be a massive spy ring. The rebels wouldn't be able to go anywhere without your network finding out, Harriet."

"Spy?" Harriet repeated.

"We could help you," Sarah replied. "Osumaka and I. We could help you."

"Yes!" Harriet exclaimed.

Sarah looked at Osumaka and then turned to Harriet. "Don't you think that we need to do something?"

"But I be a cook, and I does de laundry, and I even does nursing," Harriet replied. "Ain't that e'nuf?"

"But, Miss Harriet, we could do so much more," Sarah replied.

Frederick took a seat. "You know, Harriet, they have a fine idea. This war is very much about slavery. If the Union wins, then our hope for a free black people, for slaves, and for this nation could be realized. I believe that these United States will never be truly free until all of its people are free. If the South prevails, then I fear for our future."

"But spies," Harriet said again. "I'm guessin' we could. Spies. I need de Lord to help me. Lets me confer wid de Lord first."

"I have a meeting set with Mr. Lincoln soon," Frederick said.

"You have a meeting with the president?" asked Sarah.

"I do. In August," he replied. "I have written to him many times, and he has replied to each and every letter. I have beseeched him to provide equal pay to black soldiers. I would be happy to also tell him of what you all have planned. Perhaps he can provide some help. Clearly, a network of black spies across the South would be immensely important to the success of their struggle."

Suddenly, Harriet shouted out, "A'mighty's far-seein' eye'll find you an' deff'll come after you."

"What does that mean?" Osumaka asked.

"Miss Harriet," Sarah asked, "what do you mean?"

"De Lord jus spokn' to me. We be his far-seein' eye," she replied.

"So we'll do it?" Sarah asked.

"Yes," Harriet replied. "We be de' A'mighty's far-seein' eyes."

"Wonderful!" Frederick exclaimed. "That's just wonderful. I think it is an outstanding idea."

"I'm not sure," Osumaka replied. "Don't they hang spies?"

"Oh, Osumaka," Sarah retorted.

"I'm just saying, the white men are fighting other white men. Why should we get involved?" Osumaka replied. "It's not our fight to fight."

"Young man, you could not be more wrong," Frederick replied sternly. "This is a fight not only for freedom for our people but also to reform the injustices that have been going on for years."

"They will never reform their ways," Osumaka retorted.

With that, Frederick Douglass rose from his seat, straightened his back, and proclaimed, "Let me give you a word of the philosophy of reform. The whole history of the progress of human liberty shows that all concessions yet made to her august claims have been born of earnest struggle. The conflict has been exciting, agitating, all-absorbing, and for the time being, putting all other tumults to silence. It must do this, or it does nothing. If there is no struggle, there is no progress. Those who profess to favor freedom and yet depreciate agitation are men who want crops without plowing up the ground. They want rain without thunder and lightning. They want the ocean without the awful roar of its many waters.

"This struggle may be a moral one, or it may be a physical one, and it may be both moral and physical, but it must be a struggle. Power concedes nothing without a demand. It never did, and it never will. Find out just what any people will quietly submit to, and you have found out the exact measure of injustice and wrong that will be imposed upon them, and these will continue till they are resisted with either words or blows or with both. The limits of tyrants are prescribed by the endurance of those whom they oppress. In the light of these ideas, Negroes will be hunted at the North, and held and flogged at the South so long as they submit to those devilish outrages, and make no resistance, either moral or physical. Men may not get all they pay for in this world, but they must certainly pay for all they get. If we ever get free from the oppressions and wrongs heaped upon us, we must pay for their removal. We must do this by labor, by suffering, by sacrifice, and if needs be, by our lives and the lives of others."

"I agree with all you have said, but this is my point," Osumaka replied. "This has been going on for years, and it will not stop just because they are fighting with one another. They don't care about us."

"I cannot speak for every man. Each must fight his fight for his own reasons, but I can tell you that this is a just war, a war of honor and justice that has pitted brother against brother," Mr. Douglass stated.

"Each and every one of us has a stake in this, and each of us will be affected by the direction this country takes when this war is over. It is time for our community to organize in defense of the idea that all men are equal. All of us, regardless of how long we have been here or where we came from in Africa, need to help shape our future here in America."

"But I will not be here when this war is over! This is not my land. These are not my people. I did not come here of my free will. I was taken, taken not by the white man but by other Africans and sold into slavery to the white man. I care not of these people. I only wish to return to my home and to be with my wife and my son. It is different for those of you who were born here. You may view this as your home and a home you wish to fight for, to be free in. But this is not my home. This is not my fight."

"It is true that many of us were born here. Some were born free and others born into slavery. Some were born to free parents, others born to slaves. It is not productive to dwell upon the past in hopes that the future will change for the better on its own. We must be proactive and help guide the future into one that is just and fair for all," Frederick explained.

"I don't know." Osumaka shook his head. "I don't know." He sat down on the chair behind him.

"We gonna do dis!" shouted Harriet. "De Lord says so to me."

"Osumaka, just remember this: Without struggle there can be no success," Frederick spoke calmly.

Osumaka looked at Sarah.

"We can do it together," Sarah said to Osumaka. "We need your help."

Osumaka looked at Frederick. "I will help, but when this war is over and the North has won, I will go home to find my wife and son."

"And I will help you do that," Frederick replied.

"So you are with us?" asked Sarah.

"I am. I will help you," Osumaka replied.

Just then, a young couple walked into the room. Both appeared to be in their twenties.

"Ah, Rosetta!" Frederick exclaimed as he jumped to his feet. "Nathaniel."

Osumaka stood as Sarah also rose to greet their guests.

"May I introduce my daughter Rosetta and her new husband Nathaniel Sprague," Frederick said.

"It is a pleasure to meet you," Osumaka said as he shook both of their hands.

"A true pleasure," Sarah said as she shook their hands as well.

"What a bute of a couple!" exclaimed Harriet. "Lord be wid you two."

"We'd best be leaving," Sarah said.

"You should stay and be our guests for the evening. Rosetta is a fine cook," Frederick suggested.

"Then we will leave for Hilton Head first thing tomorrow after we enjoy your most generous hospitality. Miss Moses, we will set up your headquarters there," Sarah stated.

"We gonna get de word out and end dis war," Mrs. Tubman replied. "We best go see my friends in O' Camp Saxton b' fo we be goin' to Hilton Head."

"Yes, Miss Moses. We will go to Camp Saxton first," Sarah replied.

"Yes'm, but fo we go, we gonna patake in dis yun womens fine cook'n, and I gonna given you a han," Harriet said as she jumped to her feet.

"Lovely. Just lovely," Frederick said as he put his hands together and rubbed them in anticipation.

"Miss Harriet is a wonderful cook, known far and wide," Sarah said.

"Yes, she is," Mr. Douglass replied. "Yes, indeed, she is. Perhaps you can teach Rosetta a few of your recipes too, Harriet."

"Yes, indeed," Harriet said, putting her arm around Rosetta. Then she announced, "Now yuz n' I gonna wips up sum magic," Harriet announced. "Come on, Sarah, yuz gonna help."

The women left the room. Frederick motioned for Osumaka and his son-in-law to take a seat.

"I guess it's left to us to talk," Frederick said.

"I've been working with the community here in Rochester very closely," Nathaniel began.

"That is wonderful," Frederick replied.

"Community?" asked Osumaka. "What community?"

"I see," said Frederick. "Coming from the South and from slavery, I can see how you would feel very much alone in this world."

"Well, yes," Osumaka replied.

"When Nathaniel talks about community, he is talking about the Negro community in social, political, economic, and religious terms.

You see, Osumaka, we share a common destiny that binds us together. Racial injustice exists even for those of us who are free. By organizing our communities, we can sustain ourselves even in the face of oppression and injustice," Frederick replied.

"But why would you want to stay in such a place?" Osumaka asked.

"That is a very good question. Is this our home? Many of us can count back generations, some as far as eight generations, of being in this land. I can see how you would not feel connected to this place and thus feel like you need to return home," Frederick replied. "But this is the dichotomy that our community faces. What is our identity? Is it an African identity or an American identity? Some, within our own community, fear that we could lose our African identity if we assimilate into this culture. This is not a unique problem for our people. Many other minority groups have faced the same issues of assimilation within our American society."

"But, sir, Mr. Douglass, this is a society of integration. I have many friends who call this nation a mixture of cultures. Those who do not integrate and stand out are shunned," Nathaniel said.

"That is true. There are other cultures, other groups, both ethnic and religious, who have the same splits within their own communities. Some advocate maintaining traditions that separate them from the rest of American society, while others prefer to integrate into American culture. Our situation is unique, however, in that racial hatred and slavery heighten the challenges to our people," Frederick replied.

"Mr. Douglass, sir, can't we integrate and yet still maintain our own identity and African heritage?" Nathaniel asked.

"Nathan, certainly," Frederick replied. "That is not up to me to decide. It is up to our community."

"In a nation of liberty and equality, isn't it up to us? Isn't it up to us to decide and to seek liberty and equality for all?" Nathaniel asked.

"Young man, that is the question," Frederick replied. "However, the desire for liberty and equality is always strongest to those who are denied of it. It is assumed to be fact to those who have known nothing else. For some of us, like Osumaka here, it is hard to believe that it even exists. Community is the foundation for activism among African Americans who seek liberty from a slaveholding society that degrades our status as human beings. It is only through a strong, organized, African community can we effect positive change and thus liberty and equality for all."

CHAPTER 19

Port Royal

June 1, 1863, Port Royal, South Carolina

Traveling to Camp Saxton

"**I** T IS GOOD to be back," Harriet said with a sigh. There wasn't much in Camp Saxton; it was just the old Smith Plantation. The camp was headquarter for the First South Carolina Volunteers, with the exception of several buildings and a sea of tents; it wasn't much of a sight.

"I wonder if Bakude is here," said Osumaka.

"I'm sure he is," replied Sarah. "It looks like the entire first is here."

Noises of soldiers being drilled, blacksmiths hammering their wares, and the horses' hooves clacking filled the air, there was a hustle about the place, and preparation pervaded the air.

"You wait here, Miss Moses, and I'll see what is going on," Sarah said. "Osumaka, you stay here and look after Moses."

"I will," Osumaka agreed.

"It is so good to see our people dressed in Union uniforms," Harriet said. "They look so regal. My heart is warmed by this sight. We have come so far, yet we have so far to go."

"Moses," Sarah called, "General Hunter wishes to speak with you."

"De General calls, and I come," she replied in good humor.

They headed over to the general's headquarters in the open carriage. The camp was buzzing with troops. Osumaka and Sarah remained by Harriet Tubman's side. They stayed close, and she kept them next to her.

"We're here," Sarah said. "Let me help you down, Miss Moses."

"Now you let me be. De Lord takes keer of me, an' den, He ready to take me den it be my time," Harriet said. "I may be an old woman, but I still got kick in me."

Osumaka stood close to her to make certain that she did not fall while getting down from the carriage. Over time, his respect for her had grown. He was constantly amazed by her sharp wit, keen intellect, and unending drive.

"Les go," she said as she pointed to the general's headquarters.

"Mrs. Harriet Tubman to see you, General," the aide announced.

"Yes. Of course. Send her in!" he exclaimed.

"Genral Hunter," Harriet said as she reached out to shake his outstretched hand. "What can we do for you?"

"Well, I need to ask a favor of you. We have several gunboats that will be heading up the Combahee River. The object of the mission is to take up the torpedoes placed by the rebels in the river and to destroy some railroads and bridges. This will help us cut off supplies that are heading to the rebels," he said as he pointed to the seat and motioned for her to sit. He then headed to the front of his desk and leaned against it directly in front of her. "I won't lie to you. This will be a very dangerous mission."

"Well," she said as she paused to think. "I only go if Colonel Montgomery is to be de one to command de exp'dition. He one John Brown men, I'd known him for man' years, and I trust him."

"Well, then it's agreed. I will assign Colonel Montgomery to command the expedition. Any other requests?"

"Yes, sir, Genral Hunter," she said. "Sarah and Osumaka here will be join'n me. I ask too dat J. Plowden join'n me."

"Yes, ma'am," General Hunter replied. "We will make those accommodations for you."

"Jus one mo ting," she said. "I be getting de word out to all in des parts. Dey be passin' on de word o' where ol reb be a hidin' backs to me."

"That would be wonderful," he replied. "We are sorely in need of up-to-date reconnaissance of the enemy. If you could do that, it would be a tremendous help for the Union."

"Wells, as you a knowin', I be tottly behin the Union. Iz gonna get you dat information," she said with a large smile.

"Thank you. Thank you, Harriet," the general said enthusiastically.

"Why, thank you, Genral. Happy to help," she replied.

"Sergeant, take Mrs. Tubman and the rest of her party to the staging point. We need their help as scouts for the expedition. Also, give Mrs. Tubman whatever she needs to get the word out through her network. If she can help us find out what ol' Johnny Reb is up to, who knows how many Union lives she could save?"

"Sir, yes, sir," the sergeant responded.

"Thank you, General Hunter," Sarah said as they turned to follow the sergeant.

"Thank you. She is a remarkable woman!" the general replied.

"Yes, she is," Sarah said as she walked away.

They headed over to the military wagons, waiting to take them to the port. Osumaka helped Harriet onto the wagon and then extended a hand to Sarah. She looked at him reluctantly but took hold of his hand and lifted herself into the wagon. Osumaka followed behind.

"Why don't you sit up with the soldier who is driving us there?" Sarah asked Osumaka before he could get into the wagon.

"Good idea," he said as he worked his way up to the front. "Is it all right?" he asked the soldier as he pointed to the seat.

"You can sit on the right side. The left side is for the driver," the soldier said.

"Why is that?" Osumaka asked.

"Well, see that large brake back there on the left of the wagon?" he said.

Osumaka leaned over to look. He could see a large brake lever next to a seat where another soldier sat. "Yes."

"That's the brakeman. He stops the wagon when we need to stop and slows us down if we are going too fast. If I were on the right where you should be sitting, I wouldn't be able to communicate with him."

"I see," said Osumaka.

"Someday, all wagons will have the driver's seated only on the left. Sit there and put your feet on the dashboard," the soldier instructed.

"What's the dashboard?" Osumaka asked.

"See this board that is angled up, right there by your feet?" he asked, pointing.

"Yes," Osumaka replied.

"That's the dashboard. It will keep all the dirt from flying up in our faces, and it's the perfect place to keep your feet and your balance," the soldier explained.

"I see. Good to know," Osumaka replied. "How far are we going?"

"It's not far from here to Port Royal," the soldier replied.

"How long will it take us to get there?" Osumaka asked.

"I don't know exactly but close," the African American soldier replied.

When they arrived at the port, there were boats of all sizes. The Stars and Stripes flew everywhere. There was such activity as Osumaka had never seen before. Soon, he began to have flashbacks to his arrival at the port for his auction. He hopped off of the wagon as soon as it stopped, but he still felt dizzy. Sarah saw this, jumped off the wagon, and ran to his side.

"Osumaka, what is wrong?" she asked.

His head was spinning, but he didn't know why. "I do not know. I feel."

She placed her hand on his shoulder and pulled him to her. He wrapped his arms around her to steady himself and her around him. Soon, things stopped spinning, and he regained his composure.

"I am all right now," he said. "Thank you."

She leaned back and looked at him. "Are you certain?"

"Yes. I am fine now. Thank you," Osumaka said as he released his arms and waited for her to release him as well. "I am fine."

"Right," she said as she released her arms. "You are fine now."

"Yes. Fine," he repeated. "Let us help Miss Moses."

"Right." Sarah broke her gaze from Osumaka, and they walked to the back of the wagon.

"Let us help you, Miss Harriet," Sarah said as they helped her down.

"De Lord sure has put a great many men to freeing us," Tubman commented. "We mus mak'n sure dat de win dis war."

"Yes, ma'am. We will," Osumaka promised.

"Your boats are over here," the soldier told them as he walked them to the waiting gunboats.

"These boats aren't very big," Sarah said.

"They are gunboats meant to head upriver. The Combahee River isn't deep enough in many places for larger boats, and we need to get up to the railway and the bridge. These will take us there," he said.

"I hope they are strong enough," Osumaka said as he looked at them.

"This is Captain Kaplan. He will be on the lead boat with Colonel Montgomery. I suggest that Mrs. Tubman be on that boat as well."

"Then we, the three of us, will be on that boat, as we do not leave her side," Sarah said.

"Yes, ma'am," the soldier replied. "As you wish."

"We do," she replied.

"Permission to come on board!" the soldier asked.

Montgomery heard the call and came out to greet them. "Moses!" he exclaimed. "So good to see you."

"Montgomery! 'Tis always a good day when you be there," Tubman replied.

"We need your help, Araminta. You know the land we are going to, and you can help us with the Negroes whom we encounter on our journey upriver," Montgomery said.

"Why you need my help?" she asked.

"Well, when our gunboats travel up the waterways, many of the Negroes who see us shout 'de Yankee Buckra' and flee. We need them to know that we are their friends and that we are there to help them."

"Why does he call her Araminta?" Osumaka asked Sarah quietly.

"Her given name is actually Araminta Ross. She's called by her married name of Tubman, and at some point, she changed Araminta to the more Christian-sounding name of Harriet. She is the granddaughter of an African forced into slavery like you," Sarah told Osumaka.

"What can we do to help them?" Sarah asked the colonel.

"Well, they can provide us with information on our way upriver," he explained.

"And why should they do that?" asked Osumaka.

"Pardon me," Harriet said to Colonel Montgomery, "these are my friends, Sarah and Osumaka."

"Pleased to make your acquaintance," he replied. To Osumaka, he said, "I'm certain that your question is a fair one. On our way back from our mission, we can take on as many refugees from the banks as our boats can hold. We can ferry them up North to safety."

"Do they know this?" Sarah asked.

"No. It is almost impossible to win their confidence or to get information from them. But with Harriet along, we'll have no trouble— they will tell her anything and everything. She can then spread the word that upon our return, we will take them to safety," Montgomery said.

"Well, that sounds like a fair exchange," Sarah replied. "When do we leave?"

"First thing in the morning. We will head out just before sunrise," he replied. "In the meantime, we need to get our ships ready for the mission."

"Why is Moses so taken with this Captain Brown that she trusts anyone who served with him?" asked Osumaka.

"Her admiration and respect for Capt. John Brown has always been deep. After he was killed, her views of him have taken on a more religious tone. You must understand. She has no problem risking her life for her people, and to her, it was as natural as breathing. But when she met Captain Brown, that all changed. In her mind, the fact that a noble and strong white man who commanded the respect of other white men should take it upon himself the burden of a despised people puzzled her. In her mind, he could do anything with his life. Why should he throw it all away to help our people?" Sarah replied. "Her search for the answer to this question brought her deeper into religion."

"I see," Osumaka replied. "It just seemed that there was much more there."

"Well, there is," Sarah said wryly. "She often related the story of a dream she had just before she met Captain Brown in Canada. In her dream, she was in a wilderness that was full of rocks and bushes. Then suddenly, she saw a serpent raise its head among the rocks, and as it did so, it became the head of an old man with a long white beard. It gazed at her as she puts it, 'wishful like, jes as ef he war gwine to speak to me, and den, two oder heads ruz up beside 'em but yungr dan he.' As she puts it, when she stood up looking at them in her dream, wondering what they could want with her, a great crowd of men rushed in and struck down the younger heads and then the head of the old man who was still looking at her so 'wishful.'"

"What did the dream mean?" asked Osumaka.

"That was the strangest part," replied Sarah. "She had this dream again and again but could not figure out its meaning until she met Captain Brown. She was surprised that the man before here was the very image of the old man's head she had dreamed of so many times. Still, she could not make out the meaning of the dream. One day, while she was in New York, she felt that something was very wrong. She even told her hostess that it must be something wrong with Captain Brown, that she felt he may be in trouble and that they should soon hear bad news from him. The next day, the papers brought the news to her of the tragic events at Harpers Ferry. Then she knew that the old man's head was Captain Brown's, and the other two heads were those of his sons."

"Amazing," Osumaka replied.

June 1, 1863

Harriet and the others awoke to notes of a bugle. The sound halted the noise of the crickets and bullfrogs as they all silenced momentarily in favor of the bugle.

"What is it?" asked Sarah.

"I spect it be de wake-up call for us," Harriet replied as she was already up and dressed and ready to go.

Osumaka also rose from his cot and began to get dressed. Suddenly, the door to the quarters opened. A soldier stood in the doorway.

"Miss Harriet!" he announced, "Col. James Montgomery requests your presence on the dock."

"Yes, sir, of course. We be right dere."

"Thank you, ma'am," he replied. "I will let the colonel know that you are on your way. We will leave under the cover of darkness."

"Yung man," she called.

"Yes, ma'am," he replied.

"Wen we gettn the shown?" she asked.

"Ma'am?" he replied.

"How soon are we to get under way?" Sarah asked in clarification.

"Ma'am, within the hour. The colonel wants to get all our ships under way so that we have the full cover of evening for our mission."

"How many ships are there?" asked Sarah.

"Ma'am, there are three ships: the *Adams*, the *Harriet Weed*, and the *Sentinel*. I had better return and inform the colonel that you will be coming soon."

With that, he turned and closed the door behind him. The wood of the door cracked against the frame as the latch let out a metal cling, signaling that the door was closed.

"We best be gettn down der. Wudn't wan to keep the kernl wanting," Harriet replied as she gathered her belongings and motioned for the others to follow.

They stepped out of the bunkhouse and on to the soft dirt of the camp. The sun had just set, and only a glow could be seen over the horizon. The smell of campfires hung in the air, but a crisp cool breeze tried to blow the smoke away. The crickets and the bullfrogs resumed their songs. Harriet, Sarah, and Osumaka could hear noises coming from the docks—the sounds of fevered men readying the boats for the mission.

"Kernl," Harriet called from the dock.

"Yes, Moses," Colonel Montgomery replied from one of the boats as he headed off the boat and on to the dock to greet her.

"Colonel, this here be Walter. He know the riber liken the back o' his hand."

"Wonderful," Montgomery replied. "You and Walter will join me on the lead ship, the *Adams*."

"Yes, sir, we will, but so too will Osumaka and Sarah, as I be needin' them close by me."

"Of course. As you wish," replied the colonel.

"So many men," commented Sarah.

"Yes, we have three hundred soldiers from the Second South Carolina and another fifty from the Third Rhode Island Battery."

"Colonel! All ships report ready!" a soldier announced.

"Very well then. Signal all to get under way," he replied to the young soldier. Turning to Harriet, Sarah, and Osumaka, he said, "We had best get on board."

With that, Harriet, Sarah, Osumaka, and Walter boarded the *Adams*. The young soldier blew his whistle, and all soldiers raced to their respective boats. Osumaka could hear calls to "Release the lines!" and "Make way!"

"Moses, I need to go over the map of the mouth of the river with you, as we need to navigate the torpedoes laid by the Confederates," Montgomery asked her.

"Yes, sir, Colonel. Walt here has de knowin' of ebry one," Harriet replied as she motioned for Walter to follow her and the colonel up to the wheelhouse to plot out the location of the danger spots on their mission.

As the engines of the steamships whirled to life, a palpable tension grew. This would be the first incursion of Union troops using ships deep into Confederate territory in the East. It would not be an easy journey, and everyone on board knew that they would not all be coming home.

"So this is the map of the Combahee River," the colonel pointed to the map laid out on the chart table.

"Yes. Yes, I see," said Walter. "The torpedoes are laid out in a pattern like this," he plotted his finger on the chart.

"Give this man a pencil!" the colonel shouted. "All right. Now, use this to mark the spots you just showed me."

Walter took the pencil and carefully drew out the locations of the torpedoes hidden in the water. "Here, here, some here, more here, and laid out like this."

"Very good. Very good," the colonel replied.

"Nows how about yud given me dat pensel an I show you the knowin' I have," Harriet said as she took the pencil from Walter and began to draw on the map. "My scouts tell me that these here plantations have reb storehouses and piles of rice and cottn all for de takn." She mapped out the locations of the storehouses and stockpiles on the map for the colonel.

"Wonderful. Superb work, Moses," he thanked Harriet and Walter.

The paddle wheels of the *Adams* were first to come to life. They churned the water steadily as the ship left the dock. She headed out of the port and into the harbor. The *Harriet Weed* was second behind her, while the *Sentinel* was close behind. They headed southeast out of the harbor and past Parris Island. They then headed north past Pritchards Island and then turned into the harbor just after Hunting Island. There were routes more direct, but the colonel felt that it would be safest to approach from open waters, lest the force be spotted by local rebel lookouts. They slowly approached the location of the submerged torpedoes. As the first ship in the convoy, the *Adams* slowed its speed until it stopped just short of the area marked by Walter. Four men entered the water and disabled the torpedoes. They swam back to the ship, and then the *Adams* moved forward again with the other two ships, staying about a quarter of a mile behind. The *Adams* slowed to a stop again. The swimmers reentered the water and tackled the remaining torpedoes blocking their path. As they returned, the captain announced the all clear and full steam ahead. Colonel Montgomery gave Walter

MICHAEL JAY NUSBAUM

a hearty pat on the back as the three ships now steamed full speed ahead up the river. As the river narrowed, the channels became more challenging. Walter and one of the local pilots helped them navigate as their path became more difficult. The sun had set, and the darkness of the night would help obscure the ships as they traveled upriver.

"I see the plantations," Sarah called.

Osumaka came to the railing to see what she meant. He could see slaves in the fields, but as soon as they saw the boats, they dropped what they were doing and ran for the woods.

"What are they doing? Why are they running?" Osumaka asked Sarah.

"Dey be afraid o' us," Harriet said. "Look, dey peern out lik startled deer and scuddlin' aways like de wind at de sound de steam whistl."

One of the slaves hiding behind a tree at the shoreline could be heard calling out to another, "Mas'r said de Yankees had horns and tails, but I nebber believed it till now."

Sarah heard them and called out, "Spread the word that Lincoln's gunboats have come to set you free!"

Osumaka could see slaves, no different from he had been, working the fields under the whips of the drivers. He shuddered at the sight.

The boats moved deeper inland and further up the river. They finally reached one of the rendezvous spots after about an hour and a half.

"Up here," Harriet announced. "This is where we are to meet some of my scouts."

"Captain, prepare to pull to the shore," the colonel ordered.

"Fathom reading!" the captain called out.

"Sorry, Captain. We are nearly at hull depth," the sailor replied as he measured the depth of the river.

"Colonel, we will not be able to pull to the shore. Mrs. Tubman will have to use one of the row boats. We'll hold our position here as she heads to shore."

"Very well. Pull up there where she pointed, and I'll have an escort join you, Moses."

"No need, Colonel. No need. Osumaka and Sarah will join me. They's pertectin e'nuff. Sides, if de good Lord say it be my time, den it be my time," Harriet replied.

They headed to the side of the boat and lowered a launch into the water. Harriet, Osumaka, and Sarah got into the small vessel.

"Are you certain that you know how to handle it?" asked the colonel.

"We'll be fine," said Sarah as she took hold of the oars and pushed off.

It was pitch black as the light from the moon was frequently obstructed by passing clouds.

Suddenly, a voice from the shore shouted, "Moses! Moses, is that you?"

"Yes," she replied from the boat. "O'er der, Sarah." She pointed toward the bank.

Sarah rowed up to the bank.

"What news do you have for us?" Sarah asked.

"We drew a map of all the reb camps and cannons," the man said as he handed a piece of paper to Sarah.

"Wonderful," Sarah replied as she looked at the map.

"Miss Moses, please take us with you," the man begged.

"Gets de word outs. Tells all you knows. When we comes back listen for de witsel. Dat be de signl for alls whos can hear it to come a'runnin' to freedom," Harriet proclaimed.

"I will, I will," the man said enthusiastically. "I will tells everyone that Moses is here to take her people to de promised land!" He ran back into the woods.

As he left, Sarah pushed the small boat off of the shoreline and back into the water. She rowed it back to the *Adams*.

"They're coming back!" shouted one of the deckhands.

"Get ready to help them back on board!" ordered the colonel.

"We've got all we need," said Sarah. "Here's a map of all the reb troop locations, gun batteries, and storehouses."

"Wonderful!" the colonel exclaimed. "Just wonderful. You are truly a godsend, Moses."

"Thanks you kindly, Colonel," Harriet replied.

"Let's continue upriver to our first target. It will be daybreak soon, and we need to be headed back downriver by dawn," the colonel said.

They had traveled nearly twenty-five miles upriver to the Combahee Ferry. There, Montgomery ordered the destruction of the pontoon bridge. He then landed over a hundred black troops on to each bank of the river. There, they ran into the fields and woods, ferreting out any concealed Confederates. They encountered a few small groups of

Confederate soldiers, who, at the sight of armed black Union soldiers, fled in horror without firing a shot. The troops set fire to several plantations where the Confederate soldiers were guarding stores of rice, cotton, and other supplies. They burned homes and barns and rice mills. They destroyed steam engines and confiscated as much cotton, corn, rice, and livestock as they could carry. Whatever they could not take they destroyed.

"Break the sluice gates!" shouted one soldier to his comrades.

"What will that do?" another asked.

"It will flood the rice fields so that all this rice will be ruined!" the first soldier replied.

With that, the soldiers ran into the fields and broke the sluice gates. Water poured into the fields, flooding hundreds of acres of rice.

"Sir, all units reporting success and little to no resistance," the lieutenant told the colonel.

"Very well. Have all units return to the boats with whatever they have confiscated. Make certain that they destroy whatever they cannot take back. Leave nothing for the rebs," the colonel ordered.

"Yes, sir!" the lieutenant replied as he ran back into the fields.

Hours had passed and not the sun was rising. It was dawn on June 2, 1863, and the men on the boats could see fires everywhere. The fog rolled off the fields as the smoke filled the air and flames burned as far as the eyes could see.

"You've done it, Colonel!" the captain exulted. "You've done it!"

"We have, Captain. We certainly have. Now reboard our troops and blow the ships' whistles."

"All of them?"

"Yes, Captain. Have all three ships blow their whistles. Let the rebs know that the all-Negro units of the Union have struck a heavy blow."

"Aye, aye, Colonel," he replied. "Pass the word to the other ships. When we blow our whistle, they should sound theirs as well."

"But, Captain, won't that give away our position? Won't the rebs come after us?"

"You heard the order, pass it on," the captain scolded.

"Aye, aye, Captain," the sailor replied.

The soldiers returned to the boats laden with the spoils of their raids. As the last few lined up to reboard, the colonel gave the order. All three ships sounded their horns. The noise broke through the mist rolling onto the river from the fields. Birds flew from their perches in trees, and the fields stirred. Word had reached the slaves in the area. "When the sounds of the whistles blow, Lincoln's gunboats have come to set you *free*."

Slaves dropped what they were doing and began running for the shores of the river. Overseers and plantation managers tried to block their way. Some whipped the slaves as they ran past them. Others grabbed the slaves and tried to restrain them, but it was too late. Blacks headed en masse to the shores; there was no stopping this exodus. One overseer took out his pistol and began shooting. Three slaves dropped to the ground before another was able to brandish a shovel and strike the overseer before he could kill more slaves. The overseer fell to the ground, dropping the pistol that had denied a few more of their freedom. He lay in a pool of his own blood as slaves ran past him to freedom.

There were women and men, their arms laden with children, clothing, and other possessions. Some had baskets on their heads with a child in each arm and a farm animal tied to their waist. Others had arms filled with clothing and blankets stacked on their heads. Others dragged their pigs and chickens with them. One was seen carrying a child in one arm, a sack of clothing in another, a basket of linens on her head, and a chicken tied to each leg. The sounds of children crying, pigs squealing, and chickens squawking could not drown out the shouts of freedom.

"My God, there are so many of them!" Sarah said in shock.

"It be like the children of Israel comin' out of Egypt land," Harriet declared.

"Can we take on that many?" asked the lieutenant.

"Send all the launches to the shore," the captain ordered. "Bring back as many as you can."

"My God!" the colonel exclaimed. "What a sight."

"Miss Moses!" Sarah shouted. "Miss Moses, come back here."

Sarah and Osumaka ran to the railing. Harriet had jumped off of the gunboat, boarded a launch, and was on shore before they even noticed. With all the turmoil, they feared for her safety.

"Osumaka, we must do something!" Sarah cried out.

With that, Osumaka jumped from the deck into the shallow water. He swam to the shore as if he were going to save the life of one of his own children. He rapidly reached the shore and quickly got on to land. He ran up to Harriet who by now was approaching the boats.

Harried had noticed a poor sickly woman carrying a child and herding two pigs. The woman would not give up her child to Harriet, but she handed off the two pigs. As Harriet grappled the two pigs, the order "double quick" was shouted from the boat. Harriet and the others started to run. As she did, she stepped on the end of her long dress. It fell and tore almost off of her, so by the time she got to where Osumaka reached her, the dress was nearly gone, and only shreds remained.

"Get her back on board as soon as possible," Montgomery shouted as he saw Harriet get swallowed up in the onrush of people.

Osumaka grabbed her and carried her to one of the boats.

"Puts me down, Osumaka! I ain't no invlid," Harriet complained.

"No, Miss Moses. I must get you to safety," Osumaka replied.

"Osumaka, you puts me down now," she retorted.

Osumaka lowered her to the ground.

"But, Miss Moses," he said as she straightened in front of him, "I must keep you safe."

"If it be my time, den de Lord take me. Nuthin' you nor I can do 'bout dat," she said to him.

"Yes, Miss Moses. Let me help you into the boat. We need to get you back," Osumaka said as he helped her into the launch that had just arrived at the shore.

They helped the woman and her children into the boat as well. Soon, hands were grabbing at the boat, at Osumaka, and even at Harriet. The oarsmen began to panic as the boat became unsteady and began to rock. The woman fell to the floor of the boat, and Harriet fell to her side. Osumaka grabbed one of the oars and began to swing it in an attempt to fend off those who might overturn the small boat. The oarsmen began to hit those who would not let go of the side of the boat. Quickly, they pushed off from shore and headed back to the safety of the larger gunboat.

Men, women, and children scrambled to get on board the small boats. They brought with them everything that they could carry. Soon, the boats became overwhelmed with people. Some of the launches headed back to the gunboats, but others were unable to as people held on to them in fear that they would be left behind. Others became so overcrowded that they were in jeopardy of sinking. The oarsmen in the boats had to beat slaves off with their oars in order to break free and head back to the ships.

"Captain, they're going to capsize those launches!" called the lieutenant.

"They are, and all the commotion is bound to get the attention of the Confederates. If we stay here too long, they are bound to mount an attack on us. We would be sitting ducks here," the colonel was grim.

"We must do something," said the captain.

"Moses!" Montgomery called. "Moses, call to your people to calm them. Moses, you'll have to give 'em a song."

"They ain't hardly mys people," she muttered to Sarah. "Theys no more mys peoples den dey be his."

"I think that he means to say that they respect you and will listen to you," Sarah said.

"Only ting we's common was we all Negroes cuz I don't knows dem any morse then he," Harriet said.

"Miss Moses," Osumaka said, "they are your people. They are my people too. When I was taken from my home, it was not by white men but by other Africans who called themselves Kroo. They didn't think of me as their people, and they sold me into slavery because of that. I beg of you not to be like them. As Mr. Douglass said, we need to be as one people, and you can be the one to lead us all to the promised land. You can bring us all together. Please."

With that, Harriet began to sing, "Of all the whole creation in the east or in the west, the glorious Yankee nation is the greatest and the best. Come along! Come along! Don't be alarmed, Uncle Sam is rich enough to give you all a farm."

Her singing was contagious. The people on the banks of the river began to sing with her. They clapped their hands and shouted "GLORY!" at the end of every verse. As they did, they let go of the boats and allowed them to ferry the people to safety. The singing continued unabated throughout the rescue. All the while, the mass of people sang and clapped and shouted "GLORY!" along with her. The infectious tune soon had all on board, including the crew, singing along.

Tears filled the eyes of Harriet, Sarah, and Osumaka. Their emotions were a complicated mix of joy, sadness, and excitement. They were witnesses to a historic event that they all believed would be told for generations. This was, to them, just as important as the Jews of Israel being freed from their bonds of slavery in Egypt. The generations of the descendants of these rescued slaves will celebrate June 2 as the day of their exodus from slavery in the South.

"Do you have a head count for me?" asked Montgomery.

"We have 730 contrabands on board, sir," replied the lieutenant.

"You say, 730!" Montgomery could not believe the report. "I am certain, had we had more ships, we could have doubled that number."

"Aye, Colonel, we had to leave some behind, but there's hardly a square inch to stow them," replied the captain. "Best we make haste out of here and head for open waters."

"That sounds like a good idea," replied the colonel.

They headed steadily down the river. This time, all three boats were close together.

"I don't like the looks of those clouds," remarked the captain.

"Where?" asked the colonel.

"It took us a good part of half a day to get up here. My guess is that it will take us just as long to get out of here, and those clouds are rolling in here quickly," the captain said.

"You think we're in for some bad weather?" Montgomery asked.

"I'd say we're in line for a rough ride home, and these decks are packed with contrabands," he replied.

The wind began to blow, and the sun disappeared as the sky opened up and rain poured down upon them. The water became rough, and the boat rocked from side to side. Despite this, the people were so happy to be free that they continued to sing throughout the storm. Songs of freedom could be heard coming from all three boats, and the song echoed from the shores. Cracks of thunder and hisses of lightning could not dampen the spirits of these now freed people. Some became ill as the boats heaved violently from side to side. They hung over the rails with their stomachs turning over and over, yet they still joined in the singing.

Hours passed into night, and then a new day dawned. The clouds began to move off into the distant horizon as the boats made their way back to Beaufort. Soon, the sun was shining. It was as if they had been rescued from hell, brought through the violent storms at hell's gates, and released into the sunlit skies of freedom. Men, women, and children cried tears of joy as they realized that they were free from the bonds of slavery, free to live their lives as they wished. *Free at last*, the former slaves thought. They were free at last.

"We've made it!" shouted one of the soldiers. "We've made it!"

All rose to their feet, and a great joyous sound rose from the decks of all three gunboats.

"Thank God we've made it back," said Montgomery.

Soon, the cheers turned to song as the freed slaves and black soldiers joined together in hymns of liberty and freedom.

"Glory, glory . . . glory be to freedom . . ."

As the boats approached the docks, many in the camp ran to greet them, having heard the singing before they could even see the boats approaching. Cheers came out from the docks as the excitement coming from all three boats was infectious. Soon, those who stood on the docks joined with the singing.

"We've done it!" exclaimed Sarah.

"We hab at dat," agreed Harriet.

The boats positioned themselves as they reached the docks. No sooner were they tied up than the rescued slaves were jubilantly dancing off the boats and onto the dock filled with excited soldiers and civilians.

"How did it go?" one officer asked.

"It was historic!" a soldier from the raid replied.

The freed slaves continued to sing as they exited the boat and joined together in an open area above the docks.

"Where can we house these people?" Montgomery asked several of the officers who stood there, watching the jubilant celebrations.

"We have tents," one suggested.

"Why not put them up in the Beaufort church right down the road?" another said.

"Excellent idea, Captain," Montgomery said. "Let's gather them together, and I will address them."

The two officers spread the word that Montgomery was to address the crowd and that they were to all gather by the bandstand.

"Please come up here!" one officer shouted to the crowd, trying to be heard over the singing and cheering that continued unabated.

Montgomery took his position on the platform and raised his hands to quiet the crowd. "All, all of you are part of a historic victory against the Confederates and against slavery . . ."

The crowd roared with cheers of "Glory."

Montgomery continued, "Today was a great victory; a great victory for freedom against forces who mean to tear this country apart by continuing to enslave people who were, by God's word, meant to be free."

Again, the crowd cheered and shouted, "Glory."

Montgomery concluded, "This victory today would not have been possible without the black woman who led the raid—the remarkable Mrs. Harriet Tubman.

CHAPTER 20

After the War

O N DECEMBER 21, 1864, federal troops led by General Sherman marched unopposed into the city of Savannah. Soon after, a prison camp was set up on Bay Street, and temporary quarters were erected in the squares. A wealthy English cotton merchant, Charles Green, offered his mansion on Madison Square for the Union military headquarters, hoping that he could buy Sherman's goodwill and thus keep his inventory of cotton safe from confiscation. It was from the Green mansion that Sherman penned his famous message to President Lincoln: "I beg to present to you, as a Christmas gift, the city of Savannah, with one hundred and fifty guns and plenty of ammunition and also about twenty-five thousand bales of cotton." Sherman occupied Green's home, now known as the Green-Meldrim House, until February 1, 1865.

March 3, 1868

It was a cool spring day, and nary a single cloud marred the crisp blue sky. The war had been over for but a few years as the surrender on April 9, 1865, simply marked the beginning of a long and drawn-out end to the war. There were some who refused to recognize the surrender and continued the fight.

Curtis sat in his wheeled chair on the front porch of Deborah's home. They had grown very close since he first arrived at the plantation.

"I am so happy that you and Miss Deborah got hitched!" stated Lilly as she brought freshly made lemonade to him.

"Me too, Lilly," Curtis replied as he took a glass from her and took a sip. "Oh, that is good."

"I means you two just be like a' ol' married couple already."

Mary appeared at the door. "Lilly, you best be leaving the captain alone."

"I justs come to brings him somethin' fresh to drinks," she countered.

"Why don't you go back in the house and do some of your chores?" Mary asked.

"Whys, you not my masser!" Lilly shouted at Mary as she stomped her foot in frustration.

"Nobody is your master anymore, you fool. We've all been freed, girl! What is wrong with you?" Mary said to her.

"Awwww!" Lilly cried out as she ran back into the house.

"What was that all about?" Mary asked Curtis. Sometimes, Lilly made no sense to her.

"I have no idea," he replied.

"What's that?" asked Mary, pointing down the road leading up to the house.

"I'm not sure," said Curtis. "Were we expecting visitors?"

"I best be getting, Miss Deborah," Mary said as she dashed into the house.

Curtis strained to sit up taller so he could see who was coming down the driveway. As they approached, he could see that there were two people in a carriage as it, and the horse kicked up a trail of dust.

The door to the house opened, and Deborah came out, asking, "Who is it?"

"I'm not sure," Curtis replied. "Were you expecting anyone?"

"No, but I think it's Sarah," she said as she shaded her eyes with her right hand. "It is her."

Curtis barely got out "Is that . . ." before Deborah exclaimed, "It is! It's Os!"

"Well, I'll be," Curtis said happily. He had not forgotten the debt he owed Osumaka and had wondered since the end of the war whether he would have a chance to repay him.

By now, Mary and everyone else had heard the approaching one-horse carriage and ran to the front of the house to see who was there. Sarah, in a white blouse and long skirt, was driving the carriage. Osumaka was dressed in a white shirt and dark brown pants. His hair had gray in it, and the furrows in his forehead were now very prominent. The carriage slowed as it approached the front of the house, and Sarah waved to them. Deborah ran down the steps to greet them as Mary pushed Curtis's chair closer to the railing so that he could see them too.

"Miss Deborah!" Sarah exclaimed.

"Sarah! Os! It is so good to see you both!" Deborah said sincerely as she walked over to greet them.

"Os! Is that truly you?" shouted Curtis from the porch.

"Yes, sir, Captain," Osumaka said as he got down from the carriage and walked around to where Sarah and Deborah were.

Sarah was still seated in the carriage when Osumaka came around. He reached his hand out to help her down.

"I can do it myself," she complained. "Why must you always do that?"

Deborah giggled. "Why, you two sound like an old married couple."

Sarah and Osumaka looked at each other and chuckled too.

"Osumaka, my old friend," Curtis said as he pushed his wheelchair closer to the front steps.

Osumaka leapt up the stairs to meet him. "Captain, how are you?"

"Still alive, thanks to you," Curtis said. "You two must be tired and hungry."

Sarah and Deborah walked up the steps too.

"So good to see you again, Captain," Sarah said with a smile as she extended her right hand.

Curtis reached out and took her hand in both of his. "It is wonderful to see you too."

"Have you traveled far?" Deborah asked.

"Well, no, not really. We've been with Miss Moses on Hilton Head Island these past few years," answered Sarah

"How is she?" Deborah asked.

"She's fine. She's been upset lately that the government has not paid her for any of her service though," Sarah said. "She was promised a pension, and with all she did for the Union, she deserves it."

"That's terrible," Deborah replied.

"Sure is. She's fit to be tied, and you don't tell her no. She was promised compensation and a pension, and she'll get it come hell or high water," Sarah said.

"I have no doubt," Deborah said to her.

"It's bad enough that the Negro soldiers only received half the pay of the white soldiers. That really burned her up. But now, to be treated like she didn't help the Union win this war, unbelievable!" Sarah exclaimed.

"Why don't you come inside and let's talk about it some more," Deborah said as she motioned for Sarah to come inside with her. "Would you, gentlemen, like anything?"

"Something to drink would be nice," Curtis replied.

"And you, Os?" Deborah asked.

"Whatever the captain is having," he replied.

"Very good," Deborah nodded as she opened the door and went inside with Sarah.

"Have a seat, my old friend," Curtis said to Osumaka as he maneuvered his wheelchair.

Osumaka took a seat in a white rocking chair facing the front yard.

"It's been many years, Captain," Osumaka said as he relaxed into the chair.

"It has indeed, my friend. Please tell me what you've been up to."

"Sarah brought me up North with her. We met with Mr. Frederick Douglass, and then I met Miss Moses for the first time. She was quite remarkable," Osumaka said with a grin.

"I've heard that about her," Curtis replied. "But I just can't believe all the legends about her."

"Believe. They're probably all true," Osumaka told him. "What legends have you heard?"

"Well, that she freed thousands of slaves, blew up bridges, destroyed railroad lines, and burned down storehouses and ammunition depots."

"Those are all very true, Captain," Osumaka said, smiling.

"Truly? They are? How do you know?" Curtis asked, still disbelieving.

"Because I was with her on all of those," Osumaka told him. Curtis's eyes grew wide just as Mary came out with the drinks.

"Here you go. So good to see you again, Os," Mary said with a smile.

"It's so good to see you too," Osumaka told her. "Thank you."

Mary smiled at him and headed back into the house.

His eyes still wide, Curtis took a sip of lemonade, shook his head, and instructed Osumaka, "You must tell me everything."

Osumaka recounted stories of the daring raids and the adventures he had been on. They sat and spoke for hours. Curtis was fascinated by the stories, and Osumaka tried to tell him everything.

Osumaka noticed a face at the door peering out at him. Curtis noticed that Osumaka's attention had wandered and turned his head as well.

"Ah! Your little friend has been waiting for you, but she's not so little anymore," Curtis said with a smile.

"Pepper?" Osumaka shouted as he jumped to his feet. "Pepper! Is that you?"

Pepper flung the door open and ran out into his arms, with Mary close behind her, saying, "Osumaka! Osumaka! How I've missed you."

"You're speaking!" Osumaka exclaimed as he picked her up and held her close to his heart. She wrapped her arms around him the way she used to, but her feet now extended all the way to his knees, and she could wrap her arms around his chest without a problem.

"Speaking?" Curtis laughed. "That's all she does. She never stops speaking, specifically about you!"

"Me?" Osumaka looked at Curtis then back at Pepper. "Of me?"

"Yes!" she exclaimed. "You said you'd come back for me, and you did!"

"That's all she ever talks about," Mary said. "'Os is coming back for me,' to 'rescue me and to take me back home with him' so she would be part of a family again."

"You said that?" asked Osumaka, very moved by this news.

"Yes," Pepper replied simply. "You're my family."

Osumaka held Pepper close to him and kissed her head. "You are my family. You are my little girl."

"See, Mary. I told you he would come back for me and take me with him." Pepper said as she held Osumaka tightly.

"You did child, you certainly did," Mary replied.

Osumaka sat back in the chair, still holding Pepper and then sat her in his lap.

"I am so impressed with the way you speak and how much you've grown," Osumaka said.

"Miss Deborah taught me how to read and how to write and how to sew and how to cook, and do you like this dress?" Pepper said in a rush.

"I do," Osumaka replied.

"Miss Deborah and I made it. Can you believe it?" Pepper asked. Clearly, Mary had also played a role in teaching Pepper to speak. She spoke so quickly that Osumaka could not respond to one question before she posed another.

"No, it is so beautiful. That's amazing," Osumaka replied.

"I have so much to tell you and so much to show you!" exclaimed Pepper.

"You do?" Osumaka asked.

"I do, I do. Would you like to see my room?" Pepper asked.

"I would." Osumaka nodded.

Pepper hopped off of his lap and grabbed his arm.

"Come on," she said as she pulled him out of the chair.

"Hold on now! Slow down! I'm moving as fast as I can." Osumaka pretended to complain as he got up and followed Pepper. "You'll excuse me, Captain."

"All I can say is thank God you are back, Os. Perhaps now Pepper will find something else to go on and on about." Curtis feigned relief.

"You know, Captain, you shouldn't be out here so much, you're gonna grow roots into this porch," Mary said as she gave him a newspaper.

"What is that?" Curtis asked. "Could that be the *Savannah Daily Republican*?" When she nodded, he asked, "How did you get one?" Steady newspaper delivery was difficult since they lived so far in the country and no one went to town every day.

"Well, I know it's your favorite, so I made a deal with a man I know, and he said he can get me one every day," Mary replied.

"That is amazing. But what did you have to give him in return?" Curtis asked suspiciously.

"Captain, that's none of your concern. We all just want to see you happy," she replied.

"But if he is asking for money for it, I would like to pay," he told her.

"No need for money. I do him a favor, and he does me a favor," Mary explained.

"Might I ask you what the favor is?" Curtis asked. Was it a favor he could approve? There were many scoundrels around taking advantage of the confusion of the Reconstruction. He hoped Mary had not gotten involved with one.

"I write letters for him to a woman he's courting. He can't read or write a lick, so I read and write for him. In exchange, he brings me these papers for you."

"That is extremely generous of you. Thank you, Mary. Thank you." Curtis was relieved at her answer and delighted to have a regular source of news. He glanced at the headlines on the front page. Suddenly, one of them caught his eye.

"My God!" he exclaimed. "My God! Deborah! Deborah!"

Deborah came running out of the house to see what was wrong. Before she'd arrived on the porch, she was calling from the house. "What's wrong? What is it?"

"Michael!" he exclaimed excitedly as the front screen door swung open and Deborah, a little winded, appeared in the doorway.

"Michael?" she asked. "Michael? I thought you were . . ."

"You thought I was what?" Curtis asked.

Deborah responded haltingly as she leaned over to breathe better. "I. Thought. Something. Was. Wrong."

"No, nothing is wrong. Everything is just fine now." Curtis looked and sounded happy and optimistic for the first time in several months. He was content living on the farm, but this news of Michael really gave him hope for the future.

"What is it? Who is Michael?" she asked as she sat in a chair next to him.

"See, right here? Captain Michael Smith of the Union Naval Forces has been placed in command of the Port of Savannah." Curtis pointed to the paper and slapped it with his palm. "I'll be. Captain Smith is in charge of the Port of Savannah."

"Is that good?" Deborah asked.

"It is fine indeed," he replied with a grin. "My good friend Michael—I wouldn't be here either if it weren't for him and his friendship."

"Well, perhaps if you get word to him, he may come visit you here," she suggested.

"That's not a bad idea," Curtis said, considering the idea.

"Perhaps he could even help Os get back to his family," Deborah said, wondering.

"Perhaps indeed. He is an important man now. I wonder if he would even be able to break away to visit me."

MICHAEL JAY NUSBAUM

"You'll never know unless you try," she replied. "Perhaps you should write him a letter. We could have Mary ride into Savannah and get it to him."

"Yes. Yes," Curtis said as he sat up in the chair. His eyebrows furrowed together as he thought, "Yes, he'd be happy to know I'm alive. Why wouldn't he want to see us here?"

"Exactly," Deborah said lovingly. "Mary! Mary!"

They could hear Mary's rapid footsteps in the front hall before Mary burst from the front door.

The screen door swung open. "Yes, Miss Deborah?"

"Mary, could you please get the captain here some paper and a pen?" Deborah asked.

"Yes, Miss Deborah, might I ask who's the captain goin' to write to?" Mary inquired. Deborah and Curtis were usually amused by Mary's irrepressibility, but it could be wearing. They looked at each other and shook their heads at her impertinent question.

Curtis finally answered her. "An old friend, Mary. An old friend," he told her in a low voice.

Realizing that she might have gone too far, Mary stepped back. "Yes, Captain, I'd be happy to get them for you," she replied.

"And, Mary, please bring him my portable writing table," Deborah said. "Do you know which one I'm speaking of?"

"Yes, Miss Deborah, the one the colonel got you for . . ." Her words faded out.

"Yes, Mary. That's the one I mean," Deborah told her.

"I'll get it right away," Mary said as she darted off.

"What will you say?" Deborah asked Curtis softly.

"I'm not sure," he responded quietly. "I'm not sure."

"Why not start off by thanking him for all he did for you?" Deborah said.

"Yes, yes, I do owe him that."

Suddenly, they heard a crash from the house.

Deborah jumped to her feet, calling, "What was that?"

"I'm sorry, Miss Deborah," Mary said as she picked up the portable desk from the floor. "It was too much for me to carry."

Deborah went to Mary's aid.

Exasperated, Deborah knelt to help Mary pick up the spilled contents of the writing desk. "Why didn't you just ask me for help?"

"I'm so sorry, Miss Deborah, I know that the colonel got you this for your birthday. I didn't mean to break it," Mary wailed.

"It's not broken. It just opened up when it hit the floor," Deborah said as she picked up the pieces and placed them back in order. She looked at Mary and pleaded, "Please do not mention the colonel again."

"I'm sorry, Miss Deborah," Mary said. "I miss him sometimes."

"I miss him too, Mary." For a moment, Deborah showed her grief. "But he's been gone a long time now, and I'd just prefer that you not mention him when the captain is around."

"Yes, Miss Deborah," Mary replied. "I understand."

"Good. Thank you. Now let me take this to the captain," she said as she finished rearranging the contents of the case. She then secured it with the leather strap.

"Let me help you," Mary said as Deborah rose, holding the portable writing desk.

"I have it. Thank you, Mary," Deborah replied.

Mary ran ahead of her and opened the door for her.

"Thank you, Mary," Deborah said as she brought the desk out to Curtis on the porch.

"What is that?" Curtis asked.

"It's a portable desk. A gift from a few years ago. I haven't had the time or inclination to use it very much, but I think it would be perfect for you right now," Deborah said as she arranged the desk in front of Curtis.

"This is wonderful. Thank you, my dearest," Curtis said with a smile.

"My dearest," Deborah repeated, giving him an equally bright smile in return.

"I think that I know what to say to Michael," Curtis told her.

Curtis watched Deborah walk away. When she was out of sight, he turned his eyes off her and onto the blank page before him. He dipped the nib into the ink and began to write.

My dear friend Michael,

It is with great happiness that I have learned of your new position overseeing the Port of Savannah. It is also with great happiness that I can report to you that I remain very much alive.

MICHAEL JAY NUSBAUM

I wish to take you back, some seven years ago, when you and I served on the USS Saratoga. *I was naive to many truths in this world, and certainly, you tried to show me that. It wasn't until we stopped the* Nightingale, *and I saw how those people were treated that I could recognize my ignorance.*

If you remember, there was a young boy named Bwana whom I nursed during his illness on the Nightingale. *I must say that God certainly works in mysterious ways because that boy's father, Osumaka, actually saved my life. I have sent him, along with two others, to deliver this letter to you. It is my sincere hope that you not only receive this letter but that you might see fit to help him in his quest as well. He wishes to reunite with his wife and son, whom we set free in Liberia some seven years ago. While I am certainly in your debt for all that you have done for me, I beseech you to help me repay my debt to that boy's father.*

I am currently residing on a plantation not far from your current post. I have, unfortunately, sustained such injuries that the lower half of my body fails to respond to commands, but I assure you that this infirmity has not seen fit to diminish my wit nor my intellect.

It would be my great pleasure and an immense honor if you were to visit your old friend and see if we can hatch a plot to help Osumaka reunite with his family. I would just ask that you forgive me in advance for my inability to stand and salute you upon your arrival.

I remain your true friend,
Capt. Curtis Stanton

Curtis then poured some powder on to the paper and then blew it off. The ink seemed to dry very slowly even with the powder. He opened the desk and took out an envelope. Next to the pile of envelopes, there was a stick of wax, a candle, and some now-useless Confederate stamps. Curtis checked the letter one last time and touched the ink with his finger. It was dry. He then folded the letter and placed it in the envelope. He lit the candle and used it to melt the sealing wax. Dripping sealing wax on to the area over the overlapping folds of the envelope, Curtis sealed his letter and pressed his signet into the soft wax. He looked up and called, "Mary!"

"Yes, Captain," Mary answered from somewhere in the house.

"Mary, would you be so kind as to get this letter to Capt. Michael Smith in Savannah Harbor?"

"Yes, Captain. I'd be happy to," Mary replied.

"I would like Osumaka and Sarah to accompany you."

"I'll ask them both, Captain."

When Mary found her, Sarah was in the back of the house, cleaning her pistols.

"Sarah, Sarah!" Mary called as she could see her sitting on the steps through the back door.

Sarah ignored her calls and continued to clean her guns. Mary burst dramatically through the door.

"Sarah, Sarah, the captain wants me, you, and Os to take this letter to his friend in Savannah right away," she said as she panted from running too quickly.

"He does? Let me see it," Sarah said as she put her pistol on the step next to her.

Mary handed Sarah the envelope containing the captain's letter. Sarah took it in her right hand then moved it to her left hand and back again while turning it over.

"It's sealed," Sarah said.

"Yes, ma'am, it is. It is for Captain Smith in Savannah," Mary replied.

"I see that." Sarah made a face at Mary. "It says his name right here on the front of the envelope."

"Yes, and me, you, and Os are going to take it to him," Mary said importantly.

Sarah handed the letter back to Mary, picked her pistol back up off the step, and resumed cleaning it.

"That's fine with me," she replied as she cleaned out each cylinder of the pistol. "You'd best find Osumaka and let him know we're going. I'm going to finish up here, and then I'll get the carriage ready."

"Yes, ma'am," Mary replied as she turned and went back into the house. "Os! Os! Os!" Mary ran all over the house, looking for Osumaka but could not find him. Finally, she ran out toward the barn and the bunkhouses. She could see Osumaka standing looking out into the fields.

"Os!" she shouted as she approached him.

Osumaka turned to see Mary running clumsily toward him.

"Os, the captain has asked us to take this letter to his friend in Savannah right away," she said as she panted.

"Who is 'us'?" he asked.

"He asked, me, Sarah, and you to go," she answered.

"When are we leaving?" he asked Mary.

"Right away," she said. Osumaka's matter-of-fact responses could not dampen Mary's enthusiasm for her trip to the city.

"All right. Let's go then," Osumaka said as he followed Mary around the side and up to the front of the house.

The captain was still seated in his chair on the porch, and Sarah had pulled the carriage up to the front and awaited her traveling companions.

"Don't you have anything other than that old dirty coat?" Osumaka asked Sarah.

"It's all I have, and it suits me just fine," Sarah retorted from the driver's seat.

"You three be careful now," Curtis called.

"Yes, sir. We will," Mary responded as Sarah flicked the reins before Mary had seated herself properly.

CHAPTER 21

Finding Smith

March 4, 1868, Savannah

MARY, OSUMAKA, AND Sarah arrived in the Port of Savannah. There were Union soldiers and sailors everywhere. Most of the buildings were damaged, but there were so many people fixing them that it seemed like the port was being rebuilt from scratch. Disheveled men in tattered Confederate uniforms lay in the alleys and along the sides of the buildings. Some of the men had dressings on their wounds, and others with no apparent injury just stared into the distance. Union soldiers marched by them in groups of ten or more and paid them no attention as the continued by.

"How will we ever find the captain's friend?" asked Mary.

"I'm not sure, Mary. I didn't expect so many people to be here," Sarah replied.

"Well, if the captain's friend is truly in command of this port, then any of these soldiers should know who he is and where we can find him," Osumaka said.

"That's true," Sarah said as she slowed the carriage to ask a passing white soldier. "Excuse me."

Several other white soldiers also passed by without acknowledging her. Soon a column of Negro soldiers approached.

"It's the First!" Sarah exclaimed. She raised her hand and shouted, "The First!"

The column of soldiers responded in unison, "Whoo, whoo, the FIRST!" as they continued by.

"Excuse me, Sergeant," Sarah asked the sergeant walking beside the column.

"Halt!" he shouted. The column came to a rapid halt.

He tipped his hat as he turned to acknowledge Sarah. "Yes, ma'am. What can I do for you?"

"My friends and I have a very urgent letter for Captain Michael Smith. He's supposedly in command of the port," Sarah said.

"Yes, indeed. Captain Smith is in command of Port Savannah and the harbor," the sergeant answered.

"Could you direct us to him please?" Sarah asked.

"Of course. Park your carriage up ahead by those wagons. Make a right at the corner and follow the wharf until you reach the old cotton exchange building. Captain Smith has made that his HQ," the sergeant replied as he tipped his hat once again. "A pleasure, my lady."

"Thank you again, Sergeant," she replied.

"Column, move out!" he shouted as he and the soldiers marched away.

Sarah drove the carriage to where the sergeant had instructed.

"Osumaka, why don't you stay here with the carriage while I take Mary to see the captain," Sarah said.

"If it's all the same to you, I would like to come with you. I am curious to see this Captain Smith," Osumaka said. What kind of man would the captain's friend be? Osumaka was very curious.

"All right, we'll all go then," Sarah said as she got down off the carriage and began to tie the horses up to a post.

Mary remained in the back of the carriage, watching everything that was going on around them. She was mesmerized by all the activity.

"Mary," Sarah called. "Anytime you're ready!"

"Yes, Miss Sarah," Mary responded as if just woken out of a light sleep.

"Are you going to join us and bring Captain Curtis's letter?" Sarah asked sarcastically.

"Why, yes, ma'am. Yes, ma'am, I am," Mary replied as she rapidly climbed out of the carriage.

The three of them began walking toward the wharf. As they did, the scene opened up into a large panorama of activity. A huge flagpole stood before them flying the largest Stars and Stripes they had ever seen. Ships were moving in and out of the harbor. Recently docked ships were being tied up, and others had been there for a while and were being unloaded. There were people everywhere, and everyone seemed to be actively involved in doing something productive. No one was relaxing.

"He said over to the right," Sarah said as she pointed down the long row of building fronts.

Osumaka agreed, and the three of them began walking in the direction they had been instructed.

Sarah and Osumaka walked shoulder to shoulder as Mary trailed behind them, frequently spinning around to watch everything that was happening around her.

Sarah looked back at Mary. "Will you stop that," she grumbled.

"I'm sorry, Miss Sarah," Mary replied sheepishly. "But there are so many people." Sarah just rolled her eyes.

"The sergeant, he said to look for the old cotton exchange," Sarah said as she looked at the names on each of the buildings.

"It must be that one," Osumaka said as he pointed to a large brick building with sailors guarding the door and a crowd of people gathered in front.

"Yes." Sarah agreed.

"How do you know?" Mary asked.

"The captain's friend is an important man, one who would be protected like this," Osumaka explained. "But those guards at the front door don't seem to be letting anyone in."

"Do you think that they'll let us in?" Mary asked.

Neither Osumaka nor Sarah could answer her.

"Do you?" Mary repeated.

"I'm not sure," Sarah said as they approached the two guards at the door.

"You can't go in there, ma'am," one of the soldiers said as he bodily blocked the doorway.

"We have an important correspondence for Captain Smith," Sarah said.

The other guard looked them up and down, clearly disbelieving their claim.

"Oh, you do, do you?" The first guard looked even less impressed. "From whom?"

"From Captain Stanton," Mary told them.

"Never heard of him." The other guard shrugged.

"Let me see the letter," the first guard told Sarah.

"It has to be delivered in person to Captain Smith," Sarah replied.

"Well, that is not going to happen," the first guard barked at her. "Let me see it or move along."

Sarah motioned for Mary to hand her the letter. Mary did so reluctantly. Sarah turned to hand it to the guard. Just before he could grab it, she pulled it away from him.

"Now you do understand that this is a very important letter?" she asked.

"Yeah, yeah. Just give it to me," he replied, tiring of this game.

Osumaka watched the mannerisms of the two guards carefully. The second guard noticed; he seemed a bit intimidated by Osumaka's size.

The guard flipped the letter over in his hands several times. "It's sealed," he complained.

"It is," Sarah agreed.

"You best not break that seal," Mary told them, wagging her finger at the guards.

"It's intended for the captain's eyes only. I would listen to her and not break that seal," Sarah said.

The guard flipped the letter over and over in his hands and looked at the three of them carefully. He turned slightly and knocked on the door. Another sailor answered.

"What is it?" he asked.

"These three have a letter for Captain Smith. It's sealed. They say it's important that he gets it," the guard told the sailor.

"Fine. I'll bring it right up to him. But don't let them in. Keep them out there," the sailor told the guard scornfully as he took the letter and closed the door.

The guard turned back to Osumaka, Sarah, and Mary. "The three of you need to step away now. Why don't you go over there?" he said, a little more politely, as he pointed to a stack of crates near the edge of the wharf.

"That's fine, but we are not leaving until we get a reply," Sarah said as they turned and walked away.

Osumaka did not move. He stood in place, staring down the first guard at the door.

"Come on, Osumaka," Sarah said as she tugged at his sleeve to pull him away.

The two guards shuffled their feet as Osumaka walked away with Sarah and Mary. When they got to the crates, Mary immediately took a seat on one of them. Then Sarah took a seat. Osumaka remained standing and staring at the guard.

"Do you think they'll give him our letter?" Mary asked.

"I'm not sure," Sarah told her. "I'm just not sure."

Minutes went by, but it seemed much longer. They could see the door open, and one sailor spoke with the two guards. The first guard turned and pointed to them. The man at the door nodded his head yes.

"You three!" the guard shouted. "You three, come here," he said as he motioned for them to approach.

Mary jumped off the crate to her feet. Sarah rose slowly and looked at Osumaka before heading back to the building.

"Come on," the guard said as he motioned at them impatiently.

They walked back to the door where the sailor just inside the open doorway asked, "Which one of you is delivering this letter to the captain?"

"We all are!" Mary blurted.

"Yes. Well, only one of you can come up," the sailor responded.

"I guess that would be me." Sarah decided.

"Fine. Then you follow me. Your friends can wait for you out here," he replied.

Sarah looked at Osumaka and just nodded her head yes and then turned her gaze over to Mary. "Keep an eye on her, Osumaka."

"Very well, come with me," the sailor said as he moved into the building and out of the doorway.

Sarah followed him inside. There were desks everywhere, and both white and Negro sailors and soldiers worked feverishly. The space was a large open warehouse. The brick walls were exposed on the inside with rough-hewn timbers crossing the distance and resting on evenly spaced timber columns throughout the area. The sailor led Sarah to a staircase that went up to a loft area with glass and a door at the top. As they climbed, Sarah looked around the room below them. Once at the landing, Sarah could see a soldier inside the office behind a desk. Several other soldiers were seated in chairs in front of the desk. Her escort knocked on the door.

I motioned for them to come in.

The sailor saluted once he opened the door. "This is the courier of the letter, Captain."

"Very well, send her in. That is all, gentlemen," I said, dismissing the men.

The men rose from their seats. "Thank you, Captain Smith," they replied in unison.

The men filed past Sarah and her escort. It had not escaped her attention that while she wasn't the only Negro in the building, she was the only woman.

"Come. Come in and have a seat," the captain said to her.

I recall very clearly this first time that I met Sarah. She impressed me with her confidence. She was dressed in a long well-worn overcoat. Her long hair was braided, and her man's shirt collar was open enough to expose her sharp clavicles and hint at the breasts that proved she was not a man. Her face was chiseled, but her skin appeared soft and youthful. She was clearly a very strong woman, despite her slender frame. The dichotomy of her beauty and physical strength intrigued me.

"Please have a seat," I said to her.

I waited for her to sit, and then I took a seat as well. I picked up the letter from Curtis and opened it.

"Is this truly from Curtis Stanton?" I asked her. I almost couldn't believe the coincidence.

"Yes, Captain, it is," she replied.

"And how did you come by this letter," I asked. "Do you know him?"

"I do. Very well. He asked us to bring it to you," she replied.

"Us?" I asked.

"Mary, Osumaka, and I," she replied. "The captain asked that we get this letter to you right away."

I recall leaning back in my chair and reading the letter carefully before I responded to her.

"Curtis is my very good friend," I told her when I had finished reading. "Where is he now?"

She began to tell me a bit about Curtis's story. How, after I let him escape, he came upon the farmhouse where Osumaka and the other runaways were staying; how the little girl ran out and then Curtis shielded her from the soldier's bullet. She went on to recount how Osumaka saved Curtis's life and how Osumaka and Deborah, the owner of the plantation, had taken such good care of him while he recovered.

"I would very much like to meet this Osumaka," I said to her.

"You certainly can, Captain, he's right outside," she replied.

I rose and went to the door. The sailor remained outside, waiting to escort Sarah back to the wharf.

"Please get her friend and bring him up here," I said.

Sarah interrupted me, "But Mary is with him too."

I turned back to the sailor. "And bring her friend Mary up here as well."

"Aye, Captain," he responded as he walked down the steps to retrieve her two friends.

I went back to my desk and sat down. "What else can you tell me of Curtis?"

"Well, he remains in a wheeled chair and does not have the use of his legs," she replied.

"Yes, I read that in his letter. I'm very sorry to hear that," I replied.

I looked at the letter again and read it for a second time.

"Have you read this letter?" I asked her.

"No, Captain, it was sealed," she replied.

The sailor returned to the door with Osumaka and Mary. I rose to greet them.

"Osumaka, I presume? And you must be Mary," I said.

"Yes, I'm Mary, Captain," she responded with a small curtsy.

Osumaka stood there quietly while he looked around the room. I came out from behind my desk and extended my hand to him.

"It is an honor to meet someone for whom my good friend has such high regard."

Osumaka shook my hand as we made eye contact. "Thank you, Captain."

"Please have a seat," I said as I directed the two of them to the two additional chairs in front of my desk.

"So I think that I can help you," I said to Osumaka as I returned to my chair.

"Help me? How?" Osumaka looked surprised and confused.

"Yes, how?" Sarah asked.

I explained, "Well, it seems that Captain Stanton has asked me to assist Osumaka in finding passage back to Liberia so that he may be reunited with his family."

Sarah's eyes widened, and her chin hit her chest. Osumaka looked equally stunned. Apparently, Curtis had not shared the letters contents with his couriers.

"You would do that?" Osumaka asked cautiously.

"I would," I replied. "I'm not exactly sure how yet, but we do have a naval post there, and I should at least be able to get you on one of those ships."

Osumaka jumped to his feet from the chair, his face alight with joy. "There is nothing I would like more!" he exclaimed. "Thank you, Captain. Thank you." Sarah still had not moved.

"Well, don't thank me yet. We still have to find you that ship. In the meantime, I would very much like to visit with my old friend Curtis," I told them.

"We can take you back to him." Mary offered as Sarah remained stunned and saddened.

"That would be wonderful," I replied. "Ensign!" I shouted.

The door opened, and the sailor entered, "Yes, Captain."

"Have my mount prepared. I will be leaving immediately," I ordered.

"Aye, aye, sir," he replied as he saluted and left the room.

"How far away is this plantation of yours?" I asked them.

"Not too far." Sarah finally returned to the room. "If we leave now, we should be able to arrive before sundown."

"Superb." I smiled. "How did you arrive?"

"We took a carriage," Mary replied.

I nodded and asked, "Where did you leave your carriage?"

"Out front to the left," Mary told me. "It's near the huge flag."

"Well, then I will meet you there in fifteen minutes, and you three will escort me to my friend," I replied.

CHAPTER 22

Deborah's Plantation, That Same Evening

WE ARRIVED AT Deborah's plantation just as the sun was beginning to set and the sky glowed orange and pink. I had ridden alongside the carriage the entire way, and during that time, we hardly spoke. Sarah would tell me where we were going next, how far it was from this point, and so on. I must admit that I was a bit uneasy following them into the heart of enemy territory without my usual complement of guards. I kept reminding myself that the war was over and that we were no longer enemies with the South. The only problem was in convincing myself that this was so. I knew that the last Confederate surrender didn't actually take place until November 6, 1865, and that some Confederates still refused to surrender even now, years later. The thought that this was some kind of elaborate ruse to get me alone deep into the heart of the Confederacy just to assassinate me remained in the back of my mind. I also considered the tales I had heard of vigilante groups like the Ku Klux Klan and other so-called chivalric orders. I wondered whether the war would ever truly end. Probably not in my lifetime, I decided.

When we turned down the drive to the plantation, it struck me that here was the image that had formed in my mind of the typical Southern plantation. As we rode closer to the main house, I could see a familiar face on the porch. I was relieved when I saw Curtis, and that was enough to encourage me to take my hand off my sidearm, as I had kept a firm grip on my weapon for most of the ride.

"Captain Smith, I presume!" Curtis called from his chair on the porch.

I waved back. "It is so good to see you, my old friend!"

Sarah pulled their wagon ahead and slightly around to the left side of the house. I rode right up to the front steps and a young Negro/black woman took the reins of my horse. I dismounted as my heart raced with excitement. Curtis maneuvered his wheeled chair to the top of the steps, and I ran up to greet him.

"My God," I said. "I am truly pleased to see you so well."

"I certainly have you and Osumaka to thank for that," he replied as he stretched out his hand.

I shook his hand firmly and stared at his face. *My God*, I thought to myself, *how much he had aged*. His hair was half gray, and so too were his eyebrows. He had deep furrows in his forehead and liver, and age spots marred his complexion.

"I never thought I would see you again," I said to Curtis.

"Nor I you," Curtis replied as he pointed to the rocking chair next to him. "You must be tired. Please have a seat. We have so much to talk about. So much to catch up on."

"That we do." I agreed as I accepted his invitation to sit down.

The chair was a bit flimsy, and it creaked a bit when I sat down. I hesitated to put all my weight upon it, but it seemed to hold just fine. Besides, my feet were tired, along with the rest of me from our journey.

"Mary!" Curtis called back through the front door. "Mary, could you please get us some refreshments?"

"No need, Mary, I have them," a woman's voice answered from inside the house. The door opened, and a beautiful woman, holding a tray with a pitcher and several glasses, stood there.

I rose to my feet quickly, captivated by her beauty. I had hardly seen a woman more stunning in my life and found myself speechless.

Curtis turned his chair's wheels and said, "Michael, allow me to introduce my wife, Deborah."

I looked at him and repeated, "Wife?" I was indeed disappointed that this beauty was spoken for but also happy that my old friend had found new love.

As Deborah drew closer, Curtis reached out to her from his chair. She placed the tray upon a table and took his hand. The two of them reminded me of a love I had once known but was never able to have.

"I am so happy for you. For you both," I said, a bit sad that it was true.

I admit that I felt a bit jealous. She was a stunning woman. Her lean figure, blond hair, and green eyes with just a touch of blue in them stood out to me.

"I am very lucky to have Curtis," she replied as she kissed him upon his forehead. "I understand that I have you to thank for that."

"You do?" I asked.

"Certainly. Had you not let him go free, I would probably have never met him," she replied.

"Oh yes," I said half-confused. "What has he told you?"

"Have you heard the whole story, Michael?"

"I have not," I said.

"Please," she said as she motioned for me to sit. "Would you like some lemonade?"

"Yes, please," I replied.

She poured a glass for me and then another for Curtis. I tried not to stare at her, as I felt Curtis watching me do so.

"Thank you," I said. "Please go on. You were saying?"

She proceeded to tell me the story as she stood by Curtis in his chair. I had heard it before, but I enjoyed the sound of her voice. I watched her lips as she spoke. I watched her chest rise as she took in a breath to continue with the next sentence. I watched her brush her hair off her forehead and then place it behind her ear. I must admit that I stopped listening at some point, but I noticed Curtis giving me an odd look.

"And that's how we met."

"I see. Wonderful," I said. "I mean, how you met, not your injuries or anything like that. Just the meeting part." I could hear myself babble as I often do when in the presence of a beautiful woman.

"Well, I'll leave you two for a bit," Deborah said. "I'll have Mary make up one of the guest rooms for you, Michael."

"Thank you. That would be wonderful," I replied.

As she walked away, Curtis turned to me and asked, "She's beautiful, isn't she?"

"Very beautiful indeed. Not to mention kind and generous," I replied. "You're a lucky man, Curtis."

"I am," he replied as he looked back over his shoulder to where she had just been.

MICHAEL JAY NUSBAUM

"Very lucky," I said again.

"So, my friend, how are things going at the port?" Curtis asked.

"They are good. We have finally started receiving the materials that we needed to rebuild the city."

"Yes, Sherman and his men really did destroy quite a bit as they came through," Curtis said.

"Well, they did. But I guess that they did what they had to," I replied. Curtis smiled tightly.

"Reconstruction continues though. Things should get back to normal soon." I paused and realized that my comment was not entirely sensitive to the situation. "Well, as normal as could be hoped."

Curtis was looking down at his drink the entire time I spoke and did not really seem to be listening.

"I was hoping to ask you here for a favor," Curtis blurted.

"A favor?" I asked.

"Yes, but not for me," he replied.

"Right. For Osumaka." I remembered.

"For Osumaka. Exactly," he replied.

"You told me something about this family in your letter, but to be honest, I didn't really understand what you were asking. How could I help Osumaka? I feel that I owe him a debt for saving your life."

"I want so badly to reunite him with his family," Curtis explained.

I wondered if Curtis's brain had been affected by the injury that had paralyzed his body. "With his family?" I asked. "How could I do that? Reunite one African with his family. In Africa? Be serious. I have no idea who his family is or how I would ever be able to find them for him."

"But you do," Curtis responded.

"I do?"

"Yes, do you remember the young boy and his mother from the *Nightingale*?"

"The young boy? No. The *Nightingale*, yes," I replied.

"On the *Nightingale*, there was a young boy by the name of Bwana. I nursed him back to health, and then he latched on to me the rest of the trip."

"Oh yes. I kind of remember that. I didn't remember his name, but yes, I remember the boy now."

"Well, it turns out that the boy's father is Osumaka," Curtis said.

"How on earth would you ever know that?" I protested. "There must be hundreds or thousands of children with that name."

"True, but only one who had a little ivory statue given to him by his father," he replied smugly.

"What are you talking about?" I asked.

"That little boy gave me a necklace with an ivory statue, do you remember?"

"Honestly, no. I don't," I replied.

"Well, he did give it to me, and when Osumaka was helping me, he started to sing a song that I recognized."

"Yes, and . . ." I urged him on. The entire day had been full of coincidences. I suppose one more wouldn't be so extraordinary.

"Well, that song reminded me of Bwana's singing onboard the *Nightingale* and the necklace. When I showed it to Osumaka, he immediately recognized it as his son's," Curtis said.

"Incredible," I replied.

"I know," Curtis said, suddenly serious. "He saved my life, Michael. I have to help him."

"All right, so we have to find a ship heading to Liberia and get him on it," I replied.

"Are there any that you know of?" Curtis asked.

"Well, there is one that I can think of," I replied. "She's a dual side-wheeled steamer that's set to leave Charleston for Africa. She wasn't going to Liberia, but I may be able to change her orders."

"That would be perfect," Curtis replied. "Do you think you can do it?"

"I don't think that I can swing selling the idea of returning just a freed African or two back to Liberia, but if you can help me get close to a hundred, well, that I might be able to sell to my superiors," I replied.

"Sell?" Curtis asked.

"Well, it is all political these days. The story of the U.S. Navy returning freed slaves back to the land of their ancestors, that might work," I explained.

"That would be perfect," Curtis repeated. His optimism had smoothed some of the age away from his face. I would swear he'd taken off ten years since I had arrived.

"Well, I guess that I have my work cut out for me," I said as I got up and reached my hand out to shake Curtis's hand.

MICHAEL JAY NUSBAUM

"A pleasure, my friend," Curtis said as he shook my hand.

"Give me a few days, a week at the most, to see what I can do," I said to him as I walked down the steps and over to my horse.

I had no idea how I was going to pull this off or even how I was going to propose it. I looked back at Curtis who had such hope and trust in me. I didn't want to let him down.

"I'll do the best I can!" I called out to him as I rode off.

As I rode, I considered what would make the strongest case to my superiors. After I had submitted my proposal, several days went by without a response. I contacted as many people as I could but to no avail. It looked like I would not be able to divert a ship to Liberia, nor get Osumaka anywhere near Africa.

A week had gone by, and I was ready to return to Curtis to admit defeat when an urgent telegram came to my office. I could hardly believe my eyes.

It read, "Under the orders of Naval High Command and by the command of the president of the United States and at the request of Mr. Frederick Douglass, you are hereby ordered to mount an expedition to repatriate up to 120 freed Africans and deliver them to the free shores of Liberia."

I wasted no time. I immediately headed back to Curtis to tell him the incredible news.

My horse's hoofbeats alerted all at the plantation to my presence. Curtis was again on the porch in his wheeled chair and was first to notice me as I raced toward the house.

"Michael!" Curtis shouted. He saw my face and smiled a little. "We had given up hope!" Curtis shouted out to me.

"I had given up hope too," I said as I dismounted and tied steed to the porch.

I walked up the steps and over to Curtis. "I'm not totally sure how, but we have our ship!" I exclaimed.

Just then, Sarah and Osumaka walked out of the front door and on to the porch.

Osumaka walked up to me and extended his right hand. "It is a pleasure to see you again, Captain."

Sarah approached me to shake my hand.

"A pleasure," she said.

Somehow, I hadn't noticed her emerald green eyes at our first meeting, but they struck me now. Sarah possessed beauty, tenderness, and confidence all at the same time. It was a formidable package, and her eyes, I think, truly reflected her soul.

"The pleasure is mine as well. I forgot to thank both of you for coming to reunite me with my old friend," I replied sincerely.

"Osumaka," Curtis said, "Captain Smith has found a way to bring you to Liberia to reunite with your family."

Sarah looked suddenly bereft. Her face froze, with the corners of her mouth suddenly were pulled downward and her eyes wide-open.

"My family. Reunite. Yes, the captain mentioned that this might be possible, but how?" Osumaka asked.

"Well," I replied, "I'm not exactly sure, but it seems that you must have friends in high places."

Now Curtis looked confused. "What do you mean?" he asked.

"It seems that our friend Osumaka knows Mr. Frederick Douglass," I replied.

"It is true that I met him once, but I have no idea how he would ever . . .," Osumaka said and then stopped mid-sentence.

Sarah stood, still frozen, but watched Osumaka's every movement and reaction. She tilted her head slightly to the right as if she were a little child waiting for a parent's response. Osumaka looked at her but said nothing. The two of them were caught in a tense moment. I watched this and then turned to see Curtis's response. He just looked back at me with an inquisitive look.

"It was you?" Osumaka asked Sarah.

"It was," she replied.

"How? Why?" Osumaka asked.

"I overheard the captains speaking about getting you back home with your family. I thought that a letter to Mr. Douglass might help," she said softly.

"I don't know what to say," Osumaka said, equally quietly.

"You are going to go, aren't you? That's what you wanted?" Sarah asked Osumaka.

"I." He began, then paused. "I know that they are alive and that they need me."

"I understand," she said in a very sympathetic voice. "I do, I understand. That's why I wrote the letter."

MICHAEL JAY NUSBAUM

"You must come with me." Osumaka decided.

"It is not my place to go with you," she replied. "Besides, this is the only home I have ever known. I was born here, my mother was born here, and her mother was born here. I don't have anyone there."

"You would have me," he told her.

Sarah looked at Osumaka and said sadly, "But you have your family, and they are waiting for you."

Osumaka looked back at me and then at Curtis as if we would somehow have a solution for his dilemma.

"But why would you want to stay here?" Osumaka asked.

"I know for sure that what I am here to do on this earth is to help my people. I have so much more to do, so many more to save," she said as she walked up to Osumaka and placed her hands on his cheeks. "My work is not done here and yours lies across an ocean with your family."

"But I . . ." Osumaka started to speak.

Sarah placed a finger over his lips to stop him from speaking. "My destiny lies here with my people. I must remain here to continue Moses's work, to continue the struggle."

"But I . . ." Osumaka started to speak again.

She pulled his head to hers and kissed him deeply. Curtis and I looked at each other, mildly embarrassed, and then back at the two of them. Neither of us understood exactly what was going on.

Sarah pulled away and said, "You are the most honorable man that I have ever known, Osumaka." She pulled his forehead down to meet hers and went on. "Your place is with your family. Someday, perhaps we will be together again. For now, I have my work to do. I feel alive when I am helping my people to freedom. Too many just sit back and watch things happen to us. What is happening here is much bigger than the two of us. Go to your family. I will go to my people." She held his hands for a moment then pulled away. She smiled sadly and walked into the house.

Osumaka remained in the same spot, frozen. He did not utter a word, and neither Curtis nor I wanted to say anything to interrupt the moment.

CHAPTER 23

Voyage back to Liberia

June 2, 1868

THE LOOKOUT IN the crow's nest shouted, "Land ho!" and everyone dashed to the railing to get a glimpse. But it was still too hard to see land from the deck, so the passengers strained their eyes to see the coastline.

"Where?" Curtis asked as he wheeled his chair up to the port rail.

"Land ho! Dead ahead upon the horizon!" shouted the lookout once again.

Several of our passengers darted for the bow. Others, not understanding enough English, followed just to see what the commotion was all about.

At that time, I was sitting at my desk and finishing up my review of the logs. I heard a knock at my door.

"Come in," I said.

"Captain, sir." The boatswain saluted me.

"Yes," I replied.

"Land spotted dead ahead."

"Excellent," I responded. Our journey, Osumaka's, Curtis's, and mine, looked to be coming to an end. I looked forward to its conclusion.

"Sir, one more thing."

"Yes?" I replied

"There is a passenger named Osumaka who wishes to speak with you."

"Very good. Send him in." I smiled at him.

The boatswain turned, opened the door, and called out, "The captain will see you now."

Osumaka entered the doorway, having to crouch slightly so as not to hit his head when he entered. "Captain."

"Osumaka, please have a seat."

Osumaka sat down in one of the chairs laid out in front of my desk. He hesitated and then said, "Captain, I was wondering . . ."

"Yes, Osumaka?"

"Captain, I was wondering how I will find my wife and child when we dock," he asked.

"That is a very good question, one which Captain Stanton and I pondered before we set out upon this journey," I replied. "When we were last in Liberia, we met many people. Among them were several dignitaries, as well as the president. He is no longer in power, but he still has friends in Monrovia. Before we secured this vessel, I wrote to them, telling them about you and of our hopes for your family. My hope, God willing, is that they received those letters and someone has made an efforts to find your family and inform them of your impending arrival."

"Do you think that's possible?" he asked. Osumaka's life had been so chaotic over the past eight years that he almost couldn't believe his nightmare would soon be over.

"Yes. Well, I hope so. Look, we will be here for several days before we return home. If they were unable to find your family, I will do everything I can to help you find them."

"Thank you, Captain," Osumaka replied.

"And you will be taking the little girl you have with you, Pepper, I believe her name is?" I asked.

"Yes, Captain, Pepper." Osumaka smiled at the thought of the irrepressible child.

"Captain Curtis told me about you two," I said. "Your adopting Pepper is very admirable."

"Captain?" Osumaka looked at me, clearly confused.

"It is very admirable of you to adopt her and take care of her as you have," I repeated.

"She has become my own daughter. She is so like the daughter I lost those years ago," Osumaka responded.

Suddenly, we heard a wild cheer from outside my cabin. Osumaka turned to look at the door. I rose to my feet.

"That must mean that everyone can now see land." I guessed.

No sooner had I finished that statement than our passengers burst into song. We could hear laughter and cheers interspersed with the singing.

There was a knock at the door.

"Enter," I said.

"Captain, you're needed on the helm. Liberia is now in sight," the boatswain reported.

"Well, Osumaka, we shall know soon enough if word got to the right people and if they were indeed able to find your family. No need to borrow trouble now, we will soon know," I said as I rose, put on my coat and hat, and headed for the door.

I exited to scenes of jubilation breaking out all across the deck of our ship. People were dancing and singing and crying and laughing.

I moved toward the bridge. "Position?" I asked.

"Sir, we are approximately one nautical mile north off our mark," the navigator reported.

"Not bad," I replied. "Make the necessary course correction and take us in."

"Aye, aye, sir," he replied.

Standing at the railing, overlooking the main deck from the helm, I could see that all our passengers were now out and joining in the celebrations. I looked to my right to see two passengers timidly approaching the helm from the starboard stairs.

"Captain, thank you, Captain," one said as he knelt and reached out for my hand. The other did the same. Before I knew it, there was a line of passengers waiting to thank me. Most had tears in their eyes. Some were literally shaking with joy.

"You must thank Captain Stanton as well," I said as I pointed to Curtis who had wheeled his chair up to the railing to get sight of shore.

Osumaka stood close by me. Pepper was now glued to his hip.

Several of the passengers ran up to Curtis and shook his hand, while others patted him on the back and expressed their gratitude.

When we arrived at the dock, there was a crowd waiting for us. We maneuvered the ship into position so that the gangway could be set up on the port bow. Our passengers realized that they needed to line up on the port side to see who was greeting us. Osumaka was among the first to reach the rails. He strained to look into the crowd. I watched him closely as this journey was truly started for him.

Thousands of people crowded the docks and the port. It was a huddled mass of humanity.

"They come out here for every arrival of returnees," the lieutenant said.

"Returnees?" Curtis asked.

"Yes. When word gets out that a ship returning with freed slaves is coming, thousands show up in hopes that their missing loved ones might be aboard," he explained.

"How often does that happen?" Curtis asked.

"Not as often as it should," the lieutenant replied, "but I would guess ships arrive once or twice a month."

"They all come out here each and every time," I said, shaking my head.

"They do," the lieutenant replied.

"So many," I said. "So many just in the hope that one day their missing family might return. What have we done to these people?"

"Yes, Captain," said the lieutenant.

"What a sight, Michael," Curtis said to me.

"Yes, it is," I replied.

"I can't begin to imagine what they must be feeling right now," Curtis said as he looked at our passengers pressed up against the rails. "We did good."

"I think that I can, and yes, I believe that we did," I agreed. Then I noticed Osumaka straighten up and lean over the rail, waving and shouting. I could hear him call out, "Likana! Bwana!" over and over. I noticed him lift his leg as if he might jump over the railing and into the water in his exuberance to reunite with them, so I grabbed him by the back of his shirt and put my hand on his shoulder.

"It's all right," I told him softly. "You're home. They are here somewhere. We will help you find them. It's going to be all right."

Tears were running down Osumaka's cheeks. He turned and gave me a hug, lifting my feet slightly off the deck and gently putting me down. Then he turned to Curtis, knelt down, and embraced him as well. "I don't know how to thank you both."

"There is no need," I replied. "Seeing you so happy is thanks enough for us."

"Yes, Osumaka. Michael is right. Nothing could ever erase what was done to you, but this is the least that we owe you," Curtis said.

Osumaka picked up Pepper and held her in his arms as he strained to see the faces of those who were waiting for us on the dock.

"Do you see them?" I asked Osumaka.

"No, no, I don't," he replied. I could tell he was worried.

"Well, perhaps . . ." I started to say when he interrupted me with a joyous shout.

"I think I see Likana! Can it be them? I can't tell. The boy next to her is so grown up. It looks like her!" Osumaka was alternately ecstatic and frantic with worry.

"Perhaps when we get closer." I tried to calm Osumaka.

"No, it is her! It is Likana. That must be my boy. My boy!" Osumaka said choking back tears.

"It has been a long time, Osumaka," I reminded him. "The little boy you left isn't a little boy anymore."

"I would not have recognized my own son had he not been with my Likana. I have missed so much of his life," Osumaka said as he wept.

"I am so happy for you, Osumaka," I replied.

Osumaka shouted over and over, "Likana! My wife, my love! Bwana, my son!"

"Is it them?" I asked him. I really couldn't see how he could discern specific faces in the teeming crowd.

"Yes. It is definitely Likana, but they don't see me. I'm calling them, but they can't hear me," he said positively.

Maneuvering the ship to the dock seemed to take an eternity. Osumaka struggled to get the attention of his family. My guess is that they did not recognize him either. Once the gangway was pulled and secured, Osumaka was the first to run to the deck with Pepper in his arms. I watched from the railing as he pushed his way through the crowd. The woman and young man he'd pointed out to me were still looking at the ship when Osumaka finally reached them. His appearance shocked his wife. They stood facing each other for a brief moment until they realized that they weren't dreaming, that they were truly together again. Holding Pepper the entire time, he wrapped his arms around his wife then his son. I could see him introduce Pepper to his wife and son. They didn't seem to mind at all, just accepting her as part of their family. Then the four of them just stood there with their

MICHAEL JAY NUSBAUM

arms wrapped around one another, huddled together. I could not hear what they said to one another, but I could see the tears of joy running down their cheeks. I felt my heart jolt up with emotion and could not take my eyes off their reunion.

"Captain."

"Yes?" I replied to see the lieutenant standing beside me again.

"Captain, what are your orders?" he asked.

"Orders?" I asked as I looked back at Osumaka, still embracing his family. "Let them enjoy this moment."

"Sir?" he asked.

"Secure the ship. Make ready," I replied.

"Aye, aye, sir," he responded.

Curtis and I watched Osumaka drop to his knees, take something from around his neck, and hand it to his son. It was hard to see from a distance, but I guessed it was the ivory amulet Curtis had told me about.

"Curtis, is that . . .?"

"Yes," he replied. "That's the little statue, the *ere àwòrán*, I told you about."

Osumaka's son held it to his chest and then put the necklace on.

Curtis and I continued to watch as other reunions occurred on the dock, but none moved me as much as Osumaka's. Then I saw Osumaka pointing to us as if he were telling them who we were. His wife and son soon waved to Curtis and me. We waved back, and I tipped my hat.

Osumaka slowly led them through the crowd and over to the gangway.

"Halt!" the sailor guarding the ship said to him. "No one onboard without authorization."

"That is all right, sailor, you may let them on," I ordered.

Osumaka led his wife, Pepper, and his son on to the deck, and Curtis and I moved over to greet them.

Osumaka seemed to be introducing Curtis and me to his family. His wife extended her hand in gratitude to the two of us and then said something. I looked at Osumaka inquisitively.

"She said that she would like to thank both of you from the bottom of her heart for bringing me back to them."

"Please tell her that it was my great pleasure to do so and to see you all so happy," I replied.

His wife smiled at his translation and then said something else.

"She said that they have been coming to the docks for years and have been disappointed so many times that I was not among those returning," Osumaka said. His eyes became shiny with tears.

Then Likana asked Osumaka something.

"She asked if she could give both of you a hug in thanks."

"Of course," I said as I opened my arms.

She embraced me and began to weep once again.

"Thank you," I said as I let her go.

She turned to Curtis, leaned over, and hugged him as well. I could see tears welling up in Curtis's eyes. He began to breathe heavily, and I sensed the emotion he could not mask. He was clearly struggling to maintain his composure.

Osumaka's son, Bwana, then began to speak to us.

"What did he say?" I asked Osumaka.

"He wants to thank you two as well and to tell you that he knew that his father would one day return to him. He says that a flame burned deep inside of him that could never be extinguished. He calls it the flame of hope. He knew that as long as he kept that flame burning, that we would someday be together again."

"I cannot tell him how happy we are that we could reunite all of you," I said with a smile.

"Yes," Curtis said as he wiped his eyes with his right sleeve.

Bwana asked his father something and then his mother. I looked at Osumaka, wondering what the boy was saying. As I did, I could see Bwana removing the necklace that his father had just given him a few moments earlier.

"My son would like very much for you to have this," Osumaka said as Bwana handed me the necklace with a little ivory statue on it.

"Is that . . .?" I asked Curtis.

Curtis nodded. "Yes, yes, it is."

"It is me," Osumaka explained. "I carved this for him many years ago when he was just a little boy. I meant him to keep it as a piece of me. I told him that as long as he had it, that I was with him."

"If not for that little statue, we wouldn't be here today. That statue connected all of us," Curtis said emotionally.

"I can't accept this," I replied as I attempted to hand it back to Bwana. "It is so important to your son and to your family. I could never accept it."

Bwana spoke again.

"He wants you to have it," Osumaka said. "He says, 'You have returned my father to me, and now I give this to you so that you will always remember us.'"

I felt humbled by their words. "I don't know what to say," I said. "I certainly will never forget you."

"Say yes," Osumaka urged.

I looked at Curtis as he nodded fiercely.

"Yes then," I replied, "and thank you."

Pepper came over to me and hugged me as well.

"Thank you, Captain," she said.

"You're most welcome, Pepper," I told her.

She turned to Curtis, "Thank you, Captain. Thank you for everything."

"I am so happy for you, Pepper. You have a family again," Curtis said to her as tears ran down his face.

"I have come to realize that there is good and bad in every race just as there is good and bad within every man. It is in the end, I think, the good, which we do in this life that should define us. Thank you again, Captain Smith and Captain Stanton. I am, no, we are, forever in your debt," Osumaka said as he took his family and walked back off the ship.

We watched them walk slowly away. Osumaka never looked back. I half-expected him to stop and wave one last time to us, but he never did. They just kept walking until we could no longer see them.

EPILOGUE

I NOW KNOW what his son meant by not letting that flame die within him. He never gave up hope that he would someday see his father again. Osumaka never gave up hope that he would someday see his family again. He never let anyone extinguish that flame of hope within him. No matter what rained down upon him, he kept that flame of hope alive.

Beginning in the seventeenth century and not ending until the Civil War, approximately twenty five million Africans were taken from their homes and forced into slavery. Approximately 6 percent or 1.5 million of those ended up as slaves in the colonies and then the United States. The remainder were taken to Caribbean Islands and to South America. Among those who were taken, an estimated 10 percent died during the "middle passage" across the Atlantic. Of those who were taken to seasoning camps, reports indicate that slightly more than half survived the torture and brutality.

I, Michael Smith, have now come to realize the difference that exists between me and this incredible man, Osumaka. I am the first generation born in our great land. My parents came here of their own free will to seek a better life. In this land of opportunity, there is so much to offer and much for me to achieve. The Africans who were brought to this land were brought here through no choice of their own. They were not brought here for their own opportunities. They were brought here as prisoners to be treated worse than dumb animals. Their children and their children's children were destined to the same fate as their ancestors. The bonds of slavery will always exist and will always remain a stain on this great nation's history. The descendants of these souls will not know of their ancestral homeland. They will see this country, our country, their country, as their home. I fear that there will be no desire within their blood burning to connect with the soil of their ancestors. I fear that there will be no escape from the legacy that slavery has bestowed upon them. One day, they will all be free, but I fear that the mental chains of the past will restrain them as a people. I have found them to be the most humane of humans, sensitive and caring, brave and proud, rich in culture, and more connected to nature than any white man I have encountered during my life. As with the Hebrew slaves of Egypt, they too will need a deliverer. Someone of great character, moral fortitude, and charismatic leadership will someday lead them to their promised land. Wherever that may be, I hope that they find peace as a people. Pres. Abraham Lincoln had such vision but was struck down by an assassin's bullet; he would not be that deliverer. He recognized that all men were created equal without regard to the color of their skin or their beliefs and that the rights set forth in the Constitution of these United States explicitly preserved that equality. The foresight of our founding fathers is self-evident. It is only through the moral character of individuals, such as my good mate Curtis that the struggle will carry on. When the cause is just, then the righteous shall prevail. The cause of liberty is just, and the cause of freedom for the enslaved people of Africa is just. May all those who read of my journey through life recognize this fact: all men are created equal, and no man should ever enslave another.

MICHAEL JAY NUSBAUM